Praise for R. S. Belcher

Nightwise

"Ballard is a darkly funny narrator with fascinating allies in the world's mystical underbelly. . . . Belcher tells a tense, tightly paced story."
—*Publishers Weekly*

"Like Neil Gaiman's *Neverwhere* if it was endowed with the tone of David Fincher's *Seven*." —*The Nameless Zine*

The Six-Gun Tarot

"If you love complex, fantastical worlds, this is very intriguing!"
—Felicia Day

"Keep an eye on Belcher because if this, his first novel, is any indication, he will be a must-read. *The Six-Gun Tarot* is nothing short of fantastic: a complex page-turner with philosophical, metaphysical, and mystical underpinnings." —*Booklist*

"The power of the author's storytelling and strong characters deserves as wide an audience as possible." —*Library Journal* (starred review)

The Shotgun Arcana

"*The Shotgun Arcana* confirms R. S. Belcher's position as a relative newcomer already worthy of the highest praise." —*Locus*

"Charismatic characters and a stunning blend of history, legend, religion, and modern sensibility intertwine to create a world that embraces the strange and fantastical." —*RT Book Reviews*

BOOKS BY R. S. BELCHER

The Six-Gun Tarot
The Shotgun Arcana
Nightwise
The Brotherhood of the Wheel

NIGHTWISE

R. S. BELCHER

A TOM DOHERTY ASSOCIATES BOOK
NEW YORK

This is a work of fiction. All of the characters, organizations, and events portrayed in this novel are either products of the author's imagination or are used fictitiously.

NIGHTWISE

Copyright © 2015 by Rod Belcher

A Tor Book
Published by Tom Doherty Associates, LLC
175 Fifth Avenue
New York, NY 10010

www.tor-forge.com

Tor® is a registered trademark of Tom Doherty Associates, LLC.

The Library of Congress has cataloged the hardcover edition as follows:

Belcher, R. S.
    Nightwise / R. S. Belcher.—First edition.
       p. cm.
    "A Tom Doherty Associates book."
    ISBN 978-0-7653-7460-8 (hardcover)
    ISBN 978-1-4668-4274-8 (e-book)
    I. Title.
    PS3602.E429N54 2015
    813'.6—dc23
                           2015015284

ISBN 978-0-7653-7461-5 (trade paperback)

Our books may be purchased in bulk for promotional, educational, or business use. Please contact your local bookseller or the Macmillan Corporate and Premium Sales Department at 1-800-221-7945, extension 5442, or by e-mail at MacmillanSpecialMarkets@macmillan.com.

First Edition: August 2015
First Trade Paperback Edition: September 2016

Printed in the United States of America

0 9 8 7 6 5 4 3 2 1

In memory of Torri Lyn Saunders.

"The sun loved the moon so much, he died every night to let her breathe."

NIGHTWISE

ONE

The banker was crucified on the wall of his Wall Street office, fountain pens rammed through both wrists, an Armani Jesus.

The pens are Montblancs, very nice. Each one is custom-made, decorated with emeralds, sapphires, and rubies, and then hundreds of tiny diamonds just for good measure. They run for a hair under a million dollars each. They're sturdy too, obviously. I doubt that their current function would be of much use in a marketing campaign, but still, a fun fact to know.

I left the shitty meth-lab-trailer-on-cinder-blocks I called home when I was thirteen. I remember writing the good-bye letter to my snoring, drunken mother on the back of a disconnect notice from Allegheny Power. I wrote my good-byes with a gnawed-on pencil, whittled to an uneven point by a pocketknife. I left the letter on top of a pile of past-due bills, truancy notices, and empty Marlboro cartons. No Montblancs in our clan, no sir.

Another dead end. This pattern was getting old. Every connection, every lead I had made to tracking Slorzack had dried up. To date: three strangulations, one incinerated alive while taking a shower, one exsanguinated, a "car bomb" that left no trace of the explosive device, and now, Wall Street performance art.

I considered a working on the body—wake the old boy up for a bit of Q and A—but if the killers had experience in the Life they might have set traps for any would-be necromancer.

I pulled the high-backed leather chair out from behind the desk, rolled it to where I could have a decent view of the tableau, sat down, and admired the effect, the craftsmen's work, for a moment. Every artist signs his portrait in some way.

I pulled out an American Spirit, only three left in the pack, second pack today. The Zippo snapped open with a hollow, metallic clank. A hint of sulfur stung my nose as the wheel ground against my thumb and the flame kissed the tip of my coffin nail. Pa called cigarettes that. He was a Lucky Strike man. Too bad he hadn't lived long enough for them to kill him.

The crucifixion itself had no occult symbolism that I recognized from the position of the body—hands above the head, almost crossed at the wrists but not quite. It did cause me to flash for a second to an image of an old bondage playmate of mine, the languid way she would raise her arms above her head and await the cuffs. If there was a safe word for God's snuff play, he kept it to himself.

The positioning of the body and hands didn't indicate traditional Judeo-Christian iconography; there was none of the overtly brutal but metaphorically and mystically powerful symbolism of Teutonic or Norse rites. He wasn't hanged upside down, for example, or missing an eye, and I saw nary a crow.

I took a long draw on the cigarette, ran a hand over my shaggy hair. I had pulled it back, tight, into a ponytail to keep it out of my way. I rubbed my eyes.

The murder didn't betray any of the subtle trademarks of Dalí Absurdist Chaos Magic, the telltale covert rendering of metaphysical, four-dimensional, transcendent hypercubism that old Salvador had extrapolated in his *Anti-Matter Manifesto*. A good read, by the way. Even if you didn't care for his art, you had to admit Dalí was a top-notch psychosocial alchemist.

Signs of Satanism? Please. So last millennium. Go listen to Gorgoroth and sacrifice a puppy, why don't you.

No, no hocus-pocus. This was just someone killing a man in a very nasty way. More likely two or more killers, given the strength and flexibility needed to wrestle him up there, pin him, and hold him till the blood loss did its work. I was suddenly taken by the beginning of a very bad joke: *How many faceless conspiratorial hit men does it take to crucify a banker?*

This wasn't a ritual or an execution. This was a message. For me. *Stop searching. Back off.*

Dark streams flowed from the dead man's wrists, staining the pens' jeweled lengths, ending in swollen, pregnant drops that fell down into his eight-hundred-dollar Orlando Pita haircut, saturating his hairline and trickling across his pale, downturned face. The blood split and fractured into a wet black web, finally meeting again to pool at his perfect chin and tumble down, splashing dark stains on the expensive wool carpet. The lines across his face reminded me of Alice Cooper's makeup after a long, hot show.

I wrestled a small leather couch close enough to stand on it and reach the banker's body. I braced one boot against the wall and pulled the Montblancs free with a lot of grunting and effort. They were sturdy and had been sunk deep through skin, bone, paneling, and plaster.

The body fell, bounced off the couch, and landed with a muted squish into the dark, wet stain on the carpet that had gathered below it like a lengthening shadow.

I wiped the blood off of the pens with a monogrammed silk handkerchief I found in his pocket and slipped them into my coat. He wouldn't need them.

I hopped down, leaned over the body, and tried to imagine the killers, the struggle. It wasn't as hard for me as it might have been for most and, unfortunately, most of my insights were through the eyes of the killers, not the victim. I kept thinking how I would have killed this man, how I would have left him as an example to be found. This was far from my first visit with violence and death.

Sane, healthy, normal people grew up in fucking Disneyland when it comes to evil and the beings capable of inflicting it. Monsters, human and otherwise, roam this world, I assure you. It would be nice to blame dark powers and inhuman fiends for most of the troubles in this life, but sadly, we can't. There is more human evil out there than inhuman. Our world chokes on it, drowns in it, but some of us have learned to swim.

Hitler was the Henry Ford of the infernal. He developed a production line, a process, to make horrible, soulless acts more cost-effective and efficient while removing accountability and guilt for his "workforce." He knew the importance of branding, sound-bite speeches, props, and jingles. He also knew, like any good marketer, the importance of images, symbolism, and meme, and he stole from only the best. Like Ford, Hitler developed a process other sick, sad little psychopaths could duplicate and improve on across time and space. A process of atrocity that was as clean as the faces and reputations of the American industrialists who did business with him up until the war and even after it had begun. No dirty fingernails for the boys in the home office, no hands-on work for them.

Somewhere in the process, someone has to get dirty hands, though. Someone has to strap on the IED, feed the starving women and children into the ovens, drop the bomb, or pull the trigger; someone slaughters the schoolchildren. In my experience, the best of these "men of action" are weak-willed sheep. The worst . . . well, the worst enjoy their work. Some get off on it.

Evil is out there, right now, today, maybe watching your kids play too intently at the next table in that restaurant with the overpriced pizza and the giant rat for a mascot. Fun fact: Did you know that restaurant was founded and dedicated as a temple and feast hall to Karni Mata, the bride to the rat god, Mushika. It's true. Those little gold tokens your A-B honor roll students are clamoring for are sacrificial blood coins feeding the god of plagues and vermin, and trust me, you don't even want to know why they got rid of the ball pits.

It's all out there—dirty nails, nails caked with graveyard dirt and the coagulated blood of infants.

I know these monsters, I have fought them, and if am to be honest with you and myself, more often than not I have been the monster.

The man I was hunting had nails that were very dirty indeed, and I had promised Boj I'd find Dusan Slorzack and make sure he paid his account in full. But now, a dead banker and another dead end.

Two weeks ago:
    I found my friend, Branko Bojich in a decaying hospice in Brooklyn that smelled of shit and Vicks VapoRub.

"You look like hell," I said, standing in the doorway of his tiny cell-like room.

"I'm dying from AIDS, asshole," he said with a weak grin. "What's your excuse?"

I tossed him a small gift-wrapped package. "I got your call. How are you, Boj?"

"Dying, Laytham. Just dying, that's all. No big thing," he said, putting the gift aside. "How's my favorite West Virginia cracker doing?"

"Fair to middlin', as they say at the tractor pull. Just got back from Egypt last night. It's good to see you, even like this, man."

"Thanks, thanks for coming. I need to ask you to do something for me. It's going to be messy, though. But I figure you . . ."

"Yeah, I owe you for messy," I said. "What?"

"I want you to find the man who killed me, Laytham," Boj said.

"I'm looking right at him, Boj. You put that spike in your arm, no one else."

He squinted into the afternoon sunlight that squeezed through filthy blinds. His eyes were still, and dark as opals, but his dusky skin was now washed-out and blotchy. He talked to the sunbeams, not to me.

"I told you I was married before I came to America, right?" he said.

"Yeah."

"She died in Čelebići, in Bosnia, back in '92," he said. "She was raped, every day for months, tortured. They nailed . . ." He swallowed hard and I saw him trying to beat down the vision. He let himself fail. "They nailed an SDA badge to her forehead and then kicked her to death."

"SDA?" I asked.

"It's the initials of one of the Muslim political parties over there. The stupid bastards didn't even care how little Mita thought of politics. She believed everyone was good at heart . . . look what that got her."

He looked back to me with dry eyes, dead eyes. Whatever lived behind those dark wells had preceded Boj out of this world; the rest of him was just waiting to catch up.

"I was here in the States handling my family's business. I was planning to bring her over."

Boj's family's business was called "import-export" in polite circles. The cops called them the biggest heroin production and distribution network in Eastern Europe. When I met him, he was handling everything for them from L.A. through flyover country—Middle America. I saw him at war with the Russians, the Triads. He was the Alexander of the street—bloody, raging, glorious, and terrible. Now he was a skeleton stretched over gray skin, one good bout of flu away from Hell.

"Stupid bastards," he muttered. "I found out the name of the chief stupid bastard just a few years ago. It took the last of my resources. Most of my 'friends' have abandoned me, and even my enemies pity me and wait for me to die like a rabid dog. But I knew you would come, Laytham. I know you. I want you to find him. I want you to see he gets what he deserves."

"Why the fuck me, Boj? I'm no cop, I'm not an enforcer, a leg breaker. I know some wise guys who'll do him for . . ."

"Because he's into the Life, Laytham, the Art, the Dance, *bajanje*— whatever the fuck you call it, just like you and Harel and all those other weirdos we used to hang out with. I think he used it to escape from the law, even the street's law."

Down the hallway there were echoing shouts in Spanish. Some-one named Tuni needed to mop up Mr. McGowan's piss from all over the break room. I sighed.

"This chief stupid bastard have a name? We may have bumped into each other at one of the weirdo conventions."

"Slorzack," he said. "Dusan Slorzack. He was indicted for war crimes back in '96, but he hasn't surfaced anywhere since then. He seems to have found a back door to slip away from everyone."

"That was awhile back, man. You sure he hasn't just died some-where?"

Boj said nothing. His face was sunken, a skull with tatters of skin and bone pulled over it, a constellation of sores marking his face.

"No," he finally said. "Bastards like me don't get that lucky. My karma is fucked. He's out there laughing and drinking and fucking and Mita is only a memory in my skull, and when I'm gone, she's gone too, like she never was, and that is the greatest crime I think I have ever known. I'd do it myself if I could, Laytham. I can't."

I scratched my head and sighed. Boj waited patiently with the ghost of his dead wife for me to mull it over. Slorzack. The name meant noth-ing to me. A long-cold trail. My enthusiasm must have been shining out of my face.

"You owe me blood, redneck," he finally said when he felt me try-ing to pull away from it.

"Yeah," I said, "I reckon I do. Okay, I'll look into it."

"Good," he said, and I saw his whole body relax. He smiled. His teeth were rotting, and his gums were gray and recessed, but it made me feel good to see him smile, all the same.

"Thanks," he said.

"I got to go. I'll keep in touch," I said.

"Yeah. What the fuck is this, Laytham?" he asked.

He unwrapped his present. His eyes widened as he recognized the worn, battered leather case. He unzipped it and smiled again. Every-thing was like he had left it. The hypodermic, the needles, even the cooking spoon, caked and blackened. The rubber hose uncoiled like a tan viper, eager to wrap around his arm and sink its fangs into his vein. A small red balloon filled with poisonous rapture also fell out, tied tight to keep its contents from spilling.

"I figured what the hell, right?" I said.

"Yeah," Boj said, arraying his works before him, looking at the balloon like a groom looks at a bride on their honeymoon. "What the hell."

I knelt over the dead banker's dumb face frozen in agony and terror. The dead always look fake, like bad wax mannequins or grotesque rubber sex dolls, but the death smells were there to remind you it wasn't a special effect. Sweat, shit, piss, blood, all stuffed up my nostrils to assure me it was as real as it gets.

His eyes reminded me of Granny's. All dead eyes did. I half expected him to blink, for those cold, empty windows to shift, focus past the gathering cataract clouds, and regard me from a sitting room in Hell.

They didn't. I started to breathe again and felt the cool sheen of sweat wet the back of my shirt. I closed the dead man's eyes, more out of a desire for reprieve from their regard than anything approximating respect or human kindness. My hands shook a little. I needed a drink.

A man like this would be missed—and soon. He had been here all night, and now, in the cold gray light of dawn, his office manager, or one of his racquetball buddies, or his steroid dealer would walk in and find him. I needed to be gone by then.

I tossed the room, looking for anything that might put me back on the frozen trail of Slorzack. My short-lived friend, the car bomb guy, had left a few legal pads in his desk drawer that hadn't ended up blown to hell. They led me here. Slorzack had paid a lot of money for an introduction to this man—Berman, James Berman. Why?

I skipped searching the plundered desk and the computer with its blue screen of death. The people who killed the banker had done a professional job of tumbling the place. They had found whatever it was they were looking for, if indeed they were looking for anything at all. Tossing the room might have just been a ploy to divert attention from the murder. Unlike the crap you see in the movies, nobody methodically tears up a room and then misses the McGuffin in the false-bottom chest. It just ain't so. The only hope I had was to pick through the scraps. Look for the unseen.

I closed my eyes, steadied my hands, and slowed my breathing and my heartbeat. I opened the lenses of energy that resided along the bone staircase of my spine. I exhaled and opened my eyes.

I started with the primary reason for the killer's visit: Berman himself. If they just wanted to toss the place, they could have done that when he wasn't here. No, they came to do this to him. Ransacking the office was either a secondary concern or a ruse. I examined his body. Berman was a very tan man. He had good hair and good teeth and was tall and had a body that was a testament to many hours worshiping at the temples of the racquet club and spa. He had a class ring—a big, squat, ugly thing designed to announce to the world his pedigree. On his left hand was a simple gold band and a Masonic ring, gold with a ruby glaring up at me in the harsh office light. A Mason. He was a little more interesting now.

A sudden insight, a flare of intuition, made me open his shirt, ripping the buttons off the broadcloth and pushing his tie aside, so that it now clutched his bare neck more like a hangman's noose than a banker's badge of office. His chest was smooth, hairless. Around his neck, on a thin, expensive silver chain, were two slender cylindrical handcuff keys on a simple wire loop of steel.

I touched the keys and felt the swell of tantric power roar through my mind and down in my Swadhisthana chakra. The flicker of the candles, the spatter of hot wax, the feel of warm leather in my hand, the smell of blood and sex, the scream of pain and desire, echoing. This was the first real part of this man I had come across here. These keys were soaked in secret power, hidden desire, and I could track that.

But I felt a familiar pressure squeeze between my brows as my Ajna chakra opened its petals wider. *Something else.*

I took the chain and the keys, dropped them in my pocket. I reached for the mug of overpriced, and now cold, coffee on his desk and dipped a Montblanc pen into it. I stirred counterclockwise as I incanted, *"Aperio latito conspici . . . iam."*

I took the pen out of the mug and moved it across his still chest, left to right then right to left, finishing the charm by circling his chest widdershins and touching the tip of my makeshift wand to the spot where his cool, still heart was.

This was a risk. If the killers had planned on me using the Art to search, I could get a nasty surprise, but this was a very unobtrusive bit of magic. A trap would have to have a hair-trigger to activate against this.

The skin wavered like asphalt on a hot day and the tattoo appeared, spread across the dead man's chest. Emerald ink, racing, arcing, forming symbols, finishing in the pattern of the pyramid with the All-Seeing Eye boring into me as it hovered at the apex amid a halo of brilliant radiating light rays.

Illuminating.

"Shit," I said, with more than my usual amount of West Virginian twang. I said it out loud to no one but the dead man and me, a soon-to-be dead man.

"You're with the fucking Illuminati."

TWO

I exited the office building of the late James Berman—would-be secret master of the world—faster than a preacher leaving a whore-
house. The sky was ash. Dawn was a thinly veiled threat of bruised
light only moments away. The row of streetlight orbs that stood silent
sentry glowed in perfect unison. No busted streetlights on Wall Street.
They winked out one by one as I passed them, their duty to hold the
night at bay finished.

It was September, and dead leaves, empty Starbucks cups, and
crumpled McBurger wrappers swirled in the terminus of the wind cutting between the shafts in these concrete fortresses. I pulled up the
collar on my ratty Navy pea coat, lit a new cigarette, and kept walking away from the crime scene with my aura all over it. My stupid,
unique, mega-magicy redneck aura.

The Illuminati. Fuckity-fuck-fuck.

Down the street, a group of Occupy protesters were huddled together beside a small domed tent, trying to avoid the wind's cold regard.
Their cardboard signs bent and bowed in the force of it. None of them
looked like they had gotten much sleep. I recalled not too long ago
when there had been thousands of them down here. Most had packed
up and headed home, but not these kids. They were young, college
age, and they were true believers. In other words, cannon fodder.

While their leaders gave speeches and then drove home to Rock-away or Brighton Beach, or NYU for dinner and a nice warm bed, these kids manned the front lines. They were foot soldiers, the ones who end up dead in every war, the dumbasses who most likely volun-teered.

Screw volunteering.

Belief has power. Getting someone else to believe what you believe has even greater power. I've always been all about the power, not so much with the following or the believing. I believe in me, that's pretty much it. Believe in someone else too much and they'll fail you or screw you, or both.

One of the kids handed me a flyer. It was shaking, snapping in the wind.

"Learn the truth about who is running our country into the ground, bro," the kid said. He was maybe twenty and had a mop of curly, brown hair stuffed under a Nike lid. He sported a week's growth of beard. A blue North Peak jacket helped keep him warm, and he had an iPad in his hands with Angry Birds fluttering across its glowing screen. "Help fight the corporations that are bringing us all down."

"Irony," I said. "Do you know it?"

"Huh?" the walking billboard responded eloquently. I shook my head and took his flyer. "Fight the power," I said, and gave him a fist bump of solidarity as I slid the two Montblanc pens into his pocket without him seeing. I kept walking. If he knew who really ran this world . . . well, he'd be as screwed as I was. If they found those pens on him, he'd be a damn sight worse than screwed.

And better him than me.

The Illuminati. Really? For half a second I thought maybe Boj was setting me up to get killed. I did owe him, and maybe he thought this would be a good way to get fair market value out of me. One last "gotcha."

No. I saw the look on his skull-face, in his heavy-lidded eyes: hate.

Not for me but for the man who had taken the only light he had known in this world. No, Boj had said Slorzack had mojo. If he was hooked up with the Illuminati, it might explain why Boj couldn't find him.

I fell into a booth at Jack's Stir on Front Street. For the millionth time since I saw that symbol manifest on Berman's chest, I thought about saying fuck it and rabbiting. Boj would be dead soon and I could tell him I did my best but I couldn't find Slorzack. I'd live, Boj would die either way. You mess with the "I" and you end up with someone using your nerves as violin strings while you lie somewhere and feel every draw of the bow, every note of agony. No, thank you.

The waitress was pretty, Mediterranean with long black curls and tanned skin showing in all the places to help with the tips.

"What to drink?" she asked. Her English was pretty good. The tag next to her cleavage said DANNI.

"Cheerwine," I said as I unwrapped, and tapped, a new pack of smokes. I knew I couldn't smoke in here without a lot of bullshit following me, but the ritual comforted me and made me think of the next cigarette to come.

Danni frowned. "Wine? I'm sorry, we have no liquor license for . . ."

"No, darlin', Cheer-wine. It's a soda."

"Soda." Danni nodded. "Oh, pop. We have Pepsi . . . we have . . ."

Suddenly I felt like I was in an old *Saturday Night Live* skit with John Belushi. No Coke, Pepsi. I shook my head and smiled.

"Coffee, darlin'. Black as my soul and those pretty eyes of yours."

Danni looked confused and then smiled and wrote something on her pad. "Coffee. Yes. Very good." She looked me in the eyes. I sent a little current back to her, just a nudge of power from my sacral chakra, to make sure I got a decent cup of joe and her attention while I was here. She walked away and glanced back to see if I was watching her. I was. We both smiled.

Great. Here I was in the Big Rotten Apple, no fucking Cheerwine to be had—I hated going north. No one ever carried it up here. I could make the most of this day right now by asking Danni to come back to my hotel with me.

And then there was Boj, dying. Waiting for me. Fuck.

Boj. He took a 9mm rune-carved heart seeker for me in Vegas, back in '99, when we burned Joey Dross and stole his philosopher's stone. Boj was the only one who came back for me when everything went to shit in '01, with us trying to save that little girl from the breeding pools under Carrabelle, Florida. He risked his life to pull me out of there when the Mosquito Queen was draining me dry and I was begging for her to do it. He stayed with me during the sickness, madness, and addiction that followed.

Boj, black-hearted, grinning, mean as a snake, smooth as gun oil, eager to die—happy to kill. Alexander the Great of the occult underworld, the Life. Boj.

I couldn't give this up, not now. And not for any noble reason you might attribute, not out of loyalty, or friendship, or debt. No. It was the small, cowardly, skittering part of me that had kept me alive for so long. It said that the Illuminati were now in this and they would find me, after my visit to Berman's office. No, I couldn't just drop this. The only way out was going to be through. So I needed time. Time to figure out the link between Berman and Slorzack, to find out what Berman's handcuff keys were all about, time to work some angle with the Illuminati that kept me from getting disappeared.

I drank my coffee and admired Danni's ass in her tight uniform and listened to my inner bastard tell me exactly what I needed to do.

I tipped Danni fifty dollars and walked out into the growling late Manhattan morning.

I stopped at a newsstand on Water Street. The guy running it had a Rasputin-style beard and was wearing a ratty Primus T-shirt over his enormous beer gut.

"Give me a pack of American Spirits," I said, handing him some crumpled cash, "and a white Bic lighter."

He handed me the cigarettes and a purple lighter out of the display behind his counter.

"No," I said to Rasputin, "I asked for a white lighter."

"What's the fuckin' diff, man?" Rasputin rumbled. "'Sides, white lighters are bad luck, everyone knows that."

"Yeah," I said, "I know. Now give me the damned white lighter."

I went back to the hotel and was saddened that there wasn't a hot Greek waitress waiting for me. I got my working bag out—an old, frayed canvas bag with two worn handles and a zipper that often stuck. The bag was the color of desert sand. It was covered with various symbols and runes drawn in black Sharpie. It had a few dark, ominous stains. It also bore the logos of numerous bands I had been enamored of in my youth: Kiss, Led Zeppelin, Lynyrd Skynyrd, Alice Cooper, AC/DC, Pink Floyd, the DKs, and, of course, the Stones.

Pop quiz: What do Jim Morrison, Jimi Hendrix, Janis Joplin, and Kurt Cobain all have in common? Answer: They were all awesome. They were all left-handed, they all died at the age of twenty-seven, and all the police reports said that a white plastic lighter was found in their possession at the time of death.

I stripped in the stale, silent air of my hotel room. My body was still in pretty good shape for my age. Not bragging, but I was rocking the Iggy Pop look, without the heroin diet plan. Still a little muscle, still a little cut, still a little rock star in me. My skin was covered with tattoos and scars. A lot of my ink was work related, you might say. Symbols, formulas, pacts, and wards. My scars, ah, my scars. They came from motorcycle accidents, knives, bullets, claws, broken bottles, bites, whips, self-mutilation, and a bunch of other stuff, not the least of which was the wound in my back from being impaled by a giant mosquito woman. That one still itched most nights, and sometimes, when the moon was new and far away, her wound sang horrible, beautiful songs to me.

I closed the drapes to hide from the light and to muffle the never-ending scream of the city. I wanted to make sure I didn't lose any of Berman's psychic "scent" off the cuff keys, so I put them in a safe place—the glove. I took it out of my canvas bag and unrolled it. It was the skin of a powerful *santero* down in Miami, tanned and treated with all the fingers still intact, taken from his hand, severed at the wrist. Anything put in the glove was preserved and hidden from the view of the world and those with the Art. In short, it was gruesome mystic Tupperware. I dropped the keys in the glove, folded it up, and set it on the nightstand.

I took my working bag and entered the bathroom. I set up candles of black and red around the tile floor and on the sink counter. I took a handful of ritual Klonopin pills, called benzos on the street by the nice young man I had purchased them from, and washed them down with cold champagne ordered from room service. Then I sat down on the floor, lotus style, and closed my eyes. I centered the energies of my chakras. I felt the loci of forces align and then dipped into the power building in my Rasatala chakra, a minor point of energy in my ankles. I let the forces of selfish energy build and channel up my legs. I mixed it with the fear in my Atala chakra in my hips; I began to feel the power swirl in me, like the first smoky, heady rush of heat from a sip of good whiskey. I rolled the power around in me and felt the high envelop me. The candle flames all flared, burning bright blue, illuminating the dark bathroom. Goddamn . . . Why the hell would anyone be fucking normal if they didn't have to be?

The universe was roaring through me like an open door, and I told it what to do. Yeeeeesssss. I stood, took the white lighter out of my bag, and placed it in the sink. I looked at myself in the mirror, lit up by acetylene blue light. My eyes were wide and dark, pupils dilated. I smashed the mirror with my left fist. An explosion of silver-blue fire supernova, jagged teardrops falling down into the sink. A distant, muted echo of pain, screaming from my nerves. The power welling up in my chest, in my throat.

Shape the words, carve the energy, vomit it up into the sink, into the lighter.

Ego sum mea parasitus
Nil opus hostiam vivam

pascimus off de invicem
Possumus nostrum endorphins
Doll CARNIS! Test cibum!

The words carried the power with such force, they felt like they were loosening my teeth. Even through the chemical shroud of the benzos, I felt like shit. This was dangerous magic for an old bastard like me to be trying.

Non opus est mihi molestus varius novum amicus
Non opus novum amicus tribulant me titio
Et non indiget aliquo egere me
Video balneo patet
Puto autem quod alicuius prope
Scio quod aliquis post me, O yeah.

I clutched the counter and growled the words into the sink. With each syllable, the shards of mirror snapped and fragmented.

Habitabant in speculis me auferre, cum viderem me omnes. Crepitus ego me spiritum meum et specula, nunc adest mundo videre. Etiam Castella fecit de arena, cadunt in mare . . .

Blue smoke drifted from the sink. I looked at my bleeding left hand as if it was some alien thing, unattached to me. I let the blood drip into the sink, onto the broken glass of the hotel mirror, onto the pure white lighter. *Drip, drip, drip.* Suddenly, I was in Berman's office again. His pale, blood-streaked face looked up, and his eyes opened. They were Granny's eyes, milky white, soulless.

Nosti opinor penitus infantem et non in corde recto,
Numquam numquam numquam Numquam exaudiet me cum
*   clamavero nocte*
Infantem et clamavi tota die;

Sed quotiens me, inquam, bene ferre possum dolor
Sed in armis tuis me dicis, ego iterum psallere.
Dicam age, age, agite, et sequere eam?

Power, any power, has a price. I was preparing to damn someone to a painful death, to an eternity of suffering. To save my sorry ass, to buy me a few extra days. I reached into the sink and my cut, bloody fingers wrapped around the white lighter. I was damned too. Damned again.

Tolle it!

It was done. The candles' guttering flames were no longer blue. I staggered out of the bathroom, feeling the cosmic hangover of the power departing me. Like a junkie coming down. No longer a god, only emptiness and remorse. A hollow man.

I carried the champagne bottle, taking deep, thirsty gulps, pausing long enough to pour some over the wounds on my hand, and then taking a nice long draw off the bottle. I set the lighter on the nightstand beside the glove. It was pristine, clean, and perfect.

I fell into the bed, the bottle still in my hand, and I slept, the only sleep my kind ever truly enjoys—drugged and dreamless.

I slept for about a day. I awoke to the predatory sounds of night in the city. For a moment there was a thrill of terror, that I had waited too long, that the faceless crucifiers would be crashing through the hotel room door any second.

I got up, stood in a hot shower for a long time, and wrapped my busted-up hand with duct tape. I put on clean clothes, a Bauhaus T-shirt and jeans, and I began to feel human again. I gathered all my things and finally, as I prepared to leave, I put the lighter in my pocket. The hotel room looked trashed. I left the lights on and shut the door.

The Port Authority Bus Terminal is on 8th Avenue, near the *New York Times* building. I walked there. It was cold, but the fresh air helped me. I entered the terminal and made my way to the men's room. There was a rancid lake of piss on the floor. In the gang tags and graffiti smeared across the walls and stalls, I saw the names of twenty-six minor lords of Hell, hidden.

I placed the lighter on the counter by the sink, looked at it for a second, and then walked out, kept walking.

Someone would pick it up. I didn't know who exactly, but I did know the person would be twenty-seven years old and left-handed, and would be inheriting all my troubles with the Illuminati. Whoever it was would be tracked, disappeared, questioned, tortured, and then would finally die, if he was lucky.

The sounds of the street and the cold air slapped me as I walked out of the terminal and down the street, looking like just another asshole.

I couldn't see the face of the person who claimed the lighter. And I could see them all.

THREE

The sun choked on the concrete mountains of Manhattan and died. The night was ascendant, swollen with victory, the shrill howl of sirens, the dull murmur of human misery, and the spoor of blood, sex, and garbage soaked the air. One of the reasons the night is so full of hungry things is that it is born of death and rapacity.

I took the subway out of the city. The Keep had been operating out of "the Gates of Hell"—the abandoned Glenwood Power plant in Yonkers—for the last few months. The building was impressive in its dark sprawl. It squatted like an old whore pissing in the Hudson River, its lower levels already flooded and eaten by rust. The club moved on a regular basis, trying to stay one step ahead of New York's finest. I got the address from a Haitian cabbie for a hundred bucks and a bag of weed.

The building was huge, its crumbling, filthy walls thrummed from the bass of the sound system inside. At one hundred yards my guts were vibrating. A crowd of club kids practiced looking bored as they waited to be chosen to go inside. Their breath and cigarette smoke swirled about them like warring ghosts. Two muscled myrmidons wrapped in Kevlar, armed with steel batons, stood watch over the dented fire door that was the only way into the Keep. Their faces were bland masks with cold, laconic violence leaking out the eyeholes.

I walked up to the bigger one, a black guy with a shaved head. I noticed a sheet of paper taped to the fire door. It had a symbol on it: a circle that held the yin-yang teardrops, but this symbol included a third teardrop, the trio eternally circling, like little Zen sperm.

I looked at Baldy and knew immediately he was the man to be talking to. His companion, like me, wore his hair long, for fun, not business. This man shaved his head, so that when he was kicking your ass, you didn't have anything to grab on to. No hair, no piercings, no bullshit. Business.

"Grinner here tonight?" I asked.

"I'm not his fuckin' appointment secretary, motherfucker," Baldy replied in a quiet, even voice. No anger. "You in or out?"

"In," I said, and handed him a hundred. I started to walk past him to the door, flicking away my dying cigarette.

"No fucking trouble tonight or you be pissing blood tomorrow," Baldy said.

"I look like trouble to you?" I said.

"Shit, you stink of it," he said.

I pushed open the fire door, which stuck slightly and creaked. The furnace blast of heat, music, and smoke roared over me. I stepped into the belly of the beast.

The last thing I heard before the Keep swallowed me whole was one of the club kids whining. "Hey! How come he gets to go in?" the droning, drugged voice asked.

"Because he's the real motherfuckin' deal," Baldy replied.

The Keep writhed and sweltered. Lasers strobed and burned across a sea of swirling, milky smoke—fog machines, clove, tobacco, and pot. The sky was a thousand HD monitors shifting and fading between images: Klimt paintings, a slaughterhouse, Kenneth Anger's *Lucifer Rising*, sadism-themed porn, nebulae and northern lights, napalm runs in Cambodia, *Nosferatu*, X-rays of tumors, terrorist beheadings, and Dalí's *Andalusian Dog*. The music thundered: DyE's "Fantasy." Below the video sky, hundreds of glow sticks held in sweaty hands or twirled on strings made ever-shifting constellations as the dancers surged and receded to the ethereal strains. Some dancers wore glowing, burning LED glasses, others wore lighted gloves with firefly fingertips. A few had bottles of bubble soap that had been dosed with the chemicals in the glow sticks and glowing green bubbles drifted like will-o'-the-wisps.

I drifted through this realm. The energy throbbed, swelled, and pulsed like the dark ocean at high tide. There were alcoves, ledges, and tables everywhere. A young woman, nude except for a feathered Mardi Gras mask, hung, moaning, at a ninety-degree angle with hooks, small and large, attached to chains, piercing her skin. Her bloodred lips were parted in ecstasy while fat, shirtless men in leather pants and zippered masks pulled on the chains that tore through her.

I paused at a table covered with a mosaic of colored pills, amyl nitrate poppers, ether aerosol cans, blotter acid, coke, and weed. I snorted a few lines off a black glass mirror, felt the freight train crash of my head and chest exploding in bright, sharp, white pressure. The rush made me remember everything for a diamond-edged second, and I suddenly recalled, for the thousandth time, why I stopped doing coke.

Coming up from the mirror, I saw a man on a table on his stomach, glass cups, the air within heated by the blue blade of a handheld acetylene torch, were attached, one by one, to his naked back by a slender girl with a mane of white hair. The girl was wearing a corset and skirt of bloodred leather and a gas mask. The hot air inside the cups created a vacuum that, when pressed to the man's skin, sucked the flesh up into the cup and made the man hiss in pain and sensation.

I watched the show, along with the small crowd that had gathered. As they watched gas mask girl add more and more cups to the shuddering man's back, I lost interest and turned to regard a beautiful nude Asian woman, her head shaved, a coiled serpent of emerald and crimson ink flowing down her flawless body. She stood like a queen, regarding the crowd and me with utter contempt, then lowered her eyes and knelt at the feet of three well-dressed men in suits and featureless black leather masks. Each man held a crackling neon purple wand that sputtered and hummed with electricity. They thrust the wands into the flesh of the Snake Queen. Her aristocratic features contorted in pain and ecstasy. The whole tableau was overseen by a woman in a flawlessly tailored man's suit, a leather mask, like those of her knights, obscuring her features. She sat in an antique electric chair, in rapt attention to the Snake Queen's torture.

The pain was sudden and severe, and it came on me instantly as I watched and listened to the violet wands sizzle the Snake Queen's nerve endings. The pain was centered between and slightly above my eyes, and I knew exactly what it was. I walked away from the crowd and the show and let the yawing ache in my third eye lead me. It was at a table near the terminator between the churning dance floor and the conspiratorial darkness that was haven to lovers and criminals. It was skinny, almost gaunt, with long blond hair tied back into a ponytail and a fringe of a beard. Its eyes were heavily lidded and reminded me of a lizard's.

It was feeding on a young man at a table about twenty feet away. The boy was pale, weeping, his makeup streaming down his cheeks. Black tears. I saw the kid stuff a handful of pills into his mouth and drown it with a shot of Jägermeister. The pain radiating off him was sharp and bright, like a scalpel. The blond "man" with the ponytail smiled when the boy winced in emotional pain. I stepped into its line of sight, blocking its view of the boy.

"Try me," I said. "Go on, try it on me."

The psychic vampire regarded me for a moment like a cobra preparing to devour a mouse, and then its lidded eyes widened as it encountered my defenses. It sniffed me and quickly did the math of the jungle.

"Go on," I said, lighting a cigarette, "eat me."

I leaned over the table and flicked my ashes in its drink. It started to rise. I put a hand on its shoulder and pushed it back down.

"Don't come back here," I said. "You do and I'll rip your aura off and we'll see how long you can live with every nasty entity and negative essence in here chewing on you."

I released it. The psychic vampire stood and nodded slightly. Its face remained a mask of bland indifference.

"My apologies," it said in a near monotone. "I didn't realize this was your feeding ground." It walked onto the crowded dance floor and disappeared into the forest of sweating bodies.

"Fuck you," I said to the empty table.

I found Grinner on the fifth floor of the old power station, up where the really weird shit goes down. I ascended the wrought-iron spiral staircases, rusted helixes that took me lower and lower as I climbed higher and higher. On five, two more of the bulletproof legionnaires, like Baldy outside, told me Grinner was in the cages. They looked at me as I passed with the same guarded disgust I had given the psychic vampire. When you work in a place like this, live in this world long enough, you can smell dangerous, crazy, and sick, like dog shit on someone, and you never turn your back on it.

I passed the snuff room with its burgundy velvet drapes and muted Schubert, where, by invitation only, serial killers and things much, much worse watched the murders performed on the circular stage at the center of the large, darkened room.

I paused and scanned the crowd as best I could without drawing the predators' attention. Many wore masks. I wondered if one of them could be Slorzack; this looked to be his kind of crowd.

Tonight's murders were a ritual, a tribute to Tezcatlipoca, the Aztec god of sorcery, destiny, and the night. Not that most of the shadow men sitting at their tables watching the young girl struggle and beg for her life knew or cared. I saw one shadow's arm jerking furiously under his small candlelit table. It struck me that once that would have made me puke; now it just was. A string quartet wearing tuxes and skull masks performed "La Muerte y la Doncella." The cellist turned to regard me with hollow bone orbs and cocked his head. I walked quickly away from the door.

The cages were a maze of steel wire and human degradation.

Speakers hidden in the room blasted and distorted a club mix of Depeche Mode's "Master and Servant," bouncing it off the concrete walls. I walked past people wrapped in plastic like mummies with straw holes for them to breathe through, suspended in their cocoons like alien moths, twitching to be reborn. Eyes followed me as I moved through the corridors of cells, some feral, insane with fear and high from it too, others content and serene in their enforced captivity, drooling happily behind ball gag pacifiers. And then I came to Grinner.

Grinner's real name was Robert Shelton. He was a big guy, six two, well close to three hundred pounds, covered with tats. He was nude except for a steel contraption like a cage that encircled his genitals. He hung by leather wrist restraints inside a large cage, suspended a few inches off the floor. His dyed hair was the color of asphalt, shaved on the sides and put up in a topknot. His hazel eyes were only slits. His lips were cracked and dry. He didn't seem to recognize me or even be fully awake.

"Hey, Grinner," I said, and whistled. "Rise and fucking shine, man. I need you. Got work for you. Playtime is over."

"Who," a powerfully built bald man in a black leather and mesh wife beater with a dull steel ring sewn into the chest said, "the fuck are you?"

The music faded, morphed into a home-brewed mix of Prodigy's "Smack My Bitch Up."

"I'm the client," I said, and took a long drag on my cigarette. "I need him."

"Well, I am his master, and I say when he comes out of there," the bald man said, and held up a key on a thin steel ring that had several collected on it.

"Look, Fifty Shades," I said, "I'm not looking for trouble. Just need his expertise and I know he always needs cash."

Grinner moaned, and his eyes opened for a second. His breathing was a dry wheeze.

"How long has he been in there?" I asked Grinner's master.

"Six days," the master replied. "No food, minimal water. He contracted to give me seven."

"Well, I'm sure you have gotten your rocks off plenty of times in the last six, so I'm getting him out of there now."

Master edged into my space, into my face. "He's not going anywh—"

I jammed my lit cigarette into his left eye. He managed to close his eyes in time to save his cornea. I drove my right fist into his gut, and he went up off the ground and then down in a heap. I flicked away the crushed cigarette and then kicked him a few times in the flank and stomach with my steel-toed boot. I knelt down and took the key ring out of his hand.

"Do not try that dom bullshit on me, my friend. Now roll over and play dead. Good boy."

I unlocked the cage and slid the straps off Grinner's wrists. His voice was cracking from lack of use and a dry throat, but it was still a booming bass.

"That was epic," he croaked. "I was ready to get the fuck out of this about a day ago."

"Where did the Marquis here ditch your clothes?" I asked.

"Locker over there," Grinner said.

"Lean on me," I said, and handed him the key ring. "You can unlock your own crotch cage."

"Don't be judging, man," Grinner said as he tried to laugh. It came out a jagged cough. "Seen you up in some weird shit too, Laytham."

"Yeah," I said. "But I was usually the one with the keys to the cage."

Grinner tossed the genital cage away and pulled out a pair of purple and gray camo pants and a black T-shirt with a faded Special Forces logo on the back. He sat on the chest with a groan and slid his feet into a huge pair of black Chucks.

"Look, we'll talk business at my place. You go hail a cab since you have to go outside anyway, and I'll settle up with Master," Grinner said.

"This clown is really your master?" I asked. "And why did you say I had to go outsi—"

A powerful set of hands grabbed me under the arm and behind my head, and I was down on the cement hard and fast, a brilliant flash of pain-light filling my vision as my brain flopped back and forth inside my skull.

"I told you, didn't I?" It was Baldy's voice calm and even in my ear. More hands grabbed me, most likely the security boys from the stairs who had given me the hairy eyeball. They dragged me away, and me and my headache didn't argue.

"Glad to see you still got a way of bringing out the best in people, Laytham," Grinner said as he helped his master to his feet. "I'll meet you at the cab."

One fifty-five Avenue C," Grinner told the back of the cabbie's head as he climbed in the cab. "Loisaida."

Even through the headache, that sounded familiar to me.

"That's C-Squat, isn't it?" I said. "Punk House?"

"Affirmative," Grinner said, pulling his cell phone out of his leather jacket. He frowned at the screen and then began to text someone. "I am an artiste, after all."

C-Squat was the name of an abandoned building in a part of the East Village known as Alphabet City. It had been claimed by squatters, homeless, kids from the emerging punk scene, in the 1980s. In buildings between Avenues A through D, they governed themselves and claimed the land as their own. They ended up fighting a war for it. The NYPD came numerous times in the dead of night to dispossess them. I knew secret heroes of those shadow wars—"the Alphabet War," they called it. It was driven by many of the same Secret Master Illuminati douche bags I was dealing with now. There were initiated sects within the NYPD, cults with badges and clubs, who worshiped much more than poor Lady Justice. Some of them were little more than death squads for the Illuminated. In the end, twelve buildings survived the secret war and were still in the possession of the squatters. The city had even cut a deal with most of them, to buy the buildings. That was the way of the world; if you couldn't take it by force, buy it with money.

"Where you staying?" Grinner asked as he continued to text, his fat thumbs dancing over the touch screen.

"Figured I'd crash with you," I said. Grinner said nothing, intent on the screen.

We got out in front of the building. It was still dark, and a trace of snow was blowing. A group of street people and tenants stood around old oil drum bonfires warming themselves, talking, joking, laughing, singing, living. A group of musicians, black leather and duct-taped troubadours, jammed on the crumbling tenement stairs. They greeted and fist-bumped Grinner as we passed. The elevator was a death trap, so we walked twelve flights of dark stairwells that smelled of piss and stale beer. Street artist murals were everywhere. No gang tags, just beautiful, primal art. I liked this place in spite of myself. They had fought the fucking Secret Masters of the city and won. Maybe I could survive this.

Grinner rapped on the door as he unlocked it. There was a dream catcher made of a rusted hubcap, old wires, rats' skulls, and pigeon feathers mounted on the door.

"Christie, baby, I'm home, and I brought company, right behind me."

Grinner entered and turned immediately to his left, sharp. His wife, Christine, a tiny, waiflike woman, pretty, with auburn hair, sharp, well-defined features, and piercing green eyes, was about twenty feet from me. She was aiming a big military-looking rifle straight at my guts, and she looked like she knew what she was doing.

"Hi, Ballard. Don't move or I'll cut your redneck ass in half. Hi, baby. Did I do good?"

"You did great, baby," Grinner said from behind me. I heard the front door close and many bolts, chains, and bars locked into place to secure it.

"Hi, Chrissie," I said. "You look prettier than ever and a damn sight more pretty than this sorry SOB deserves. My god, are you pregnant, darlin'? You are glowing, baby!"

Christine smiled sweetly from behind the rifle and nodded eagerly. She smiled so wide her eyes closed in happiness. The rifle never wavered. I felt a large cold barrel of steel rest at the base of my neck just behind my left ear.

"You have never, ever wanted to stay with us, motherfucker," Grinner said from behind the massive pistol resting against my head. "So I figure you are running from someone and you think me and my family might slow them down a little bit. That how it goes, buddy? I remember how you did Malcolm XYY and that sweet little girl from the Crusade of Secret Saints. You fed them to the fucking dogs, feetfirst."

"It's not like that, man," I said. "I need you to . . ."

"Erase your ass? Hide you until some trouble with a badge and a gun kicks in my door and fucks my world up while you go dancing away? That what you were going to say?"

"I need a crosshair go-to on someone, full package. Everything. I'm looking for someone, and yes, I have trouble nipping at my ass, but it won't be back on my scent for at least a few days and by then I will be gone and . . ."

"And who did you have to throw under the bus to keep your pretty fucking ass alive for a few more days, Ballard?"

I turned slowly to stare into the gun, into Grinner's eyes. I felt a great sense of peace flow over me at the prospect of the gun ripping my head off, destroying my brain. The feeling passed.

"No one either you or I give half a damn about," I said. "Now, you want the job or not?"

"Fifty K," Grinner said. "And you are a ghost in forty-eight hours, no matter what." He lowered the gun. "You can crash down the hall next to Megan's room."

Christine lowered the rifle and leaned it against a wall. She ran over to Grinner on tiptoes and embraced him.

"Missed you!" she said. Grinner picked her up, bear-hugged her, and spun her around before setting her back down. Her laugh was the sweetest, most innocent thing I had heard since getting off the plane in this city. "You had fun with your friend? He beat your ass real good for you, baby?"

Grinner laughed, kissed her, and nodded. "He was a punk-ass bitch compared to you, beautiful."

"Who's Megan?" I asked. Christine hugged me now and kissed my cheek.

"Roommate," she said. "You'll like her. She's last door on the left, you're on the right. Watch the floorboards near the window, Ballard, they're a little rotted."

"Does Megan man the damn flamethrower when company comes?" I asked, and kissed her forehead.

A wave of exhaustion settled over my bones like early-morning frost. The sun was coming up soon. The coke had lost some of its manic magic after Baldy had dribbled me off the cement. My body wanted to sleep, but I wasn't sure if I could.

"You got any beer in the fridge?" I asked Grinner as he and his wife fell on the couch into a pile.

"Been dry for about two years," Grinner said. "Got some smoke, if you want."

"Thanks. I'll pass," I said. I walked down the hall and opened the door on the right. There was a bare, stained mattress thrown in the corner. The room was about ten degrees colder than the rest of the apartment. The only illumination was the sodium light bleeding in through the broken window covered in cardboard and duct tape. Something scuttled deeper into the shadows in response to my entrance.

I dropped my bags, fell onto the mattress, kicked off my boots, and was asleep before my cigarette became ash between my fingers.

FOUR

It was 1972 when I first learned what I was, what I was capable of, and the price you pay for power.

I was five years old, my pa had been dead for two years, and I spent most of my time with my granny: Mable Thornton Pugh. Granny was the best—I know I'm biased since she pretty much raised me, taught me all the important things. But you'll hear the same from a lot of folks who are a damn sight closer to good than I am.

After Pa passed, Ma still had to work at the factory, and to make ends meet she started cocktail waitressing at the Destiny Lounge out on Route 16. Granny kept me as much as her own job at the factory allowed. She kept working until she honestly couldn't see anymore. Tough old knot.

I stayed at Granny's a lot. Cold glass bottles of Dr Pepper with narrow necks, ham sandwiches on Wonder Bread. Horehound candy, half-moon pies made with the green apples off the tree in her backyard and fried up in a cast-iron skillet. She'd play Buck Owens songs on the old guitar she taught herself how to play as a girl.

I remember being snuggled up under heavy quilts she made herself. We would sing old mountain songs, spirituals, hymns. She'd sing Elvis, Hank Williams, and George Jones. She would tell me tales— Fool Jack stories and the Three Billy Goats Gruff and Br'er Rabbit's foolishness. She always smelled of talcum powder, and that scent still has an association for me with love. Her arms were saggy and strong and could defend against the fiercest nightmare monsters the dark could hurl at me.

Going to sleep, nestled over Granny's arm, hidden under her covers, I think was the safest I ever felt in this world.

Over time, I learned the history of our clan, the stories. Old stories from back before people wrote stuff down. They told it, felt its truth in their bones, like the cold, or love, passing it along as best they could.

Granny's mother, my Great-Gran Beulah, used to order medical books from the Sears, Roebuck catalog. When someone was in trouble having a baby, and there were complications and she needed a midwife, she would call on Great-Gran Beulah. If a whole family was down sick with the black vomit or the flux, maybe whooping cough, Great-Gran was all they had to count on for a hundred miles in any direction, and they would call for her. Granny told me her mother would often get calls to help from counties far away. She was the closest thing to a doctor, a sage, or a protector most folks in that part of the West Virginia wilderness had back then.

Sometimes folks came running to Great-Gran for help with things people didn't like to talk about, hell, didn't even fully know how to comprehend. Once, Granny told me, a little girl named Eda Pruitt got hexed when she fell down an old well. After they rescued her, she started talking in the voice of an old, dead German farmer. The voice said it was a servant of Scratch himself. Hogs started dying on the farm, and then people started getting sick. That's was when Sears, Roebuck failed you, when reason and rationality failed you, and you had to go back to the old ways, the secret ways. Our clan was steeped in them too. Great-Gran would take up her waking stick and put her medicines, herbs, poultices, amulets, and books in a satchel and set off to help, walking there most of the time. Granny still had her mom's walking stick and satchel. I remember it from a hundred walks, Granny's bony fingers wrapped about it

"It's in our blood, Laytham," Granny would say as she grunted at the exertion of climbing higher and higher, me trailing behind her with my own stick Granny had cut from a tree branch with her ubiquitous, never-dull pocketknife. "It's our way. When people are hurtin' and wickedness is being done, it's our load to help them, darlin', the sick and the defenseless and the just plain stupid, any way we can. It's the price of the gifts the good Lord has given us."

Those gifts had many different names, depending on where you grew up. I've studied all over the world, and I've heard many of those names. Great-Gran Beulah and Granny were known as Wisdoms— wise women. They had the power to traffic with the unseen, the haints; the Waiting, spirits of the dead; and the Elementals, the old, green spirits of the land; the Little Folk, the Fae and their tricks and beauty; even the High-Named: the Watchers, gods, angels. They knew the names and signs of the fallen spirits too: the Hungry, the things squatting in the Void, but it was folly to truck with them. Folly—Jesus, looking back, how far I've fallen. They knew the secrets of the plants and herbs, how to dowse to find water, or objects, or people lost; they could heal or hex, cure or curse. Dreams spoke to them; Granny taught me everything speaks to you, if you just shut up and listen.

And I believed it all, especially the parts about helping people in need and punishing the wicked. Hell, back then I still believed in the Easter Bunny.

The power did run in our blood. Granny was the first to see it in me, to really see me at all, truth be told.

Now, there has been a lot of bullshit written, said, and whispered about me—urban myths, legend, and outright lies about how I got my power. A lot of the stories sprang up from that Dutch filmmaker's documentary about me and the gang back in 2000. Some from that little blogger pissant. He ended up writing a book about me, published it in 2008. Lying piece of garbage didn't even use a good photo of me for the cover. Thought about suing him, but I just covered his junk with acidic boils for six months instead.

Most folks figure the power comes to you from God or a deal with the Devil, some near-death experience, or a past-life revelation, or getting struck by lightning, or bit by a radioactive necromancer, blah, blah, blah. There is no anointment; the universe has no time for pretentious shit like that. Power simply *is*. It flows like water, it seeks paths of least resistance into this world, conduits through which it can work with minimal effort. It transmits, and some folks have the hardware to receive. There are no Chosen Ones, but there sure as hell are a lot of grifters, like your humble narrator, who make a living off of self-important marks who think there are.

You end up able to access and comprehend the power the same way you end up with anything else of real value in this world—either through pure dumb, blind luck, or you get born to it. You can't get it by choice, any more than anyone chooses to be born Angelina Jolie or Stephen Hawking; beautiful, autistic, brilliant, alcoholic, wealthy, or gay—the cosmic lotto simply has its few winners and lots and lots of losers.

My granny was the only one who ever thought I was a winner. The day I was born, Granny made a big deal out of the fact that I was a caul bearer. She said it was rare for the men in our clan to be born with the placenta, or the caul, stretched over their head, like a veil. She insisted mine be kept and rubbed onto paper for safekeeping, and she was its guardian. My folks thought she was crazy, but they did it. It was unwise to cross Granny.

Even if you end up with power, that's no guarantee of anything. It takes discipline and a very fluid mind to make something of power. It is also takes will, unshakable will to believe, to control it, and to have the balls to use it. And there is a price you pay for power. Like everything in life, there is always a price.

When I was five, Granny picked up her walking stick and her satchel. She packed it with ham sandwiches, fried apple pies, Dr Peppers, and a few other things.

"C'mon, Laytham," she said, "let's go for a walk, darlin'."

The "walk" was a hike about two miles up the rocky side of a mountain. Granny's backyard opened onto shallow, rocky rises that grew to become the giant of the Appalachian Mountains, and we often climbed the gentle slope full of moss-covered rock outcroppings, thick oaks, and green brush. We'd find a big, flat, comfy rock high up to give us a good view and sit down and have our picnic. Today Granny was looking for something particular, and we kept climbing, higher and higher.

"Your legs tired, boy?" Granny asked, smiling as she paused. Her thin gray hair was a curly, wiry mop. She wore a simple thin flower-print shift with tattered stockings that ended below her knees and simple navy blue sneakers. Her nose was like that of a hawk, and her dark eyes held a wicked light—humor and maybe a touch of something smarter and just a hair mean. Granny did not suffer fools.

"Uh-huh," I said, nodding.

"Well, why didn't you say something to me, then?" she asked. The few teeth she still owned flashed. The two in front were small and side by side. Sometimes when Granny smiled I thought of a rat.

"I didn't wanna make a fuss, be no lazybones, Granny," I said.

Granny groaned. She planted her walking stick and rested her weight against it. "I know, Laytham, but don't be a fool either, darlin'. Something stuck in your craw, you speak it. You tired, then you stop and rest."

So we did. We settled on a large, flat boulder covered in a cool carpet of green moss. Granny unpacked the satchel while I struggled to climb the side of the rock that wasn't gently sloped into the ground, my legs kicking and fingers grasping for a hold.

"Always like to go the hard way, don't you Laytham?" Granny said as she opened the two bottles of soda.

I grinned and pulled one leg, then the other onto the green surface of the bolder. "Uh-huh. It's more fun!"

As a reward for my climbing skills, I devoured my sandwich and two (!) apple pies. Granny kept looking about, and I could feel she was waiting for something.

"Why'd we go up so high today, Granny?" I asked.

"Came up here to show you something important, Laytham. You gonna need to see it sooner or later. I cotton to sooner," Granny said.

"Now, Laytham, I want you to do something for me," Granny said. "I want you to feel the sun shining down on you from above, sparkling through the leaves of the trees, feel the warmth on your face. Close your eyes, darlin'.

"I want you to feel the cool stone under you, the soft living moss, feel it beneath you. Feel it connected to the dark soil, to the roots of the trees, and feel it all connected to you."

I could feel it, everything around me was alive and cradling me. It felt like I had Granny's arm around me. I kept my eyes closed; my breathing was slow and even. I felt anchored, like I belonged. I could feel Granny's smile, like the sunlight kissing my face.

"Very good, Laytham. Now, I want you to reach out and tell me what you feel, different, in motion. When you have it, I want you to open your eyes."

My heart beat faster, my breathing quickened. I could feel energy, wild, uncontrolled, a tiny pulse thudding like a 1-1 drum. It was in me, part of me. I slowly let it move away from me, like pushing a balloon away, to the proper spot, to where it was supposed to be in space, and opened my eyes and gasped. There was a little gray squirrel with a bristly tail. I saw it scamper down a tree and bound across the field about fifteen yards behind me. It stopped, stood on its hind legs, and regarded me. I was its lightning heartbeat, I was its panting breath and twitching nerves, but I was also me. It was an effort to keep the space between us. I looked back to Granny. She was still, calm. She was the mountain we stood upon, she was the trees and the rocks, the sun and the soil. She rested her hands on her mother's walking stick and regarded me with as serious a face as I had ever seen.

She narrowed her eyes and nodded slightly toward the squirrel. "Now be still and watch," Granny said.

Suddenly there was a whirring sound in the tall grass and the squirrel froze, its eyes wide and dark with fear. I felt the other flowing along the ground, cold, muted thrumming, like meat machinery, a steady pulse, no fear, no joy, only hunger and terrible emotionless purpose. The squirrel began to jump, but it was too late. The rattlesnake struck a whip-crack blow. I felt the jolt of impact, felt the venom, like acidic ice, slowing the racing little heart. I saw the squirrel stagger and then drop. My emotions were a nova that shattered the connection, and I was me again, alone in this universe and cut off from everything by the blinders of my perception. I started to rise to help the squirrel.

"Laytham, no!" Granny shouted. Her voice stopped me. "What do you think you are doing?" she asked calmly.

"I'm . . . the squirrel, Granny. I could feel it, it's dying. I gotta . . ."

"Help it?" Granny said. "How, darlin'? Poor thing is dying, Laytham. Everything living has got to die."

"Why?" I said. My eyes were hot and welling with tears, my whole body was shaking, and my fists were at my sides clenching and unclenching. I could see the squirrel twitching and the snake crawling closer to it. "It ain't fair, Granny, he didn't do nothing to nobody, least all that mean old snake!"

Granny's eyes softened as the sobs shook me. She looked like she was going to come hold me, but then she tightened her grip on her mother's walking stick and the steel settled again behind her brown eyes.

"I know, darlin'," Granny said. "And you're right, it ain't fair one bit. Not even one drop of fair, but it is right, Laytham, and you need to learn the difference.

"Life has to be fragile for us to understand it, to not abuse it, to cherish it, and each other. Snake's just doing his job. Did you feel any mean in it, feel anything at all, darlin'?"

"It was hungry," I said. "It's cold, up in its head, though, Granny, it's cold and scary."

"That's 'cause it lives its life cold, honey," Granny said. "It's made that way; it's not warm, like us. But that don't mean it's evil, it just means it's made to do what it does as best it can."

"Kill," I said. "It's made to kill, Granny? Why would God do that?"

"No, don't be puttin' this all on the Almighty," Granny said, wagging a bony finger. "When you are tryin' to put together a puzzle, and you haven't seen the whole picture and you don't get all the pieces to finish it at once, it's easy to blame the puzzle maker. God puts the pieces here for us. We are pieces of the puzzle, Laytham, just like that squirrel, and that snake, but he also gave us the ability to put the pieces together any fool way we want, to build our own picture. But like any puzzle, it has to have boundaries to frame the picture."

The squirrel shuddered one last time and was still. Granny pointed at the dead creature. "That," she said, "is a boundary."

"No," I said. The anger welled up in me, anger at the puzzle maker, anger at the snake. It wasn't fair, and I didn't give a damn about how pretty the picture in the puzzle turned out. I remembered the state troopers and the men from the mine office calling on Ma and Granny to tell them Pa was gone. It was the same feeling, only mixed more then with paralyzing fear and sadness, confusion, and a feeling of powerlessness, smallness.

I grabbed my crooked little walking stick, jumped off the boulder, and ran shouting in rage toward the rattler and the dead squirrel. Granny was shouting too, but I couldn't hear what she was saying over the sound of my anger and the blood hammering in my ears. I stood on one side of the dead squirrel, and the coiled rattler was on the other. I swung widely and missed the snake with my stick. It struck too, but I didn't feel anything. I swung again, and this time landed a solid blow. The snake looped in pain and confusion. I hit it again and again and again. I felt Granny's hand on my shoulder.

"Laytham, honey, stop, the poor thing is dead."

I did stop; I gulped at the air and looked at the snake. I had bashed in its head, and its body was still looping, mechanically. It was horrific: a biological robot trying to continue its function while its bloody, crumpled skull lolled lazily to one side, its broken jaws trying to open and close, to bite, to perform its function.

"Do you feel better now?" Granny asked. There was no malice in her voice, only concern.

I kept looking at the snake. And suddenly I understood the lesson I was supposed to take away from all of this, and the anger was stoked in me again.

"Yeah," I said, "I do. But I ain't done yet."

I knelt by the squirrel and I tried to slow my heartbeat, tried to calm myself. I had no idea what the hell I was doing and I had no names for the techniques I was trying to undertake. I did notice that, for some strange reason, my anger made me feel calm; it helped me focus. Everything slowed, expanded, merged, like it had under Granny's guidance. It was easier now. I knew it was possible and, therefore, I could do it again.

"Laytham Ballard, what are you getting into?" Granny asked. I ignored her and regarded the squirrel. It was cold, dark. The frenetic light that had filled it was gone. There was no difference between it and the dirt it lay upon. Dust to dust.

I knew what I needed to do. It came to me. At five years old, it came to me as easily as breathing. I dropped my bloody walking stick and picked up a sharp, thin stone. I raked it across my palm. The pain was as distant as Granny's protests. She was talking, but she wasn't stopping me, wasn't about to stop me, either. No one could stop me. No snake, no Wisdom, no God.

I squeezed my hand into a fist, and the blood swelled and leaked between my fingers and dripped onto the squirrel's body. The blood was fire—my anger, my life, my power. Mine. I felt the drops, was the drops. As they soaked into the dead animal's fur, each drop was an exploding sun, a dying star, life and death in its purest, most beautiful form. I drew a deep, powerful breath and then exhaled. The world exhaled through me. The squirrel's chest expanded then, contracted, in time to my breathing, again, again. I held my breath and the squirrel kept on breathing.

I stood. Everything was indistinct and bright and dreamlike. My head was swimming. I heard the world's heartbeat and it was my heartbeat. Sunlight flashed through the roof of trees, and a flock of black birds exploded into flight across the constellations of scintillating emerald light. I felt soft, strong hands hold me up and smelled talcum powder close to me.

"I got you, darlin'," Granny said. She led me back to the rock, and I lay back as she began to remove items from her satchel to mend my cut hand. The last thing I saw before my eyes closed was the squirrel scampering away back toward the tree.

It was getting dark by the time I was well enough to make the walk home. Granny and I descended the mountain quietly for a long time. Finally, I broke the silence.

"Granny, are you mad at me?" I asked.

Granny's hawklike profile softened in the growing shadow. "No, darlin', I'm not," she said, and then laughed. "Always like to go the hard way, don't you, honey?"

I didn't reply. Granny stopped. She hugged me tightly and kissed me on the cheek.

"I love you with every breath left in this old body, Laytham. I brought you up here to try to teach you your first lessons as a Wisdom, and I'll be if you didn't end up teaching me."

She checked the bandage on my hand as she continued. "What you did back there, Laytham, it's beyond me, beyond any worker I've ever seen. I've heard tell of it, but I've never seen anyone who could use, command, the power so fluidly, so instinctually. Do you understand what I'm saying to you, darlin'?"

"You're not mad, and I did good," I replied with a smile.

Granny frowned, tightened the bandage, and stood with some help from her walking stick.

"I'm not mad, and I am very, very proud of you, Laytham, but there is something I was trying to teach you today and you didn't understand it, and now that I know you have the power that you do, I need you to try to understand. It's going to be even more hard now that you know what you can do, honey.

"Laytham, you must not ever, ever bring anything back like that again, darlin'. Never again. Do you understand me?"

"Why, Granny?" I asked. "I saved it, it's okay and it was dead. Why is that bad?"

"The world just ain't that simple, Laytham," she said. "Everything has a balance, everything has a price, and some prices, baby boy, you can't afford the debt it brings."

She nodded at my bandaged hand. "That cut will leave a scar, that scar will never heal. That is the price you pay for that act, and trust me, boy, you got off cheap."

"I don't care," I said, but I was a little freaked out that the cut on my hand would never fully heal. It was my first bite of mortality, and I have to admit it both terrified me and thrilled me.

"When a life ends, and the spirit passes, it is not our place to interfere with the Almighty and his plan," Granny said, and began walking again. I followed and rubbed at my bandaged hand.

"Doctors save people all the time. Like on *Emergency!* on TV, Granny. They ain't interfering with the Almighty, are they?"

Granny sighed. "Dear Lord, we are all in so much trouble when you become a teenager. It's different, Laytham. This will be hard to understand for you, darlin', but the power, the gifts you have been given, they are not the same as what doctors do; it's better, it's outside of how things work. We are not part of the natural cycle of things, us Wisdoms. We have a responsibility that is hitched to that power."

It did make sense to me, perfect sense. I had felt it when I first decided to do something about what happened to the squirrel. A sense that nothing was impossible and that I could do anything.

"So, us Wisdoms are like the Almighty, right, Granny?" I said.

Granny spun around. She moved quicker than I had ever seen her move before. She grabbed me by the shoulders hard, before her walking stick had even hit the ground, and had her face up in mine.

"Don't you ever, *ever* say that again!" she said, and shook me. I couldn't tell if she was angry or afraid. "Don't you *dare* think that. We are people, Laytham, just people. Our power is a cross, not a crown, you understand me, boy? We serve, we witness, and we protect. We don't rule. You think you're above common folk, you start thinkin' you're a god, and you will end your days in a place far, far worse than any hell you can imagine, son. You'll end up alone."

She scared me, and I trembled and was quiet the rest of the trip home. As the mountain began to gently slope back into the familiar terrain of her gardens and my tire swing and the kitchen door's porch light, Granny stopped and turned to address me.

"Laytham, darlin', are you okay? Granny is sorry she got so upset, honey."

She hugged me tight and I cried a little, and slowly I began to feel better, like I always did in Granny's arms, in Granny's love.

"It will make sense in time, darlin'," Granny said as she held me. "Granny will help you find your way."

The cicadas hummed, nature's monks chanting in a hidden cant. I looked up, red eyed, from Granny's shoulder and saw the squirrel I had raised from the dead perched on Granny's cement birdbath, watching me. Its eyes were darker than the night.

FIVE

I woke to daylight clawing at my eyes through the broken window and the sound of sirens, car horns, and millions of human rats all going mad in too small a cage. There was also someone pounding relentlessly on Grinner's apartment door. It sounded like a sledgehammer.

I groaned as I got to my feet. My whole body ached from the beating Baldy had given me the night before. My face was sore, swollen, and cut, and my mouth tasted of copper and decay. I was only wearing my jeans, and someone had covered me with an old wool army blanket. I staggered out into the hall.

"What the hell?" I called out. The door opposite mine opened a little bit and a woman's face peeked out. She was lovely—long black hair and warm brown eyes. Her complexion was olive. And I saw a flash of skin ink on her bare upper right arm.

"It's for me," the woman said in a voice with a strange accent. It was French mixed with something else. "His name is Roman, and he's here for me."

"You don't sound like you want that," I said.

"No," she said, "I don't. It's kind of a long story."

"You can tell me all about it after I send . . . um?" I said, jamming my thumb toward the front door.

"Roman," she said, a ghost of a smile on her lips.

"Right, Roman. After I send Roman on a little holiday. Get it?"

The smile widened, though it was still guarded. "I do, actually," she said.

The pounding continued, and I sighed.

"Be right back," I said. "You just hang back. Any messages for Roman?"

"Tell him I want the pictures he owes me."

"Pictures, right," I said, and walked down the hall. I heard her door shut with a click behind me. I walked through Grinner's apartment. The lights were out, and I was pretty sure if Grinner or Christine was home, one of them would have dealt with the elephant trying to knock down their door by now. For one horrible second, I thought it might be Illuminati bagmen here to collect me, but I knew my white lighter working had been solid, better than solid. I had days before I needed to move on. No, Roman was the kind of pain in the ass I could very much handle.

I unlocked the door, which took a second because of the half dozen locks and bolts Grinner had installed. The pounding stopped as soon as I began.

Before the final lock was snapped and door opened, I placed my palm on my chest.

"*Strenuorum quasi lapis,*" I said, and opened the door.

Roman looked exactly the way I expected him to. No, strike that, he was about 25 percent more Guido than I expected. He liked a little hair with his product, and his spray tan was so orange it made him look like an Oompa Loompa. His shirt was open to his navel, and there was enough bling around his neck to gold-plate the state of New Jersey. The only thing remotely interesting about him was the hand cannon he had in one of his massive fists that he had been using to pound on the door. Like I said, a rocket scientist.

"Where the fuck is she?" Roman said as he started to push past me into the apartment. I didn't budge. Literally. The big goombah tried to shove me out of the way with one hand, but he could not move me. He stopped and his mouth hung open in confusion. I smiled.

"She's washing her hair, Roman," I said. He backed up a little and ran at me in a classic football tackle. He hit, and I didn't shift an inch. I did, however, give him an uppercut that closed his mouth pretty solidly. The force of it staggered him, and I felt the satisfying crunch of broken teeth. As he stumbled backward, I relieved him of the gun. I cocked it and aimed it at his bloody face. It seemed Roman only had two facial expressions, rage and confusion. I was getting confusion now.

"What do we need to do to make this not happen again, Roman?" I said. "What does she owe you?"

"Thuck yoth," Roman said through torn lips and shattered teeth. He sounded like a little boy.

"Now, Roman," I said, "you still have your kneecaps." I lowered the pistol to his knees. "One last time, or I cripple you and go back to my Cocoa Puffs? What is your beef with this girl?"

"Da bith owth me twenty K," he said, backing away from the door, getting ready to bolt with his pristine knees.

"That include the vig?" I asked. "She gives you twenty grand and she is square, no interest, no more visits from you and your mouth guard?"

Roman was slowly shifting back to rage. He nodded.

"Okay," I said. "I'll have it to you by this afternoon. She have your number?"

Again the nod.

"We will call you and tell you where to meet us, understand? And bring the pictures you owe her, or no deal. You got that?"

"Yeth," he said. The eyes seethed with hatred.

"Now go get yourself some breakfast through a straw," I said, and shut the door in his face. I turned around and the girl was standing there, her arms wrapped around her chest, holding herself. She wore a black wife beater and purple panties. The ink I had seen on her shoulder earlier was part of a whole canvas. She had a slogan in Italian running along her left shoulder and collarbone, partly obscured by the sleeveless T-shirt; there was a skull with a bloom of roses behind it on her outer left thigh. With her raven hair, dark eyes, and olive complexion, she looked like she could be Greek, or Italian, or Middle Eastern—maybe all of them. I finally decided on Gypsy. Superman has kryptonite, I have Gypsies. She was small, about a half foot shorter than me, and she had very feminine curves. Her eyes and her body language reminded me of a doe—shy but curious, ready to bolt at the first sign of aggression. The guarded smile returned.

"Thank you," she said again with the accent that hinted of many places. "He would have hurt me very badly."

"Yeah, I kind of got that," I said. "Why are you into him for twenty grand?"

She moved to the couch and settled in a corner, her knees tucked up and a pillow now clutched tightly in both arms. I joined her, dropping Roman's gun on the coffee table.

"I'm a fool," she said. "That's the short version. I have been in the city for about a year now, I came from Canada—Calgary, in Alberta."

"That where you from originally?" I asked.

"I'm not really from anywhere originally," she said. Her smile widened for a second, and then she withdrew it.

"Anyway, I work as a model, a fetish model, mostly. I met Roman at a club, and he told me he was connected and could get me a professional photo shoot and some good gigs, he'd pay for it." She shook her head and chuckled; it was a sound of slight amusement and disgust. "He said I was his 'investment.' Yeah. So, the photo shoot was amazing, great stuff, would really enhance my portfolio. The jobs, they were . . . less amazing. They sucked."

"Porn," I said, more than asked.

She nodded. "Nasty, raunchy warehouse porn. I've done a lot I'm not proud of, but I've never done anything like that, Mr. . . ."

"Laytham," I said. "Laytham Ballard."

She extended a hand, and I saw a tattoo of a boxy little robot on her wrist. I shook her hand. "My model name is Miss Magdalena. My real name is—"

"Megan," I said, shaking her hand. She looked surprised as she drew her hand back. "I have scary wizard powers," I said. "And Christine told me last night. We're roomies. Hi."

I got the full smile, and it was worth the wait.

"Megan McGilvey," she said. "I like Magdalena better, though. Hi. Thank you for buying me some time with Roman, but I don't have the money he says I owe him for the photo shoot and backing out of the pornos."

"I got it," I said. "I just got paid for a little job I did in Egypt, and I feel like sharing the wealth." I could feel her emotionally withdraw. She was wary, had been down this road too many times with men.

"No strings," I said. "No porno, no sleeping with me, no nothing. Scout's honor."

"You," Magdalena said, "were never a Scout."

"I was!" I said, feigning insult. "For about two weeks, until there was an incident involving the den mother and my knot-tying merit badge."

Magdalena laughed. "I like a man who knows his knots," she said.

A wonderful, unspoken exchange happened then. The acknowledgment of a secret shared and offered. I smiled back.

"Okay, I'm trusting you," she said. "And I will pay you back, I promise."

I nodded as I groaned and stood.

"Things tend to balance themselves out," I said. "Okay, I'll figure out a good, safe place for us to meet Roman tonight and then get dressed and get some work done."

"Thank you, Ballard," she said.

I almost told her not to thank me yet, but then I thought better of it.

This," Grinner said, spinning in his high-backed swivel chair and holding up a thumb drive that looked like Boba Fett, "is everything from every dark, greasy corner of the Net about Dusan Slorzack, who, I might add, sounds like an enormous tool." He handed the drive to me.

By the time I had showered and changed clothes, Grinner and Christine were home, and Grinner took me into what he lovingly called "the lab." It was a cold, dark room honeycombed with rows of metal shelves full of server slices, microwave transmitters, satellite jammers and receivers, and shit that I couldn't begin to guess at its function. They all had little yellow, green, and red lights twinkling like fireflies. Cables and cords flowed everywhere and in every direction. Grinner's throne and the monoliths of computers and massive flat-screen monitors were islands of light in a sea of shadow. A little blue police call box bobble was bouncing gently on the upper edge of the massive monitor that sat behind him. The monitor currently showed the feed from all of the police traffic cameras in lower Manhattan. Rob Zombie's "Living Dead Girl," one of Grinner's favorites, thrummed over the speakers mounted to the ceiling and hidden in the air-conditioned darkness.

"It's not sexy," Grinner said, nodding to the thumb drive. "He's covered his tracks very well. Elite well. It's mostly old news reports, a few really decrepit docs from his political days, and a few hints about his connections and hobbies. Some kink stuff and some of the occult stuff, but it's all old and not really a huge amount of help.

"To summarize, Dusan Slorzack was born in 1945 in Belgrade. His father was a Nazi war criminal, Erich Gebhardt, who incidentally was a member of the SS and the Studiengruppe für germanisches Altertum. You know them, right?"

"The Thule Society," I said, nodding. "Occult society that cozied up to the Nazis." Grinner nodded, then went on.

"His mom was a barmaid, and prostitute on the side. Here's a tidbit, he was born a *zduhać,* someone whose birth caul, or placenta, is intac—"

"I'm familiar with that," I said, interrupting. While it's pretty much a crap shoot as to who is born to work magic, there are no coincidences when it comes to most magic itself. There is pattern, form, and direction, omens and portents. Sometimes the patterns are so complex, so chaotic, you can't see them, and sometimes they smack you in the face.

"Anyway," Grinner said, noticing my agitation, "supposed to mean you are born with innate magic powers. Big-league stuff.

"In his twenties, he was a supporter of numerous nationalist groups that opposed Tito's regime. He also studied mysticism, psychology, and philosophy, and was a disciple and eventual leader of the Black Hand. Ever hear of them?"

"Vaguely," I said.

"They were founded in 1911, kind of an occult terrorist group," Grinner said. "They were all about Slavic reunification at any cost. They were responsible for assassinating Archduke Franz Ferdinand, which started World War One, which eventually led to World War Two."

"There are a bunch of occult theories about the assassination," I said. Grinner nodded as he continued to sort through what looked like video files on the monitor.

"Back when I was in the navy, in CYBERFOR," Grinner said, "I was working in Bosnia. We hacked the Serbian air defense system, spoofed it so they couldn't shoot down our planes. The Black Hand was still creeping around the region even then. Lots of rumors they were mixed up in the ethnic cleansing going on. Two world wars, mass genocides. Damn. For such an obscure little group, they know how to make a statement."

"Yeah, resulting in the murder of millions," I said. "That much death is a hell of a lot of energy for a working, like nitrous in a car. Maybe the ethnic cleansing was the same kind of thing."

Grinner turned, gave me a hard look. "You think a bunch of occult assclowns started two world wars and practiced genocide just to charge up their Ouija boards? That is pretty fucked-up, man."

"I've seen worse," I said. "What else you got?"

He shook his head as he turned back to his keyboard.

"Well, by the early '90s, Slorzack was in Radovan Karadžić's inner circle and apparently helped push him to become president of the Republika Srpska—the Serbian territory carved out of Bosnia.

"From there, he weaseled his way into a position associated with Ratko Mladić, the scumbag who established and oversaw the ethnic cleansing and rape camps. Omarska, Čelebići, Keraterm, Trnopolje, Manjača, all the camps. Your boy Slorzack was hardwired into the administration at all of them, not just the one Boj's lady was at."

"Excuse me?" I said. "How did you . . ."

"You think you are the only one who can be all Dr. Strange, bro?" Grinner said, obviously very happy to have surprised me. "I found your muddy tracks all over Slorzack's trail. I cleaned them up as best I could, which is to say, epically, and also covered the track back from you to poor old Boj. That man was truly badass, the patron saint of stylish violence. It's a damn shame what happened to his wife. If anyone did that to Christine, I'd . . ."

He got quiet, looked away, lost in the click of the keys. This was a place I really couldn't gain admittance to. I had never had a Mita, or a Christine. Almost, a few times, but I was too chickenshit to see them through, to make it work. And then there was Torri Lyn and that . . . didn't work out.

I spent my life at the frayed edges. I didn't have anyone to be that invested in, to make my breath catch or my heart race. No one to protect or to avenge. Most times I was cool with it, part of the price I had chosen to pay for the power and the Life. But sometimes, sometimes . . .

"Thank you," I finally said. "For covering my ass and Boj's too."

"You'll get the bill," he said. "And by the way, I saw you got some big-ass bloodhounds on your tail too, serious mojo, lots of money and power. Long-ass reach. I'm keeping you to your word. I want you completely gone in the next twenty-four hours, Ballard, you feel me?"

"Yeah, of course," I said.

"And don't screw Magdalena over either, okay," Grinner said. "She's a good girl, and she doesn't need your special brand of fucked-up, okay?"

"Got it," I said.

A grainy black-and-white video image bounced into focus on the massive seventy-inch flat-screen monitor. It was a cluster of men in very bad suits talking, joking, and glad-handing as they got into a row of boxlike little cars on a rubble-strewn street in what appeared to be a partly bombed-out city. There was no sound, and a video camera time and date stamp in the corner of the video image said these pictures were taken on October 21, 1994.

"This is the last-known picture I could find of Dusan Slorzack. That's him there, talking to Mladić." Grinner froze the image. Dusan Slorzac was smiling, a cruel razor cut of a smile, and he was shaking the hand of the man who orchestrated the death of hundreds of thousands. Slorzack was tall and broad from bone and muscle. He had the build of a brawler more than a magus, with a mane of black hair that feathered away from his wide face and fell below his collar. It was a terribly out-of-date haircut looking like something a teen idol in the '70s would sport, and it looked even more incongruous on Slorzack, whose weathered, craggy face and bent, formerly broken nose marked him to be in his fifties at least. I was paying more attention to his eyes. They were dead. Black, immortal eyes—shark eyes, cobra eyes, the dead places between the stars. The slit smile was a poor attempt to appear human. He wasn't very good at it. I felt a pang of understanding, and that troubled me.

"Now check this out," Grinner said, and tapped a key. The flow of time resumed on the video. Slorzack glanced over Maldić's shoulder. I saw the moment he caught sight of the camera. The slit of a smile faded, and my prey narrowed his eyes. It was as if he was looking right at me, across time, across the electron sea. I looked back and I felt the power in my body begin to coalesce, to rise. It was pure fight or flight. We locked eyes and we knew each other. He arched his head slightly. The video distorted, warped, as if a powerful magnet had been suddenly put beside the camera. Slorzack's face twisted and blurred, and then the images were lost to a wall of electronic rain. Grinner was facing me again. We were both silent. The static made the shadows in the room dance.

"You sure you up for this, man?" Grinner finally said.

"That all you got for me?" I said. "Not much to go hunting on. Pretty light for twenty grand."

"Fifty," Grinner reminded me. "And I'm not done yet, corn pone.

"People like Slorzack find me all the time to erase them from the Net, from life, to make them cease to be, and I charge them plenty for that. From the moment you are born, you are named, marked. A person's true name used to be a secret thing, a sacred thing—it gave someone power over you. Today your true name is your social security number and we hand it out like it was candy at Halloween. So many agencies, so many powers and principalities have dominion over us, Ballard, and we have no clue, man. Credit score, police record, taxes, DMV, online shopping, GPS. We give strangers on the other side of the planet our exact location every time we walk into a fucking Starbucks with our cell phone. We are owned, Ballard, from the day we are born until the day we die. He's out there, and he has chains, just like the rest of us. I've got a few more places to look, a little more voodoo programming to do, before I call it a day."

"Like what?" I asked. "Where else is there to look?"

"You remember those shared computer projects in the late '90s and early 2000s," Grinner said. "SETI used them to look for Klingons and shit, and a bunch of other research groups got volunteers from all over the world to let them co-opt their home computers, to boost processing speed to churn the huge amount of data these groups had to mull over."

"Yeah, I remember," I said. "So?"

"So, some of the beautiful bastards that own everything saw some real potential in that, saw a way to forge another chain. The social media stuff—Facebook, Twitter, MySpace, Instagram, Tumblr, all that shit—well, they networked them, all of them, into something called an SI, a swarm intelligence. It's a nebulous, churning, cloud-based thing, made up of a population of simple agents interacting locally with one another and with their environment. In this case, us and our social network. There are few rules in a swarm intelligence, no centralized control structure dictating behavior. Local and, to a degree, random interactions between each little cog in the swarm lead to the emergence of intelligent, predictable global behavior, and all of it is unknown to the individual parts of the system. Turns out we're not so special, Laytham. We work on the same level as bacterial growth, ant colonies, flocks of birds, schools of fish. Animals being herded."

Grinner chucked drily, the way a guy dying of lung cancer might if asked if he was going to quit smoking now. "Herded. Jesus, we did this to ourselves. Stupid bastards, tending their virtual farms and sending out duck-lipped bathroom pictures, building fantasy football leagues and composing one-hundred-forty-character missives on what they had for lunch at Burger King. They are being used to mine data, like slaves, mining the data that shackles them, that defines their lives."

He shook his head slightly, his tiny eulogy for the human race.

"Is this another pitch for Anomyous?" I said. Grinner flipped me off and went on.

"The good news is that I know how to get into that system, know how to read the patterns, the trends and forecasts. I can read the human race's guts like the fucking Oracle at Delphi. Even if Slorzack managed to erase most of his trail, a rock hitting a pond produces ripples, and I'll trace those back to him by scanning the pond."

"Big damn pond," I said. "What if he's in some third world shit hole, no Internet and no online stuff?"

"Don't exist anymore, man," Grinner said. "If he's on this earth and he has had any human interaction, I'll find him. When Kalahari Bushmen have fucking cell phones, there is no place to hide from me anymore."

"Damn," I said. "And they say *I* do black magic." For some reason, the handcuff keys around Berman's neck jumped into my mind. "You said he was into the Lifestyle. He frequent clubs anywhere?"

"Here in the Apple," Grinner said, "but it was a long time ago—about ten or eleven years ago. Before me and Christine's time, way before Magdalena's time too. That's like a geological age in the scene. Pretty cold scrap."

"Is Didgeri still around?" I asked.

Grinner laughed and I smiled.

"Didgeri," Grinner said. "Yeah, yeah she is. Still owns the

Dreamtime too. Hell, yeah, man. If anyone in this town would re-member old Slavic Frankenberry, it would be Didgeri."

I got up and slapped Grinner on the shoulder and started to walk out of the lab.

"'Preciate it," I said. "I'll tell her you said hello."

"Screw that. Tell her she still owes me a grand for getting that Ko-rean ghost out of her iPad," Grinner said as he pulled up a wall of code on the monitor. "Good hunting, hillbilly."

SIX

Magdalena and I took a cab to the West Village. It was a little after nine and a cold drizzle was spitting on the city, not that the city gave a damn. Magdalena pulled her worn leather biker jacket tighter around herself. She was wearing a black-and-red leather corset, tight black jeans, and high-heeled boots. She had on a little black-and-purple-striped knit cap and matching wool scarf to ward off the rain. I wore a beat-up old olive-drab military trench coat I had found in Goodwill in Atlanta fifteen years ago. I had an Adventure Time T-shirt on under a threadbare black sweater, my ripped-up jeans, and my combat boots. I lit up an American Spirit as soon as we got out and paid the cabbie.

"You smoke way too many of those hipster cigarettes," she said. "Those things are going to kill you."

"Something's goin' to," I said. "Might as well be something I enjoy."

"Better ways to go," she said.

We walked down the sidewalk past deep wells of shadow. Pale, gaunt faces, smeared in paint to provide the semblance of life, floated up out of the darkness to mumble offers of pleasure and pain to both of us. It's a sad testament to the endurance race that life is that their offers didn't move either of us. It was the same anywhere you went.

When you hit low enough, all you had left to sell of any value was your skin and your soul.

We turned the corner and crossed against the light, arriving at the threshold of the Dreamtime. The windows were all blackout tape, and you could feel the thrumming power of the music vibrating through them. A small crowd milled under the tattered awning by the main doors: trannies, club kids, a few slumming B-list celebs. Dirty idling taxis were queued up by the curb, awaiting fares.

"I've heard about this place," Magdalena said, "but I never made it here before. You told Roman to meet us here?"

"Yeah," I said. "I know the lady who owns the joint, and she won't allow any bullshit in her domain."

At the entrance, I handed the doorman a hundred. He was slender and porcelain, save the vibrant peacock tattoo on the left side of his face and the machine pistol under his white Edwardian coat. Every part of him was bleached except the shimmering color of his tattoo. He unhooked the shabby, frayed velvet rope and gestured for us to pass.

"You actually know Didgeri Doo?" Magdalena said, a wide smile with the warmth of daybreak crossing her face. "She's a legend in alt and fetish modeling. She was one of the only transgender fashion models to make it big in the mainstream. Without her there never would never have been any Malika, no Tula Cossey, no Lea T. Wow. You met her here in New York?"

"No," I said, opening the door for her. The music, a club mix of "Afterlife," by Arcade Fire, rolled out into the street. "I met her back in Australia, when she was a skinny little Abo boy named Adoni and got beat nightly by Outback shit kickers for dressing like a girl."

We walked down a narrow hallway painted black, with strands of white Christmas tree lights adorning the walls. It narrowed, funneled into a vast room. Beams of light and darkness rained down with the music. The dance floor was painted, covered with a rainbow-colored serpent with scales of black light paint. The serpent coiled, slithered, twisted, and glowed across the floor. It was everywhere, and the dancers flowed, moved among its coils. The serpent was the dancers and dancers were the great snake.

"Now," I said, "she's the queen of the world, holding court."

Above the glowing, undulating snake-floor, on a stage just in front of the DJ's perch, was a shifting, swirling figure with twin neon-burning poi ropes in her hand, spinning a hypnotic pattern around herself—a cocoon of electronic fire. She had bronze-brown skin shimmering with body glitter, a dress of golden metal mesh, golden knee boots with six-inch heels, platinum hair raining down like Lady Godiva, and eyes the color of clove. I couldn't help but smile. She was a goddess.

"Didgeri-fucking-Doo!" Magdalena said, jumping up and down and tugging on my arm. "Come on, old man, let's dance!"

The music changed, slid, morphed into Sultan and Ned Shepard's "Ordinary People." I could feel the power flowing through Dreamtime, I knew Didgeri was using that power, was in the middle of a working. I knew I had Roman to deal with and Slorzack and the Illuminati, and, and, and. But in that second, in that moment of heat and sound, with this beautiful girl, so much life and passion shining out of her, I laughed and nodded.

"Okay, let's fucking dance, darlin'."

And we did. A lot. For the first time I could remember in years—hell, decades—I felt the joy the power could bring, the beating heart of magic, the power of humanity, of release, of emotion not guarded behind a wall of discipline and paranoia. I laughed and I sweated and I danced. And Magdalena was the center of the storm; she moved with fluid grace, navigated the serpent coils flawlessly with instinct and passion, and I felt the power shine off of her, out of her like a geyser from Heaven. In that moment I saw what she was, what she could be.

I looked above the dance floor to the stage, and my eyes and Didgeri's locked. She had sensed it too.

Magdalena and I eventually collapsed in a booth, our clothes soaked. I'd ditched my sweater within ten minutes of starting to thrash about. I bought an ice bucket full of obscenely overpriced bottled water and paid extra to make sure it wasn't dosed with X. Magdalena and I both downed two bottles before either of us could talk.

"You dance pretty good for a seasoned citizen," Magdalena said, raising her bottle in a toast. I tapped my bottle to hers, smiled, and uttered a quaint vulgarity. We turned to look at the dance floor, and Roman was standing in front of our table, both eyes blackened and tape on his nose. He was damp from the rain outside and had slid one of his hands under his raincoat. His eyes burned with fantasies of payback and petty anger.

"Enjoy your dance, bitch," Roman shouted over the pounding beat of the music. He started to draw, and I began to rise, but I was tired, sore, and caught completely off guard. I tried to think of a simple ward, anything to stop him, but I had let all my defenses down. Idiot. I suddenly felt a flare of power, like the sun bursting to life from behind storm clouds.

A perfectly manicured hand rested lightly on Roman's shoulder. The skin was slightly darker than the color of cinnamon, and two bracelets of bone and gold clattered as the fingers touched Roman.

"Is everyone having a delightful time, Laytham?" Didgeri Doo asked.

I smiled. "We are now," I said.

"Absolutely deadly!" Didgeri exclaimed happily. "It is so unlike you to come down here and to let yourself go so completely. I think this lovely creature at your elbow simply must be the cause."

Roman was frozen; his hand hovered under his coat but did not move. The look of confusion was back, and this time he reminded me of a caged animal. He was trying to move the gun, trying to will his hand, will any part of his body to move, but nothing was happening. Didgeri simply ignored him, removed her hand from his shoulder, and leaned over the table, extending the hand to an awestruck Magdalena.

"Such a pleasure to meet you, dear," Didgeri said. "Any friend of my balla, Ballard, is welcome here. Especially one that can so thoroughly enchant him to loosen up. The man is a clenched fist with legs. I'm Pangari. You might know me by my working name."

"I do!" Magdalena said eagerly, shaking her hand.

"She does," I added, and leaned back to wave at Roman. He looked truly terrified now. I smiled at him. "You look beautiful, Geri. This is Magdalena, she's a fan girl and a model as well. And this very, very unfortunate man is Roman. He's learning impaired."

Didgeri smiled and leaned in to give Magdalena a kiss on the cheek. She turned to regard Roman, and the smile faded.

"No one brings anger and destruction into my domain," Didgeri said. Her voice was a steel whisper, and I could hear every icy syllable over the blasting music. I knew Roman could too. A small, brown scorpion scuttled into view on Roman's arm, the one partly concealed under his jacket. Didgeri placed her hand slowly, deliberately on his left shoulder. Roman's eyes were dilated in fear.

"Do you have any idea who you are pissing with you silly, ugly gubba?" she cooed. "You come into my initiated place, my place of power, and try to start something with your silly hunk of dead steel. You might not recognize it anymore; it's crawling up your arm."

I watched Magdalena's reaction to all this—relief at the protection and the apparent end to Roman's threat before it started. But she was also fascinated and frightened by the show Didgeri was putting on for us. What I didn't see was confusion or panic. It just confirmed what Didgeri and I both had already sensed.

"I am the Goddess Eingana's agency outside the Dreamtime," Didgeri said softly in Roman's ear. The scorpion was now making its way up Roman's arm and toward his shoulder. "I clutch the Black Sinew, the threads of life and death. Your life or death, Roman. I let go, and you slip into darkness."

With the supreme effort only life-or-death terror can fuel, Roman made a faint, whimpering moan. The scorpion was poised on his shoulder, its claws nipping at his earlobe, its tail arched to strike. Didgeri looked away from his frozen face down to Magdalena.

"Is there anything you'd care to see happen to him, m'dear? His energy seems to be mostly focused toward you. Would you care for him to die?"

Magdalena blinked and turned her head. She rubbed her face. I knew what Didgeri was doing, and I found it cruel, though my inner bastard admired the flawless way it was being executed. I almost extended my perceptions to see what was going on inside Magdalena, but it would be a terrible breach of etiquette toward our hostess, who had kept the nasty goon from gunning us down where we sat. So I waited, like the rest of the universe. Magdalena looked Roman in the eye, and I saw the flash of anger there. This man had used her, hurt her, and made her feel foolish. I knew what my answer would be.

"Let him live, let him go," Magdalena said. "Please."

Didgeri smiled. Her brown-gold eyes shined. "A very wise choice, darling."

"But first," I said, "get the pictures from him. They belong to Magdalena. He was supposed to bring them." Magdalena laughed and hugged me. Didgeri nodded and turned her attention back to Roman. She slid her hand into his coat.

"It seems Laytham is not as forgiving as Miss Magdalena, here. I hope for your sake you brought the pictures, gubba."

The scorpion was still teasing and pinching Roman's ear. Didgeri's hand returned from under his coat with a thumb drive. She handed it to Magdalena.

"Thank you," Magdalena said.

Roman blinked and then began to move again. Very stiffly. Didgeri remained next to him.

"You know where the door is," she said. "Old Man Scorpion is with you and will stay with you until I tell him to leave you be. Any trouble, these good people see you ever again, and he will kiss you. Do you understand, wagala?"

Roman nodded very slowly. The scorpion snipped at the air next to his ear.

"Thank the pretty girl for your life on your way out," Didgeri said.

Roman looked scared. His eyes were wet. This had all been a little too much for his mind to process.

"Bye, Roman," Magdalena said, smiling. It was sincere. She stood and placed the envelope with the twenty grand I had given her earlier in the night in his trembling hand. Roman walked away, trying to avoid the crowd of dancers between him and the door like a man carrying sweating dynamite. He vanished into the laser-drenched mist of the Dreamtime, lost in a curtain of bodies.

"That," I said, "was very cool. Thanks, darlin'."

"Deadly," Didgeri said, laughing. "I only get to do stuff like that when I hang out with you, Laytham."

Didgeri nodded toward the thumb drive Magdalena was examining.

"Why don't you go check that on the office computer, dear? Make sure it's what you were looking for."

"That would be great. Thank you so much," Magdalena said, and hugged Didgeri. "It should be pictures from a shoot with James Stiles."

"Ah, yes, James," Didgeri said as she gestured to one of her bartenders, a powerfully built black man. "Quite the charmer, as I recall, and an excellent eye; made me feel like Cinderella. I hope the photos are intact, dear. I'd love to see them." She turned to her employee. "Keane, take Ms. Magdalena here back to the manager's office and help her with the computer, please. Thank you, dear."

Keane and Magdalena walked away, and Didgeri moved around the table to sit down. I slid out of the booth and pulled out a chair on the other side of the table for her.

"Alone at last," she said, sitting. I pushed in her chair. "I do so adore southern gentlemen. Even when they aren't terribly gentle. Especially when they aren't, actually."

I offered her a bottle of water. She refused with a dismissive wave and gestured to summon one of her bottle service hostesses.

"I need your memory, Geri," I said. "I'm looking for someone in the Life, an Initiated Man. He was also a player in the Lifestyle here in New York about ten years ago. His name is Slorzack, Dusan Slorzack. He may have been hooked up with a Wall Street suit named James Berman—also in the Lifestyle, I suspect," I said, and held up the handcuff keys Berman had been wearing when I found him. Didgeri shuddered as the power from them passed through her like a painful memory. The hostess arrived, a slender Asian woman in a short black dress.

"Bring us a chilled bottle of Ley .925, and three glasses, darling," Didgeri said. She looked back to me. "Still a tequila man, Laytham?"

I nodded and addressed the smiling hostess. "And a Budweiser as well, please, darlin'. Can is fine."

The hostess seemed a little confused, but Didgeri nodded and she took her leave to get our drinks.

"I'm certain there is a special place in Hell for a man who drinks two-hundred-thousand-dollar tequila with a Budweiser chaser," Didgeri said blandly.

"So," I said, holding up the keys again and shaking them, "ring any bells?"

"Ugh," she said, and rolled her eyes. "There is power coming off that, but you already knew that, didn't you?"

I nodded. "This Berman guy is dead, murdered. A few days back. Wasn't in the news. He's connected, but I'm not sure how much."

"I know him," Didgeri said. "By reputation only. He was a switch— liked to play dominance and submission roles, I am led to understand. More into kink as a gateway to power than to passion. I'm sure you know the type." She smiled at me.

"Yeah, yeah," I said. "Guilty. I wouldn't be lucky enough for you to know Slorzack too."

"Again, by reputation, balla," she said. "They used to call him 'the Pain Eater' in the clubs. He was a sadist, and he combined that with tantric traditions. Very much a horror show, from what I heard. His play partners tended to go missing after a few months. Rumor was a few of them ended up in his fridge."

"He still creeping around, Geri?" I asked. I felt the slightest hope stir in me that this was going to be easier than I had anticipated.

"No, he left the city around 2002. A lot of people did back then. There were a few police investigations into missing people he may have been involved with, but nothing ever came of them. Berman stayed active on and off in the scene, but the Pain Eater just disappeared. There are rumors that he was, well, never mind."

"No, c'mon now. Don't be holding out on me," I said. "Spill."

"Well, that he might have had something to do with what happened on nine/eleven," Didgeri said.

The hostess returned with the chilled gold-and-silver bottle of Ley .925. She poured both of us a shot and then set a frosted mug of beer next to mine. I tipped her a few hundred. And I waited until she departed to continue.

"You are kidding me, right?" I said. "This guy have a secret lair too? Henchmen?"

"First the drink, balla," Didgeri said, "then the smart ass."

We raised the slender tubelike crystal shot glasses and clinked them gently together.

"A thousand-mile journey begins with a single step," she said.

"May as well be 'here we are' as 'where we are,'" I replied. We both tossed back the tequila. Cool, bitter smoke clawed down my throat and caught fire in my belly. I felt a twinge of something warm stir in me, but I pushed it aside.

"Nine-fucking-eleven," I said. "Really?"

"That was the rumor," Didgeri continued as she set her glass down and dabbed the corner of her lips with her finger. "That he was connected to that evil somehow."

"You know any of Berman's long-time play partners you might be able to reach out to for me?" I asked. "I need as much of a bead as I can get on Slorzack, and I need to know how deep into the Life Berman was too."

"I can make some inquiries. Give me twenty-four hours," she said.

"I can give you fourteen, darlin'," I said. "I threw some pretty ballsy misdirection magic at the hounds on my tail, but I don't have long to get the hell out of Dodge."

"Very well," she said. "I will perform my customary miracles and make it happen. I only do this for you Laytham, I hope you appreciate that."

"I do," I said, and I meant it. "It's damn good to see you again, Adoni. May I still call you that?"

"Name I was born with," she said. "Name I died with. Boy's name. After what you did for me back in Brisbane, balla, you can call me whatever you want."

"You hear anything from your dad?" I asked, pouring another shot.

"He's alive," Didgeri said, picking up and examining her empty glass as I filled it. "And he'll stay that way as long as I stay clear of him. My uncle occasionally sends something mauia lurching out of the Dreamtime to try to piss with me, but his power is weak this far across the sea. He'd love to send a Kurdaitcha man to point a bone at me, but he doesn't have the balls to do it."

"Well, you certainly do," I said, smiling, and raised my glass. Didgeri laughed and raised hers as well; the crystal clinked. "You say the word, sister girl, and we're on a plane back to the land down under to deal with your uncle and grandfather."

"No, Laytham," she said as we both set down our empty glasses. "I miss my da', but I understand your way, my balla. An Initiated Man, a Secret Man, needs to walk alone in his world. It's too dangerous to have people you care about who can become collateral damage. Too many things that can make them bleed, drive them mad. Don't you agree, yes?"

"Yeah," I said, as I watched Magdalena walk out of the back room, talking to Keane, smiling, laughing, completely unaware of her power, her beauty. Heat stirred in me again, but now, looking at her, I had no desire to push it away. But I did. I suddenly saw her on the other side of the meat grinder that was my life, and realized I couldn't do that to a work of art. "You're right."

"Still," Didgeri said, smiling and pouring three new drinks, "even if you walk alone, doesn't mean you can't have a little company with you for part of the trip."

I turned back to Didgeri. "You are up to something, you scheming witch."

"Always, darling," Didgeri said. "Magdalena, she has no idea what she is, what she has the capability to become?"

"I didn't even feel it until tonight, in here," I said. "Whatever working you were doing, it caught her up in it, and you could feel her power like a bomb blast."

"Caught her, yes, I see," Didgeri said. "It's a simple bit of yilpinji. Quite common back home. I do it with the crowd on good nights. They seem to enjoy it."

"That sounds familiar," I said, sipping my beer. "Where do I know that from? This is some damn good tequila, Geri."

"She will be back over here in a moment," Didgeri said. "Any thoughts on how we proceed? Each tradition has its own ways of—"

"I don't have a damn tradition," I said. "You know that. I'm a mutt. I can't take on a fucking apprentice! I'm in the middle of caper! The way my life is, especially an apprentice that looks like that."

"Then perhaps it is time to change the way your life is, balla. You want to die alone? No friends? No lovers? Some nightmare thing locked at your throat?"

"But you just said you agreed with how I live my life," I said, draining more of my beer. "What the hell, Geri!"

The music, the lights, everything was diverting. I was getting tired of Didgeri's mystic master bullshit. I looked over to Magdalena. She was dancing alone, well, she had several men and women dancing around her, dancing to the rhythm she set. They wanted to dance with her, connect with her. The voice in Fashion's techno version of Bowie's "The Man Who Sold the World" was blasting across the Dreamtime. Magdalena was smiling, laughing. She looked very young, life incarnate. I vaguely remembered feeling that way once—a long, long time ago, like the song says.

"I said I understood it. That doesn't mean it's what I want for you, balla," she said. "You used to work with others—Harel, Boj—your 'Occult Rat Pack.' Now you walk into places alone that can get you killed, or worse. You could take this girl as an apprentice, settle down and teach her, prepare her. She's a Star Soul, a High Magician, like you and me. She will work miracles in time. You could help her, like you helped me."

"Shit, I helped you into a mental hospital, Geri," I said, draining the last of my beer. "A real master would have stayed with you, taught you. I just strapped you into a roller coaster full of explosives, lit the fuse, and walked the fuck away when the credits rolled. Like I always do."

"I seem to recall it a bit differently," Didgeri said. "If people follow you, join you in your journeys, it is their choice, their walkabout. It is arrogant and selfish of you to deny them a destiny, and egotistical, I might add, to think it's all about you."

"Whatever," I said. "Bottom line, I can't teach her. Can't. I'll give her the pitch and explain to her the options she has. Can I send her to you to study?"

"Of course, but you and I both know you are the one who can prepare her for the Life far better than I."

Magdalena was walking to the table now; she was glistening, laughing from the dance. Her eyes were damp and dark and focused on me. The deer I met in the apartment this morning was gone. She moved like a panther, my breath caught in my throat.

"Damn, look at her," I said, and then shook it off. I glanced back to Didgeri.

"I don't want her in the Life. You can teach her how to live, not just survive, Adoni. Please?"

The Queen of Dreamtime smiled at me, and it was like the sun warming my face. "Of course, balla, of course."

SEVEN

We grabbed a cab out front of the Dreamtime at four A.M. and sloshed into the backseat. Magdalena told the driver, a slender, dour-faced Indian man in a maroon windbreaker, the address, and off we went.

It was still raining, but it felt cool and good after the heat of the club, and we both felt the exhaustion and strange marriage of calm and exhilaration that come after a night of dancing your ass off. A random thought wandered through my tequila-enhanced brain. *Cocaine would ruin this feeling right now. Even pot would.*

"You got kinda quiet after you and Didgeri talked," Magdalena said, taking a sip on a bottle of water. "You okay?"

"Right as rain, darlin'," I said. "We just got to talking all serious council of wizards stuff. Very weighty, cosmic shit. Who's taking the sorting hat to prom, and such."

"Umhm," she said. "Have to do with this guy you are looking for, that you still haven't told me anything about?"

"How the hell did you know I was looking for someone?" I asked.

"You have Grinner working on something for you," Magdalena said. "People usually hire him to find people or to get lost. I had a fifty-fifty shot. Besides, you don't seem the type to be trying to hide."

"You'd be surprised," I said. "What time is it?"

She looked at her phone. "Four ten. Why don't you have a cell phone?"

"They are a tool to control you economically and mentally," I said.

"Paranoid much?" Magdalena asked.

"I know a guy in L.A. who has developed an entire form of sympathetic magic through cell phones," I said. "He's a twittermancer—he can read your thoughts, control your actions, and know your secrets through your cell phone traffic. Of course his workings have to be a hundred and forty characters or less to work, but that keeps him on his toes."

"You're not serious about the phone stuff are you?" she asked.

"Think about it for a second," I said. "What is one of the most personal, idiosyncratic talismans you carry with you everywhere—to bed, to the bathroom? Your phone. The cell companies are drug dealers; they push minutes and data plans instead of crack and meth. Most folks would pay for their phone before they pay their rent. No one seems to notice that one of the major cell companies has the fucking Elder Sign from H. P. Lovecraft as its corporate logo."

"Oh, come on," she said. "You're ranting. You sound like a Luddite, for Christ's sake."

"Arcane, binding contracts," I went on, "the addictive quality of having the phone close by, to check it, to talk through it by texts instead of actually talking to people. The constant hunger and envy for the newest one, the thinnest, the biggest screen, even if you just got one. The incessant monitoring of where you are by GPS, the dependence on it. Tell me, the people closest to you—do you know their numbers, or do you just push a button and the phone takes care of it? And the constant use of the things mutates your brain, alters the organ you use to interpret reality, to reason. Give it a few decades, you will have them implanted inside you—part of you. I'll pass on Candy Crush, thanks."

She laughed. I could get used to that sound.

The tires of the cars swooshed on the wet streets, smeared with the reflections of city lights. The cabbie was listening to some AM talk show going on about Bigfoot being an extradimensional entity. He was, but I really didn't need that in my ear right now.

"You feel any different tonight, in the club?" I asked.

"Yes," she said, "I did. At one point, I thought maybe I had been dosed with Ecstasy. I felt connected to everyone and everything in there. The people, the music, the light. It was amazing, but it didn't feel . . . synthetic, like X can. It felt like I was breathing with the world."

I nodded and fished out my cigarettes. "Well said. You were." I held the pack up so the driver could see. "Hey, pal, you cool?" The driver glared at me with eyes that smoldered of hate and practiced patience. The window on my side of the cab hummed down and the cool air and rain blew in. I nodded and went about the business of lighting up. "Tell me, did you feel connected to me or Didgeri in there?"

"Some when we were dancing, early on, some when she was doing her poi thing, but now that you mention it, no. It was like you two were outside of everything."

"It's a defense," I said, "something you learn to do so you aren't naked and vulnerable. That beautiful world you were breathing with, it has teeth sometimes, sharp ones."

"I don't understand," she said, turning toward me.

"Yeah," I said, "part of you does. You're afraid to go with that intuitive knowledge yet; you'll learn that in time too. Your instincts can guide you. It's the universe whispering in your ear."

"You were serious about all this magic stuff you been talking," she said. "You meet guys all over this town that claim to be into occult stuff—usually it's a pick-up line, or an excuse to wear black and be an asshole."

"Listen," I said, "inside. Listen, hear the music between things, between you, in you."

I saw her open herself to her own inner voice; the knowledge crossed her face for just a second, then she shut it down, hard.

"Are you trying to tell me I'm some kind of psychic or something?" she said. I saw the driver's hate-filled eyes flick back to us in the rearview mirror. The noise from the radio had diminished.

"Turn it back up," I said, blowing cigarette smoke out the window, "right now. And if you look back here again, I know several very reputable rakshasa in this town that I will personally invite to feed on your liver. Now drive."

The cabbie muttered a prayer in Hindi and turned the radio back up.

"Psychic is a word," I said. "My granny called us Wisdoms. Geri's kin call us Secret Men or Initiated Men. Wizards, warlocks, witches— lots of w's there. Magus, Illuminate, hoodoo, Drabarne . . ."

"Drabarne. My grandmother used that word," Magdalena said. "You are saying I can do magic? I'm some kind of witch?"

"I'm saying you have the potential to open yourself up to a wider universe, to new perceptions, to power, real power. Yeah, darlin', I am."

She looked out the window into the darkness between the islands of city light. She placed her hand on the cool glass, and I could see her shadowed reflection in the window, a face filled with rain. "Why me?" she asked softly. "I'm not anything special, I'm nobody."

"I don't know why," I said. "I don't think there is a why. You have choices now. Decisions about what you want to do with it."

"Can I just ignore it?" she said, the ice cracking in her voice. "I don't want anything to do with it, okay? This is fucking crazy. Magic isn't even real. This is bullshit."

"You don't believe that," I said. "Not even as the words are falling out of your mouth. You know it, you feel it, and you've felt it most of your life. You can run from it, pretend it isn't real, and ignore it. It won't ignore you. It's no coincidence that we found each other. The people who exist in this world—most of us call it the Life—can sense each other. We're like lodestones. The Life tends to drag us toward one another, and toward trouble, weird trouble.

"The power doesn't really give a damn what you want. I'm surprised you haven't run into one of us before. So, yes, you can keep on keeping on. But even if that is your choice, you needed to know about all this, so when the weird shit comes a-knockin', you can at a least be ready to run, not just piss yourself and lose your mind."

The words seemed familiar to me, and when I realized their origin was my grandmother, a terrible sadness filled me. I wish I had listened.

We were quiet for a bit. Her hand found mine and I took it. She was tough, I'll give her that. Most people who just find out that all the paranoid, schizophrenic shit they thought was bad juice in their heads was actually not madness but hyperreality, they tend to lose it. She didn't. She took my hand and we rode through the endless city.

"I was with someone for a long time," she began. "I . . . enjoy submission, I like having someone take control and take me out of my head. I had a lot of bad things happen when I was a kid . . . that doesn't really matter. I like it and, at times, I need it. This woman, I met her, and we fell in love, and she gave me that, and I gave her what she needed too, I thought—a sense of being in control of me, of protecting me and caring for me. I thought . . ."

She was fighting the tears, and so far, she was winning. She turned away from the night and looked me in the eyes.

"She was like you, into all this occult shit. She was powerful, like you, like Didgeri, maybe more powerful. She scared me. She was building a cult around submissives who worshiped her like a goddess. She was buying up land in Mexico, recruiting medical personnel, military types, as her slaves."

"She have a name?" I asked.

"Yes," Magdalena said, nodding, "but I don't want to say it. I can still feel her regard sometimes, like she's looking for me, and if I think about her too hard, if I say her name, then she will come get me. I know it's stupid, but she fucking terrifies me."

"No, no," I said. "That's actually a very good idea. Don't think about her if you can help it. So things went bad and you left?"

"Yes," Magdalena said. "She started dominating me all the time, not just when I consented to it. She forced me to take part in her rituals. She . . . used me in them. Now I think that I was some kind of . . . battery for her. She used me. I always felt so bad afterward, like I had the flu. I liked her putting me into a submissive mind space, but then she started trying to addict me to it, try to crush my free will. I ran away, took another name, and hid. I got help, helped myself. Started over. So, yeah, I have met someone in the Life before, and she was a psychopath and nearly ate my soul."

"I know you don't want this," I said, "and I understand why, but if you accept this part of yourself, master it, then if this crazy bitch ever does turn up one day, you at least have the tools to protect yourself, to keep running, maybe even to take her down."

"I don't want to take anyone down," Magdalena said. "I just want to focus on beauty, on creating things. This 'Life' seems to all be about control and power and using people. I don't want that."

"It doesn't have to be," I said. "Didgeri was doing a working tonight; it was part of what you felt in the club. It was about making people open up, making them feel good, feel connected. The power is a tool; you can make of it whatever you want, whatever you have inside of you."

"Could you teach me?" she asked. A cold knife slid into my guts.

"I . . . wouldn't be a good teacher," I said. "I suck at that. I'm just telling you what your choices are and letting you know you have options. I'm trying to help you, Magdalena."

"If this is some bullshit scam to get me to sleep with you," she said, "it is the worst ever."

"No," I said. "Unfortunately, after all of the psychic vulnerabilities we've been ripping open tonight, it would be really, really shitty of me to do that. Bad wizard form, I'm afraid. Could get my pointy hat revoked for that. Just a confidante and a friend."

Magdalena gave me a very strange look and squeezed my hand.

The cab pulled up in front of Grinner's building. The rain had canceled the usual ongoing block party. We got out, and I reached for my wallet to pay chuckles, the cabbie. The second we were out of his cab, he gunned it and roared away.

"Come on," I said, putting my arm around Magdalena, "let's get out of this damn rain."

The apartment was dark. Grinner and Christine were either asleep or not home. We shed our coats and walked down the hall to our rooms.

"Well, thanks for a very . . . unique evening," she said. She held up the thumb drive. "And thanks so much for this! I can really make some things happen in my career with these in my portfolio. You're a hero, Laytham."

"Bullshit," I said, "but I appreciate the sentiment."

She moved a step closer to me. "Well, you were a Boy Scout," she said, resting her hand on my chest. I felt my pulse jump at the touch.

"For at least a week," I said. Awkward silence. No one moved, no one stepped away. The feeling I had when we had first met and talked was back. The unspoken thing that is either there or not, granted or forbade.

I knew what was right; I just really didn't give a damn.

I ran my hand through her long, thick raven hair, still damp from the rain. Our eyes locked. I clutched a handful of her hair tightly and pulled her head back. She gasped. Excitement, and a touch of fear, flared in her eyes. I felt a cool sense of control settle over me, wrapping itself in my arousal, my desire. Our mouths, hungry, insistent, clumsy in need, opened, fell onto each other, upon each other. She moaned under the crush of my lips, my tongue.

She pushed me against the wall next to my door. Her nails were raking down my back, her legs wrapping around my waist. Her tongue, teasing, flicking my own. It was my turn to moan.

"You going to get in trouble for this?" she said, gasping as our mouths separated for a moment.

"Trouble is my business," I said, with apoligies to Raymond Chandler, and pulled her by her hair back to my mouth.

We crashed into her room, the only light spilling in from the hallway. There was a vanity with a cracked oval mirror, a dumpster treasure, a dresser from the same back alley store, and a proper bed with tarnished brass head- and footboards. There were dark candles everywhere, on every milk cart pedestal and bookcase, on top of the dresser and the vanity, and there was a brass stand that held a large white candle near the window.

As one clumsy, thrashing organism, we stumbled to the bed and fell onto it laughing and moaning. Clothes were flying everywhere. I sat up and put my hand to her pale, perfect throat. She gasped, then relaxed against my hand. I kissed her bare shoulder and then kissed my way up to the tender junction where shoulder met neck. I moved her head backward slightly with pressure to her throat.

"You want this?" I said. "You need this?"

"Yes," Magdalena hissed. "I need to be outside my head. I need to feel out of control, to be under control. I want it."

I tightened my grip on her throat and sank my teeth into her alabaster shoulder. She gasped and her head flew back. Her body shuddered as pain and pleasure burned through her nerves.

My hand slid from throat to her breast, clawing at the corset. My mouth was at her ear again. I chewed on her lobe for a moment. She gasped again; her hands were clawing at my chest, pulling at my sweater, tearing it. Her hands were running through my hair, tugging on it.

"Mine," I growled into her ear. "Mine, tonight."

Her lips found my cheek and then chin as she covered me in sweet wet kisses.

"Yours," she said, her voice muffled against my neck. "Yours, tonight."

Magdalena fell back on the bed, her hands sliding under my sweater and T-shirt, teasing, raking my nipples with her nails. Sensation surged through me. Still crouched on the bed over her, I turned my gaze to the harsh light of the open door.

"*Propinquus quod obfirmo!*" I said, and stabbed at the door with my finger. The door slammed shut, and the lock turned with a click. I made a sweeping gesture with the same hand all about the suddenly dark room, and said, "*Candela exuro perspicuus!*"

All the candles in the room flared to life as one. Magdalena's eyes were huge, full of honeyed darkness in the flickering candlelight.

"Power," I said as I pulled my shirts over my head and tossed them into the darkness. "Control, will, submission. All of these are the first

principles of magic, the currency of the universe. You'll learn that sometimes you control the power and sometimes it controls you."

Magdalena traced the scars and the tattoos across my skin with
her nails. "Which is better, control or submission?"

"Yes," I said, and we both laughed. We kissed again. She raked my
chest with her nails and I caressed her face, tracing my finger along
the pulse in her throat.

I pointed at the beat-up old boom box she had sitting next to the
vanity, surrounded by towers of loose CDs.

"Lascivio Al Viridis," I said.

"Love and Happiness" by Al Green began to play.

"Turn over," I said.

"Yes, sir," Magdalena murmured. She rolled onto her stomach, like
a great sleek cat stretching. I began to unlace the corset, revealing more
and more of her porcelain skin and more of her tattoo ink. She was
magnificent. I pulled back on her hair, like the mane of a mare. She
moaned and reached for the small nightstand next to her bed.

"In the drawer there . . . I'll get them," she said, breathless. The last
seams of the corset popped loose as she stretched to reach the drawer.
I climbed off the bed and quickly removed the rest of my clothes. Magdalena rolled off the bed on the other side with a squeak and a giggle
and did the same. Wrapped in shadow and guttering candlelight, she
was a dark goddess. It was impossible to tell where the darkness of
her hair and her eyes ended and the night began. The smile on her
face could make saints fall, gladly. She held up a pair of steel handcuffs, the chain between the bracelets suspended by her single slender finger. She climbed onto the bed and crawled toward me.

"Think you can get these on me?" she said, purring.

I stepped forward and climbed on the bed, grabbing her by the
wrist. She gasped. We rolled and struggled, biting, kissing, tumbling,
snarling, and moaning. My mouth found its way to her nipple, and I
teased it with my tongue as her hands slid to my waist and then lower.
Her teeth sank into the biceps of the arm I was holding her wrist with.
My teeth scraped the skin of her hard nipple, and we both gasped at

the sensations. I rolled and forced her onto her back. The cuffs were in my free hand; I snapped one of the bracelets onto the wrist I had already captured. She grinned, and with her free hand slid her nails down my back; the pain was sharp and warm and it made my loins stir and made me gasp. I captured her other wrist and pulled it forward, looped the handcuff chain between the posts of the headboard, and snapped the other cuff on. She struggled against the cuffs, her arms now stretched above her head. For one horrible second, I saw Berman nailed to his office wall, his arms stretched the same way, but I shoved the profane thought away. No ugliness tonight, just beauty and passion and power. The rest was waiting for me tomorrow.

I ran my hand over her face, traced her lips. The struggling began to diminish. We were both panting, sweating.

"That," Magdalena said, gasping, as she reached up and kissed me, "was fun."

"Mmmhmm," I said, our eyes locking.

I put my hand back to her throat and she closed her eyes, a sigh escaped her lips. My other hand traced a line from her lips to her breasts. I took her nipples between my thumb and forefinger, teasing, pinching them, then moved my hand lower. She moaned and squirmed under me.

Magdalena had numerous colored scarves wrapped and knotted around the bedpost. I released her throat and stopped my teasing of her body to undo a beautiful black-and-blue-patterned one. I raised her head and we kissed for a long time, deep, sweet, and slow.

"Do you trust me?" I asked. I ignored the thoughts stabbing me in the back of the brain, shoved them in the hole with the crucified banker and listened to my reptile brain.

"Yes," Magdalena said, almost whispered. I slid the scarf around her head and covered her eyes, knotting the blindfold tight in the back. I kissed my way over her body, down her body, exploring, lingering, and learning where she most enjoyed my attentions.

I picked up one of the candles, a red one in a glass jar. I held it a few feet above her body and slowly tipped it until a stream of the hot wax splashed on her shoulder and flowed down to the top of her cleavage. Magdalena gasped and then moaned. I did it again, this time the wax splashing over her hard nipples and running down the sides of her breasts and onto the sheet.

"Oh," Magdalena said, writhing, as the next stream of hot wax made contact with her pale skin. I picked up a white candle, then a black one, and used each one in turn to paint her skin with wax and pain. The patterns merged, melded, bleeding, flowing like a Monet, like a Rumi poem in flesh.

The hot wax dribbled on her stomach . . . lower, lower.

"Yes," she mouthed, her voice a whisper.

The orgasms began, rolling, building, crashing like the thunder that heralded the storm. Magdalena could hardly make a noise, barely convulse, as the pleasure flared in her like dying stars. Again and again and again, until time was a frozen, broken thing.

I could feel her retreating into a secret, private place inside herself, as she became more and more engrossed in the sensation itself, moving past the place where pain and pleasure had definitions and boundaries, past reason, past the waking mind to something far more intimate, far more intuitive.

At the heart of the ecstatic mystic tradition is the understanding that reason blocks the path to understanding, to hearing the pulse of the world, its beautiful voice. Much of the practice, regardless if you talk to a Sufi or a snake handler, is to let go of the prison of the self, of reason. Here, blindfolded and bound, Magdalena had reached that place when the division between goddess and flesh were gone. Freedom. The inebriation of the infinite.

I put the candles away and gently touched her hair. She shuddered, soundless. I found the cuff keys in the open bedside drawer and unlocked her. She moaned at the feel of the cool steel leaving her skin. Magdalena was covered in dried candle wax, as were the sheets. I pulled her close to me and covered her with a quilt. She mumbled and rested her head on my chest.

"Thank you," she muttered. She wrapped her arms around me and slept.

"No, thank *you*," I replied, but she could no longer hear me.

In the silver, overcast dawn, the gunmetal sky of a rainy morning, she woke me with her body moving against mine, her mouth to mine. The need between us was hunger, thirst, gasping for air. It couldn't be ignored or denied. Both of us were half asleep, and we moved in perfect symmetry, becoming one, feeling the pulse between us quicken, rise beyond the ability of reason or understanding, expand to encompass everything, all of us, both of us, one.

Magdalena's eyes opened wide as we both came; they had changed from dark and hot, like an August midnight, to brilliant, acetylene blue. Power welled up between us, through us, and in the instant of our communion, every candle in the room erupted with a brilliant blue flame and then snuffed out, dead.

The two of us held one another tight, gasping. I watched as Magdalena's eyes faded back to their normal color.

"That," I said groggily, "was magic. We did magic, you and I."

We fell asleep in each other's arms.

EIGHT

The light had changed from overcast dawn to overcast day. I was being jabbed harshly. It was insistent, strong, and I couldn't ignore it. I opened my eyes and felt the grainy, steel-wool-in-my-skull ache of too much $200,000 tequila. Grinner was standing over me, poking me in the collarbone.

"Good morning, asshole" he said, jabbing me again. "Your fucking time is up. Get up and get out."

"What the hell is your problem, man?" I said, trying to sit up. I was covered in bits of candle wax.

"My problem, Ballard, is I can always count on you to make a fucking mess on your way out the door. What the hell happened to not messing with Megan?"

I rolled over to look. Magdalena was on her side, facing away from me. She too was still covered in little globs of wax. She was breathing deeply, obviously asleep.

"Shit," I said.

"Yeah," Grinner said as he walked to the bedroom door, "shit. Get the fuck up, get dressed, and meet me in the living room. We are going to conclude our business." He exited and then poked his head back inside the door. "Asshole," he said, and left again.

I staggered nude down the hall to the bathroom. Showered, brushed my teeth. My head was full of grease-soaked cotton, and my stomach was a rock tumbler full of gravel and bile. I wanted to puke so badly, but I couldn't.

I wiped the condensation from the shower off the bathroom mirror above the sink and looked at my reflection. I looked old, too old to still be making the same stupid mistakes.

"Asshole," I said to my mirror self. He nodded in agreement.

My bags were packed and on the floor next to me on the couch. I was dressed—jeans, boots, and a black T-shirt. My hair, still wet from the shower, was pulled back into a ponytail. Grinner sat on the couch next to me and sipped his coffee from a square mug fashioned to look like the head of a creeper from Minecraft. I drank my coffee out of a mug with the seal of Grinner's old naval unit on it. I was trying not to hurl all over his rug.

"He's dead," Grinner said. "He has to be. No other answer."

"What did you find?" I asked.

"Nothing," he said, shaking his head. "Not a damn thing. Not a ripple in the whole damn Net. Dusan Slorzack is gone. Gone, daddy, gone. The stuff I gave you before is stale, useless to track him. After 2002, he simply doesn't exist, no footprints, no smudge to indicate his passing. He simply falls off the earth. And anyone even tangentially related to him ends up gone too. Forever."

"Well, if he's dead, shouldn't there be some kind of trace or trail?"

"You ever hear of Jimmy-fucking-Hoffa, motherfucker?" Grinner said. He was red, flushed, excited, and this just wasn't about me getting with Magdalena. He was scared.

"You told me you knew where Hoffa was," I said.

"Yeah," Grinner said. "He's an animated corpse serving drinks to a bunch of old toothless Sicilian necromancers at a spelleasy in Cleveland. That's not the fucking point, motherfucker! The point is some folks you simply do not want to find, and your boy is one of them, man. He is protected by angels from on high, or demons from the fucking pit. He is gone, Ballard, you hear me? Gone. And now, so are you, *capisce?*"

"You cover your tracks well enough, Grinner," I said. "You know I don't want this showing up on your doorstep."

"Fuck, Ballard, you're like dogshit on your shoe, track it all over, stink the whole place up. I am about ninety percent. Me, Christine, and the baby are golden. We're taking the money you are about to pay me and getting the hell out of the city for a while."

I handed him an envelope I took out of my bag. It was close to the last of my money from the Egypt caper, after helping Magdalena. Back to broke again. Grinner counted the money and nodded.

"Okay, thanks," he said, starting to calm down a little. Fifty thousand dollars had a way of helping with that. "I'm sorry I couldn't get you more, man. But this guy is a ghost.

"I do have another avenue you could try, but it's a long shot. I know a guy in Virginia, he owns a farm there. He was with IBM a long time ago, back in the gray flannel suit days. CIA too, part of Project Stargate—that psychic stuff they screwed around with. He was a big part of Project Midnight Climax too, those LSD experiments. The old dude's totally BAMF!"

"You think he can find Slorzack?" I said, taking the slip of paper Grinner offered me with a name and address scribbled on it.

"I've exhausted all the technological means at my disposal," Grinner said, "which is to say, everything technological. I think you may need to try other avenues of information retrieval. Magic is kind of the ultimate in social engineering, you know?

"'Bruce Haberscomb,'" I said, reading the name on the paper. "Never heard of him. He's in the Life?"

"Dude's an Acidmancer," Grinner said. "An Akashic hacker. If it's information contained within the human experience, he can find it and even alter it."

"Acidmancer, huh?" I said.

"Yeah, dude has trained himself to reach a heightened state of creative visualization while on LSD. He's a seventh-brain adept, a neurogentic alchemist. He works his magic with a computer while he's tripping his balls off," Grinner said.

"I know what an Acidmancer is," I said. "I just didn't think they existed anymore. They were Timothy Leary's Knights of the Round Table. There were eight of them, hand-picked, one for each of the Eight Circuits of Consciousness Leary discovered. I just thought they all died in San Francisco, fighting Charles Manson's nightmare Tulpas in the Helter Skelter War in 1969."

"Well, Bruce is no poser," Grinner said. "He should be able to tell you everything about your boy there."

I stood and slung my bags on my back. I offered a hand to Grinner. "Thanks, Grinner, I 'preciate it."

He shook my hand and nodded down toward the bedroom hallway. "Anything you want me to tell her?"

"Tell her to get to Didgeri as soon as she can. She can protect Magdalena, or at least hide her if there is any blowback from me. You guys will make sure she's okay before you cut out, right?"

"Yeah, man. Christine loves her; we'll make sure she's okay. But do you want me to say anything to her, y'know, from you?"

"No," I said. "I fucked this up enough already."

"Classy as always, Ballard," Grinner said. "Oh, yeah, Didgeri texted me this morning. She said to meet a guy named Trace at Café Sage down on John Street. She said he'd be there about one thirty today. He'll be gone by two."

"Okay," I said. "See you around, Grinner. Kiss your girl for me, and that baby too."

"Affirmative," he said, opening the front door. "May the road rise to meet you, and may the doorknob not hit you where Mother Nature split you."

I walked out. Homeless, again.

"Hey, asshole," Grinner said. I looked back.

"Christine loves you too. Surprise me, don't go do something stupid. Be safe, bro."

I ditched my bags in my reserved locker back at the Port Authority bus station. Dropped off stuff that might cause trouble and hung on to a few tricks that might help. I ditched my ID and pocketed the last of my cash, then took a cab to John Street.

I wanted to eat a pound of greasy Cajun fried chicken, wash it down with an ice-cold two-liter of Cheerwine, which was nowhere to be found in this god-forsaken town, and then sleep and sober up, but I was running out of time and I knew it. In a very short period of time, no hotel, no flop, no crack-house fortress would be safe for me to stay at for more than a few hours. The All-Seeing Eye, well, sees all. I needed leverage to stay alive long enough to find Slorzack, and to keep breathing even after I found him.

Café Sage is a cozy little Thai restaurant, a few blocks from the Federal Reserve building. The walls were painted with vibrant colors—yellow, red, and green plants reaching to a happy orange sky. The lightness of the place was stark compared to the cold, rainy gray day outside. I walked in and shook off the rain. There were only a handful of people in the café. None of them looked like faceless occult assassins, so I chalked that up as a win. The lunch rush had ended, and the staff was catching their breath, a few of them eating at a table near the doors to the kitchen. Crowded House's "Don't Dream It's Over" was playing on the stereo behind the bar.

A handsome young Asian man in a crisp white shirt and flowered tie greeted me at the door with a smile. You could cut yourself on the pleats of his slacks. I told him I was meeting someone, and he nodded and pointed to a table near the windows occupied by an equally handsome black man, who looked to be in his early thirties. He was dressed in a perfectly tailored suit, Valentino, I'd guess. His trench coat hung over the back of his chair, drying. As I approached, he began to give me the look usually reserved for dismissing street bums, then the lights went on, and he rose and extended his well-manicured hand.

"Mr. Ballard? I'm Alex Trace. I was told you could help me."

"Depends," I said, sitting and turning to the waiter. "You have Cheerwine? It's a soda?" He smiled and shook his head. "Of course you don't. Thai ice tea." I regarded Trace as the waiter departed. "I might be able to help you if you help me. Tell me everything there is to tell about James Berman and Dusan Slorzack."

He picked up his coffee, his hands trembling. "I'm with . . . was with James since 2000. I was twenty-one, he was thirty. He'd just become a senior partner at his firm; I was finishing up my internship and starting my job at the Fed. James was into . . . strange things. He fascinated me. He . . . had a wife and children. They don't know him, not really. They know the mask he had to wear to move through the maze. But I got the real him, all the ugliness, the beauty, the secrets, the lies. I'm the caretaker of the true James Berman."

"You're scared," I said, thanking the waiter for my tea. I took a long drag on it. It was cool and sweet, and my head cleared a little. "They come asking after they found him?"

"Yes," Trace said. "The police, a few days ago. I have no idea how they knew about me. James was always very discreet."

I took the handcuff keys out of my pocket and held them up for Trace to see. His eyes widened, then he began to tear up. He looked down into his coffee. "Very," I said.

"We explored every aspect of the senses," he said. "James had such a high-pressure job, so much responsibility, so much weight on him from above and below. Sometimes he needed to feel in absolute control of everything. I was his everything. Sometimes he needed that control stripped away from him, so he could feel helpless and have permission to feel that way. I couldn't give him that; it's not in my nature, but . . . others did," Trace said, wiping his eyes.

"Look," I said, handing the handcuff keys to him. He clutched them in his fist like they were solid faith. "I'm sorry for your loss, but Berm . . .

James was messed up in some very bad stuff with some very bad people, and I am trying to find one of them. It's quite possible James is dead now because of this man."

"The Bosnian," Trace said. "Slorzack. The Pain Eater."

"Yep," I said. "You've obviously met."

"That creepy son of a bitch," Trace said, and crossed himself. I smiled.

"You a religious man?" I said.

"I haven't stepped into a church in fifteen years," he said. "When it comes to the Prince of Darkness, yes. That bastard scared the hell out of me, and James too."

"I heard they were tight?" I said.

"If by 'tight,' you mean Slorzack used and manipulated James to get what he wanted, then yes," Trace said, sipping his coffee. His fear seemed to be losing out to his anger. "Topping, evil bitch. James worshiped him. Kissed his ass. Literally.

"We met Dusan and his slaves at Paddles. It seemed like a coincidence, but I think the evil SOB set it up. He wanted James from the moment he laid eyes on him, and Slorzack had this . . . power, like a sick little god, to make things happen, to seem to know everything, to just . . . appear. God, he made my skin crawl."

I felt something moving, unseen. A power was in motion, something set loose and coming my way. I couldn't track it. My Ajna chakra was no help; it was not functioning properly. I couldn't tell what direction it was coming at me from, but it set my teeth on edge, and it worried me that it rose up the moment Trace began describing Slorzack. I began to gather my will through the static of my hangover and exhaustion. I was off, and it was at the worst possible time for me to be off.

The storm picked up outside, and there was distant growl of thunder.

"Then we started running into them at the private parties, the secret clubs," Trace said. "Next thing I know, we were part of Slorzack's inner circle. James was his slave, and his apprentice. Like I said, James was into high weirdness—there was some kind of cult or secret society on Wall Street that he was part of. He practiced magic, fucking magic, and let me tell you something, it's real! That crazy shit is real!"

"Do tell," I said, gesturing to the waiter that we were leaving. I dropped fifty on the table. I really couldn't afford to do that now, but I couldn't afford wasting the time for checks and change, or the attention of cops if we dined and dashed, either. Whatever it was, it was accelerating, and I had to get us moving before it locked on us.

"What are you doing?" Trace asked, rising. "Didgeri said you could protect me, help me. I can't go home, I can't go to work. They're everywhere. They think I had something to do with James's death."

"I'll protect you," I said, palming the rectangular glass salt shaker off the table. "Get your coat on, we're going. They're making their move, and we have to keep a few steps ahead of them if we're going to stay alive."

"How do I know you're not with them, that I can trust you?" he said as he put on his raincoat.

I opened the salt shaker and poured the salt into my right palm. I focused on the energy in my Muladhara chakra; it was like slogging through mud. I envisioned the red four-petal lotus opening. The image wasn't easy, and my sacral and gonad energies were, let us say, less than at optimal.

Training overcame as much of my stupidity and poor choices as it could, and I felt the protective energies, the sense of security, of fight-or-flight fill my lower spine and travel down my arm. I made a fist, cradling the salt. I carefully synchronized the harmonics of the crystalline matrix of the salt with the energy as best I could and filled each grain with my power. They were beautiful in my blurry third eye's perception, looking like blocks of frosted glass, filling with the crimson energy of my seventh chakra.

"Fair enough," I said, walking toward the front door. "I need you to finish your story, and I may need you as insurance to help keep them off my ass too," I said. "I'm your best bet to survive right now. Magic is real? No shit. I am a fucking magical rock star, and I can tell you if we don't fucking run, right now, Alex. We are both dead."

He paused for a single heartbeat, then nodded and began to follow me out the door. Outside, the rain became a dark curtain, knifing down. Lightning flashed. I didn't have to wait for the thunder.

Contact. Shit.

The door of Café Sage exploded in a hail of broken glass and steel. Over the sound of the door disintegrating was a horrible organic sound, an angry guttural snarl mixed with an almost plaintive whine. It was an animal sound—plural, animals.

I grabbed Trace by the arm and pulled him, hard, over the table I was sliding across. I flipped it to shield us both from the fragments of the exploding door, but I felt pinprick stings across my cheek and hand, and when I looked at Trace, he was bleeding too, from his forehead and cheek.

"What the hell!" Trace screamed. I got my ass off the floor and grabbed him with my free left hand, jerking him to his feet.

"Run!" I said, heading back into the restaurant. The customers, the staff were shouting, screaming; there was a barrage of frightened English, Chinese, Thai. The snarls again, and the table we had been hiding behind flew through the air and was shaken, splintered, ripped apart.

"Run!" I screamed again, pushing Trace ahead of me. I didn't know what else to say.

NINE

Fear tends to affect people in a couple of different ways. There is blind, mindless herd panic—stampede. Trace was in near stampede mode, as were the majority of the people in Café Sage. I, fortunately, have lived through enough stampedes to be graced with a different way to process terror: A hyperacuity settles over me when everything goes to hell and I am in fear for my life. It all slows down, and it all becomes very high-def.

Trace was ahead of me, running toward the back of the café, while most of the patrons and staff were trying to push past us to flee through the shattered front door. The invisible, snarling creatures sounded about fifteen feet or so away from my back.

As people bumped and pushed past me, screaming, I shouted to Trace. "Kitchen!" I yelled, and gestured toward the swinging door to our left, past the bar.

Trace veered and hit the kitchen door like a linebacker on steroids. He vanished into the kitchen and I followed, running. Behind me, the invisible things were buzz-sawing through the customers who were trying to get past them to the street. A few people, seeing others lifted off the ground by an invisible force and then shaken and rended to a screaming, painful death opted for the other way fear can claim you:

They curled into a fetal ball under a table or against a wall and lost their will and their minds.

The kitchen was stainless steel islands, bays of stoves, and massive monolithic freezers and fridges. The cook staff was evenly divided between those headed into the restaurant toward snarling faceless death and those who were cutting out the back door to the alleyway. I gestured for Trace to head out the back door. I grabbed a discarded white apron off a steam table and knotted it up into a makeshift satchel, careful to not spill the salt I was still palming. I began to move quickly between the aisles, grabbing items as I saw the need for them, and stuffing them into my new bag.

"What the fuck are you doing?" Trace screamed from the door. "Come on!"

I quickly grabbed a few more things. The snarling was coming closer, and the screams were fading away, one by one. I made it to the back door.

"This way," I said to Trace, pointing left. Once he was out in the alleyway, I joined him but held the kitchen door open. The rain was a heavy, pounding curtain of cold water.

"What the hell is that thing?" he asked as I knelt by the doorway. "And you picked a great fucking time to start grocery shopping."

"I don't know what it is yet," I said. "I have a few ideas, but I need more information." I knelt on one knee and carefully began to pour a line of the salt along the inner edge of the door, going left to right, trying to keep it as dry as I could while Heaven pissed on us. *"Non pertransibis, ferreo canis exprimamus,"* I incanted, then turned back to Trace. "The stuff I grabbed is the closest thing to weapons we have right now. Calm down, Alex. Stick with me, do what I say, when I say it, and you'll be all right."

Inside the kitchen I heard the door to the dining room explode and fly across the room, clattering. There was another scream and the snarling, mixed with the whine. Something was hovering at the edge of my memory, but I didn't have the time to pause and shake it loose.

I stood and brushed the last of the salt off my hands and began to sprint toward the mouth of the alley.

"Come on, this way," I said. "Time to put that P90X shit to the test."

Behind us I heard the things chasing us crash into the ward I had placed on the kitchen door. From the howls of anger and pain, and the fact that nothing was shredding our flesh, the protective spell had held. The things would have to backtrack, and that would give us precious minutes.

We ran out of the alley and made our way onto John Street, turned left, and sprinted across Cliff Street. Cars honked and drivers flipped us off. We kept heading west, our feet splashing as we ran.

"What did he want from James?" I shouted above the rain and the bellowing cars.

"Who?" Trace said.

"Slorzack," I said. "You said he used and manipulated James. To what end, exactly?"

We crossed Gold and headed for the intersection of John and William Street. A few blocks up was the Fulton Street subway station and, I hoped, escape.

"You have got to be kidding me," Trace shouted back at me as he jogged against the downpour. "We got invisible monsters that shake apart people like nothing chasing us, wanting to eat us, and you want to keep talking about that evil bastard!"

"He is most likely the one behind those things," I said, wiping my wet hair out of my eyes. The cuts on my cheek and hand were stinging, but the worst part was my thudding heart and my four-packs-a-day lungs. They were beginning to burn, and my breath was coming in faster and faster gasps. "The more I know, the better chance I have of getting us out of this alive." Suddenly, the horrible boom of multiple collisions thudded over the hiss of the rain. Something tore through the cars that were ahead of us on William. The windows exploded in blooms of blood, brains, and bone chips, like the dye packs in stolen bank bags. An instant later, the car windows shattered, and there were howls as the rolling coffins jumped the sidewalks and crashed into buildings. Pedestrians screamed and scrambled for cover. I managed to grab Trace and pull him back, narrowly missing one of the out-of-control juggernauts.

"I'll . . . be . . . damned, they . . . flanked us," I said, pausing to gasp for breath. "They . . . knew. They knew where we were headed."

"Why didn't they just jump us up the street, then?" Trace said, staring at the twisted knot of mangled cars that now blocked the intersection of William and John. Panicked civilians were running everywhere. A few were trying to snap pictures or video with their cell phones.

The things chasing us moved through the debris and the rain, snarling, without a single piece of broken glass crunching, without the slightest indication of a shape or form, moving between the raindrops. They were cunning, completely invisible and intangible, making them effectively invulnerable. I didn't think they got tired, and they had a taste for blood. It was a brilliant summoning, but luckily not by a master.

I slid my hand into the satchel and took out a sealed plastic container in the shape of a cylinder. I had taken it from one of the kitchen's fridges.

"Because they're enjoying the hunt," I said. "You remember when I told you to run awhile back?"

"Yeah?" Trace said, nodding, his breath a white mist trailing from his mouth and nostrils.

"Do it again. Now!"

We hauled ass heading south, toward the Wall Street subway station. The irony of how this whole mess had led me right back to Wall Street was not lost on me. We ran two blocks, passing One Chase Manhattan Plaza—the temple of the god of credit—on our right, and past Our Lady of Victory Church, the home of an equally venerable god, on the left.

The howls behind us, closing, were colder than the rain. We weren't going to make it to the subway unless I tried something. I stopped, turned toward our unseen assassins, and opened the container. This was a long shot, but it was all I had left.

"What the hell!" Trace had stopped about half a block ahead of me and was staring in disbelief.

I tried to forget the rain, forget the cold and the ice of fear in my bowels, forget the hangover, the low blood sugar, the DTs, and the fire in my lungs. I tried to forget the world. I could do this—I was one of a handful of badasses in the Life that could do this, and of those limp wands, I was the only goddamned rock star in the lot. Elvis-fucking-Mandrake-Presley.

The power came. I reached into the sopping-wet apron-satchel and pulled out a hunk of raw ginger. It resembled a gnarled hand. I took a bite of it and swallowed, the numbing fire of it scratching and clutching at my throat. The power flared in me, strengthened by the ginger. I held the root like a wand as I cast the contents of the container, raw minced garlic, into the air before me.

"Non habetis accessum ad hoc dimensionis. Tu es ingrata! abire, ardens!" I shouted into the storm. The lightning came, drawn to my words as if to copper. The garlic caught fire in the air, hissed, and popped. The invisible things howled in pain. I turned and ran, dropping the garlic container and laughing at the storm, in spite of myself. I saw Trace sprinting ahead of me toward the subway entrance, a huge gray stone building on the right with wide arched windows high up and a skeleton of pipe scaffolding enclosing it. It looked a bit like an old train station. He stood at the doors, looking inside and then back to me.

"What the fuck is wrong with you? Why are you laughing?" he shouted, eager to begin his decent into the underworld.

"It worked! Son of a bitch if it didn't actually work," I called back, grinning. Something growled and snapped with fangs that did not touch this world but grabbed my coat tight. I spun and tried to slip out of the trench coat as a second invisible thing clamped down on a sleeve my arm had been in a second before. I tugged on the remains of the coat, and the captured sleeve and tail tore free. For an instant, I caught a whiff of something—it smelled of rancid, decaying organic things—methane, rotting meat. Then the whimper in the middle of the angry snarls. In that instant, when I was close enough to our invisible assassins to catch that whiff of them, I named them, and I knew how to beat them, if I lived that long. I took the tatters of my raincoat, rolled away from the savage ghosts, and ran toward an umbrella-wielding silhouette making its way to the subway entrance. Trace was shouting something to me, but I couldn't hear it over the storm, the howls of the phantom killers, and the blood pounding in my ears. I needed seconds, and I didn't own them anymore. There was one more trick, and it was a dirty one. I crashed into the stranger with the umbrella.

"Hey! What the hell, man?" Mr. Umbrella said. He smelled of menthol cough drops. "Watch where you are going!"

I draped the trench coat over him and rolled away again. I didn't want to see his face. I ran as fast as I could to the doors. I heard the snarling, the shredding, and the screams. Trace's face was a frozen mask of horror. He looked at me like I was an alien thing, a monster.

"Y-you . . ." Trace stammered. I shoved him through the doors and into the echoing halls of the station.

"Go, go, go, go!" I shouted, and pushed him ahead of me. We ran down the escalators. I heard the tone signaling a train was preparing to leave.

"What is the busiest street on the island?" I asked Trace as we thudded down the moving staircase.

"What?" he said. "Uh, Forty-second Street, I guess."

We reached the lower platform. The uptown train was ready to depart. The warning tone was sounding, and the final streams of passengers were flowing through the open doors.

"Times Square, right?" I added, "We have to get on that train."

As we ran toward the turnstiles, shouting and gunshots sounded on the upper level. The MTA cops hauled ass to respond but didn't have time to do more than curse as Trace and I jumped the turnstiles and sprinted to the train. We fell into seats, gasping as the tone sounded, the doors shut, and we began to move.

"We . . . We . . . made . . . it," Trace gasped, then laughed and started choking and coughing. I shook my head and slid back the wet hair plastered to my face. I'd lost my ponytail holder somewhere on the run. I'd lost my wallet, my cash, and, worst of all, my cigarettes. We both looked like drowned rats—me more so without my trench. My T-shirt with Alan Moore's bearded face looming out at the world, my jeans, and chucks were all saturated. A small lake was forming on the plastic bench around my ass.

"The pack is still out there, still hunting us," I said. "They won't stop until they kill us or we dispel them."

"Pack of what?" Trace asked.

"Inugami," I said. "I'd guess about four of them, and since they can't possess people and they still seem to be pretty feral, they must have been summoned in a hurry and not properly enshrined yet."

"This is the same kind of crazy shit James and Slorzack used to talk about for hours," Trace said. He paused, leaned on his lanky knees, and stared at the scarred floor. "You killed that man with the umbrella, led those things right to him. They tore him apart in front of me."

"Yes," I said, "I did, and yes, they did. Now, since the Inugami have been summoned half-assed and don't demonstrate their full range of abilities, it means we're dealing with someone other than the Inugami-Mochi, and that is most likely why we are still alive right now."

Trace shook his head in dismissive disgust. "You and Slorzack, man, are cold-blooded bastards." The subway shuddered to a stop. "Chambers Street," the conductor's weary voice said.

"You rather it was you, bit to death, bleeding out at the entrance to a New York subway? You feeling all Jesus on me? Because I'm pretty sure you could have gotten their attention and you could be dead now, instead of that poor bastard. That what you want?"

"No," he said sullenly. "Fuck you anyway, Ballard."

"Relax," I said. "It will take the pack awhile to reorient itself and get a fresh lock on you."

"Me?" Trace said.

"You said the cops came to see you," I said. "They had a search warrant, right? All nice and legal. They searched your apartment, and they took things they could use to create a magical sympathetic link to you, a resonance. The magical law of contagion: Once two items interact, they are bound, linked."

For a second, I wondered if Didgeri had set me up by arranging this meeting with Trace, but I tamped down that thought. Trace was right, I was a cold bastard.

"The cops?" Trace said. "NYPD flatfoots? They are part of this bullshit occult underworld?"

"Some are," I said as the door chimed and shut. I was starting to shiver from the wet clothing. "Just another form of dirty cop. They join up with one of the badge cults, some are born into them. Some of the cults actually fight to keep the force clean and wage perpetual war with the other cop cults. It's complicated."

"Yeah, no shit," Trace said, rubbing his eyes. And these origami chasing us . . ."

"Inugami," I corrected.

"Yeah, whatever. Tell me what's tracking me, what's trying to kill us," he said, almost pleading.

"Okay," I said, "and then you are going to answer all my questions about Slorzack and what he and Berman were up to. And remember, you asked."

The train lurched ahead, squealing out of the station. More people were getting on now as we crawled toward the close of the business day. The other passengers ignored us, they ignored my words. Live in a city like this long enough, and your brain starts to produce novocain.

"How to make an Inugami, or dog god," I said. "Take a beloved household pet, a dog that loves you unconditionally and thinks you are the most wonderful thing in the universe, the way only something as stupid, loyal, and innocent as a dog or a child can. Bury it up to its neck in graveyard soil, or soil mixed with the ashes of the dishonored dead. Place food and water just outside the reach of the poor dog and wait. When it's going mad from hunger and thirst and about to die, you chop off its head."

"Jesus," Trace said. "Who the hell thought something like that up?"

"The ritual originates in Japan," I said, "home of tentacle porn and dirty schoolgirl panty vending machines. That's the basic ritual to make one of these things, but the Inugami-Mochi perform much more elaborate rituals to create theirs. Makes them more powerful, smarter, and more ruthless. Believe it or not, we got lucky."

"Inugami . . . Moochie?" Trace said, shaking his head.

"Close enough," I said. "Very old, very powerful families in Japan create Inugami the way the Dutch used to breed new kinds of tulips. They keep the dog gods as family pets, use them as servants, assassins. Some of the oldest families are tied to the Yakuza as Shugenja—the Japanese mob's sorcerers."

"This . . . this is just too much for me," Trace said. He was close to crying. "Rabid ghost-god-dogs, ninja wizards. I . . . I never wanted any of this. I loved James. He was cute and well-off and cultured. I wanted a life with him, but not all this . . . madness."

"Yeah," I said. "It's not a life for everyone. I wouldn't recommend it to anyone I liked. And it's Yakuza, not ninja; they get kind of testy about that. Why did Slorzack want him?" I asked.

Trace closed his eyes and shook his head. "At first it was kink and attraction," he said. "But then Slorzack saw James had real connections, real power. I think that was his plan all along. They started doing magic together—what the hell do you call it?"

"Workings?" I offered.

Trace nodded and continued. "Workings. Slorzack knew a lot more than James about most things, but James knew something Slorzack was desperate to learn about. They talked about it a lot, and Slorzack was always trying to wangle more information about it out of James. It made James happy to hold it over that creepy old bastard's head. Once Slorzack let James whip him just to get a scrap of a some weird formula about it."

"What was it? Was it a spell? A charm? Something they were trying to summon? What?" I asked. As much as I just wanted to find Dusan Slorzack and end this, there was that itch in my back of my skull, a scrap of knowledge, of power, I didn't have, and I wanted it. Revenge for Boj was the last thing on my mind as I leaned closer.

"Greenway," Trace said. "They called it the Greenway."

"What was it?" I asked.

"I don't have a clue and I don't care if I never know," Trace said, "especially after what they did . . . for it."

A chill wormed its way through my guts. "What did they do, Alex?" I asked softly.

Trace looked around and lowered his voice when he spoke. "They . . . they were both in on it, what happened . . . back in 2001."

"You're serious," I said. "I heard a rumor, but come on, man, really?"

"They helped plan it. Slorzack and James and . . . someone else. They worked with the terrorists. There was lots of money and magic involved. Slorzack and James planned out some kind of working. They said it had to be that specific day, because of the numbers or something, and the targets . . ."

"You are telling me that Dusan Slorzack and James Berman were behind nine/eleven?" I said.

A few people on the train turned in my direction when they heard. While the default in this town is unflappable, there are some words that always hold power in the proper places, still maintain an emotional connection, for good or bad, like a live wire.

"Yeah. I heard them working one night, and they said it was necessary for whatever the Greenway was."

"Do you remember exactly what they said?" I asked. The train lurched again as we continued north, passing into shadow and then light, falling into shadow again.

"They said the towers were the pillars of the temple, a symbol of wealth and power that had to be sacrificed to open the way. They said the Pentagon was the 'sacred star' or some shit. Something about the White House being sacrificed too—and Shriners or something?"

"Masons," I said. "Maybe Masons."

"Yeah, Masons. Once James was mixed up in that, I got really scared. Especially when it actually fucking happened. I mean, what kind of mind can kill all those people for some insane rite?"

"Slorzack," I said. "He's had plenty of practice at it."

"Whoever was mixed up in it with them, I think that person directed things," Trace added. "James seemed to know them better than Slorzack."

"Mystery scumbags have a name?" I asked. In the back of my head I felt a movement across the city, a stirring of my instinct to flee, to hide. The Inugami pack was on the move again.

"Like I said, I really didn't want to have anything to do with any of this," Trace said, shaking his head. "Fucking insanity. Wait. Gerry? Giles? Giles. Yes, James slipped once and used his name. Giles."

"Well, it's better than nothing," I said.

"Before they did . . . what they did, James asked me a lot of questions about my work at the Fed. I'm pretty sure it had something to do with what Slorzack was after."

"What did Berman want to know about?" I asked.

"Printing and engraving," Trace said. "The history of it, what happened to the old engraving die plates for money once they were retired."

"What do they do with them?" I asked.

"They are in vaults at the Bureau of Engraving and Printing in Washington," Trace said. "Those master dies are used to make the printing plates that are used on the presses to produce money."

"Why the hell did he want to know about that?" I asked.

Trace shrugged. "He was interested in that shit from the time we met. He and Slorzack actually traveled to D.C. to do the tourist thing. Part of my job at the Fed is to coordinate the shipments of damaged and worn-out currency once it's taken out of circulation. I know a lot of people at Engraving and Printing. I got them full access."

There was a long pause, the train shuddered and rocked.

"How long after you met Berman did you two bump into Dusan Slorzack?"

"A few months," Trace said. He looked up, turned, and stared at me. I shut up. My inner paranoid bastard had already run through the scenario in my mind. I hoped Trace's hadn't. The man he loved was dead, and I had just pissed all over his memory. Something crossed his face like a cloud drifting across the sun. Then it was gone.

"What happens to me now that you got my whole story?" Trace said. "You going to kill me, cut me loose?"

"No," I said. "You held up your end, for all your screaming and freaking out. I'll get you out of the city and find a safe place for you to hole up. We're square."

Trace nodded. "Thank you. Thanks."

"Don't thank me yet," I said. "We need to banish the Inugami before they find us again. I can already sense them getting closer. We got a few more stops till Times Square."

"Why Times Square?" Trace asked. I didn't answer. I needed supplies.

I stood. Between the swaying of the train and the numbness and ache in my legs, it was hard not to just fall back into my seat. I had lost most of my goodies with the trench coat, and if I was going to locate what I needed to be able to end this, I would have to rely on the kindness of strangers. I walked up to a guy in a very nice Hugo Boss two-button, slim-fit suit. He was sitting, earbuds from his iPod jammed in his head, reading *Forbes*. He had a raincoat and a leather satchel next to him. He looked to be in his early thirties and seemed comfortable with a look of soft disdain on his narrow face. I stood in front of him, holding the overhead rail to steady myself.

"Excuse me," I said. "I was wondering if I might have a pen and a piece of paper, please. It's kind of urgent."

He pretended to ignore me and kept listening to his music and reading his magazine. I pushed the magazine down with one hand while keeping the other clamped on the rail. He looked up, glaring at me. I saw the fear peeking out too, but he was trying to hide it well.

"Excuse me," I repeated.

He popped an earbud out. "What?" he growled. Somehow I managed to not swoon in fear.

"A piece of paper and a pen. May I have those, please? It's an emergency," I said.

NIGHTWISE   111

He scowled and opened his satchel and rooted around.

"It's always an emergency," he grumbled. "People like you make me sick."

"People like me?" I said.

"I work my ass off to have the things I do," he said. "People like you think everything just falls outta the freakin' sky."

"I see," I said, nodding. "And what do you do, exactly?"

"I work on Wall Street," he said. "In banking, if it's any of your business."

"Mmhhmm," I said, taking the piece of notebook paper he ripped out of small Moleskine notebook. He handed it to me like I had a disease. "Teller?"

He stopped his search for a pen and looked up at me, his eyes narrowed, burned.

"Maybe collections?" I said. "You enjoy taking old women's last dollars to cover the fees you shit on them? You like tricking and lying to people about how much you care about them, their family, and their future, and then rape them and take that future away.

"You bust your ass for your company, and you are caged up in a little box, like a dog waiting to be euthanized. You make them millions every day and you can't afford a car, a parking spot downtown? You live in a shit hole apartment and feel the ulcer burn into your guts every night because you can't pay your own damn credit card bills to keep up the kind of life you get told you should be living, but you hound people every day for not paying their bills, for doing the same damn thing. Went into debt for that suit, didn't you? Are you a good dog? That how you make your living, Bubba?"

"Fuck you, you white trash bum," he spat. I smiled.

"Pen," I said. "Please. You can get another free one at the bank."

He tossed it at me and I caught it. He flipped me off as I walked back to my seat and then put his earbud back in.

The truth is I am a bum and a criminal and a villain, and very proud to be white trash, but I'd rather eat out of a Dumpster and sleep on a subway vent than be a bottom-feeder like Mr. iPod. There is no intrinsic nobility in poverty, I assure you, but there damn sure isn't any in wealth, either.

"You enjoy that?" Trace asked quietly.

"Yeah, I did," I said, smoothing out the paper on the dry parts of the bench. "You?"

"My pops worked for a company for thirty years," Trace said, looking down at the floor. "Long days, short nights. No vacations. More work, more responsibility, not much more pay. Too tired to read to me, to play with me. Always saying he had to be perfect, had to not give them any reason to call him a shiftless nigger, to whisper behind his back. Being a paragon is damn hard on a man, can kill you.

"I missed him so much, and then I kind of hated him for it, like it meant more to him than me. He was just trying to do right by me and Mom, trying to win a rigged game. He dropped dead at work, and the people he had given his life for didn't give a damn. They replaced him, gave the job to someone right out of college for half the pay, like changing a spark plug. I think we got a fruit basket after the funeral.

"When Mom got sick, they did everything they could to drop her from the insurance Pops had paid into for most of his adult life. The creditors hounded her, made her sicker. She died a nervous wreck about the bills she still owed to millionaires. James was the only thing I had in my world beside my job at the Fed. I realized when they told me he was gone that I had nothing anymore. Just the job, just like Pops."

"Not too late to change that," I said. "It's your life, free and clear."

Trace smiled and looked at the pissed-off Mr. iPod. "Yeah," he said. "I did enjoy that."

The trick to dowsing is to free your mind to the compass of instinct. I knew the place I wanted to go, and I knew we were close. I didn't have a witching rod—those Y-shaped sticks dowsers traditionally use, or a pendulum, or even a ring on a chain, so I had to make do with some automatic writing tricks I picked up. I put my waking mind away. The rocking rhythm of the train actually helped with that. It took a few moments. The last conscious thought was of the wave of hunger and confusion from the dog gods that hit me like a power washer full of acid. My hand jerked and shifted across the paper. Then, trance over. I blinked and looked at the paper. We had our map.

I tossed the pen back to Mr. iPod as Trace and I departed the train at the 42nd Street stop.

"Much obliged," I said, and kept on walking.

After the train roared and squealed away into the tunnel, I examined the map I had drawn and pointed after the train into the darkness.

"There," I said. I could feel a pressure in the back of my skull, a flare of my Ajna chakra. The pack was coming, drawing closer.

"Into the tunnel?" Trace said. "If we don't get electrocuted, or break our necks jumping down, the MTA cops will—"

"Have you noticed an overabundance of cops interested in us at all today?" I asked as I walked to the edge of the tunnel. "Do you have a key on you?"

"What, your cult cops?" Trace said, digging into the pockets of his still-damp raincoat. "They ordered to leave us alone?" He handed me a small key ring. I slid one key off the loop and handed it back to him.

"Maybe," I said, "but we start mucking around down here, and they may get interested real quick. Be ready for that. You're not going to ask me what the key is for?"

"Figure some messed-up shit you're going to show me presently," Trace said. "Why bother?"

"Good," I said. "You're learning."

The gravel that surrounded the tracks at the edge of the tunnel crunched as we dropped down. I held the map and started walking. There was a narrow ledge with a rail on either side of the tunnel, and we shimmied up. It was cold and windy in the darkness. A row of feeble yellow lights in oval metal cages were strung along the wall. It was enough for me to read the directions and images my back brain had scrawled onto the paper.

"Maybe we can get directions, if we get lost," I said as the warm circle of light from the tunnel entrance grew smaller and became a moon, then an eye that finally closed, and it was as if we were in deep space.

"That's not funny," Trace said, looking around nervously.

"Not intended to be," I said. "There're about six thousand mole people living down here, have whole societies and cultures."

"You're talking about some kind of mole creatures living down here, right?" Trace said. I stopped and looked at him.

"No, I'm talking about human beings," I said. "They just call them mole people."

"Under New York? That's just weird, man," Trace said. "Urban myth."

"As real as it gets," I said. "No telling how many died down here during Hurricane Sandy. No myth. Just people trying to live, to stay alive, the way people do."

I went back to walking and following the magic map.

It took some time. We reached cross corridors and junctions, narrow metal stairs leading down. The only light was from the screen of Trace's cell phone. I insisted he disable the GPS in it. No mole people showed up, but we did encounter plenty of rats. Eventually we found the door, just as the map said we would. It was a heavy steel security door with an outdated Con Ed logo stamped into it. It was secured by a heavy chain and padlock. I dug Trace's key out of my jeans pocket, knelt before the padlock, and held the key in front of my eye.

"*Obfirmo aperire,*" I said. The lock resisted my spell and remained closed. I narrowed my eyes and rubbed my chin. There was a counterspell on the lock, designed to keep someone from doing what I had just tried to do.

"Why Latin?" Trace asked.

"Huh?" I said, looking up.

"You're a country boy," he said. "Why do you speak your spells like you're late to Snape's potion class?"

"It's a focus, a trigger," I said as I studied the complex knot of frozen will around the lock through the lenses of my Ajna and Sahas-rara chakras overlapping. "Different workers do it in different ways. A lot of magic is based in belief and perception married to will. I've known some spell-lobbers who pray to a god or sing hymns, some chant mantras, or fall into glossolalia, others evoke Satan or Cthulhu. It's all a matter of what makes the power work best for you, through you—it's what you believe in. The guy who taught me a lot of the basics used Latin. He was kind of old school like that."

"So what do you believe in?" Trace asked.

I held the key up again and spoke to the padlock. *"Cincinno, vos nominantur a me, et ego EXTEXO incantatum est illud tenet vobis. i provocare voluntatem urget vobis. Ego sum superior! Yield! Et cum clavis nodum nostra. Aperi!"*

The padlock snapped open, and the lock and chain clattered to the damp stone floor.

"Me," I said with a tight smile and fire in my eyes. "I believe in how amazingly badass I am."

Far off in the darkness, past the circle of Trace's phone light, there was a chorus of howls.

"Shit," Trace said, "they found us."

"Come on," I said, pushing open the door. "Let's finish this."

The chamber beyond was a network of aluminum tubing, meters, and junction boxes housing cables—the arteries and veins of the city, the thrumming heart of Times Square.

"The ritual requires that once you decapitate the dogs, you bury their heads under a busy street, so the spirits can know no peace," I said.

"That's why Times Square." Trace nodded, then he gagged. "Oh, God, I'm going to be sick!"

The stench hit both of us. Rotting meat, putrid blood. The air was filled with flies. The light of Trace's screen panned down to reveal four decaying dog heads, the shiny white bone of the skulls peeking out between bloody fur and the squirming attentions of maggots. The soft jelly of the eyes still held the dumb, confused look of the dead. The heads were arranged in a circle, each laid on top of Japanese kanji, painted in blood. Small scraps of paper containing spells and phrases of power were placed between the heads, completing the circle of the spell. The papers were also in each dog's mouth. A traditional Shugenja ritual arrangement.

The howls again, growing closer. I closed my eyes and tried to re-member my Japanese. It was always better to try to unweave a spell using its own traditions, if you knew what, or who, you were dealing with. The lock spell had been Western tradition, I'd bet good money on it. So a different caster had secured the room, or . . . I dismissed the thought. I didn't have time for it right now, but it troubled me. "忠実なものは、犬の神が、あなたはよくあなたのマスターを務めている。あなた自身とあなたの主人の家に敬意を表する。食べ物や獲物と冷たい水と日陰の場所で、今では休み。あなたは、あなたの義務とあなたの痛みから解放されます。犬良い。残り," I said. The spell papers all flared to life and began to blacken to ash.

There was a chorus, a quartet of mournful wailing in the darkness just outside the door, and then it was gone, only an echo that was smothered by the weight of the earth. Then silence.

"Thank God," Trace said.

I looked up from the flickering flames of the broken spell and smiled at Trace. "Thank me. I told you I'd get you out of this," I said. "Now let's—"

Trace's head exploded. Hot blood and brains splashed over my face and chest. As his body crumpled, I heard the thud of the silenced gun that had ended him. At the doorway stood a group of NYPD SWAT. I could see the bouncing flashlights of more beyond the door. They were in full combat gear: night-vision goggles, gas masks, helmets, and body armor—giant insects with Kevlar carapaces. One of them held up a small black box.

Two sharp stings in my chest and I was suddenly on fire, shaking, convulsing, as every nerve, every muscle in my body was sheathed in tingling, throbbing agony. My legs betrayed me and I fell, twitching.

"He's down!" a voice said. All I could see were black combat boots and the bloody body of the man I swore to save illuminated in the flames of a burning dog skull. Voices, shouting.

Hands grabbed me, pulled me. A black bag was slipped harshly over my head and another charge of current applied to me. I fell into oblivion; my last thoughts were a realization that the darkness was just. It came to saints and villains equally, and a sad wish passed through me that the darkness would never end.

TEN

Granny passed away in 1974. She came back to visit in the summer of '75. Probably getting a little ahead of myself.

I was ten years old in 1975 and unable to articulate, even to myself, the alien feelings I experienced near Kara May Odam—my first awkward brush with my slumbering sexuality and my first, and last, babysitter.

Kara May. Sweet Jesus in a Mustang. Jailbait-ponytail-wet-dream-prom-princess. All hay-colored hair, halter-top tits, and bare, tanned legs that were slender and firm and kept on going like a John Bonham drum solo, all the way up to her Daisy Duke perfect ass. She smelled of Bubble Yum bubble gum, strawberry lip gloss, pot smoke, and stale sex. Seventeen years old with vacant brown eyes that shifted between dull incomprehension and a fluid, sensual cunning. No disrespect intended there, Kara May. Most of the people I grew up around were pretty damn stupid, but many of them possessed acute and often uncanny instincts, and those instincts served them in good stead more often than any fact, figure, or tome. There is book learning, and there is knowing things. Thinking back on the whole incident with Kara May and Granny, I was the stupid one. Again, getting ahead of myself.

To my eyes, Kara May was the perfect woman, a goddess. If I

had been a bit older, she would have been the stuff of epic jerk-off fantasy. I never did, though, because of how things turned out on Halloween.

I was a little shit at ten. Made it hard on my momma. Pa had been dead five years, Granny, not even a year. Ma lost everyone she counted on to keep her safe and sane, and was left with my vicious, useless, whiny little ass to take care of. Some of the men Pa used to work with who hadn't died in the mine with him would come around. They'd knock on the door of the trailer, holding a six-pack of PBR. They'd smile and sit for a spell. Ma was thankful for the attention and the help they would offer—fix the old Nova, keep it going for another inspection, mow the lawn, and the occasional friendly date to avoid the madness that comes with death and loneliness.

So when Cecil Wheeler came up with two tickets to go see Conway Twitty Saturday night at Lakeside Amusement Park over in Roanoke, across the Virginia border, Momma jumped at the prospect. Her friend Gloria from work over at the Destiny Lounge had a niece, and she babysat. That was Kara May, and she had kept me a few times over the years when I was sick and Mom couldn't get out of a shift at work, or simply couldn't afford to miss work. It had been a few years since I had seen Kara May—Granny had kept me, but now Granny was gone.

After what happened with the squirrel, Granny had tried to work with me as much as she could, and as much as I'd let her. I actually got tired of Granny's little tests and games and practice. It had started out as something secret and fun and had suddenly turned in to a chore. There were so many rules, so many things I was never supposed to do or even think. Eventually, by the time I was seven or eight, I told Granny I didn't want to be a Wisdom.

"Now Laytham, honey," Granny said. "You can run from the things you can do, pretend it isn't real and ignore it. But it won't ignore you, darlin'. The power doesn't really care what you want; it's like water in a flood, looking for a way to flow. Like water, it can be a comfort or it can be destructive. Sooner or later, you will have to deal with it. I'm just trying to help you, sugar. I know it's difficult, especially to have so much talent and to be so young."

"I don't want it, Granny," I said. "It's hard. I don't like it no more."

Granny sighed, and I waited for the guilt and the sermon. They didn't come. She smiled at me. "Want to play checkers?" she asked. I hugged her and went back to being a little boy.

She was right. I wished I had listened to her, wished I had taken the time to learn more from her. Not the lessons about focus and projection, no, the real lessons she tried to teach me—about compassion and wisdom, patience and humanity. The ones I really needed were the ones I failed at, still fail at. I didn't learn them, though, and a few years later, she was gone. Like the old Merle Haggard song says, "Mama tried."

So there I was with my long-lost babysitter making me feel all kinds of things for the first time, and Momma and Cecil headed out the door to the concert and then some square dancing. Cecil looked and tried to act as much like Richard Petty as he could, he had on the Ray-Bans, the big cowboy hat, and the mustache. A toothpick danced at the corner of his mouth as he spoke.

"We'll be back by two or three in the mornin'," Cecil said.

"Your momma knows and that's okay with you, Kara May, honey?" Mom asked. "Laytham usually goes to sleep watching them monster movies, and that's fine. He ain't got no bedtime on the weekends. You leave him be to watch those silly things and he'll drop off before midnight."

"I understand, Mrs. Ballard, and it's okay," Kara May said, smiling. "Me and Laytham are gonna git along jist fine."

Momma kissed me, and I hugged her, and then her and Cecil were gone. Kara May went the kitchen and made us popcorn and cracked open one of Mom's beers.

"Let's watch some TV, Laytham," she cooed and plopped down on the couch. It was Saturday evening, so we watched *Hee Haw* and then *Emergency!* on WSAZ, and then *Mary Tyler Moore* on WOWK. It was dark by then.

"Kara," I said, "I'm hungry. What's for dinner?"

She finished her beer and nodded toward the half-empty popcorn bowl. "I made yew popcorn, Laven, that's plenty. Now hush."

"Laytham," I muttered under my breath. "It's Laytham."

The front door was still open, with the screen door closed. It was July and still hot as hell. Outside, the trailer park was quiet except for the cicadas. Fireflies, like orphan stars, drifted across the field where all the kids who lived here played football and pretended to be Evel Knievel on our bikes.

We had a single oscillating fan pushing warm air back and forth between us on the couch. Kara May was sweating, and I kept looking at her but not wanting her to see me staring, and I honestly didn't know why I felt so excited and shy all at the same time. I felt something stir in me, around me. I know now it was my Muladhara chakra, my root chakra, opening and acting up.

Kara had knocked back about four or five of Mom's PBRs by now, and she was laughing and smiling a lot more. Kara's teeth were crooked and yellow. I didn't care. For some reason, that just made me think she was prettier. The flaw made the rest stand out more.

We had switched the TV back over to WSAZ to watch the last half of the *McCloud* mystery movie on NBC. I told Kara I liked Columbo more because of his cool coat and how smart he was. Kara said that McCloud was sexier and began to tell me what she would do to Dennis Weaver if she got the chance. I suddenly really hated McCloud. An empty beer can on the coffee table crunched itself flat at the instant I felt a pang of jealously. I noticed it, but Kara May didn't, because she was too busy jumping up to answer the banging and shouting at the screen door.

Two teenage boys and another girl came into the trailer. They were loud, clumsy, and smelled of beer and, what I would realize years later, pot. Kara May was really happy to see them and hugged and kissed one of the boys, a skinny guy with black curly hair and wide sideburns. She called him Chip. The other girl looked a lot like Kara May but wasn't as developed and had black hair. Her name was apparently Jessie, and her boyfriend, Bobby, was wearing a mesh tank top and had long blond hair and a mustache kind of like Burt Reynolds in *Smokey and the Bandit*. They proceeded to help themselves to more of Momma's beer.

"Y'all, this is Layman. I'm watching him, and it's his bedtime," Kara May said, shooing me off the couch so her friends could pile on it.

"Umm, Kara May, it's Laytham," I said softly, kind of scared and embarrassed and hurt she didn't remember my name. "You . . . you said I could go to sleep on the couch and, um . . . watch the monster movie after the news."

The boys hooted at this and Kara May shushed them, then turned to address me. "Well, now I'm telling yew to go to sleep in your bed right now. Come on." She took my hand and led me down the dark hallway that ran along the length of the trailer and back to my room, Mom's room, and the bathroom.

Her friends laughed and jeered as she pulled me out of the living room. Jessie burped from the beer. Kara May let go of my hand when I got to the door of my dark room.

"Okay, Lay-tham," she slurred, "git on to bed now. We're gonna be havin' grown-up time."

"Kara, I'm scared," I said, and I was. She shook her head, obviously disgusted with me.

"Oh, fer fuck's sake," she said. "Yew watch those dumb-ass horror movies. How can yew be scared?"

She flipped on the lamp next to my bed. "See, no booger-man. Now git on in that bed, Laytham."

"I'm not scared of monsters," I said, climbing into the bed. "I just . . . I just miss Momma, and I miss Granny real bad. I'm scared of being alone, Kara. Please sit with me till I go to sleep. I'll try to go real fast, Kara, please."

If Kara May Odam had sat at the side of my bed and been a decent human being, hell, done her fucking job for about a half hour, my whole life might have been different. Hers too.

She snapped off the light and shoved me into the bed, under my

Spider-Man sheets. "God, yew is such a little sissy-faggot!" her silhouette said. "Reckon it's on account of your pa being dead—he's not
here to man you up. Go to sleep, Layman."

She walked out of the room and shut the door. I was in darkness.
My eyes adjusted to it. I became acclimated to the shadow. I felt my
fear turn into something else, something I would struggle with my
whole life—anger.

The fault is ultimately mine. If I had listened to Granny, really listened, I might have had the strength inside to weather her passing, to
not feel so alone in a hostile universe. "Mama tried."

Granny tried to teach me compassion and understanding, tried to
show me how beautiful it all was and how we were each part of that
beauty, never alone. However, I fear it simply wasn't in my nature. The
universe taught me different lessons—taught me its indifference, its
cruelty, and its love of irony. It taught me how alone we truly are in
this world, in this skin, in ourselves.

So my response was a cold, angry resolve. A petulant, childish response. If the universe was gonna pick on me, be mean to me, then I'd
be mean to the universe right back and hard. I still have that response upon occasion; I am still that angry, frightened child more often than I'd care to admit. Unlike many, though, in an act of ultimate
cosmic irony, I was born with a way to strike back, and I did. Granny
tried to warn me about that too, but I was just too angry to listen.

I got up out of the bed. I heard laughing and music from the eight-
track tape stereo in the living room. It was Lynyrd Skynyrd's "Simple
Man"—maybe one last desperate plea from Granny, from the beyond.
I didn't listen.

I opened my door slowly and darted across to the hall to Mom's
bedroom. The door was open and it was dark in there. I could smell
smoke—Kara May and her pals were hitting a bong and were obliv-
ious to me. The music was loud and they were louder.

Under Mom's bed I found the book. It was Granny's old scrapbook.
It was full of pictures of her and her sisters and brothers and Momma
when she was a child and baby pictures of me. I pulled it out from its

nest among shoe boxes and dust bunnies. I held it to my chest like a holy book.

Next stop was the bathroom at the very end of the hall, between my room and Mom's. Momma always kept the light on for me but Kara May or one of her buddies had turned it off. They had pissed all over the toilet seat too.

Granny's old wooden hairbrush was on the top shelf of the medicine cabinet, and I had to precariously climb the sink to reach it. Momma hadn't had the heart to throw it out. I held it and memories flooded me. I could feel her, see her—her smile, her brown eyes, her love like the sun on my face. I took a clump of the gray hair from the brush. I took a pair of scissors from the medicine cabinet too.

Back in my room, I shut the door and welcomed the darkness. It whispered to me, nurtured the hot coal in my chest. The universe was unfair and uncaring, Kara May was unfair and uncaring. So I would adopt their methods and get back what had been taken from me. It made perfect sense to an angry little boy with the power of a demigod inside him.

I closed my eyes and moved through the album a page at a time—feeling, not looking. I felt the power move up and down my spine, pulsing in time to my anger, my breath. The power is different when you are calm and when you are angry. There is a different sensation about it. Your perception of yourself is different too. Anger makes you feel powerful; it pumps you up—high on hate. Now, after decades of training and practice, I see that anger, that energy is not sustainable, and therefore is weaker. It's like a sugar rush, a boost of power, then it's gone. But as a ten-year-old alone in my dark room, I felt like an angry sun full of power and righteous cause.

I paused; there was a flare of power, of energy, on one of the pages of the book. I opened my eyes, and it was my favorite picture of Granny. She was holding me as a baby in her rocking chair and smiling. I took the photo off the page. I had a cowboy doll—sorry, action figure. I used the scraps of tape on the page to affix the picture and the hair to the doll. The hair still had a vague shiver of energy to it, very faint, but I could feel it. Now I only needed one more thing.

I took the scissors and cut my left palm deep. I still have the scar to this day. My blood welled up as quickly as the pain.

Outside my room I heard Kara May and Chip saying loud, drunken good-byes to the other couple. I heard an engine start and gravel crunch as headlights briefly wiped across my narrow open window. The gravel sounds ended, and the purr of the car's motor lessened and then faded away. I heard Kara May and Chip moaning and laughing as they staggered down the hallway to Momma's bedroom. They hit the walls and laughed harder, then they fell into Momma's room and onto her bed.

I took the doll and held it in my bloody, throbbing hand. I closed my eyes and I reached through the memory of the photo, through the DNA of the hair, through the lens of my love and my loss. I had no idea what I was doing; it was all instinct. I ached, and I missed her, and I would do anything, pay any price, fight any monster to have her in this world again. I felt the tendrils of the energy welling through me, all my chakras pulsing along my spine like stars, I felt the power flow out of me into the tenuous links I had forged to her in space and time. I reach out for Granny and tried to pull her back here, pull her to me. I felt the power throb with my heartbeat, with the gushing of my blood. I could feel something, like the nibble of a fish on your line, so faint but there and close. I needed more power. I simply didn't have enough myself and the universe was stone silent beyond me, offering no aid, no encouragement. I would have to do this all on my own, and I knew, instinctively, where to garner more power.

I took the scissors in my undamaged right hand and crept, still carrying the doll, to the door to my room. I opened it slowly. Across the hall, I could make out Chip's skinny naked ass pistoning up and down between Kara May's open legs in the bed. She was moaning and clawing his back with her nails. I walked across the hall, padding quietly in my bare feet. I stood by the bed.

In my mind, I was still teasing the connection I had felt, working it. I felt the heat coming off Kara May and Chip, and it fanned the power in me. I drew that energy, stole it greedily, carelessly, and I saw the envelope of energy about each of them, joined as one in the passion of their union, rip and tear like gauze as I harvested the power of their sex. I found out years later I had torn their auras in the act, and how horrible a thing that is to do to someone. At the time, I didn't know. I was a stupid, careless child ripping the wings off butterflies because they were beautiful and I wanted them, killing what I desired in my greed for it.

I drove the scissors deep into Chip's back. Again and again and again. He screamed and the blood splashed everywhere. A geyser of fiery energy roared out of him, and I was ready, I took in all of it. The connection became stronger, became a hard link, a certainty, and I pulled with all my will, all my might. I called out into the void and something answered, something approached. Granny was coming.

Chip backhanded me, and I flew across the room. The scissors and the doll were out of my hands. Kara May was screaming. Chip was too. He stood and staggered toward me. He punched me in the face. There was a flash of bright light and numbness spiked with pain, and then he punched me in the chest, and I suddenly felt like I was made of jagged, broken glass.

"You little prick!" Chip bellowed. "That fucking hurt!" He hit me again and again. I tasted blood in my mouth, and I pissed myself. It was hard to think, and everything seemed to be immediate and in my face and far removed all at the same time.

Kara May gasped and then shouted, "It's still in your back, it's still in your back, oh God, we got to call the rescue squad!"

While Chip shouted at Kara May to pull the scissors out of his back, I crawled to Momma's closet and hid inside. I had never been so afraid in all my life. Everything took on a sharp, bright, dreamlike quality, like being drugged, as my little brain tried to process so much violence, so much screaming, so much blood and trauma. There was a wet sucking sound and then Chip moaned. The scissors landed a few feet from me, black with his blood, outside the closet's leveled door.

"I'm going to kill that little faggot," Chip screamed.

"Baby, yew dun lost a lotta blood," Kara May cautioned. She was naked and covered with much of the blood Chip had lost. "Lay down! Let's jist call an ambulance."

"Call one for this little sumbitch!" Chip said as he tore open the door to the closet, ripping it partly off its hinges. The carpet squished with his blood, and the room reeked of copper, sex, and urine. The only light in the room was from the hallway. Chip was backlit, and his shadowed face didn't look human. Blood dripped down his back, ass, and legs to splash on the floor. He steadied himself on the doorframe.

"I'm gonna choke you, you little bastard," he growled, slurring his words. "Wring your neck like a fucking chicken."

He reached for me, murder in his eyes.

There was a crash in the living room. Everyone froze from the noise. It was the screen door flying open. The crash of furniture being knocked aside in the living room and then the *thump, thump, thump* of heavy steps down the hall toward the bedroom, toward us. There was a smell—mud mixed with putrefied blood and flesh, something sour, something gone bad, the shit smell of methane, like the smell of swamp—wet and stagnant and peaty.

Kara May saw it first. I couldn't see her, or it, from my bolt-hole in the closet, but I heard her losing her mind. It sounded like a bird made of pure terror banging into the chimney of her throat and then flying out and away, dragging her tattered reason in its razor-sharp claws. Human beings aren't made to sustain pure emotion. It burns us out, damages us.

Chip turned toward it, and he pissed in fear, like a frightened dog, when he saw it. He stumbled and lunged at it, screaming. I heard Kara May scream in response, but her mind was already gone. It was a parrotlike response to stimulus. There was a wet sound like a plunger creating a vacuum in a toilet, and then Chip stopped screaming. Kara May did as well. I heard her mumble, and then retching sounds. Chip's body thudded dully to the floor in front of me. His eyes were wide, the blood vessels all around them ruptured. His face was frozen, a rictus of fear.

"Laytham, honey," the voice said from outside the closet. It sounded like Granny, but her throat was packed with phlegm, and the words bubbled as she spoke. "He ain't gonna hurt you now, darlin'."

"Oh, Granny!" I said. "I missed you, I love you."

"Granny's here, Granny's here, Granny's here . . ." Kara whispered.

"I know, Laytham, but you did something we are never supposed to do, baby, and there is a consequence to that. The power demands a price," Granny said.

"A price, a price," Kara May babbled, "price, price, price . . ."

I knew I should stand, step out, and see her; I could tell she was standing right by the door to the closet. My instincts screamed *no!* A clod of putrid dirt fell to the floor. A fat worm squirmed and crawled free of it and began to slither across the carpet.

"I'm sorry, Granny," I said. "I'm sorry if I did bad. I just missed you and I was so sad."

"I know, Laytham, and for what it's worth I'm trying so hard to forgive you—you didn't know what you were doing, what you cost me."

"Cost?" I said.

Kara May began giggling. I heard a thumping sound, rhythmic.

"I . . . I can't go back, honey," she said. It sounded like she wanted to cry but wasn't capable of that anymore. "It's a one-way trip, darlin'. You pulled me out. I . . . I'm not allowed to go back no more."

"But . . . but I thought you were missing me too, Granny," I said. "I thought you were sad."

"Now, Laytham Ballard, don't you be fibbin' to your old Granny," she said. "You weren't thinking about me. You were thinking about yourself, now weren't you?"

The thumping became louder, and Kara May was humming a tune in time to it.

"I missed you, Granny," I said softly.

"Honey, you have to learn to let it go. You are not the Almighty, and you can't use the power to do whatever you please. There are rules, and when you break them, there are consequences."

Hot tears finally came, and I sobbed. The terrible awareness of what

I had done settled over me like a moonless night. "I'm so sorry, Granny. Were you happy where you were, Granny?"

There was a long pause, I saw the shadow of the thing that had been my grandmother shift.

"Aww, it weren't all that great, I suppose," she finally said, but there was anguish in her voice.

I cried.

"Now Laytham, you have to promise me you won't do this again, son—promise me! The price is too high, for everyone."

"I swear, Granny," I said. "I'm so sorry, Granny. What will you do?"

Another long pause. Kara May's pounding and humming continued unabated.

Finally, Granny spoke. "Well, I can go to the place that welcomes all comers. At least misery will have company. Or I can stay in my skin until it turns to dust and then just wear away with it."

I screamed in sorrow, in pain unlike any I could fathom—I still remember that feeling, that pain, to this day. It's the feeling that makes us eventually long to pass from this world. Kara May joined me in the wailing.

"Oh, God, Granny, I am so sorry!" I screamed. Can't they take me? Please take me instead and let you go back to Heaven! Please, God!"

"It can't work that way, Laytham," Granny said. "We are each responsible for what we do, the damage and the healing. It ain't God's fault—that's like blaming the landlord when you burn the house down. Folks like us got a lot more ability to harm or heal than most, but in the end we still stand for what we've done with our life. We all do, no hiding from that.

"For what it's worth, I forgive you, honey. And I love you, Laytham. I always will."

I heard the wet, heavy footsteps recede back down the hallway. Then there was only the thudding sound of the door again and the rhythmic pounding and Kara May's animal-like mewling.

I crawled out of the closet, over the damaged door, over Chip's cooling body. And I pulled myself up by the edge of Momma's bed. Kara, naked and covered in her lover's blood, was in the corner of the room by the night table, beating her head against the wall. With each impact, a new dark stain. Clods of wet, slimy mud led out into the hallway.

Kara May stared at me with the look of a broken toy. She no longer existed in the same world she had, and I felt myself strangely envious of her. Everything was spinning, dizzy. I was at the threshold of her new kingdom, and I yearned for it.

"Price, price, price, price . . ." She giggled in between impacts. Then she stopped and turned to look at me, her face harlequined in blood. She pointed to me and made a noise at the top of her lungs. It was laughter and rage and absolute fear. It was the sound madness makes when it scratches upon the wall of our world.

"Priiiiiicccccceeeeee!!!!!!" she screamed and pointed at me. I picked up the bloody scissors at my feet and, without any hesitation, I tore them across one wrist, then the other as deeply and as hard as I could. I lay on the floor and waited for, welcomed death.

Looking back, I was incredibly lucky; I shouted out into the dark well beyond this world and begged for someone to come to me. No protection, no wards or charms, no training. It's a miracle I wasn't possessed by the Waiting, what Granny would call a haint, or a ghost, or something far, far worse—the Hungry, the Unnamed. I like to think it was Granny's doing, her looking out for her stupid, crazy grandson, one last time.

It's part of my legend now, the myth of the rock star. "He raised the dead at the age of ten." The part of me that had all the feeling burned out is kind of proud when I hear that, and that is very sad. Only I ever view the event in its proper context, as, "He took a human life and damned a good soul at the age of ten."

To this day, I wish something had clawed up out of the Void, vomited into the lands of light and matter, and claimed my body and soul. I wish I had been eaten, instead of what I did to the only person who loved me all the way through in this shit house world. I wish they hadn't breathed life back into me, wish they had let me bleed out on the floor of Momma's bedroom. I wish I had listened, wish I had learned. Wishes are the currency of the foolish, the helpless, and the damned, lotto tickets that never pay out.

I saw Kara May a lot after that. Every day when it was meds time in the common room at Weston State Hospital. The asylum is closed down now, in part due to the hauntings, but that's a story for another day. I spent a year and a half in Weston, after Granny came to visit. Kara May Odam never left the hospital alive, another bloody bill on my account.

They never found Granny's body.

ELEVEN

The Seraphim were waiting for me on the other side of oblivion in the interrogation room. Always in the interrogation room—in my dreams, after the beatings, the torture, the drugs, I was always in the interrogation room. A loop of horror, like a serpent choking on its own tail. Always in the interrogation room.

I came to, leaning against someone in ballistic armor with a black bag on my head and my chest burning, throbbing from the Taser. The bag was ripped away. I blinked under the harsh light of the room, which looked the same in a hundred different police stations, right down to the stains and scratched declarations on the table.

The armored SWAT cop nodded to the two plainclothes detectives, gave them an odd salute and a bow, almost ritual in nature, and exited the room with my black bag. I tried to stand still and look cool, but I was teetering. My hands were cuffed, and my mind was flat and dull.

"Sit," the skinny one said, gesturing to the chair across from his own at the table. Soft, strong voice, Bronx accent. Skinny was balding, he had strands of salt-and-pepper hair combed over his pate. He had a thick, bushy, gray cop mustache standing sentry under his nose, and his complexion was pale with splotches of florid pink. His eyes may have been kind a few eons ago; now they were just tired. He wore the detective uniform—a short-sleeved, white-collared shirt, a cheap-looking tie (this one was brown-and-beige striped), and a sport coat that was at least ten years old. He didn't look well enough dressed to be a dirty cop. He had a little police union pin tacked to his lapel. I'd wager the keys to these cuffs that he had a Saint Christopher medallion around his neck.

I sat. His friend, the fat one, lurked menacingly in the corner off to my left. He was a good foot taller than me and Skinny and outweighed us both by at least 150 pounds. He dressed about the same as Skinny, except he shopped the big and tall bargain bin. Anger came off of him in waves, like heat off asphalt on a summer day. I could see the scars on his knuckles without needing to see his hands, and at home there were holes in the sheetrock walls and a discarded wedding band on the dresser in the bedroom next to a dusty wedding album and a letter of reprimand. He had a mop of black hair and a face that was too old, too busted up, too wrinkled, and too damn mean to have such a crown. At first glance, you'd think he was sporting a toupee, but on second viewing, you'd realize that he was just an old guy who got lucky enough to keep his hair, kind of like me. I wasn't feeling an overabundance of lucky right now, I have to admit.

Fat was waiting; I could see it in his dog-shit brown eyes, glazed with hatred, in his posture. Waiting for me to give him a reason, any reason, to let it loose, to use the plant gun, to break me down so he could live a little longer outside of himself. To teach me a lesson. I knew exactly what not to do here, to avoid the ogre, to avoid the rage. I knew, but we all have our weaknesses, don't we?

I smiled at Fat as I sat down. "Hi," I said, and waved as best I could with handcuffs on.

Fat walked over and kicked the chair out from under me. I hit the dirty tile floor hard. His steel-toed shoe was in my side, kicking me, hard, over and over and over, like Gene Kelly doing a buck-and-wing. I felt red blossoms of pain as several of my ribs snapped under his attentions. I tried to roll into a ball. He pulled me up by my hair with one hand and punched me a few times in the face with the other. A strobe of white light flashed behind my eyes and my face became numb.

I was pretty sure my nose had just been broken, again. What was this now? Six, seven times?

My exercise partner held me up while he picked up the chair off the floor and slid it back to the table. He deposited my sorry ass in it and let me go. He stalked back to his corner.

"Who are you?" Skinny asked. "We tried to print you, of course, while you were out. The ink wouldn't stay on, it ran off your fingers every time we tried, and the partials we managed to get weren't actual prints. They were like tiny paintings, seemed to be small parts of some painter's work . . . who was it?" he asked Fat, who was wiping blood off his hands with an old handkerchief. Fat shrugged.

"Some fuckin' faggot," he opined. Accent straight out of Brooklyn.

Skinny snapped his fingers. "Bosch," he said. "Hieronymus Bosch. Nice trick there.

"No wallet. We tried blood tests, DNA unraveled and the results were inconclusive. One genetic test told us you were Alex Trebek. We drugged you, of course, tried to get intel out of you that way. You were very resistant, obviously not your first time being interrogated. We tried digital scans of prints and facial recognition. Your images crashed the computer, crashed the network, or sent us to Russian porn sites, every time. So, we figure you for being in the Life. Figured we'd just ask you. Who are you, cowboy?"

I sucked back in through crushed sinuses, winced at the exquisite pain, and hocked a glob of black blood onto the folder in front of Skinny.

"Phuck youh," I said through loose, bloody teeth. "There's anuder sanple ford youh. I wan' a lawyer."

Skinny smiled, sighed, and shook his head, the way you might at an errant dog that pissed on the new carpet again.

"No, pal, fuck *you*. Hard. You understand that there will be no lawyers coming for you, don't you?" Skinny said. "You are alone here with us, and when we are finished with you, you go to the Tombs—you know, Lower Manhattan. We have a special section there just for guys like you."

"Gee, I didn't knowd there wa' anybody like me," I said.

Skinny smiled big, and ice filled my bowels. "Guys like you—people who fuck with the Secret Masters, asshole."

"Isn't dath a golfth tournament?" I said.

He nodded to Fat. I didn't need to see the bigger cop to feel his smile.

Everything jerked back into the frame-jump world of violence and pain. There was blood, mine, everywhere. There was no clock in the room, so I measured time in the intervals between new expressions of hurting and the pauses between pain.

I remember crawling across the floor, trying to hide in a corner, but Officer Friendly would have none of it. His kick caught me in the diaphragm, and I felt all awareness abandon me with the air in my lungs. The panicked feeling of not being able to breathe, not pull a breath out of the air. The thrill of thinking you are going to die and realizing how unimportant you are, how meaningless your life is to the continuity of the great show. Trauma strips away all our pretenses; it leaves us naked and small.

Eventually, I was dropped back into the chair. I couldn't see very well. One eye was swollen, and the other didn't seem to be working the way it was supposed to. I couldn't feel my left leg at all, and there was a sharp knife in my lungs with each breath.

Skinny had a can of soda now. I guess he had stepped out during Fat's quality time with me. Surprisingly, I hadn't noticed. I had taken enough beatings in my day to know Fat knew exactly what he was doing. He freestyled a bit, but he was an artist of suffering. I was right at the edge of life-threatening, permanent damage.

"Why did you kill him?" Skinny asked. "Tell us your name and confess your crime. Why did you kill him?"

"Killh who?" I asked.

"The banker," Skinny said. "You were in his office on Wall Street about five days ago. Remember him now?"

"Node," I muttered as I put my head down on the table.

"You a freelancer, a Sellspell? A Hexhitter? Maybe you're an

Athame, a ritual assassin with another lodge, and Berman got in your way? Tell me I'm wrong."

"Who's Berdman?" I said, looking up and rubbing my swelling face.

"You led us a merry chase, I'll give you that," Skinny said. "We had been looking for you for days. It was fortunate we picked you and Berman's boyfriend up on the city cameras we have hardwired into the Sphinxes."

"Finxes?" I asked. Skinny handed me a paper towel to stanch some of the blood dripping from the train wreck that was my face.

"We take political prisoners, like you. Some homeless, if they haven't wrecked their nervous systems with too much Sterno, orphans of the state that have fallen through the cracks, and we do a series of surgeries on them. Remove all their external sensory organs: eyes, ears, nose, tongue. We destroy parts of their brains and enhance other parts, and then we wire them up to the over 2,397 traffic and surveillance cameras in the city. They become eternal watchmen, scanning, seeing, unblinking, unsleeping. They live in coffins—devices that feed their shriveled bodies. They sift data for us, churn it, and, lucky you, they spotted you and your dead friend, Trace.

"Were you fuckin' him too?" Fat rumbled, and smacked the back of my head. "That why you snuffed Berman, lovers' spat, homo?"

It was hard to think, but a few wheels were turning in me. A hypothesis was formulating, but I didn't have the brain power to reason it out right now. They were either playing games with me, mind-fucking me, or I was missing some things. I decided to keep doing what I was doing, clam up and keep fishing.

"Whyd you killh him?" I asked Skinny, looking him dead in the eyes. "Trace. He wad a civilian, a nobody."

"You liked him," Skinny said.

I nodded. "Yeah, he was okay. Why killh him and keep me? Why?"

Skinny looked genuinely pained for a second and rubbed the bridge of his nose. "It was not supposed to go down that way," he said. "Someone on the extraction team screwed the pooch, got a little overenthusiastic and dropped Trace. We'd already interrogated him about Berman and had pretty much written him off. It was sloppy and bad form. You're right."

Fat seemed not to be too happy with Skinny's line of discussion with me. He resumed brooding and pacing in the corner. But I saw what angle Skinny was working here, and it was brilliant. Establish trust, demonstrate honesty, and share information, just enough to keep me going but not enough to give me the full picture.

These two cops were not just pulled out of a hat; they were both experts in their arenas. Fat in breaking my body and Skinny in hacking my mind.

"Why did you have him with you at the ritual site?" Skinny asked. "What did he know?"

"I thin' the real question is whyd yourth man killed him," I said. "I'd look to yourth own house, firs', pal. That wasn't an accident, id was an off-the-books hit."

The muscle in the left side of Skinny's jaw twitched.

"Your ass is about to be disappeared," Skinny said. "Now, why did you kill Berman?"

"I'm ready to disappear now," I said.

"Ballsy little prick," Fat muttered to Skinny. "Want me to bounce him around a little bit more? See if he gets more helpful?"

I looked up at Fat. He was panting, but he actually looked healthier after our session. There were all kinds of things I could say. They would all get me killed or in a wheelchair, turned into a vegetable, breathing through a machine. Sometimes you have to listen to your survival instincts and not be a fool.

I smiled through bloody teeth and shredded lips. "Thad wha' youh and yourh boyfrien' call fordplay, Salad Barh?" I said to Fat. I heard Skinny laugh.

I don't remember anything after that, until the Tombs.

The second worst thing about being beaten to within an inch of your life by professionals is that after it's all over, you have the time to stiffen up. Time for your back to become a fused steel rod, for your head to feel like it's full of gravel, for your skin to feel tight and numb over the brutal topography of bruises and split skin. The worst thing, of course, is getting the shit kicked out of you in the first place.

They call the Manhattan Detention Center "the Tombs" for good reason. In the caves of crumbling concrete, between curtains of steel, it's easy to feel lost to time, to life, to daylight—a thing of dust, frozen pain, aborted from the memory of the world. Prison is Hell's waiting room.

On the way to my new home, they paraded me through the general population. Imagine walls six stories high, made of screaming, hungry faces and steel. It rained down on me; I was baptized in shit, blood, puke, moonshine, and cum from my new neighbors. The guards just smiled. They knew I was headed for the special cells.

I sat in my dark cell in the deepest bowels of the prison and felt the beating I got at the precinct house stiffen me up real good. Welcome to the rest of your life.

I was unsure how long I had been out. I had been drugged, I felt that much and, like any effective drug designed to incapacitate you, it played hell with my sense of time. My head buzzed, and I was dizzy, and my mouth was dry. The puncture wounds and burn marks from the Taser's barbs in my chest were scabbed over and healing. The looked like they had been treated. That gave me a rough idea: I had been in here for at least a few days.

My new world consisted of a six-by-nine cell. Facing the corridor were steel bars with an electronic sliding door of bars built in. On the back wall was a cot bolted to the floor, a thin, slightly moldy old mattress, an army blanket, and a plastic hospital-style pillow. A sink with a square of polished steel for a mirror bolted to the wall, a stainless steel toilet with no seat. When I used it, I pissed bright red blood.

I tried to focus my energies and see if I could perceive any enchantments on the bars or locks, or any kind of scrying, but I was too broken, too weak, and still too drugged to make anything happen. I tried to cry, but my eyes were too swollen and raw from bruises to summon tears. I groaned and rolled over on the cot, falling into a deep narcotic darkness—a land of no dreams. If there was mercy in this universe, I would die in my sleep, but my last waking thought was that I knew there was no mercy, and even if there were, I was the last soul on earth deserving of it.

TWELVE

Sleep was a knotted, broken thing. Nightmares of the beatings Fat had given me, Trace's head exploding and showering his brain meat on me. Restraints, the smell of rubbing alcohol, and questions droned in my ear under surgical lights. ECT sessions at Weston, Boj's sunken skull of a face. Slorzack staring at me from the video, killing the video with a stare. Static. Tangled, wet sheets, awake.

I woke in my cell to guards over me, guns pointed at my face. Men in white coats were holding me down and injecting me with hypodermics. I tried to fight, but I was made of pain and stone.

They departed, and I fell back to sleep. It was hard to keep my eyes focused; my brain was slippery. Whatever they were planning to do to me, it could wait till after a good nap.

I awoke later; time had no meaning anymore. My face itched, and I scratched it. I had a beard now. I sat up in bed, and there was no pain, but there was a powerful, gnawing hunger in my gut. I was starving, and my mouth tasted like a diseased raccoon had taken up residence in it.

I stood and walked to the mirror over the sink, again amazed that there was no pain, no stiffness. I twisted on the faucet and water sputtered out. I knelt and drank great greedy gulps of the cold, silver liquid. It was the best water I had ever tasted, and I drank until I couldn't drink any more. I straightened and regarded myself in the mirror. I had a full beard now and my hair had grown at least a few inches. For a second, I thought they had kept me drugged and under for weeks, maybe a month, but then I touched the bloodstains on my pillow and mattress. Some of them were still damp.

I went back to the bunk and sat down, waiting, craving food.

"Hey, hey man," a voice called to me from the darkness of the other side of the corridor of cells. "You okay, brother?"

"Surprisingly, yes."

"Dude, you grew that beard crazy fast," the voice said again. "They brought you in yesterday, and you were clean shaven, and beat to hell."

"Yesterday?" I said. "Thanks. My time sense is kinda fucked-up with no windows or clock and the drugs and all. So I've only been down here a day?"

"Yeah," he said. A horrible voice inside me whispered that this could all be an Illuminati psyop designed to feed me false information and screw even more with my brain. I wasn't quite that paranoid yet; for example, I had drunk the water and shoved down the thought that it was most likely dosed with chemicals. If I lost myself to that level of crazy already, then I was as good as dead. "Yeah, man," the voice continued. "We get three meals a day—that's part of how I have been keeping track."

"Good, I'm starving," I said. "When's food?"

The guy laughed. "You slept through breakfast, so lunch should be coming soon."

"Great," I said. I felt so much better, I felt like pacing the cage, running laps. I didn't understand what was happening inside me. To pass out in so much pain and so tired and sore and wake up feeling brand-new, it was exciting and frightening all at the same time. I knew they were doing something to me, inside me, but at the same time I felt like I was in my twenties again.

"I'd tell you my name, but they are listening in," I said to my friend in the shadows. "You can call me Crowley, if you like."

"Cool," he said. "Like the Ozzie song. They already know who I am, so I don't give a shit. My name is Darren, Darren Mack. Nice to meet you, man."

"Likewise," I said. "Don't take this the wrong way, Darren, but . . . are you real?"

He laughed. "Yeah, they do kinda play with your head, man. But no, I'm real, bro."

"Good," I said. "How long you been in here?"

"Well," Darren said, "the protests were in October, and if we go by the clock of the belly and count each three meals as roughly a day, then . . . I'd say . . . about five years."

"Jesus," I said. "Five years? Alone?"

"Mmmmhhhmm," Darren said. "I kind of thought I'd lost it when you showed up, maybe I was finally hallucinating, so I started some shit with a guard to see if this was real or if it was just me going bat-shit. He fucked me up pretty good, so I got my answer. Totally worth it, by the way."

I laughed, and so did Darren. I got off the bunk and knelt by the iron bars and the door, examining the lock. I closed my eyes and felt the power flow through my bone and nerve staircase. The defensive enchantments glowed and danced like live current. The place was warded against my kind of trouble. Given a lot of time and tools, I might be able to unravel the defenses, but then where exactly would I go? I was out of the world, in the bowels of one of the greatest prisons on earth. In a cell block that could be designated "the George Orwell Wing."

"Hey," Darren called out, "what you doing, Crowley?"

"Sussing out the locks," I said. "They are pretty thorough."

"Yeah," he said. "I gave up on breaking out of here a long time ago."

"You said something about protests," I said. "What happened?"

"Times Square," he said. "It was a huge protest in October—that would have been . . . 2011," he said. There was a long pause, and I knew he was doing the calculus of imprisonment, reviewing all the birth-days he had missed, wondering if loved ones were alive or dead, search-ing for him, or if they had forgotten him. Missed chances, missed loves, life eaten up by the sharp maw of time, eaten and gone. I remained silent.

"Yeah, so I was part of a group, we went after Citi's mainframe."

"You a gray hat?" I asked.

"Hells yeah," he said. "Damn good one too. Just not good enough. They busted me after I put some stuff up on their Web site."

"Bullshit," I said. "They did not drop you in the sphincter of the universe over some spray paint manifesto on a corporation's home page."

I heard Darren chuckle. "Yeah," he said. "I guess it was a tiny-weeny bit more than that. I coordinated the cyber attacks against the IMF during those months. Sent all those documents to Wikileaks. They busted me. Had a whole G.I. Joe black helicopter assault team come get me in the dead of night. Been here ever since waiting for my due process."

He laughed again. I was amazed by how human a sound it was, laughter in the heart of the labyrinth. Pissing in the eye of the Minotaur.

"You," I said, "you are Fawkes? The Fawkes?"

Laughter again. "Yeah," he said. "Guilty. Did Wikileaks ever get that stuff out?"

"Uh, yeah," I said, "about Wikileaks . . ."

I spent the time till our jailers brought us lunch catching Darren up on the news of the last few years. I have to admit, by the time the guards rolled up with the carts with the Styrofoam boxes containing our food, I was dizzy and groggy from low blood sugar. I could usually go days without eating and be cool. They had done something to me, were still doing it, but I didn't care. I wanted food more than answers.

A detail of SWAT myrmidons showed up at the same time, in full combat gear. One of the riot cops pointed at me.

"No time for lunch, asshole, you got a date at the precinct house."

And away did I go. As they marched me out, I saw Darren. The kid in the cell across the hall from me, the scourge of the Secret Masters, was maybe twenty-five, tops; he had a full brown beard, long hair, and a hell of a shiner. He was dressed in filthy street clothes. His shirt had a complex circuit board design on it. He gave me the peace sign as he grabbed a second Styrofoam lunch box.

Sometime later, I was sitting at the table again in the interrogation room. Always in the interrogation room. There was a cold soda and a pack of cigarettes in front of me. Skinny was still sitting with the same smile twitching at the edges of his face. He had his folder open in front of him. He recited a litany of names. One of them was my real name—the one that had power over me.

"So," he said as he finished the list of names, "which one is really you? We gave your profile to the Hidden Oracles at Quantico, along with all of the proper tributes and blood sacrifices, and got all of these possible results back. Your face is hidden in shadow from the Oracles' sight. That is an impressive bit of working. So we do this old school. Save yourself the aggravation of another session with Lou, just tell me who you are."

"Why, so you can put a compulsion glamour on me to answer your questions?" I said, fumbling with the pack of smokes. I wished they were American Spirits, but these would do. It was hard to tell if the look on Skinny's pinched face was amusement or controlled anger. I held out the cigarette, and Skinny lit it with a white lighter.

"Those are bad luck, y'know," I said. Skinny's face split into a smile.

"So, we have a player," he said to Lou. After all Fat and I had been through together, I figured I should call him Lou. "They are bad luck, funny guy, they are real bad luck."

Lou worked me over real well. He went up to the edge he had taken me to the day before and gave me hope it was coming to an end, and then he went over that edge, hard. I was in agony, and then terror welled up in me as he kept going. He took my partly smoked cigarette and burned me on the face, in one of my eyes, with it.

"Your name," Skinny said, "and it stops."

I said nothing. I have no fucking clue why. I knew if they kept this up I would break and I would do anything they asked me to do, tell them anything. Give up Grinner, Christine, the baby, Magdalena, Geri, anyone, everyone, to just stop this pain and the disfigurement. But then I got pissed at myself for that and decided I rather fucking die than be that little snitch bitch. And there was still that nagging thing in my head if I could just think, just have the time to reason it out without a concussion, or pain, or hunger buzzing in my head.

"Askh Lou's mom," I muttered, and spit blood in Lou's wide face.

More "quality time" with Lou followed. More questions, more witty replies that resulted in new and startling levels of pain, disfigurement, and permanent injury. There was no longer a line; Lou was destroying me in as painful a way as possible.

"Your name?" Skinny said again and again. Sometimes it was, "Why did you murder him?" or "Who do you work for?"

Each time my answer was a nonanswer, sometimes smart-ass and defiant, other times just sobbing sounds. I couldn't cry. Lou had put out cigarettes on my tear ducts by that point.

Lou took out a straight razor, and he cut one of my ears and most of my nose off. He whispered in my ear, "Your eyelids are next." I felt his raging erection against me as he began to cut at the corner of my one remaining, squirming eyeball.

"No," Skinny said, and he stood. "Lou, that's enough."

"The little fucker is about ready to crack," Lou said defiantly, like a kid pleading with his mom to have five more minutes to play before he has to come in for the night.

"No, save it for tomorrow," Skinny said. "Bring him over here."

Grudgingly, Lou planted me back in the chair. I slumped over, my face hitting the table. Lou pulled me back and then smashed my face back on the table several more times. Blood flew everywhere.

"Jesus, watch it!" Skinny shouted. "I don't want to have to go home to Sally and the kids with this skell's fucking blood all over me. Pull him up."

Lou did. It was hard to focus; I was more out of it than aware. Skinny leaned close as he dabbed the bloodstains off his tie.

"Do you know why I let Lou go so far with you today?" Skinny asked. I couldn't answer. A bubble of blood swelled between my shredded lips and shattered teeth and popped.

"Because tonight you will be injected with the same potion they pumped into you last night—a combination of alchemy and biotechnology. Microscopic golems. Magical nanotech that accelerates your whole body's metabolism and heals you completely. And tomorrow morning, you will be fine. You will have aged a few months, but you will be fine physically and ready for another day of this and another and another. Do you understand, funny guy? You get the punch line?"

I stared stuporously at Skinny, but the awareness must have registered in my one functioning eye, because Skinny nodded and smiled broadly.

"That's right, no dying here, no matter what I let him do to you, no escape, no release. And the memory of each thing he does to you, the dreams of it, the dread of the next time you come to this room and what will await you—those are forever."

I made a little sound. It was very weak and feeble, but it made both men laugh. I didn't have enough of me left to be angry or even fully afraid. I was like a suffering animal, and I just wanted it to stop.

"Tomorrow, I will not ask you any questions," Skinny said, "and I will make sure Lou here cuts your tongue out first thing. So have a good night's sleep, funny guy."

And after a little more "me time" with Lou, they buried me back in the deepest, darkest part of the Tombs.

Skinny was as good as his word the next day.

Time became intervals of torture and healing.

The only food I got was what Darren managed to steal for me. I was so broken by the time they returned me in the evening, I was unaware of dinner. And the healing coma that the tiny magical robots in my cells put me into ensured I missed breakfast. If I was lucky, I caught a few lunches a week before the detail came to get me for my time in the interrogation room.

I felt my humanity slipping away, my mind turning to liquid that couldn't hold a tight thought or defend a position, and reasoning was getting harder every day. Between the lack of food, the drugs, and the torture, they were breaking me, it was working. Darren became my anchor to objective reality. Part of me was waiting for him to be gone one night when they returned me, another prop, another way to give me a scrap of hope and then take it away, but so far he seemed to be real.

I woke as usual, feeling fine physically, but now, daily, my mind was dull, and it was hard for me to do much but stare. Thought was like pushing against a wall of mud. I counted on Darren to tell me how long I had been here. It was about a month now, he said. Thirty days, thirty trips to the interrogation room. Thirty healing treatments. I had fantasies at one point of Geri, Grinner, and the gang crashing into Rikers in some daring *Matrix*-like raid and saving my ass. I didn't dream that anymore; I didn't dream at all except of the torture in the interrogation room. Sometimes I couldn't tell the dreams from the reality.

My beard stretched to my stomach now and my hair to my mid-back. Both were streaked with silver. I had no clue how much the healing elixir was aging me, but I knew that the rush of my accelerated metabolism was now being checked by my near constant starvation.

A white Styrofoam box sailed across the corridor. It landed with a thump by my bars, and a second later another food box fell.

"Two?" I asked Darren. My voice sounded strange to me now, alien. Words felt thick and odd in my mouth.

"Yeah, man," he said from the darkness of the other cell. "I think it's your anniversary or something, and you deserve a little treat, Crowley."

I worked the boxes through the bars and opened the first one. It was piled with food—bacon, sausage, hamburgers, fries, scrambled eggs, ham sandwiches, potato chips, and a baked potato. The second one contained pizza slices, tacos, mashed potatoes, even a hunk of steak.

Sitting on top of the piles of food were two joints, one in each box.

"Merry Christmas!" Darren said and laughed.

"Where the hell did you get this?" I said, and I think I smiled for the first time in a thousand years.

"Don't got matches, though," Darren said, and I saw him standing with a big grin of his own and a joint dangling between his teeth. "Don't got a light, do you?"

I slipped my hands out past the edges of the bars and pointed at his blunt with my index finger.

"Accendere," I whispered to the stale air. The tip of his joint became cherry red, and smoke coiled away from it.

"Whoa," he said, and then laughed.

"Yeah." I nodded and sat back down on the bunk. "I get that a lot."

"How, how'd you do that, Crowley, man?"

"Sweet old lady taught me how to do it," I said. "I learned the fancy words some other places, but she taught me to listen to the fire and the air and the water. I wish I'd listened better."

I got off the bunk and lifted one of the legs. The leg was hollow, and I pulled out a crumpled cigarette pack. Inside were four cigarettes and the white lighter I had palmed on the first day.

"How did you get this smoke?" I asked.

"Shit, man, it's prison," Darren said. "Even in this part, it's still prison. I used to suck off this guard in exchange for part of the weed he confiscated in the cell searches in the general population. I stockpiled it. Like your food there."

"Darren, my man, I think I have a notion." I began to eat, wolfing down the food eagerly. I set the two joints, my cigarettes, and the lighter to one side and kept stuffing food into my mouth. "Do you know who the Seraphim are?"

"The what? Angels, right? Angels in Heaven," Darren said.

"Yes, but wrong Seraphim. They are the secret police of the Illuminati. They make the Secret Masters' enemies disappear. They are smoke and shadow, everywhere and nowhere, and they have our asses in the belly of the beast."

"New World Order, yeah, I hear you," Daren said.

The food was helping. I paused, went to the sink, and filled it with water. Then I muttered a simple purification spell Granny had taught me. It worked. The wards were on the bars and locks and were keyed to destructive or countermeasure-style spells, complex magics. But Granny's simple old-as-the-hills purification spell worked just fine. The old ways, the simple ways. Magic, like water cutting into rocks, finding its way. The narrow focus wards were a cheap solution to keep magical cons from busting out. It was a loophole. And I just loved loopholes.

"So, if these guys are the all-seeing, all-knowing, and all-powerful masters of the world, and we are their prisoners, then why don't these cops know more than they do?"

"Maybe they are trying to trick you into confessing?" Darren offered, taking a long drag on his joint, holding it nestled in his lungs, and then slowly exhaling the mellow smoke. "Trying to get you to slip up."

"Why would it matter to them?" I said, tossing one empty carton away and starting to work on the second one. "They know, right? They are going to play cat and mouse with me for a fucking month and keep asking the same damn questions?" There was a long pause. I got up and drank half a sink full of clean water. My head was clearing fast.

"They don't know," Darren finally said. "They are fishing. They don't fucking know."

I laughed and licked my fingers and wiped my lips and beard. "Yep. They are on a fishing expedition. They said something the first few days, about the Inugami . . ."

"The what?" Darren said.

"They were asking why I had Trace at the ritual site. They thought I had summoned the Inugami, so it wasn't them that sicced them on us; it was someone else. Not the Secret Masters, not the Illuminati. I made the assumption because the cops grilled Trace, but I could have been giving them too much credit. Maybe it was Slorzack after all, or someone clearing the path for Slorzack."

I tossed the second empty box on the floor and burped. It felt so good.

"What the hell is an Inugami?" Darren asked. "What the fuck is a Slorzack?"

"I'll tell you when we are out of this shit hole," I said, lying back on my bunk and smiling, holding my belly. "I'm going need you to do a few more things for me, Darren, and one of them is going to be very hard to do. Very."

"Okay, Crowley," Darren said, choking a little on the smoke from his joint. "What you need, man?"

"I'm going to need all of your dope, any rolling paper you got."

"Okay, man. Done. I got the better part of a dime bag."

"And, here's the really tough part," I said.

"Yeah," Darren said, leaning against the bars and taking another drag.

"I need you to believe me when I say I'm coming back to get you the hell out of here, man."

THIRTEEN

Another eternity in the interrogation room. Another fugue
of nightmares and hypodermics. I had told Darren to try as
hard as he could to wake me earlier. He did. It was like
fighting my way up from dark, warm water.

I pulled my ass out of bed, groggy, starving, and still hurting a bit.
The pain actually felt good to me. It was bearable, and it spurred me
on.

I told Darren what I needed. He didn't even balk. He tossed me a
box of breakfast with his bag of weed inside with the food. It was time
to get to work. When Lou had been carving on me last night, I swore
it was going to be my last night in that room and in this cell.

Darren had pretty good shit. I began the ritual after I ate breakfast. It took some effort to coax my body back to the practice of magic.
They had almost broken my will, and a Wisdom without will is nothing. I sat on the floor of my cell, crossed my legs, and straightened
my spine. My breathing became my universe: slow, even, in and out,
in through the mouth, out through the nose. Slowly, I opened each
petal, each chakra, wide. My body became a distant shadow. I sensed
the forces flowing, crashing, moving, blocking all about me. The winds
of the world howled through me like an open window, they cleansed
me, renewed me.

I had wondered to what degree we were being watched here in the Tombs, and now I could perceive the forces arrayed against us. It was mostly passive glamours—colored threads of frozen power, welded by will, crimsons and emeralds, azure and gold tripwires, invisible to human eyes. It was a very passive, but elaborate, web of magics. As long as you weren't trying to break out, the spells slumbered. However, it was keyed to a specific array of spells—apportation, for example. Other magics, like the one I was using to view and the one I planned to undertake with Darren's dope, would be virtually invisible to the wards, wouldn't cause a quiver in the web. Again, I was surprised at how low-rent the Illuminati were being. Something was missing. There was a part of the story I was not privy to. But I was going to get my answers before I walked away. I had paid for them.

Tobacco would have worked better for this, but I was down to three cigarettes from the pack I had palmed on my first day, which didn't give me much to work with. A lot of the brands out there, this one included, were doped with certain spirit- and will-killing chemicals. The more industrially processed the plant material was, the harder my job was going to be. So wacky tobaccy it was.

Now that I knew our surveillance was passive, and my working wasn't going to set off bells and whistles, I spread the marijuana on the floor before me. I resumed my cross-legged lotus position, closed my eyes, and filled myself with cleansing air, cleansing energy. I was made of sunlight and cool breeze, in a frame of ivory bone; I had a staircase of swirling, pulsating divinity running along my spine.

I opened my eyes and fell into a universe of emerald, a forest of cool green light. The spiritual essence of the marijuana embraced me like a mother's arms. This forest was old, older than man. It knocked down the puny concrete walls that tried to bind me, undid the wonder of the city that enfolded me, choking it to dust with relentless, clinging tendrils and the acid of time. I was small, puny meat in the cathedral of the Green Man. I called out in the chartreuse air. My voice echoed in a space where life had no vocal cords. The world was silent. I had to go deeper, push deeper like a seed screaming, sliding, tearing its way to the sky and to light. I had to shift my energy, my thoughts away from the rigid, independent animal brain to the thought-stream of spores and roots. Knowledge and language flowed like water, settling, spreading in the damp soil, both slow and quicksilver fast—a knowing without the foundation of logic or the handholds of sensory perception. I was flying across the high wire without a neural net, so to speak.

I called out again, seeking an audience with the force that inhabited this temple of leaf, stem, and seed. My voice was no longer human; it was impulses, emotions softer and less blunt than the boot of words, subtle, with nuances like the perfume that seduces the bee.

The spirit in the leaf answered me. When it finally spoke, it had a Mexican accent. By that, I mean it conveyed its geography of origin to me in such a way that it made an association in my physical human brain. It was an old spirit, a powerful one, tied closely to the founding of magic and the rending of veils between worlds. I called it "Red."

I told Red what I needed it to do. Naturally, it was reluctant to do much of anything; most nonhuman-inhabiting spirits are pretty chill. Then I told it what I would give it, and it agreed. Blood buys a lot.

We concluded the bargain, and I slowly moved my awareness, my consciousness, back into the lonely, cold world of animal autonomy. It felt a little like the BDSM condition they call sub-drop, a feeling of loneliness, disconnection, disorientation after intense emotional and physical sensation. Anyone who ever came off an acid trip gets the same kind of feeling, an intense perception of not being in sync with the world anymore. It takes a while for your senses and your mind to reboot.

"Hey, Crowley, you okay, man? You were zoning for a long time. I don't know how much more time you got before they come."

I groaned and crawled off the floor, gathering the pot back in its baggie. I took one of the few tobacco cigarettes I still had, laid it on the bed with the pot and a pen cap I had managed to acquire during my last visit to the interrogation room, and I began the slow and very careful process of swapping out the tobacco for the newly awakened marijuana in the paper. I ruined one of the three remaining cigarettes trying, but I learned from my mistakes and managed to stuff the other two with the pot. I put them back in the crumpled pack with the lighter and stuffed them in my jeans pocket. I tossed the remainder of the bag of Red across the corridor between the bars to Darren just as the door at the end of the cell block thudded and groaned open. He scooped up the bag and gave me a huge grin and a thumbs-up.

"Don't forget me, Crowley," he whispered.

"Never," I said. "Thank you, man."

When they took the hood off my head, I was back in the interrogation room. It hadn't changed. Skinny and Lou hadn't changed. Lou had a chili stain on his tie. I decided not to mention it to him. The three of us were alone again. Skinny told me to sit.

I did.

"So," Skinny said, "what shall we do tonight? You ready to talk now, to fill in the blanks?"

I nodded stiffly. My body language was that of defeat, of a broken little scuttling crab of a human being. It actually was very easy to pull off. I had been so close to cracking, to breaking. I was scared of these two men, and I would have nightmares about this room until the day I died. I was pretty sure my Hell would be the interrogation room.

"Good," Lou rumbled. He didn't mean it. I was pretty sure he went home every night and jerked off to what he had been doing to me. Lou wanted this to keep going forever. He was good at his work, and like most people who are, he loved it.

I took out the crumpled pack of smokes, my hands shaking. I pulled the first one out and put it to my lips. Skinny lit it, like he was rewarding a good child. Smoke swirled around the terminator of the overhead shade. There was still enough tobacco in there that the scent of the pot wasn't immediately noticeable.

"Let's start with your name," Skinny said, opening his folder and clicking his pen. He had a fresh yellow legal pad at the ready. He seemed relaxed. I was broken, now came the easy part.

"Ballard," I said. "Laytham Ballard." Skinny nodded and scribbled a note.

"You're the cracker asshole that was stupid enough to tangle with that trickster god thing that was screwing with that family in St. Louis," Skinny said. "What did they call that thing, Jimmy Squarefoot, a few years back? Biggest supernatural discharge since the Tunguska Blast in Russia, I heard."

"Yes," I said. "I am indeed that stupid cracker asshole."

"Bullshit," Lou said. "Ballard is a fucking occult legend. He raised the dead at ten, ripped off the philosopher's stone from Joey Dross in Vegas back in 1999. He's fucking James Bond, Gandalf, and Jim Morrison all rolled up into one. Bullshit some sniveling little pissant like you is Laytham Ballard."

"I know it's hard to meet your idols, Lou," I said, smiling, and took a puff on the cigarette. "If you meet the Buddha on the road, kill him, right?"

Lou began to move toward me menacingly, but Skinny stopped him with a gesture.

"You've demonstrated some occult aptitude and pulled off some impressive stunts I can't explain and my superiors can't either, so I'm willing to give you the benefit of the doubt about who you say you are. And you are telling us now that you killed James Berman, correct, Mr. Ballard?" Skinny said, back to focus.

I took a long drag on the cigarette and regarded Skinny. "So you guys didn't kill him because I was coming to talk to him about Dusan Slorzack?" I said, watching his eyes, his posture. Skinny looked down at his pad and scribbled another note. He avoided my gaze. Lou shifted nervously and glared at me.

"We're asking the questions here. What was the link between this Slorzack and Berman?" Skinny said. I smiled, and the fear went up out of me, like the mellow smoke I blew toward the ceiling. I leaned forward in my chair, across the table.

"So the others, the other people that died on my way to Berman, that wasn't you guys covering your tracks, was it? You weren't tying up loose ends for the Secret Masters, for the Illuminati? The Illuminati doesn't have a fucking clue what Slorzack and Berman were up to?"

"The All-Seeing Eye . . ." both Lou and Skinny droned.

"Yeah, yeah, yeah, 'sees all.' I got that. But whatever caper Slorzack pulled off blinded even the All-Seeing Eye. Wow. That's Dr. Strange-level badass."

I crushed out the cigarette on the table and regarded Skinny and Lou with a newfound contempt. They really didn't have a clue. My hands glided to the crushed pack and the last smoke. They didn't shake anymore. I took the last cigarette. The room was full of pot smoke now, drifting in swirling, milky pools around the light.

"Y'see, I knew something was wrong with this picture. The way you guys were going about this, the really low-budget magic being used. The Illuminati is top-shelf all the way. If they needed info out of me, they would have ritually killed me and had my spirit worked over by some hard pipe-hitting demons from the Dante Union. The things you gave away without even meaning to, I just couldn't figure it all out. Until now."

Lou had his straight razor out. He moved toward me. Again, Skinny gestured to hold. He kept making notes as I wrote, but I could tell he was getting angry. This was not part of his script.

"I needed to know just how fucked I was, guys," I said. "If this was a top-to-bottom Illuminati operation, then I was pretty much dead. But if Berman was freelancing, and I just happened to bump into you guys while hunting for my war criminal, then it was all good. You feel me?"

"Listen, you little maggot," Skinny said. It had taken awhile, but I had finally gotten on his nerves. "We don't give a damn what you were running. You are the prime suspect in the death of a member of the Inner Cabal of the Five Boroughs and we are going—"

I laughed and pulled out the white lighter. I slipped the cigarette between my lips. They were dry, swollen, and cracked.

"The Cabal of the Five Boroughs! Jesus, that's like the occult equivalent of the Lions Club. So your boy Berman was a flyweight. And I'm guessing you guys are too. What crew you with, Seraphim? The Fists of Gevruah? Give out occult parking tickets and pick up the Secret Masters' dry cleaning?" I laughed again. They were out of position, out of control, emotional. I was ice. I was going to enjoy every second of this.

Skinny sputtered at his slip. Lou moved beside me. He dropped the straight razor on the table in front of me. Teutonic runes of power were etched onto the mother-of-pearl handle. A +1 magic straight razor. Cool. I never noticed that all the times he had used it on me. Must have been distracted. He leaned down next to my face. I could smell Aqua Velva, garlic, and decay.

"Say hello to your new girlfriend, shit kicker," he hissed.

I flicked the white lighter and flame caressed the tip of the cigarette. I drew a deep breath in and let the smoke nestle deep in my lungs.

"We got a man in this precinct who is going to blow your head off, because you came at him with this," Lou said. "Let's see how smart you are without a face, redneck."

"*Suscitare,*" I said as I exhaled.

I blew smoke in Lou's face. His eyes clouded and then became milky white. He gasped and staggered back, rubbing at them franticly, then clawing at his throat as if he were trying to ward off a strangler. I exhaled in Skinny's direction as his eyes widened in understanding. A cloud of rich, pungent marijuana smoke grabbed him like a long-lost lover. He fumbled to stand and groped for his piece as his eyes failed him too, behind magical cataracts.

I grabbed the razor, flicked out the polished silver blade, and opened up Lou's neck in one smooth, fluid motion. His blood was a hot curtain that sprayed across the table.

I was up now, and I sidestepped behind Lou and held his massive, convulsing body as a shield. Skinny fired his 9mm wildly. It made virtually no sound inside the swirl of living smoke, dull thuds like shoes being kicked off onto the floor. The first round went into a wall; the second hit Lou in the chest and knocked both him and me over onto the floor. Skinny was screaming for help, but the smoke held the air in his lungs. He dropped his gun and clawed at his throat.

By now I had Lou's gun out. I pulled myself clear of his twitching carcass and carefully aimed. I put a single, quiet bullet into Skinny's forehead. There was an eruption of skull, black blood, and brain across the back wall. He dropped like a puppet with his strings cut and was still.

I wiped off the gun and put it in Lou's hand. I walked over and placed the straight razor next to Skinny, close to where his hand lay. The smoke swirled around the room like fog. It obscured sound, sight, and even surveillance cameras. In the smoke, I could hear the spirit of the leaf licking its chops at the cooling Seraphim.

"Edere," I said to Red.

I collected the Seraphim's notes, the legal pads, the folders, and the clipboards. They were in code and not on normal NYPD report forms. Good, I hadn't legally been put into the system at all. I checked their wallets and was not surprised to find they had more money than clean cops could possibly possess. They sure didn't spend it on clothes. I took enough money to get me away from here but left enough to keep them looking dirty. I scribbled a quick note on a sheet of yellow legal paper. It said, "He knows about the Trace hit and the mole, eliminate him." I slid a few thousand dollars in with the note, folded it, and stuck it in Skinny's coat pocket. I pulled my hair back, stuffed as much of it as I could under my collar, and took Skinny's coat, which had managed to avoid the spray of blood.

I slipped Skinny's lanyard ID around my neck, picked up the joint off the bloody table, and took another long drag, crushed it out, and gathered up both cigarettes from the ashtray. The smoke in the room was dissipating. I could hear Red's sated chanting in my mind. It reminded me of Aztec pyramids and bloody sand. It made me smile to imagine these two men's souls being digested in the silent green. I shuddered at what I was capable of. Then I walked out the door of the interrogation room for the last time.

In the hall, I kept my head up, my clipboard prominent. If you have an ID and a clipboard, you can navigate most bureaucracies with virtual impunity. A few hundred footsteps, two flights of stairs, and I was out the door, free.

Outside it was night and cold—January in New York cold. The sky was gray light pollution. It looked beautiful. I paused on the stairs of the precinct house and thought about Darren locked away in the Tombs. I pushed it out of my mind, because I knew I deserved to be there a million times more than he. But here I was free and relatively clear.

I never saw Darren Mack again.

Some flurries fell. There was sky above me, not concrete, and I felt exhausted and wired all at the same time.

Dusan Slorzack was not a made man in the Illuminati and therefore not untouchable. He was out there, somewhere, and now he owed me too.

I walked toward the street, pausing to stop a uniformed cop who was entering the precinct.

"Excuse me, Officer," I said, raising the red-flecked cigarette to my lips. "Do you happen to have a light?"

FOURTEEN

One cab ride, a shave and trim, and a quick stop at a thrift store to grab some clothes, and I was back on the job. I didn't want rest; I didn't want to go inside anywhere if I didn't have to for a while. A gentle snow was falling, and I felt like a kid again. I bought a throwaway cloned cell phone off a street hustler and made my way up to Brooklyn Bridge Park. One of the best views in the city. I leaned against the railing and enjoyed the city's lights and the cold, quiet snowfall.

I called the Dreamtime and asked for Didgeri. The bartender screamed to be heard over the noise of the club. After a moment I was transferred from the rumbling bar phone to a private office. Didgeri's warm, mahogany voice kissed me. I said hi.

"You're alive," she said. "I don't believe it! How do you do that?"

"Luck of the hillbilly, darlin'," I said. "This line clean?"

"Silly boy, do you even need to ask?" she said.

"Magdalena with you?" I asked.

"Yes," Didgeri said. "She came to me after Grinner and Christine left town. I've been letting her stay with me. Delightful young lady. She's been very worried about you. We thought you were dead and gone."

"I was," I said. "I got over it. I need you two to meet me somewhere.

New York is going to get a lot of heat very soon, and we all need to change venue for a bit."

"Where to?" Didgeri asked. "Rome, Paris, Ibiza?"

"Harrisonburg Virginia," I said. "Farm country."

"Oh. Well," she said, "and you are sure this is preferable to imprisonment, torture, and death?"

"Nice," I said. "There's a place down there called Foxglove Farm. I need you two to meet me there in about two days." I gave Didgeri the directions, just as Grinner had given them to me.

"Any idea how I can get hold of Grinner?" I asked her. "I need him."

"No, but Magdalena knows. She wants to speak with you," Didgeri said.

"No, just . . ." I said.

"You okay?" Magdalena's voice now. "Grinner said you had some real badasses on your tail. You shake them?"

"Eventually," I said. "You okay? Didgeri been taking good care of you?"

She laughed. "Yes. Very. Now what's this about you sending us to some chicken ranch in Virginia?"

"The city is going to get hot. Regular cops and cult shields are all going to be looking for me, and they will make their way to you two. I need to get to Foxglove too, but I need to make a side trip first."

"Where?" Magdalena asked. "And why can't we all go together?"

I sighed. I fished out the last partly crushed Red-weed cigarette and found the white lighter in my new thrift store army parka. I cradled the bootleg cell phone between my ear and neck as I lit the joint.

"Because I am going to go do something bad, and possibly bloody, and I don't need a fucking audience for that."

"Audience?" Magdalena said, contempt dripping from her voice. "I figure you need help. I'm not the one who has been out of circulation for over a month, grandpa."

I laughed and nodded. "Okay, okay. Easy with the grandpa shit. Want to give me a complex?" I exhaled the cigarette smoke, it felt good. Her voice felt better.

"And if I say no?" I said.

"Then good luck finding Grinner," she said.

I sighed again, took another drag on the cigarette. The city was like a fortress of light and glass stretching in every direction. It was beautiful.

"So we're in?" Magdalena said. I could hear her smile across the lousy connection.

"There is a place on Oceanview, in Little Odessa," I said, and gave her the address. "Meet me there tomorrow afternoon, around two. I'll fill you and Didgeri in when you get there. No guarantees. This is a hasty caper and it is almost one hundred percent to get our shoes wet. This is no fucking field trip."

She laughed and gave me the number to reach Grinner. I said good-bye and hung up.

This was bad. I kept closing my eyes and seeing Darren in his cell in Rikers. I had meant every word, that I would come back for him, meant it with all my blood, bone, and balls. I could put the energy and firepower I was putting into this new excursion to gain knowledge of whatever Slorzack and Berman had been up to, this Greenway, into getting Darren out. I wasn't doing that. But I would, I swore to myself, I would find a way to get him out. Settle accounts with Boj and Slorzack and then Darren. And I was dragging Magdalena into shit she was not ready for. I had wanted to keep her away from the Life as much as I could.

I called Boj's hospice. After a lot of bullshit and waiting, they got the phone to him.

"Hey, look who's finally decided to check in." His voice was weak, strained. "How are you, asshole? Any good news?" I told him everything. Well, most of it, anyway.

"You paid up, redneck," he said. "Man's too big, got too much *chara*, too much juice."

"Bullshit," I said. "I am on this fucker, and now he owes me too. I am going to find him and I am going to make him pay. Gonna be a hell of a story too, Boj. Best stick around to hear it."

He laughed; it turned into a burbling, hacking cough. "Okay, I'll try," he said and hung up. He was dying, and I was running out of time to make this right. So many things to make right in this world, so little time to clean it all up, to make it pretty and square.

I finished my joint, crushed it out on the snow-covered ledge, and flicked it into the night. The view was just a view again, and the snow was no longer wondrous, it just made me cold.

I stopped by my bus locker and picked up a few things I'd need for the caper and scooped the last of my emergency cash. I ditched the cloned cell phone and bought another one off the street. I managed to find a decent flop for fifty dollars a night. I also picked up some cheap soul food, a few packs of American Spirits, and a six-pack of PBR. I asked for Cheerwine at three places. No one had it.

After I ate, I lay on the bed and dialed the number I had for Grinner. He answered on the second ring.

"Go," he said.

"Hello from hell, asshole," I said. "The AC's shitty, wish you were here."

"No fucking way," he said. "How did you . . ."

"Clean line?" I asked.

"Hold," he said. Beat of five seconds, then, "Affirmative. I figured you were dead, Ballard. Holy shit, man."

"I need some work related to that thing," I said. "I still got any credit, or frequent-flyer miles? And I need part of it by tomorrow afternoon just to make it sexier."

"Talk to me," Grinner said. And I did. I told him what I needed by tomorrow afternoon and where I needed it to be for me to pick it up.

"Should be doable," he said. "But that quick means quality is going to suffer. It might get bad quick, y'know?"

"Yeah," I said. "I'm covering that. Getting some high-end artillery for backup."

"Anyone I know?" Grinner asked. I ignored him.

"I also need you to find any connections, and they do exist, between James Berman, a guy named Alex Trace, the Federal Reserve Bank, the Bureau of Engraving and Printing, and the Life. Slorzack may have cleaned up his own mess pretty well, but Berman's the chain around his neck. They were into some deep shit together. See what you can dig up, okay?"

"Yeah, and then your credit is all used up, sport," Grinner said. "Only reason I'm doing this for you is I'm kinda curious what you are going to do next, you crazy son of a bitch."

"Love to your girl," I said. "She's better than you deserve." And I hung up.

I sat by the open window and the fire escape and watched the snow fall lazily and drank my beers. By four A.M. I could sleep, and I did.

In the morning I got up, reluctantly, out of my warm bed, to meet the Gun Saint.

Brighton Beach is a neighborhood near Coney Island. Its rows and rows of houses are tombs for old working-class Jews. In the last twenty years or so, it has also become home to more and more Russian immigrants.

At the edge of the ocean is a small park. Today it was filled with children and parents enjoying the snow, building snowmen and forts, having snowball fights. The rows of chess tables had been cleared, and dozens of old men sat playing the game of kings in the cold air and bright sunlight. A portable radio was playing big band music off an AM radio station—Glenn Miller.

Alone on a cleared park bench, an old Asian man sat watching the children play and looked beyond them to the cold blue, foaming waters of the Atlantic. He was short and stocky, but not fat. He had a salt-and-pepper crew cut and a broad, unsmiling face. He looked to be in his sixties, but it was hard to get a handle on his age. While everyone else was bundled up in heavy coats, parkas, scarves, and gloves, he was in a simple maroon windbreaker and white oxford shirt and work pants, with work shoes. He sat with a great deal of serenity and power, as if all before him—the ocean, the sky—was arrayed for his viewing alone.

"Hello Ichi-sama," I said in my best Japanese. I bowed, low.

"Your Japanese is atrocious," he said in English. "You've had ten years to improve it."

"Yeah, kept meaning to get that Rosetta Stone thing. Never did," I said. "May I sit?"

He rose, a smooth, fluid movement, and bowed slightly. "Yes," he said. After I sat, he returned to the exact position he had been in before and regarded the waves crashing on the frozen sand. His eyes were black mirrors.

"It has been ten years, hasn't it?" I said. "Still do tai chi here at sunup?"

"Yes," Ichi said. "I occasionally have to dismiss a few *Bamusu* who have decided to sleep here after gorging themselves on wine. I don't like them here when the children come to play. It frightens the children."

I nodded. "It's a lovely park. Still play chess?"

"I do," he said. "There is an eighty-five-year-old gentleman from a little town on the White Sea. He is very good. We talk about his grandchildren and how we both grew up in fishing villages. There is also a man who was the only survivor of his family from Treblinka. He beats me on a regular basis. Very good."

I nodded toward an open table with a board painted on the top. The pieces were bunched on top of the board. "Care to play me?"

"No," he said. "You would lose."

"Humor me," I said. He stood, regarded me, and walked to the table. I followed. We sat on the cold benches, Ichi seemed not to even notice the cold and began to set up the pieces. He gave me the first move.

"How is your daughter?" I asked.

"Well," he said. "She completed her schooling at Oxford six years ago and is now a respected barrister in London. She has met a man, an Englishman. I am not completely unsatisfied with her choice. I anticipate a wedding and grandchildren shortly."

I lost a knight. Ichi lost a pawn.

"Congratulations," I said. Ichi grunted.

I lost two pawns. Ichi was relieved of a bishop. He paused and looked across the board at me, as if he were analyzing me a molecule at a time.

"I believe the last time you saw my daughter was at my wife's funeral," Ichi said after a time.

"Yes," I said. "Your wife was a wonderful woman. I loved the tea she always made me when I visited your home."

Something approximating a smile crossed Ichi's face, and his cold, dark eyes warmed by a degree.

"Yes," he said. "She was . . . wonderful."

I took a rook, but it was a trap and it cost me a bishop.

"I've come to ask for your assistance, your expertise, in a rather urgent enterprise," I said. Ichi said nothing but continued to look over the board. "I am planning for some resistance at one point, and I would be honored if you would lend me your experience and your skill, Gun Saint–san."

Ichi's eyes flicked up from the board to me.

"You 'planned' for resistance?" he said. "I trust your planning of this mission shows more foresight than your chess game."

I took Ichi's queen. He looked up at me and narrowed his eyes again. I held the queen between my fingers.

"You were off your game just a hair from the moment your wife came up," I said. "I saw an opening, and I saw your trap. I worked very hard to make a riposte happen. I sacrificed my bishop, but it got me your queen. You are right, by the way. I am going to lose."

The old man nodded and actually smiled. "I see now what you have been doing instead of improving your Japanese," he said. "However, all that energy, all that maneuvering to still lose. It seems pointless to me."

"It is," I said. "It was to show you I had improved. It was a childish act, poorly executed."

"You know that is your greatest weakness, Laytham-kun," Ichi said. "It always has been. Your emotions overcome your reason. It is a fatal flaw, and it puts those who trust you in danger. A man your age should have overcome it by now."

"Is that your way of telling me no?" I asked, looking at the queen and setting it on the table.

"It is my way of saying the man I knew ten years ago would not have been able to acknowledge a weakness, or even see it. You have grown, Laytham-kun. I will undertake the mission with you. Are there any others I will be working with?"

I smiled and tipped over my king. "Didgeri Doo. I didn't want to involve her or her new apprentice, but I will need Didgeri to give us evac."

"Oh," Ichi said. "I see, Didgeri Doo—the *fukusō tōsaku-sha*, the transvestite."

"I think she prefers transgender," I said. "I know that stuff didn't fly too much in your time, but it's a different world now."

"I am one hundred and fifty-nine years old," Ichi said. "Men are men and women are women. I do not believe that will ever change. However, I can work with him, and he is a competent Shugenja, despite his perversions."

"Yes," I said. "She is. A very powerful Shugenja, at that."

I decided to not try to argue or explain gender politics to Ichi. One, at his age it was doubtful I was going to change his mind about anything and, two, he might just kill me if I got too annoying.

I stood and bowed low again. Ichi stood and bowed as befit his station. I told him the address in Little Odessa to meet me at tomorrow, where I would lay everything out about the caper. I started to walk away from the beach.

"Laytham-kun," Ichi said. "The thing you wear about your neck, I would have it please as payment for the service I do you."

I turned and smiled. "How the hell could you know?"

"I have studied with blind Buddhist monks and Sufi masters older than I. I have traded wits with Rasputin, the mad, immortal monk, himself. Did you honestly think that you could hide something from me? Your posture screamed that you were concealing something around your neck."

He held out his hand, and I slipped the talisman off and tossed it to him. It was a simple leather cord with a small leather pouch. Ichi opened the pouch, and a worn ivory chess piece, a white king, fell into his hand. He looked at it and then at me.

"It belonged to Bobby Fischer," I said. "It's a very powerful charm. You may want to hang on to it the next time you play your chess buddies."

"I see," Ichi said.

"I needed you," I said. "I needed to get your attention, and it's a little hard to engage you, Ichi-sama. So I figured I needed an edge. Like I said, I knew I was going to lose."

"No, Laytham-kun," Ichi said as he flipped his own king over. "I think you have mastered the game far more than I had previously given you credit for. Until tomorrow."

I bowed again and took my leave of Ichi.

FIFTEEN

Washington, D.C., is a city of marble, blood, secrets, and lies. My kind of town. It was bright and cold when Ichi and I ascended the escalators from the Smithsonian Metro station with the teeming swarms of morning commuters to downtown D.C. Islands of snow turned to ice were packed around the bases of streetlights and parking meters along Independence Avenue.

I was dressed for success in a navy Versace suit. My hair was pulled back tight from my face in a severe ponytail. I was wearing Ray-Ban Aviators, and I was carrying a briefcase. Ichi was dressed in an older Hugo Boss suit, black, and he had a wide black tie and aviator sunglasses as well. He looked like a Yakuza undertaker. People moved out of his way. He didn't seem to notice.

We turned left off of 12th Street onto C Street. The Bureau of Engraving and Printing was two blocks up. It was an old building, neoclassical architecture with traditional Greek-influenced pillars, looking something like an ancient temple. Large worn stairs led up to the columns and the doors beyond them. A pair of BEP police officers, in dark blue baseball caps, with gun belts, radios, and scanning rods, greeted us on the other side of the glass doors.

Waiting nervously at the cops' station beside the door was a young woman in her twenties, dressed in a very flattering but functional navy power suit dress. Her hair was blond and her Treasury Department ID said her name was Elizabeth Compton. When she saw us, her face switched from worried to confident in a flash. I smiled my best corporate asshole smile and pocketed the sunglasses.

"Mr. Breenan, Dr. Isaku? Hello, I'm Liz Compton. I'll be your guide today."

"Hi, Liz," I said, shaking her hand. "Please, call me Larry. Dr. Isaku doesn't speak much English, I'm afraid. Pleasure to meet you. Thanks so much for getting the tour together for us so quickly."

"Well, when Senator Hawlsey's office contacted us and told us about Mr. Isaku's time restrictions on his trip, we were happy to oblige."

I nodded. So far, Grinner's covers for us were working great. He hadn't gotten back to me yet on the research I had asked him with, but as far as this operation, everything was looking good. I nodded to the rope line leading to the metal detectors.

"This way?" I asked.

"Yes, please," Liz said. Ichi and I walked up to the metal detector. I placed my briefcase on a conveyor belt, next to the arch. One of the federal cops popped it open. There was an iPad, some yellow legal pads, a tin of Altoids, pens, and today's editions of the *Washington Post* and the *Wall Street Journal*. The cop took the iPad out of the briefcase.

"Sorry, this has to stay at the station. No electronic devices back in the press rooms."

"Of course," I said, smiling.

The case ran along the conveyor through an X-ray scanner, which showed exactly the same contents to the seated guard. So far everything was going smoothly. Ichi and I passed the metal detector walkthrough and wanding with flying colors, and I retrieved my case, minus the tablet. Ichi and I showed all the appropriate identification to the guards, signed the log book, and were both issued visitor badges to clip onto our suit pockets. Liz smiled at us both as we passed through into the wide lobby. Smiles all around. Happy happy joy joy.

"Okay, well, let's get under way, shall we?" she said.

"Please, let's," I said.

Liz took us past the lobby and down a series of corridors with numerous displays. Some were electronic and interactive, and others were simply wall displays with pictures explaining the contents of various cases. Most included different types of currency and a few dummy plates used to make currency. The halls were empty except for us and a few employees. The regular civilian tours didn't start for a while yet, and I wanted us to get this done with as few other people around as we could.

"The Bureau of Engraving and Printing," Liz said, "is an arm of the Department of the Treasury. The Treasury Department was founded by an act of Congress in 1789 to manage government revenues. The first secretary of the treasury, Alexander Hamilton, was sworn into office on September 11, 1789 . . ."

"September 11?" I said.

Liz laughed. "Yes, the conspiracy theorists have a field day with that one," she said, and then continued walking and talking. "The Treasury prints and mints all currency in circulation through the Bureau of Engraving and Printing and the U.S. Mint. That's what we do here and have been doing since 1862."

We paused at a large observation window overlooking a massive room full of printing presses. They were huge, over fifty feet long, churning out rivers of currency sheets. There were dozens of employees moving about the press floor in an intricate dance, sliding between the machines, avoiding the constant stream of wealth being created out of thin air. There were computer console stations at several locations above and on the press floor, manned by operators directing and controlling the creation process. The sound of the presses was muted behind the thick shatterproof windows, but the powerful vibrations of the machines could be felt through the floor and the walls. This was a place of power, but not my kind of power.

"Our Simultan sheet-fed, high-speed rotary offset presses and our I-10 Intaglio presses produce the traditional images on U.S. currency.

Our facility here produces approximately 10,000 sheets per hour, roughly 541 million dollars a day at all of our locations."

"Dr. Isaku's research is into the history of the engraving process of American currency," I said. "The senator's office said we would be allowed access to the archive for the dies and the plates. It sounds like an amazing process."

Liz smiled. "Oh, it is." She sounded as thrilled about this as I did. It was clear that this was not her normal job for Treasury. Someone on the senator's staff had pulled strings to get her here for this private tour. She was bored with this, and she could tell I was too. It gave us a sense of camaraderie.

"Right this way," she said.

She led us down a side hall, past more well-lit glass display cases mounted into the curving wall to a small lobby with two elevators. She raised her own ID badge, about her neck on a lanyard, and slotted it into a panel beside the elevator doors. The doors opened, and she ushered us into the car.

"So, would you rather see the engraving gallery first, where our master engravers work, or the archives where we keep the master dies and plates, dating back to the beginning of the republic?" she asked.

I looked at Ichi and asked, "Heads or tails?" in my lousy Japanese.

"I love the intricate details of your master plan," he responded. "Truly I am in the presence of a tactical mastermind." Then he bowed slightly to Liz, and she smiled and bowed back.

"Engraving, please," I said.

The offices of the engravers were on an upper level in the newer annex building. We got off the elevator, walked down a hallway filled with framed photos of the building and its history, and eventually turned onto a corridor with a small office. A glass wall and door announced we were in the Engraving Department. A receptionist at the desk was listening to some music on computer as we passed. Liz waved to her, and she smiled back.

"The engraving for the dies used in paper currency and coins is all developed in these offices," Liz said. "There are seven engravers that each work on different parts of the dies. They develop the patterns and symbols that are put onto the plates and have input into the designs themselves, always with an eye toward how to produce a superior artistic effect while making the currency more difficult to copy or counterfeit."

"Only seven," I said. She nodded. "Again, a strange number coincidence. Seven is a very powerful number in numerology."

"Really?" Liz said, looking at me like I was a complete moron she was being forced to endure. She hid it well, but I had seen the look enough times to recognize it. "That's fascinating."

"Very strong link between seven and the Masonic lodges," I said. "But I'm sure I'm boring you."

She smiled and laughed. "No, not at all. Now down this way . . ."

I had kept a tight lid on my senses and powers, but now in the corridors of the engravers, I opened my perceptions slightly. My Ajna chakra opened, and I sensed vague wisps of mystical energy floating between the offices like a scent of subtle perfume. There was power at work here, but it was elusive, alchemical perhaps. I peeked into an office where a slender man in rolled-up shirt sleeves was working at a drafting table on an intricate series of lines and forms, which I recognized as the tracery on American currency. There were wisps of magical energy coming off the drafting pens and tools he was using. The symbols and patterns he was creating occasionally flared and flashed with power as he muttered quietly to himself and continued to draw. The engraver, a gaunt man in his late twenties with thinning black hair and gold wire-rim glasses, paused and looked over his shoulder at me. Something about him looked unhealthy, ill, in a way no medicine could help.

"Please, this way to the conference room for the presentation," Liz said in a hushed voice. She had backtracked and was right beside me. I smiled and waved to the engraver. He didn't smile back. As I walked down the hall past the other offices, all of the engravers, all slightly ill, slightly wrong men and women, had turned away from their work to stare at me. I left the scribes to their master's work.

We were shown a thirty-minute video about the engraving process, which included interviews with several of the engravers I had just passed. In the video, they seemed to be normal, healthy, and excited government employees.

During the video, Liz left for about fifteen minutes. I'm pretty sure she was checking our covers and clearance again. I had spooked her, but at this point I was cool with that.

"The woman is distrustful," Ichi said softly in Japanese. "You have put her on edge with your crazy Yamabushi talk."

"Yeah, well, there is something going on here," I said back in broken Japanese. "They are building something, reinforcing some kind of working here. We need to get a look at those archive plates."

Ichi snorted. "They think this engraving is detailed, that this is intricate design? Bah."

"Did you . . . did you just say 'bah'?" I said. "No one says 'bah.' Not even super villains. I mean no one."

"I do," Ichi said. I shrugged and shook my head.

"Things are about to get messy," I said.

"Very well," Ichi said.

"Bah," I said.

After the presentation, I stood and stretched. "So, if it is not too much trouble, the doctor wanted to look around a bit down in the archives, if that isn't too much trouble, Liz."

"No," she said, smiling, "not at all." By now her smile was an utter lie.

We took another elevator after leaving the land of the engravers. It took us down, deep. The doors opened into a vast warehouselike room. It was temperature controlled. There were steel wire cages, each with its own lock, which stretched as far as the eyes could see. Each cage room contained different items—chests, drawers, lockers, and who knows what covered by canvas tarps. I figured the Ark of the Covenant and the formula for KFC were down in here too. Two BEP cops were stationed at a guard desk with a bank of monitors, showing security cameras all over the faculty and across the archive as well. One of the cops, a burly black guy, stood as we got off the elevator. He said hello to Liz.

"There is a conference room down here where we can bring most of the items in the archives for Dr. Isaku to examine," Liz said.

"Terrific," I said to Liz. I turned to Ichi and said, in Japanese, "Ready, Doc?" Ichi nodded. "Nonlethal please," I added. Ichi looked at me with mild disgust, as if I had just passed wind in his presence.

Liz directed us to a large leather ledger next to a set of clipboards on the guard desk. I offered the pen to Ichi, and he took it, looked at it, and frowned, and then looked at the ledger and frowned. He was as good at that as Liz was at fake smiling.

He leaned over the ledger and seemed confused about where exactly to sign. The other cop behind the desk grunted as he stood. He was white with a thin mustache and had a bit of a gut. He leaned over the desk to show Ichi exactly where to sign. Ichi grabbed his head and smashed it down onto the desk, hard. As the guard went over, Ichi reached over the desk, turned the guard's arm over, and pulled his pistol free of his holster in one smooth motion. As he was bringing it up, he fired a round at the burly guard, who was just now beginning to resister what this little old Japanese man was doing. He began to draw. Burly's head snapped back and he fell to the ground, a pool of blood forming on the concrete floor about his head. The guard whose head had been smashed into the desk received another powerful blow to the head from Ichi, who used his own gun to pistol-whip him. He slumped over too, onto the floor near his partner. Liz was just beginning to scream at the sound of the gunshot.

It's okay!" I shouted. "Liz, it's okay! Goddamn it, I said nonlethal," I said to Ichi, gesturing toward the burly cop's still form.

"It is a scalp wound," Ichi said in English. He was already moving over to the two cops and gathering their guns and ammo. "He will bleed a great deal from it, and he will have a concussion, but he will not die. Question my craftsmanship again in this endeavor and I will shoot your eyelids off."

Liz had gotten hold of herself and stopped screaming. She was pale and obviously frightened but was keeping her shit wired tight. Alarms were going off now. The cameras in the archives had caught what just happened, and already the building was being locked down.

"Liz, we're not going to hurt you, I promise," I said. "I need to know, are there any other ways down here other than this elevator? Stairs? Loading bay?"

She rubbed her face and looked at me with a mixture of fear and anger. "Yeah," she said in an even voice. "There is a stairwell in the northwest corner, and there is a cargo elevator about halfway along the southern wall. What are you guys doing? What do you want?"

"If I told you, you wouldn't believe me," I said.

"Elevator coming," Ichi said. "They will endeavor to flank us at the stairs as well. My guns, please."

I slapped the briefcase on the desk and clicked it open. The concealment enchantment I had laid upon the case had worked perfectly, and now I pulled out the false panel, grabbed Ichi's two pistols, and handed them to him. The guns were custom-made modern variants on weapons used during the Civil War, called LeMat revolvers. They were .44 Magnum pistols with a 12-gauge shotgun barrel under the pistol barrel.

I also handed him his speed loaders for the two guns and a handful of 12-gauge shotgun shells. He put the bullets and the shells in his pants pockets. He stuffed the guards' pistols in his belt.

"You'll be able to handle the stairs too?" I said. He nodded curtly.

I took the Altoid tin out of the case and opened it. I popped a small, powdery white mint into my mouth. I offered one to Ichi. He made a sour face, then opened his mouth and allowed me to pop the mint in.

"Bah," he said.

"What the hell are you two doing?" Liz asked.

"We like to have fresh breath while we violate federal law," I said. I looked at Ichi. "Mine's working. Is it working for you?"

Ichi, a LeMat in either hand, nodded and then turned to face the elevator. *Get to work,* his back said to me, silently. *I will give you the time you said you needed.* I took Liz by the arm and led her into the rows of cages.

I heard the elevator doors begin to creak open, as Liz and I lost sight of the old man.

"Come on," I told her. "Let's leave him to his work."

SIXTEEN

Liz and I ran down the corridor of cages. I led her by the arm, but she seemed okay with getting away from the sounds we were hearing behind us. There was shouting. A man's booming voice, "Drop the guns now, or we will fire."

There was a barking of gunfire, like a cannon firing as rapidly as a machine gun. The whole archive echoed with the rumbling. Liz looked back and then ran faster. People tend to do that with gun battles.

My so-called third eye, the Ajna chakra, was opened wide, in part because of the enchantment on the mint in my mouth. Didgeri and I worked pretty hard to come up with a working that would function the way we needed it to through the candy. I slid part of my awareness toward Ichi and was rewarded with a view in my mind of what was happening. A cloud of gun smoke drifted around Ichi. The elevator doors were closing. BEP cops were screaming and shouting as the doors thudded closed and muffled their excitement.

I disarmed them, Ichi thought to me, and I heard it in my head. He was moving and reloading his pistols as easily, as thoughtlessly, as someone would swallow. *You understand that when the soldiers arrive, I will not be able to be so merciful.*

Yeah, I thought back to him. *I hope we will be out of here by then.*

I could perceive that Ichi was moving quickly, in a shuffling run, down a hallway toward the stairwell. He turned the corner just as the fire door to the stairwell began to open. Ichi slid like a baseball player rounding third and headed for home, toward the door, a gun in each hand. The LeMats roared with cordite-laced thunder in his hands. More BEP cops began to swarm thought the door and were greeted by a curtain of exploding lead.

A few of the cops returned fire until their guns were shot out of their hands. One cop stepped into a bullet, and his shoulder exploded. His partners pulled him back as they slammed the fire door shut. Ichi stood gracefully, rising as if gravity did not own him. He shrugged the empty casings from his hand cannons and reloaded them. His breathing was even and normal. His mind was calm as oil on water.

I shifted my awareness again and called out, "Didgeri, you in position for evac? Any problems?" In my mind's eye I saw Geri and Miss Magdalena on a sandy beach, near the water. An immense bearded giant made of cast iron was struggling to arise from the sand. His massive arms, legs, and head were all erupting from the ground. Didgeri stood looking at his face, studying it. From her point of view, I could see that the sculpture, called *The Awakening*, was actually moving, shifting somewhat. The Initiated Man's perceptions were slippery, bright, and distorted.

Magdalena's thoughts, clear and sharp, came through to me. *"We're at the National Harbor in Maryland, just over the border from D.C. Didgeri said that this was the spot where it was easiest to slip into the Dreaming. She's already started her meditation. She took some stuff too, drugs maybe, I'm not sure what."*

"This giant is the metal shadow of the Wandjina," Didgeri thought. Her thoughts were vibrant, full of swirls of matter, mind, and energy blooming like erupting stars, novas of association, power, and beauty. Breathing cave drawings, spiral trails, and black suns with white triangular rays. *"This place is good for stepping between the three worlds; it is a realm of fluid hypertime,"* Didgeri thought to us all, *"the spider web, the frame upon which the worlds were thought-born in the Dreamtime. We are ready for you, Laytham. I begin to walkabout. Find you on the path,*

balla. *Bring you home. Magdalena is my anchor stone, my fire to lead us back out."*

"Walk safe, thurdu," I thought back to her, but already her bright kaleidoscope of thought and perception was diminishing into an unknowable darkness, like a light on a raft drifting away into the ocean at night, growing smaller, fainter as it was carried on dark waters.

"She . . . oh, my God . . . she just walked between the statue's head and arm and just faded away." Magdalena's thoughts, bright and real, and tinged with panic and disbelief. *"It looked like she was walking on the ocean, then she was . . . gone . . . How . . ."*

"Don't ask how," I thought. Liz was talking to me, and I heard more gunshots. We were running out of time. *"Never ask how! Believe what you see, trust your senses and your gut. Didgeri is traveling, and she needs you to be her lifeline, her way back. We all need you, Magdalena. Focus, feel her. Reach out to her thoughts through the link we are sharing. Call to her, sing to her. Be her beacon."*

I turned to Liz. "What did you say?"

"Are you on something?" she asked. "I said, what was it you wanted to steal? There's a lot of stuff in here."

"I'm just high on Thoughtoids," I said. "Minty fresh. I think I'm looking for some old dies and engraving plates, the earlier the better and moving forward. Also any old writings related to the founding of the Treasury and the original federal script."

"You don't sound like a terrorist or a counterfeiter," she said. "Why are you doing this?"

She led me to an intersection of four corridors. There were columns that had small plates on them denoting archive location numbers. She studied them for a moment, and then we turned left. I switched my brain-cam to Ichi. He had repelled another elevator assault and was now headed toward the cargo elevator, reloading, trotting, calm, like a machine.

"I'm trying to find a man for a friend," I said as we walked briskly down the hallway and Liz scanned the lot numbers on each cage's tag. "That man is very hard to find, and he came here about a decade back to research something, something occult and having to do with currency."

"Oh, my God, you are some kind of militia conspiracy nutcase," she said. We stopped in front of a cage and she opened the door with a loud click.

"Yeah, I am," I said. "I'm a member of the Leprechaun Liberation Front, here to uncover the secret magical formula George Washington created to make fluoride into a mind control substance. This the right cage for what I told you I was looking for, right?"

"Yes," she said.

I ushered her in and then followed. There were large, older wooden cabinets with dozens of different-sized drawers in each of them. Some drawers had labels; others had pieces of old peeling yellow masking tape with dates or code numbers on them.

I opened my senses, as I had done upstairs in engraving. The chests in front of me dripped with power, eldritch and a flavor that was unknown to me. I knew what was coming next, though, due to the spells woven around the chests. They were primed to alert whoever had placed these wards on them to sound a silent mystic alarm if they were tampered with or even sensed to be magical in nature. The bells and whistles were going off somewhere. I slid open one of the drawers and looked inside. There was a very old, worn engraving die for a continental note, the precursor to the dollar bill. The die was what was used to make the actual printing plate. This one was from 1775. It had a few odd markings on the edges of the die that emanated a very faint magical charge. The really odd thing was that the style of the marks bore no resemblance to any form of occult or magical system I had ever seen.

"What the hell," I muttered. I reached into the briefcase and pulled an old Kodak Brownie camera from the hidden compartment. The camera was a thick black box with a fixed lens. I set the plate on the edge of the chest and began to snap pictures.

"What is with that camera?" Liz said.

"It's a very special artifact," I said as I opened another drawer and removed another die, this one from the first production of the U.S. dollar coin in 1793. The unknown mystic symbols were on the edges of the die too. I took another picture. "It belonged to Philip Jones Griffiths."

"Who?" Liz said.

"He was a famous photojournalist that chronicled the Vietnam War," I said. The camera has a very special ability. It shows truth, pure, objective truth. It can't be blocked by obscuring spells, illusionary glamours. You can't hide things from it."

"Like what, exactly?" Liz said. "Secret satanic scribbles on the dies?"

"Look," I said, "I am a bit of a nutcase, I'll grant you, but I am also a fucking Encyclopaedia Britannica when it comes to the occult, and I have never seen symbols like these before. The dies are marked with occult power channels that are holding a magical charge more than two centuries after being made."

I opened more drawers, took out more dies: the first dollar bills from 1811 and then the first "greenback" bills from 1862. The odd mystic symbols continued on the dies, becoming more intricate, more complex, but still unknown. The enchantments were worked into the plates, leaving a residual charge. This was old, powerful magic, and it was completely unknown. I couldn't even fathom its purpose. I snapped pictures of everything and tried to piece it together.

I suddenly felt a spasm in my Swadhisthana, my sacral chakra, as if I had been stabbed with a blade of fire. Something was ripping its way into the world.

"Didgeri, please tell me that is you," I thought, but her mind and presence were still far way and dancing in place settled somewhere just past my Vishuddha chakra. No, whatever the hell it was, it was from a far more terrible place, a place of baser matter.

"Soldiers are here." Ichi's mind was cool stone. *"No more Mr. Nice Guy."* I switched to his point of view. He stood before the cargo elevator as the massive gate slid upward. He bowed, arms crossed, gun in each hand. These were Special Forces troops, black operators, paladins of plausible deniability. Twenty of them, looking like jagged,

bulletproof shadows with gas mask eyes. They moved like oiled smoke, missionaries of death. They fanned out, tossing smoke and CS gas before them, like a dragon's breath. Seeing them through Ichi's eyes frightened me, they were antibodies of order and control. Then I caught a slight razor-edged thought as it slipped from Ichi's disciplined mind, and the fear changed in me.

"*Finally,*" he thought. "*I was getting bored.*"

Ichi raced toward them even as the clatter of their machine guns began, spraying death. Ichi spun, swirled into the clouds of darkness and pain, moving along their left flank. Blasts from his guns now— two of the twenty fell, and now the old man was wearing one of their gas masks. He felt the bullets whine past his ears. He jammed a barrel under a chin and pulled the trigger, snagged the pins on a pair of grenades with the hammer of the other gun, twisted them loose with a violent jerk of his arm, and fired, putting a bullet through the eyepiece of another's mask. Two more down. Two seconds. The whole archive shook as the flash bangs Ichi had detonated went off in the middle of the black ops teams. Ichi was deaf now, and blind. I pushed out of the contact, trying to avoid the nausea, but as I did I saw in his mind serenity, as he moved on, killing, dodging, using senses that still functioned past sight and sound. And I pitied these warriors, for they played at death, and today they had met it.

"What the hell was that?" Liz shouted.

I was back, ripping open cabinets. I found the 1935 dies with the All-Seeing Eye of the Illuminati on them. The symbols now were small and intricate with elements of sacred geometry, Sanskrit, hieroglyphics, but mixed in a bold, almost reckless way that made me admire the artist. This was a wizard who was unafraid of breaking structures and rules, creating something new from the shattered pieces of the past. I was in awe of it. I had found my Rosetta stone. The magical script covered the edges of the 1935 die completely. I began to see the hazy mechanics of the working, but I needed more information to even begin to backward-engineer it, to understand it.

This was lost art. I snapped pictures quickly, as I felt the horrible thing bore closer and closer to the really-real world. I had minutes if I was lucky. The gunfire intensified on the other side of the archive.

"Liz, are there papers, letters, anything from the early days of the Treasury? Please, I'm close." She opened her mouth to protest, but the pleading in my voice must have convinced her. She started opening drawers of the other cabinet.

"There are some packets of letters here from the late 1700s and the 1800s; I assume you are looking for documents from the 1930s as well, the way you orgasmed over the 1935 die. Right?"

"Yes," I said. "Thank you, Liz. Thank you from the bottom of my crazy-ass heart."

I opened my mind to Magdalena. She was on the beach, calm, controlling her panic and her disbelief. She was focusing on something far away that I could only vaguely perceive.

"Okay," I said. *"I need you to call the number on the throwaway cell phone now. Dial it, wait for the connection to happen, then hang up and toss it in the ocean. Got me?"*

"Yes," she said. I felt the distaste in her thoughts. *"What is that? It feels like someone just vomited in your skull. I can feel it, smell it. Ugh. It's making it hard to receive you."*

"Psychic chaff," I said. *"Something bad is coming through, summoned up once the trip wires were hit. This place had someone on speed dial to conjure up something major so quickly."*

Tumblers were tripping in my head, but there were too many channels flipping in there currently for me to pay it much mind right now. I filed it away, to review if we lived past the next five minutes.

Liz handed me the letters and packets of documents in plastic bags. The lights died and the archive fell into darkness. The emergency lights clicked on with a *thunk,* and everything was painted in harsh halogen and deep shadow. The gunfire was getting more sporadic.

"Now what?" Liz said as I opened the packets.

"One of our people on the outside just activated a virus that was in that tablet we left up at the guard station in the lobby," I said, unfolding the first letter and squinting at it in the dim light. The paper burst into flame.

"No, No!" I shouted. The other papers in my hand erupted into flame as well. I dropped them to the floor, where they quickly turned to curling black ash. "Damn it, damn it, no!"

I held on to the one I had been trying to read; it was from the late 1800s. I saw the words "endeavor," "esoteric," and "sacrifice required," before the flames performed their rendition on the secret knowledge and gave me the cosmic finger.

"Fuck!" I said, trying to squeeze one more word out of the blackened paper as it began to drift away like leaves in an autumn wind.

"Larry," Liz said. "Larry! Whatever your name is! Your hands, you're burning yourself."

My arms dropped and the black paper slipped from my fingers. It was ash before it hit the cement. Gone. The secret, the knowledge, the magic trick. Hidden by jealous, greedy little minds. Gone. Fuck.

"Wouldn't be the first time, Liz."

I groaned as the abomination shit itself into our world and my Swadhisthana chakra clenched at the affront to space-time and my personal aura. Liz clutched her stomach and gagged at the close proximity to the manifestation.

"God," she said.

"Doubtful," I said, rubbing my red, swollen hand. I tucked the camera into the briefcase and grabbed it.

"Liz, I know you think I am insane, and I want you to keep thinking that. You run up to the stairwell and keep running. It was nice to meet you. Thank you for everything. Run. Don't look back."

She started to say something, then thought better of it, and ran. She didn't look back. I stepped out of the cage and walked toward the well of darkness between the terminator of two emergency lights. The thing was there. It had been sent for me. I cleared my mind and summoned my power. I could feel Didgeri swimming between the worlds, coming closer. I reached into my pocket and took out a small bullet of chalk.

"*Ichi,*" I thought, "*time to go. Head for your pickup like we planned. Geri is almost here.*" I drew a simple hexagram on the floor. The thing in the dark made a wet moaning sound from multiple mouths, as it solidified, like Jell-O, in the skin lands.

"*You are in danger,*" Ichi thought. "*This creature is not part of the plan. I will—*"

"*You will stick to the plan and your part,*" I thought back. "*I got this. Your guns can't help with this. I got it.*"

Ichi was silent; he headed to the location we had already selected for Didgeri to pick him up. Something was moving in the darkness, part of the shadow dislodging itself. I knelt and touched the chalk markings.

"*Geri, if you can hear me,*" I thought. "*I'm going dark. I'm going to be in a seal, cut off from you, and when you see that seal open you have to grab me quick, darlin', or something else is going to.*"

The thing in the darkness lumbered into sight. I filled the Seal of Solomon with my power and my anger, and stood. The seal flared and the thing snarled. All the voices were gone in my head. I was alone. I suddenly remembered the lyrics to the Pixies song "Hey"—don't ask me why.

It was nine feet tall, four feet wide, a column of black, leathery skin leaking medical waste from fist-sized, fanged sphincters all across its body. Glowing red eyes, mouths, barbed breasts, hooked penises, and human arms were scattered across the surface of its trunk with no semblance of design or reason. A ring of arms at the base of it, bent at the elbows like tree roots, held it up and allowed it to lurch forward, toward me. A circle of arms flailing toward accursed Heaven was at the top of the pillar of filth and atrocity, a beautiful, perfect blue eye in the center of the palm of each hand in the crown. It moved toward me, hissing, leaking, and stinking.

"Hold," I said. "By the power of the Silver Seals and the Compact of Shiva, by the Sacrifice of the Bodhisattva, by the secret saint Alice Weinstein of Fort Worth Texas—destroyer of monsters and guardian of life, by the Court of the Uncountable Stairs, you are bound to stand down or name yourself."

The thing lurched to a stop. It made a sound kind of like an eighteen-wheeler having congestive lung failure. It started to speak from all its mouths at once in a language I didn't recognize.

"No," I said. "Nice try. You know the rules, lurker at the threshold. Your name or you must depart the angle worlds."

"And you, you who stink of fear and petty evil," the thing rumbled in a phlegmy, amplified voice, "you claim to be of the Nightwise, a protector, a guardian of these lands?"

"Yeah, well, my membership card may be a little out of date, but yeah, I am. Now stand and name yourself, or depart."

"I am Neva," it said, shuddering. "The twelfth maiden of Chernobog. Bringer of All Ills."

"Chernobog," I said. "Eastern European. The Black God. Older than Lucifer. You're one of the twelve Likhoradkas, evil demigod things. What are you doing here?"

"Killing you," it said, and shuffled forward. "Do you think your little ward and your tiny powers can match the might of the Goddess of Plagues? One touch and you will die the most horrible death a human can imagine, every illness, every disease cast upon you. Such is the fate of those who interfere with the works of Chernobog."

Neva was right in front of me, now, a wall of oozing hatred and death. I slid my toe to the edge of the chalk.

"And now, little guardian, little Nightwise, tell me your name, before I devour you," it rumbled.

"Dusan," I said. "Dusan Slorzack." Neva shuddered as it laughed. The sound of the demon goddess's laughter slid into my brain's greasy folds. No human was ever made to hear that sound.

"Very funny, Nightwise," Neva said. "But you are not the Avatar of Chernobog, and such a pathetic lie will not save you."

I slid my toe over the chalk, blurring it. "Then come and get me, you poxy old bitch," I said. *"Now, Geri, now!"* I thought.

Neva was on me, the useless chalk island was nothing. Wet, oozing hands reached for me. A black weeping wall was my universe.

Something grabbed me by the ankles and pulled. I closed my eyes and tried not to piss myself. I was too scared for a last thought.

Water. I was under cold, salty water, something had hold of me, and I flailed and twisted, fought and tried to run. I was up, out, in bright daylight—blue sky, fresh, cold air. I snorted seawater and the stench of the twelfth maiden out of my nose.

Didgeri had my shoulders, helping me up. She was soaked. Ichi was standing next to me in his suit, also completely wet. Magdalena had waded in and was laughing and shouting. The water was freezing. A crowd of tourists on the sand, near *The Awakening* statue, were looking at us. I couldn't care less. I looked at Didgeri and hugged her as tight as I could. She hugged me back.

"Great job," I mumbled. I coughed up some water and coughed and laughed again. "Great job, guys."

We all couldn't stop laughing, except for Ichi, of course. The gulls laughed with us as we slogged our way back to the shore.

SEVENTEEN

Didgeri and Magdalena had acquired a Jeep. We climbed in. Ichi refused to sit anywhere near Geri, so he and Magdalena sat in the back. We were all so fucking happy to be alive, no one minded Ichi being an old stone ass. We drove to a mall parking lot, found a public restroom, and everyone got on clean, dry clothes. I now sported jeans, boots, a Bella Morte T-shirt, a leather jacket, and a shit-eating grin at being alive. I treated my rowdy pirate band to a luscious lunch of fast food from the mall food court. Ichi, the party animal, got some steamed rice and water. Magdalena, for such a tiny girl, put away more sushi than I thought a human being of any size could consume. Giri had a decadent choco-foamy-coffee drink thing of about eight thousand calories and a chocolate scone, and I, their fearless leader, had tacos—the perfect travel food. Tacos—exotic. That's me, International Man of Mystery. I asked the girl at the counter of the taco joint if they served Cheerwine. She asked if they sold that in 40s.

"Let's get the fuck to Virginia," I said.

The sun was bright and the air was cool bordering on cold for early February. We glided onto 495, headed toward I-66 and then I-81, to Harrisonburg.

I missed WHFS, the old alt-radio station I used to listen to whenever I was in D.C. or Maryland. It was long gone, so I surfed the channels and eventually was delighted to find that HFS had moved to a new frequency and was alive and well. "Seven Nation Army" by the White Stripes greeted my ears. It seemed fitting, so I put on my sunglasses, rolled down the window, ate my taco, and smiled.

"You are insufferably pleased with yourself," Didgeri said.

"I am, darlin'," I said around a mouthful of taco. "The caper was cherry. I have some very solid leads as to what Berman and Slorzack were up to, and I got to face down some evil, skanky Eastern European demigoddess and live. Yeah, I'm that good."

"Ballard?" Magdalena said from the backseat. The music on the radio changed to "Kerosene Hat" by Cracker. "That . . . goddess thing you were talking to back at the Treasury, it said you were a Nightwise. What is that?"

I sighed, and Didgeri and Ichi both chuckled.

"Nothing," I said. "It's nothing."

"Ballard doesn't care to recall it, but there was a time when he was a cop," Didgeri said.

"The Nightwise are an honorable association of knight-magicians, who dedicate themselves to police those in the Life from excesses and protect this world from unnatural threats," Ichi said. "They are legends across the known worlds for their integrity, doggedness, and power. Naturally, Ballard did not remain with them long."

"I quit," I said. "Wankers, the lot of 'em."

"I heard you were kicked out," Didgeri said, the smile growing.

I turned up the radio and kept driving.

Many miles down the road, Ichi muttered something to Magdalena in the backseat.

"Bah. This noise I am forced to be subjected to. Perhaps we could listen to some good American popular music—Count Basie, Glen Miller," he said.

Magdalena laughed. "I love those! I think that is a lovely idea."

Ichi kind of sort of smiled; it looked like his face was breaking. "It is good to meet a young person who appreciates real music."

"I enjoy all music," Magdalena said. "May I ask you a question, Ichi-san?"

"Yes, of course," Ichi said.

"Is it true what Didgeri told me? Are you really one hundred and fifty-nine years old and a descendant of the author of the *Book of the Five Rings*?"

Ichi nodded curtly. "Yes. I am of the blood of the Sword Saint Musashi, and I was born in 1854."

Magdalena leaned toward the old sourpuss. "Please, tell me about your life. I'd really like to know."

"Well . . . it is not that interesting a story," Ichi said. "But, since you are so respectful and such lovely company, very well."

Ichi began to talk. I tuned out. I'd heard the legend of the Gun Saint many, many times, and the story got better if you could slip a little hot sake into the old stone ass. I had to hand it to Magdalena, she had held up her end of the job, backed up Geri, and she even got along with Ichi.

"That old camera got very wet," Didgeri said. "You sure you got what you came for?"

"Yeah," I said, popping the last bite of taco in my mouth. "It doesn't even have film in it, works completely by magic. I want you to look at the pictures too. These symbols . . . It's a whole magical system I have never seen before. I'd love your take on it."

"And I'd love to see them too. A new system centered around American currency, evolving and developing over the span of hundreds of years. Fascinating."

I popped a mint in my mouth and offered the small red-and-white tin to Didgeri. "Telepathtoid?" I said.

"Give me that," she said. "I shudder at the thought of the most powerful juvenile delinquent in creation with a box of telepathic mints. Visiting your mind gave me a real appreciation for New Jersey. I see now there are worse things." She made a face and took the tin away, stuffing it in her purse.

"It's nice," Didgeri said.

"What?" I asked.

"Seeing you happy. It's been a long time," she said.

"Yeah," I said, "it has."

The music played, and we drove down the highway chatting occasionally about nothing. It was what normal people feel like, and for me it was a vacation.

Foxglove Farm was out where the buses don't run, off of State Route 796. We turned right opposite Newdale School Road. Rolling green hills and distant blue stone mountains stretched as far as the eye could see. It was farm country, acres, miles of minimal human presence, of green and dust and gravel swirling in clouds about the Jeep. Mailboxes, dozens of them, clustered near a main road, combed like a wasps' nest. It made me feel good to know that not every square inch of every corner of the world was paved and known and just three minutes from a Starbucks.

"Do you hear banjos playing?" Didgeri asked.

"This is home, darlin'," I said. "Be it ever so humble."

It was early afternoon, still a few hours of sunlight. We bounced down the private access road past entrances to farms and private estates with colorful names like Hermitage Hill, Buttermilk Road, Morning Sun, and Thorny Branch. After close to an hour, a small sign guarding a large mailbox told us to turn, and we began to ascend a wooded hill. In moments, we were surrounded by oaks and pines, the surrendering sun's brilliance flashing though barren and emerald branches.

"This place is beautiful," Magdalena said.

"And easy to defend," Ichi said matter-of-factly. "A single path in, dense foliage, the high ground to see invaders coming. Very wise."

After a few more turns, we passed a rusted, open metal farm gate with a chain and padlock hanging off it. The skeleton of an old Ford pickup lay next to the decaying husk of a vine-choked barn. A worn sheet metal sign on the gate announced we were indeed at Foxglove

Farm. The dirt and gravel road got bumpier, more ruts, deeper from snow and flood. We saw fences and pastures on our left.

"Oh! Look!" Magdalena shouted, pointing, excited like a little girl at the zoo. "Sheep, cows! Oh, I hope they have horses!"

I felt us hit the wards like slamming into a brick wall. They were tight and strong, the work of a master spell crafter. Didgeri winced and looked at me, then back to Magdalena.

"Oh," Magdalena said. "That didn't feel good at all. Kind of like a change in pressure. Was that some kind of magic barrier?"

"Yep," I said. "We just rang the doorbell."

"We are being watched, and weapons are being aimed in our direction," Ichi said absently. "I hope they have food; I am rather hungry. Tea would be pleasant as well."

The old man had dried, cleaned, and oiled his weapons on the trip up, but he didn't seem in any hurry to pull them, so I took that as a promising sign.

The blue sky was fading, graying, as the early winter night approached. The wind had picked up, and the forest's shadows were growing longer and darker. A final, wide turn, and we were at the top of the hill. The main house and barns jumped into view.

There was a beat-up old Ford F-150 with faded red and white paint parked in the wide circle of dirt and gravel where the road abruptly ended. It had a tag in the back window of the cab that said simply FARM USE. There was also a dark green Range Rover with Virginia plates and an old Black Mazda RX-7 with New York tags parked in the circle. Off to the left was an island of asphalt that had been poured as a basketball court. From the condition of the backboard and rim, it hadn't been used in a while. A huge barn and stable ran off to the right, beside and behind the main house. A massive two-story work building stood off behind the basketball court.

The main house was painted white with dark green shutters, a wraparound porch, and a shingled roof. A small group of people stood on the porch, near the parking area. A woman cradling a shotgun walked down off the porch and headed toward the Jeep. She was skinny with pale skin and a wide constellation of freckles across her prominent nose. It was difficult to place her age, somewhere between thirty and forty. Her hair was a coppery red and fell in ringlets down past her narrow shoulders.

There are usually two types of redheads: striking individuals with an almost unreal beauty and then those possessing a fascinating ugliness. She was both. She wasn't beautiful by the conventional wisdom, but there was sexuality and confidence about how she carried herself that gave her a magnetic quality. She was dressed in a thermal T-shirt, jeans, and hiking boots. Did I mention the shotgun?

I rolled the window down. "I'm Laytham Ballard," I said. "I'm here to see Bruce Haberscomb."

The woman lowered the gun to her side and jerked a thumb toward the others, who were coming off the porch to join her. "They beat you here," she said. "I'm Pam, I'm Bruce's wife."

Grinner and Christine walked up behind Pam. Christine smiled and waved. She had a baby bump poking out of her HIM T-shirt. Magdalena squealed and jumped out of the car to run around and embrace her.

"Right on time, I see," Grinner said, giving me a fist bump as I climbed out of the car. I turned and shook Pam's hand.

"Pleased to meet you, and thank you for the hospitality," I said.

"We're used to it," she said. "Bruce tends to accumulate a lot of occult fanboys, no insult intended."

"None taken," I said. "Grinner told me about him. He sounds like a remarkable man."

Pam shook her head and rolled her eyes. "Yeah, okay. Come on in, dinner is almost ready. The Great and Powerful Oz will join us later."

Ichi and Didgeri were getting out of the Jeep. Ichi started grabbing bags out of the back. Grinner and I helped.

"The tablet virus worked okay back in D.C.?" Grinner asked.

"Yeah, perfect. Killed the whole building's power right when we needed it, and the IDs were solid too," I said. "I didn't expect to see you two here with all these wanted fugitives. I thought you'd be south of the border by now."

"Yeah, well, I wanted to see if you pulled it off, and I wanted to give you a face-to-face intro to Pam and Bruce. And . . ."

We carried the bags onto the porch and through the bay doors into the living room. It was an enormous room full of packed blond oak bookcases, a huge stone hearth with a comfy-looking couch and over-stuffed chairs huddled around it, and a wide wooden spiral staircase headed upstairs. To the left was an arch leading to a large dining room. Grinner, Ichi, and I followed the girls, who in turn were following Pam upstairs.

"And?" I said to Grinner.

"I found something," he whispered. "Our missing link to Slorzack, Berman, and Trace. It's kind of hard-core, so let me tell you after dinner, okay?"

I nodded. "You really think Haberscomb can find him?"

"Yeah," Grinner said. "And you will too."

Dinner was . . . well, it was something I have had maybe two or three times in my whole life. There was amazing food—all kinds, fresh—a lot of it grown or raised at Foxglove, and Pam was an exceptional cook. There was good drink—wine, beer, coffee, tea, hot sake for Ichi and Grinner. She even had Cheerwine for me! There was conversation, stories, jokes, laughter, remembrances, toasts. It was a family dinner for a bunch of people who had no families. It was beautiful.

This day had started with the potential for death, failure, or imprisonment. It was ending like something out of a storybook. I tried so hard to not listen to the bastard part of me, the survivor part, the realist part who told me this wouldn't last, couldn't. I tried to just enjoy it while I could.

Pam seemed to relax once food was on the table. She enjoyed having company, and she, Geri, Christine, and Magdalena all became very thick. Ichi and Pam actually struck up quite a conversation about gardening and farming, most of it in Japanese, and Grinner and I played the old remember-that-time game.

After dinner, we all helped clear the table, do the dishes, and put away leftovers. Pam fixed a plate for her husband and put it in the fridge. The kitchen at Foxglove Farm was like an industrial kitchen, designed to feed a lot of folks in a hurry and clean up quick as well.

"Sorry your husband couldn't join us," I said. "Everything all right?"

"Yes," Pam said, wiping down a marble countertop. "Bruce was away for a few days, and he just got back. He needed to crash pretty hard. He should be up and about by tomorrow, Mr. Ballard."

"Please, after a meal like that, and all this hospitality, I'd sure appreciate it if you'd just call me Laytham," I said. "Where did he go, if I can be so nosey?"

Pam seemed to have trouble articulating. She tried a few times, then stopped. Finally, she put her dish towel away and said, "He travels all over the world, over several worlds, but he never leaves his workshop out back," she said. "I hope that makes sense to you."

"It actually does," I said.

"I'm glad it does to you, because it damn sure doesn't make sense to me. You can't call what he does hacking. It's . . . that's like calling life a 'chemical process.' Bruce . . . travels, and some of the places he travels to take a toll on him. So he's resting. I hope he can see you in the morning."

"No hurry," I said.

Pam leaned against the counter and shook her head.

"You'll forgive me, Laytham, but men like you are always in a hurry. You're used to having people come out to meet you with shotguns, used to being a few steps ahead of some new disaster. You see, Bruce isn't the only one with a reputation, and yours precedes you. So I appreciate you being patient—you really don't have a choice in it, but I know you are racing some clock, and Bruce knows too."

I sat down at the small round table in the breakfast nook. Pam joined me.

"I have an old friend, older than Grinner. I don't have too many friends, old or otherwise, left. My friend, he's dying. He lost everything in this world that mattered to him and he took a slow and pain-ful way of killing himself.

"He doesn't have much time left and he asked me for one last fa-vor, one last debt called in. He wants me to find the man who raped, tortured, and killed his wife, who took all the reason and hope in this world away from him. Bruce may be my last hope to find him."

Pam looked at me, through me. "Why didn't you help your friend before he was dying?" she asked. "Why didn't you help him find some-thing else to live for? Help him survive the pain, endure it, instead of run from it in self-destruction?"

I couldn't hold her gaze. I looked out the bay windows into the ut-ter darkness of a country night.

"Because I was too damn busy," I said, "too much up my own ass, into my own little drama, my 'legend' to care. Because he had pissed me off, and part of me wanted him to get exactly what he has now, because he hurt me, and he betrayed me, and I am a vindictive son of a bitch, Pam."

"You think finding this man for him and, I assume, killing him, will change anything for either one of you? Honestly?"

"No," I said. "Men like us, we're thrice damned already. The things we've done . . . There's no redemption, no magic satori at the end of the road. His life is still shit and my life is still shit, and we're both evil bastards. Almost as evil as the bastard I'm hunting. Nothing changes that.

"I just saw him all frail and decaying from the inside. And he asked me to help him one last time. And I do owe him; I owe him my life a dozen times over. And he asked me . . . he asked me.

"When your whole life is ugly and dirty and broken, when you have fucked up so many times, in so many ways, Pam, a tiny spot of clean looks mighty good to you."

She was silent. I was too. There was laughter from the other room. I heard Grinner's booming voice.

"You saw him and you saw yourself," Pam finally said.

I nodded. "Yeah, and all us evil bastards, all of us, hate thinking about dying alone. 'Bout the worst fate for any of us. We know we deserve it. We know it's the most likely outcome of where we've driven our lives to, but . . .

"Pam, today I faced off against a thing from another place—a thing that was pretty much a god—and while I was scared shitless when I thought it was going to kill me, part of me thought, 'This would be a good way to go out. They'd be talking about this for years.'

"Hell is having the time to reflect back on the train wreck of a life you've made. Having time to recall the faces of everyone you fucked over, wish you hadn't said all the things you said, agonize over the 'if-only-I-hads.' Regret is the deadliest poison of all, and it works slow. So, if I can give Boj one tiny drop of something other than regret, it's worth it. And he won't be alive long enough to realize how pointless and meaningless it really is."

Pam looked at me, and then leaned over and hugged me. It was the most alien feeling I could recall from the day, more than the evil goddess, more than running between worlds, more than magic.

"Bruce and I, we had a son," Pam said. "He died. Bruce blames himself, and truth be told, a part of me blames him too. If we hadn't had each other, I . . . I don't know if I would have survived it. I fell, I wanted to fall. I could have been your friend Boj. But I had Bruce. And Boj, Boj has you. That's why he reached out. Everyone tries to find someone, something to hang on to in the darkness, in the fall. Even evil bastards don't have to be alone. A truly evil bastard wouldn't care."

She released me and walked toward the kitchen door. "Coming?" she said. "I think they are playing some stupid board game."

"I'll be along presently," I said. "Thank you, Pam."

She walked out. I sat for a moment and recalled days gone by. Boj at his prime, a dark underworld prince full of violence and twisted honor. Harel, innocent and so wanting not to be—full of life and compassion and eager to live a life of adventure, to help people, to master magic. And me, the fucking rock star, so eager to make a legend, to make my name, I was willing to do anything, use anyone. To use them.

I looked toward the other room, I saw the people in there in my mind. I saw my old friends, my old crew, and how they were now. Nothing changes. People can't change, even if the world would let them. I wanted a cigarette really bad.

More laughter from the other room. It felt better, easier, to be alone, to keep your distance and your guard up. How many people in that room would end up dead if they stuck with me? How many dead inside? How many would betray me? Wound me? How many of them would I let down, or throw under the bus in the name of my own pride, my own ego, my own lousy hide? No answers. Just do the job, make things square for Boj. One foot in front of the other.

I stood and made my way to the living room. I opened the door to the sounds of life and light, and stepped through.

"Okay," I said, "I'm on the team that doesn't suck."

EIGHTEEN

The beds were huge, soft, and clean. It was almost noon when I got up. There was a little folded note on my bed stand, next to the magic Kodak camera and the empty scotch glass. The paper smelled like purple lollipops. The note said simply:

You are amazingly hard to wake up when you are drunk and tired. Gods know I tried.

Mag

P.S. Who is Torri Lyn? You talk in your sleep.

I sat on the side of the bed and smelled the paper again. I remembered the scent. I refolded it and left it on the night table.

Showered, shaved, and wearing clean clothes, I headed downstairs. It was quiet, and early afternoon sun was filtering through the numerous windows. The only sound was the old grandfather clock's steady, oiled-metal ticking.

"Hello?" I called.

"They're gone," a voice said just out of sight to the right of the stairs. "Took the Jeep and went into town. Ichi-san is walking in the woods, and Pam is at her clinic in the main barn. She's a rather busy veterinarian in these parts."

I came off the stairs, turned toward the dining room. A heavyset man in his late sixties with thinning black hair, sideburns, and thick glasses—what they called in the military BCGs, or "birth control glasses"—stood from the dining room table to greet me. He was dressed in what they used to call "the uniform" at IBM—a white collared shirt with short sleeves, a pen protector with actual pens in the shirt pocket, dark slacks, and sensible shoes. He had a slide rule case on his belt. He crossed to meet me and thrust out a hand.

"Howdy," he said, shaking my hand. It was a firm, vigorous shake. "I'm Bruce Haberscomb."

"Laytham Ballard," I said. "Pleasure to meet the legend."

"Likewise," Haberscomb said. "I know I'm not exactly what you were expecting . . ."

"No, no, it's just . . ." I said.

"Old habits die hard," he said with a chuckle. "Back in the day, this outfit was pimp. Pam has been trying to get me to at least wear an occasional sweater vest, but I just can't do that. Freebirds got to fly, I say."

"Please," I said, "never wear sweater vests. Ever. Please. They suck."

"Yes," Bruce said with a great deal of solemnity. "Yes, they are just about the worst thing in this universe, ever. They do suck. Yes. Please have a seat. We can talk about why you are here."

We sat at the dining room table. He poured me coffee from a stainless steel pot and then refreshed his own cup.

"Did Grinner tell you much?" I asked.

"That you are looking for someone, someone who has erased every trace of himself from human society."

"Yes," I said. "He told me you can hack the Akashic Record and locate him."

Bruce nodded and took a sip of coffee. "'Hack' is a crude term, but it's essentially correct," he said. "Do you understand the Akashic Record—what it represents?"

"I have some experience with it," I said. "I studied in the East for quite a few years, but I'm afraid my understanding is far from complete, Bruce."

"The Record presents itself in many different ways to each pilgrim," he said. "Edgar Cayce described it as the Hall of Records. Others view it as a photographic or holographic experience. Some claim it is the reflection of curved space-time off the twenty-sixth dimensional wire-frame.

"To me, it has always been presented as computer code, a logic puzzle to be studied, line by line, and sometimes carefully modified."

"So you can actually see . . . what?" I said, leaning forward. "Everything?"

"I can access all the desires and experiences of our world, the life experiences of every human from now until the last human, the empathic experience of the entire nonhuman bio-aura of earth, and the aggregation of the tuplaic architecture formed by the interaction of the dynamic of karma with thought-form structures based upon the desires, the dreams of every human that has been or will be. Didgeri Doo would call that aspect the Dreaming."

"That has got to be a bitch to process," I said, shaking my head, "to not get lost in that. I felt a little taste of that when I first discovered the Art, that feeling of interconnectivity, and it must be much, much harder."

Bruce nodded. "Yes, precisely. Only someone with the proper training and the right hardware in their skulls can distinguish between actual 4-D experience and experiences created by imagination and keen desire."

"LSD, acid," I said. "Grinner said you were an Acidmancer, and now I understand why—it helps you navigate the Akashic Record."

"Yes," Bruce said. "As you well know, each of us comes to the Life a different way, and we find our own paths to access the power. I am led to understand from Grinner that you found what works best for you is chakraic visualization and somatic reinforcement. For me, it was programing. Building objects in code was like solid curtains of music, sculptures of thought. It still gives me goose bumps. Turns out, as I kid I was coding when I didn't even realize I was doing it.

"I had a real knack for it too. I was recruited out of UC–Berkeley by IBM and, in a few weeks, I was promoted over to their covert Defense Department programs. You know, the Blue Magic Initiative: Bell Atlantic, Book and Candle, Deep Ouija, all that stuff, mixing magic and computer technology. I worked side by side with Marcel Vogel— he's actually who recruited me. That man was a visionary and a genius, a true pioneer in merging hard science with occult and paranormal theory. He did things with luminosity, magnetics, liquid crystal systems . . ." Haberscomb smiled. He was looking back at Camelot. The memories were green and golden. "The man was a living, breathing wizard—the real deal, a Pythagoras, a Tesla, a Feynman. He was my hero, my inspiration. Those were exciting days, Latham. You wouldn't have even been born yet."

"Reckon not," I said with a wide grin. "So, how do you get from IBM black ops to Acidmancy?"

"Well, I discovered a little problem with coding and magic for me," he said. "The code became too rigid in my mind. I sometimes overlooked elegant intuitive solutions to simple formulaic models because I was too tied into the dogma of the code. I wasn't creating items out of thought and math, I was merely utilizing the artifacts others had created. I fell into the abyss of assembly. My workings suffered for it. I wasn't the only one, either; it was one of the reasons Blue Magic eventually folded, the basic dilemma of coding versus programmer, samurai versus rōnin. I was stuck in between two worlds. I had been trained to illuminate manuscripts, if you will, but I ached to write my own stories, and I lost the power somewhere in between. I wandered in some pretty dark places trying to get the magic back. I know you understand paying a price for power, Laytham. Grinner told you I was with the Company for a while?

"Yeah, Project Stargate, Project Midnight Climax. Midnight Climax was where the CIA was covertly dosing U.S. citizens with acid to see how it would work as an interrogation and mind control drug. Pretty deep black, Bruce."

"Yep," he said. "Not my finest hour. Thank goodness for Timothy. He helped me solve the problem, brought me back to myself."

"Timothy Leary?" I said. "Right? You were one of the original Acid-mancers?"

He nodded, sipped his coffee. "There was more than just the war in Vietnam going on back then, Laytham," he said. "There was a cultural war, a spiritual war, waging across the world. So many young, brilliant minds, so much will and desire to change the world, to create a golden age out of dross. So much hatred and madness and reck-lessness. So many casualties, in all the wars. Those boys coming home in aluminum boxes, kids getting shot down and beaten in the streets, bastards like Manson turning kids who wanted peace and love into murdering robots . . ."

He removed his glasses and wiped his eyes. "I won't venerate Leary. He had great ideas and short-sighted ones. Many young men and women fell on the battlefield of the mind, causalities of their own burn-ing desire to experience, to evolve past that point of human social evo-lution. For every Acidmancer, every psychonaut, there were a legion of burnouts—lost lives, chemically burned souls. Was it worth it? I can't say. I can tell you this, though, we made a difference, and we stood against evil. The Agency's evil, Manson's evil, Nixon's evil. We stood . . . and we fell.

"I'm the last one of the originals. I retired here in the eighties, when it was clear that all the things we were fighting for, we had lost. I have visitors—folks like you and Grinner, some who come to apprentice. I try to do what I can to help people. That's what it's all about, right? We couldn't change the world, not in any real, lasting way. So we change our little part of it, right? That's what we wiz-ards do, isn't it? Change the world at the fringes, defend it in the night."

He was quiet. The clock ticked, and I sipped my coffee. Finally, he looked over to me and smiled.

"Sorry. An old man rambling. Okeydoke. You want me to go into the Record and see if I can find your man, Mr. . . ."

"Slorzack," I said. "Dusan Slorzack."

"I will. I understand from Grinner he is one bad guy, so I will go find him for you. Did Grinner do a full search for you using all the conventional methods?"

"Yes."

"Normally to hide your tracks from someone like Grinner, you need pretty powerful friends—is he Illuminati? Neomasons? Purrah? The Mazekeepers of Pamukkale? Id of Warhol? Assassins of the Magic Bullet? One of the other superior secret societies?"

"I thought he might be Illuminati," I said. "But it appears he's free-lancing. He's mixed up with some low-level Illuminati types in some kind of caper, but the home office seems clueless."

I stood and held up a hand. "One second. I want to show you something I recovered yesterday. If you have some blank paper—photographic or computer paper—that would be great."

I ran upstairs, grabbed the old Kodak, and came back down. Bruce had a small ream of paper waiting.

"That's a beaut of an old camera there," he said. "That a Brownie?"

"Yeah," I said. "Special one too. Watch."

I placed the camera on the stack of papers and laid my hand lightly on it.

"Veritatem revelare estis testificata," I said. Images from the archives at the Bureau of Engraving and Printing slowly developed on the paper underneath the camera, like an old Polaroid Instamatic, only faster.

"Very nice," Bruce said. "An artifact of power. Someone loved this camera very much, and you took that love and power and turned it to a like-minded purpose. So you are an artificer too, Laytham. Impressive. It takes a bit of social engineering to make an item of power."

I removed the camera and checked the paper; each sheet held one of the images I had taken of the mysterious occult symbols on the engraving dies for the U.S. currency.

"Not as impressive as you think," I said. "I dabble. If I can't make the artifact I need, or find it, I steal it. It's got me in trouble quite a bit over the years. I almost grabbed a very badass straight razor a while back that would have cost me worlds of hurt."

I handed the photographs to Bruce one at a time.

"What do you think? You ever see anything like this before?"

"No," Bruce said. He opened a drawer in the buffet behind him and retrieved a magnifying glass. "I haven't." He studied each picture carefully.

"It's an evolving system," Bruce said. "Looks like they hit their stride in the 1930s. It looks pretty realized by then. I can see where it's derivative of a few Western traditional sources, but such bold, almost reckless innovation. This work is genius."

"Any clue what it is, what it's doing?" I asked.

"No," he said.

"You ever hear of anything called 'the Greenway'?" I asked.

"I'm afraid it doesn't ring any bells," he said. "However, I might be able to put some of this into a historical context for you. Ever hear of Henry A. Wallace?"

"'Fraid not," I said.

"He was Franklin Roosevelt's secretary of agriculture and second vice president," Bruce said. "Not surprising you haven't heard of him. He's part of the history of the Life—one of those dark alleyways in history most folks don't wander down. He might have a connection to your mysterious new magic here, as well.

"Wallace was a damn good man, saved thousands of family farms during the Great Depression as agriculture secretary. He was also a seeker of truth and an avid occultist and mystic. He was into all kinds of stuff: astrology, Native American shamanism, Theosophy, Tibetan Buddhism. I don't know if he worked the power, but he sure as hell studied it and knew more about it than most.

"He was FDR's right-hand man and a heartbeat away from the presidency in the middle of the crucible of World War Two. I often wonder what path our world would have taken if he had become president at such a critical juncture.

"The reason I mention him at all is that he made many comments publicly that implied there were powers at work behind the economy of the United States. This was in 1935, the same year the dollar acquired the All-Seeing Eye, the same year this printing plate of yours, here"—he pointed to the photograph in front of him, the one with the unknown mystic symbols covering the edges of the die plate— "with a fully actualized and completely unknown magic system embedded into it, came into reality."

"You think he was trying to warn people about whatever this is?" I asked. My coffee was cold. I didn't care. My instincts were screaming to me that I was on the right track here, and that this was much, much bigger than I had imagined.

"Or maybe he had been part of it and then saw where it was going and wanted out. You know how that works, Laytham. Sometimes there is no turning back. You're in too deep."

"What happened to him?" I asked.

"Like I said, he was a good man, "Bruce said. "We both know what happens to good men in politics."

"So maybe you can see if Wallace knew anything about this"—I held up a picture of one of the plates—"when you go into the Record."

"I will try," Bruce said. "Running the Akashic Record is like kayaking on a river full of rocks and falls. The more I go in trying to find, the rougher the ride, but yes, my interest is piqued." He grinned. "I want to know too."

NINETEEN

"May I study these photos? I have certain techniques to commit them fully to memory, but it takes a bit," Bruce asked as he stood from the dining room table.

"Sure," I said. "Any way I can assist? I'd like to see an Acidmancer in action, if I could?"

Bruce laughed. It was a soft, comfortable laugh, like mellow pipe smoke, or worn leather. It made you feel safe. "Come on, I'll show you the office," he said.

He grabbed an old, worn dark green barn jacket off the hook by the living room doors, and I grabbed my leather jacket. He folded the pictures and stuffed them into a pocket of his coat. He led me out of the house and toward the big two-story metal prefab work building. The sun was bright again, but the wind had picked up. It was cold and our breath trailed out of our mouths.

We walked across the asphalt basketball court with its rain- and snow-faded chalk drawings and its lone post and goal, a rusting sentinel with a rotting net, a flag to an age of bright summer evenings, fireflies, and laughter.

"Pam mentioned our boy to you?" he said.

"Yes, I'm so sorry. A parent should never outlive a child."

"Kids shouldn't outlive their parents, either," Bruce said. "It's a mess, either way, this whole death business—poorly thought out, you ask me. And if you look back in the Record to the beginning or forward to the end, it doesn't change and it never makes sense in this world, ever. If I ever find God, I need to have sit-down with him about that."

Bruce paused at the door and rummaged in his pockets until he found a key ring. He selected a key and unlocked the door. I felt a surge as powerful mystic alarms, wards, and defenses lifted like a stage curtain. He opened the door and gestured for me to enter.

Inside, the first level of the building was mostly taken up with what looked like a medical clinic. There were exam rooms, a well-stocked lab, and a waiting room and reception counter. Pam, in a Mumford & Sons T-shirt, red-and-black flannel shirt, and worn jeans, was doing paperwork in a small office just behind the waiting room and reception area. Her wall was decorated with pictures obviously drawn by children thanking her for healing their pets. She looked up and smiled at Bruce. He came around the desk and hugged and kissed her.

"I see you two found each other," she said. "How are you feeling?"

"Better," he said. "I'm taking Laytham down to the office to show him around, and then I'm going in to find his mystery man."

Pam tried to hide the disapproval on her face but failed pretty badly.

"Your loss," she said. "I was making those scalloped potatoes you like so much for dinner."

"Save me a plate," he said. "I'll be home for dinner, just late. I want you to come fetch Laytham in about an hour or so, if you don't mind. I will be out in the Record by then, and I don't want him crashing any of our wards or our defenses crashing him while he's trying to get out on his own."

"Okay," she said, smiling. "I love you, old man. No wandering. I want you home by midnight."

Bruce laughed, kissed her again, and then led me out of her cramped office. She waved to me and I waved back. I paused just long enough to see the worry slide back onto her face before she tried to outrun it in the paperwork.

The "office" of Bruce Haberscomb, the last Acidmancer, was a re-inforced concrete-and-steel bunker hidden under the work building and accessible only by a hidden staircase. The secret door, the stairs, and the door to the office were all booby-trapped and dripping with magical and mundane alarms, detectors, and weapons.

"I need all of the security so that this doesn't end up with the wrong people," he said, gesturing at the glittering womb of computer tech-nology that laterally made up the walls of the large, cold spherical room. "It's the world's first fully functioning quantum computer. About twenty years ahead of its time. I had a friend at Los Alamos Lab. I hooked her up with an alchemist buddy of mine—funny story—they ended up getting married. They helped me get it up and running to deal with a little problem I had with a higher-order entity that was messing about with the world through satellites."

"A higher-order entity?" I asked.

Bruce pushed his glasses back up the bridge of his nose. "A dragon, actually . . . Tiamat, actually, the um . . . the Mother of Chaos. She's not bothering anyone anymore, no siree."

Bruce walked down a set of steel grid stairs to a large ring-shaped platform that surrounded the center of the room. The ring was edged with large flat-screen monitors, worktables covered with various elec-tronic, computer, and alchemical gadgets, tools, bits and pieces, and lots and lots of computer servers and workstations. Another set of stairs descended from the ring platform to the floor of the chamber and granted access to another series of computer consoles, some lock-ers, a bunk, and additional workstations. Suspended from the center of the ring by massive steel and data cables was a dull steel capsule that reminded me ominously of a coffin with rounded edges. Bruce shrugged off his jacket and hung it on the back of a chair at one of the workstations.

"It comes in handy," he said. "I need to keep the things I work on quantum-encrypted. I can't let the information I receive from the Akashic Record fall into the wrong hands."

"So," I said, "to sum up, you fought an ancient dragon-goddess with your magic quantum computer. Do you have a fan club? 'Cause if you don't, I'd like to start one."

Bruce chuckled. He began to punch codes and commands into computers. The coffin-looking pod came to life. It lowered a few feet, and then a powerful gyrostabilized arm turned it until it was lying horizontally.

"We'll, I've heard a few of the tall tales about you too, Laytham," Bruce said. "Needless to say, a whole heck of a lot more people know about Laytham Ballard than ever heard of me."

"Yeah," I said. "Only because you were busy saving the world, and I was busy trying to get all that attention."

The pod opened with a hiss, and the top half of the capsule swung aside on hydraulic hinges. Inside was a grayish foam material with a vaguely human-shaped cavity cut out, allowing Bruce to lie down? Numerous hoses, cables, and sensory terminals lay coiled like snakes inside the cavity.

"Is it full sensory deprivation?" I asked.

"Yes," he said. "I like to narrow my perceptions to specific stimuli. I have contacts that function kind of like Google Glass, only more so. I have fast-twitch nerve-mouses built into those finger terminals there. All my vitals and brain patterns are registered at that terminal over there, and it regulates fluids and waste as well as the drip rate for the LSD. I have trained myself now so that, under normal circumstances, I can do with very minuscule doses of acid to achieve the state I need to metaprogram and navigate the Akashic Record."

"Bruce, thank you for doing this," I said. "I really have run out of places to look. Thank you."

"Sure thing," he said, smiling. "People like you and I have a gift. We get to see things, do things that normal folks would never, ever believe, never get. And the flip side of that is we have a duty to help when we can and to fight the bad guys where we find them. It's a privilege and an obligation." Granny's words coming out of Bruce's mouth. "I'm glad to help you fight the good fight, Laytham."

He set a few more parameters on the consoles before him, and then he took the photographs out of his jacket pocket and excused himself to the lower gallery. I sat, and I waited. After about twenty minutes, Bruce came back up in a white bathrobe. He was wearing swim trunks under it and had taken his glasses off. His eyes had a strange bright blue-white sheen, which made me think he was wearing smart contacts.

"Ready?" I asked. He nodded and checked a few readings on the screen. Bruce walked to the sensory deprivation pod and began to hook small sensor terminals to his chest and side.

"I've meditated and committed the symbols on the money dies to memory. Once I'm in, the pod will deliver the proper dosage of LSD to me through my skin, and I'll begin. You can sit quietly until Pam comes for you, Laytham. I'll see you by midnight, and I should have your answers."

"Bruce," I said, "I'm no hero. I'm nothing like you. I never wanted to be. I've always been the bad guy, or, at best, the selfish guy."

"I know," he said. "You don't think I'd jump into this without looking into you. I know what you are, I know what you've done, and I also know what a lot of people think of you. And I know what you think of yourself."

"Then why the fuck are you doing this?" I asked. "You know what a bastard I am."

Haberscomb tossed me his robe and chuckled. He climbed into the pod and got comfortable. He connected the terminals to his fingers and plugged several of the small cables into devices embedded in the sides of the pod.

"A person is his actions, not his intentions, and all I can say is that I looked you up and down in the Akashic Record, and I saw enough to convince me to help you. I haven't given up on you, Laytham Ballard, even if you have."

With a gesture of his fingers, the pod began to close. Bruce gave me a peace sign and a wink before he was swallowed whole by the machine. Banks of computers began to hum and whirr. The air-conditioning in the office kicked into overdrive, and it became even cooler. The walls of the room throbbed with power as the quantum computer began to spin itself up to full power. The lights all dimmed. Music filled the chamber, and I realized I had seen Bruce pop small earbuds in. The music was slow at first, a piano, the whisper of strings. It enveloped the room, and it made me think of snow falling silently, gently in a deep woods. I looked on one of the monitors and it said "Metamorphosis One" by Philip Glass and Bruce Brubaker. I sat back and watched as the pod bearing Bruce Haberscomb rose on its metal arm of hydraulic tubes and cables, higher and higher, and then swiveled and turned over, around, rolling, moving Bruce through space as his mind now moved past the walls of flesh and bone into a realm of omens and portents, principalities and power, galaxies drifting like snow.

"Safe journey," I whispered.

The music faded, only to be replaced by another Glass composition, "The Hours." I sat and tried to not think. It didn't work too well. And I began to listen more and more to my inner bastard, and I began to plan my endgame as best I could with the limited information I had.

Pam was suddenly at my side. She looked tired.

"Time to go," she said. "Field trip is over." I let her lead me out, and I tried to ignore the worry and the sadness on her face whenever she looked up at her husband twisting and writhing in a synthetic heaven of his own design.

TWENTY

Ichi, home by four from his nature hike, was his usual chatty self and proceeded to trounce me soundly in chess a few times. Eventually I got up the nerve to ask.

"Ichi-sama," I said as I reset the chessboard, "I mean no offense, but why are you still here?" The old Gun Saint did not look at me as he reset his pieces.

"Why have I not returned home or moved on now that our mission is complete?" he said. "When you reach a certain age, you find yourself locked in a press of days, more binding than any chain, any dungeon cell. You can feel yourself getting cold and brittle inside, and you . . . miss anything, anyone who distracts you from the grindstone your life has become. You and your associates are . . . distracting, and you remind me of myself and my old friends, all of whom I have outlived. I am in no hurry to go home."

He finished setting up his pieces and looked across the board to me. "I know why you are asking, Laytham-kun. And I do understand what you must do now, even if the others do not. If I may add, as a lonely old man to a lonely young man, I urge you to not drive them too far away, regardless of the reason. You will regret it in the end."

"Your move," I said. "And thank you."

Everyone was back to Foxglove by six that night. They came in from town laughing and happy.

"There's nothing on any of the news channels, the radio, or the papers about what happened in D.C.," Magdalena said as she set a few grocery bags on the dining room table. "I mean nothing, like it didn't happen."

"Same on the intrawebs and the TV," I said. Grinner plopped down on the sofa next to Christine and Geri. Ichi stood, arms behind his back, palms clasped.

"So that's good, right?" Magdalena asked. "We're clear?"

"Not necessarily," Grinner said. "It could just mean they plan to hunt us down quiet."

"Exactly," I said. "It's basically a cost-benefit analysis for them: Is it worth more to hunt us, find us, interrogate us, and kill us, or is it less hassle to just let us scuttle off like cockroaches?"

"A poet," Didgeri said blandly. "You are a poet."

"It isn't pretty, but he's essentially right," Grinner said. "The next forty-eight hours will determine how in the clear we are."

"Who is 'they,' exactly?" Magdalena asked. "Is this the Illuminati we're talking about?"

"That is a very complicated question, dear," Didgeri replied. "Most powerful and far-reaching secret societies are more incestuous than Ballard's family tree."

"Nice," I said. "Thanks."

"It is often difficult to determine where one ends and another begins," Didgeri continued. "I'd say that, given the close ties to banking and the federal government, Illuminati involvement would be primary."

"But from what Ballard said," Grinner interjected, "this is an off-the-books job Slorzack and Berman were doing, which means the powers that be may be as clueless as we are about it."

"The covers Grinner gave us are sealed tight—doubtful they will blow back on us—and the mystic cleansing Ichi and I underwent should wipe a lot of the psychic fingerprints off us," I said. "Our exit, however, is another matter. I am thinking that Neva wasn't a guardian of the archive; I think she was summoned by some third party to stop whoever was messing with those plates. An entity like her sets off all kinds of bells and whistles the all-seeing eyeholes will want to investigate. We also jumped space on our way out, and that leaves some really big mystic skid marks . . ."

"You need to not talk anymore," Didgeri said, wincing.

"So, what's our next move?" Magdalena asked, sitting down in the chair next to the couch. I stood and turned off the TV news.

"There is no 'our next move,'" I said. "First rule of a caper is knowing when to cut bait and run. And that time is now, gang. All of you need to get the fuck gone, now."

I tried hard to ignore the look of hurt and confusion on Magdalena's face. Geri just shook her head to make sure I understood just how stupid I was being right now.

"Laytham," Christine said sweetly, "you're being an asshole again. Stop it. We all came to help you."

"And you did, Christine," I said, standing and looking at everyone. "You guys saved my ass and kept me going, but if, in the next ten minutes, black helicopter thugs like the ones Ichi played with in Washington crash in that door, your life is over, your baby's life is over, your husband's life is over, the Haberscombs' lives are over. We all go into a black bag and we never come out."

"You did," Magdalena said, with bitterness in her eyes and voice. "You came back out of the black bag."

"He is right, Megan," Ichi said. "Together, in one location, we are too visible a target, too vulnerable. We need to scatter. And we do endanger our hosts. We should all depart soon."

Christine snuggled in deeper to Grinner's shoulder. He looked pissed at me too. Good. The more the merrier.

"I'm done talking," I said. "The caper's over. I have to wait to hear what Br . . . Haberscomb has found for me to get me back on Slorzack's trail, then I'm fucking gone. As for the rest of you, good job. If there was a take from this, I'd be giving you each your shares. Much obliged. Now get the fuck out. Tonight."

The room was silent as I grabbed my jacket off the peg next to the door and walked outside.

It was damn cold and the stars boiled and burned, distant and wordless in their sharp, painful beauty. So many. I wondered for the thousandth time today where exactly Bruce Haberscomb was and what he was communing with.

I fumbled in my jacket and cussed. I was going almost two days with no cigarettes. I heard the door open, then close, and Magdalena, her hands thrust deep into her black leather-and-cloth hoodie, looking like a cross between a nun and a ninja, stepped down into the gravel parking circle with me.

"Nice show in there," she said. "You really are a natural at working that. You're like an antimotivational speaker. Tony Robbins with a goatee."

"I'm not trying to motivate anyone," I said. "Just giving them the facts, and you should listen too. This is the Life, darlin': running, hiding, surviving. Waiting for faceless killers to come for you. Glamorous as hell, ain't it."

"You didn't seem to mind a few days ago when you were planning this little field trip and you need them, needed me."

"Yeah, well, like I said, caper's over. I don't need them anymore. Time for everyone to pack up their shit and go home before we all get busted."

Magdalena stepped closer to me. Her eyes were huge and dark, liquid and perfect in the light from the full moon. Her breath was the wings of gray moths fluttering past her cheeks, silvered. She reached for me, to touch my face. I felt her fingers brush my cheek. It was the gentlest touch I could recall in a long time, since Torri Lyn. I looked up at the moon and tried to fight down the storm in me.

"You don't have to do this alone," she said. "These people aren't here for money or power. They are all here because they believe in you, respect you, love you."

I took her wrist and moved her hand away from my face. I was stone.

"You think because we spent one night together, that I am the dark prince of your little Gothic fairy tale?" I said.

"Don't do this," Magdalena said. "Don't."

"I don't do that," I said. "I'm not for anyone. I'm not your romantic lead, and I find your schoolgirl crush sad and misguided. In case you didn't notice, in case Grinner didn't tell you, I left you in the morning and had no intention of ever coming back, ever teaching you, ever seeing you again, and I was cool with that."

Hot tears welled in her eyes. She fought them, valiantly. Her wet eyes never left mine.

"I was like you a long time ago," I said. "Then I wised up. I met enough people like me, watched enough dumb, sentimental lemmings die because they didn't know that things like loyalty and friendship and love are parlor tricks we play on ourselves to keep from losing our minds in this asylum. Consider this your first real lesson in magic. Know when to walk away, and don't drag dead weight."

I let go of her wrist, and she stepped away, back toward the house. "If that's true, then why are you going after Slorzack? Why are you helping your friend?"

"Because I want to see if I can take this prick," I said. "Nothing noble, just ego and balls and bragging rights. Boj just gives me cover. And now, because I want to know what this Greenway is, I want the secret, I want the power. It's really simple when you look at it without all those tears in your eyes, darlin'."

"Trust me," she said, flint in her voice, wiping her tears away on her sleeve, "these will be the last ones you see for a long, long time, Professor. I'm a fast learner."

She walked back in the house without another word. I felt my balls in my stomach and copper in my mouth. First times and beginnings are rare and fragile, like spring flowers in the late winter frost. I had just destroyed another one. I was the prince of frost.

I walked toward the work building, under the bright regard of the swollen moon. I didn't want to go back inside. Light and warmth and everything from the night before, it was a dream, it was for others, never for me. I looked down and noticed as I walked I had no shadow—an old debt to a harsh loan shark, the harshest in the Life. It was a jarring reminder of how far I had fallen and how right my choice was to send them, to send her, away.

I heard the groan of the metal door to the building and saw Bruce emerge, clothed again and in his barn jacket and a stocking cap pulled down to his brow. He seemed to teeter a bit as he tried to close the doors. I sprinted over to help him. Motion lights caught me and painted me and the Acidmancer in a circle of harsh halogen light.

I helped him with his keys to lock the door. "You okay?" I asked. He seemed a little out of it, his pupils slightly dilated, but he righted himself quickly.

"Yes, yes," he said. "I am fine. The words feel funny in my mouth—jagged, like they don't quite fit, but I am already readjusting to this dimensional harmonic, and I'll be . . . I'll be okay. I want cheesy potatoes."

"I'm pretty sure Pam has those waiting for you," I said. "She smacked Ichi's hand when he made a move for thirds, that's no mean feat—old guy's spry for his age. C'mon, let's get you inside."

"No, no," he said waving me off. "You need to know first, you need to hear."

Behind me, I heard voices exiting the house and the sound of a car engine starting. Shouts and returned voices. I heard Grinner's booming voice and several female voices. I thought I heard my name. I looked intently at Haberscomb, and he leaned in.

"He's been excised from the Record," he said, his lips trembling in the cold. "Slorzack, his entire beginning, middle, and end, it's all gone. His thread has been removed from the skein."

"How is that possible?" I asked, holding Bruce up. "How could anyone erase himself from the memory of Humanity?" I heard the engine growl to life and then the crunch of gravel as the Jeep turned and headed down the road, leaving Foxglove Farm.

"He didn't," Bruce said. "He couldn't. It would require a higher-order entity to alter space-time on such a comprehensive level. He's got friends in high places."

"Or low," I said. "Any idea who? The Watchers? The Court of the Uncountable Stairs? The Lodge of the Animal Lords? The Hungry? Who, Bruce?"

"Don't know, don't know," he muttered. "No resonance I could trace. Same with the magical operations on that money—all space-time adjuncts to it had been just wiped away, unraveled and allowed to be lost in the roar of the Styx, black waters rushing . . ."

A cold coil tightened in me, and I had a sudden insight into exactly who had done these things for Dusan Slorzack. However, I needed to be sure, to cover all the dwindling possibilities funneling down into a singularity, a certainty. Down to him and down to me.

I got Bruce inside. Pam helped him up the stairs to their bedroom; she had to promise him a big plate of scalloped potatoes would be brought to him. While I had been talking to Bruce outside, Didgeri, Ichi, and Magdalena had left—headed back to New York eventually. They were going in a very roundabout way to ensure that they were not being hunted. They took the Jeep. That would be a hell of a road movie.

While Christine and Pam said their good-byes, I helped Grinner pack the Mazda.

"You," Grinner said as he tossed a duffel bag in the backseat, "are king of the dumbasses, you know that, right? You had a fucking army ready to roll for you, and you just had to go and fuck it up, didn't you?"

"I didn't ask for an army," I said. "And what the hell happened to 'Fuck you, give me the money and get the fuck out'? I respected that guy; he had his mind on his business and his family."

"Hey, fuck you, Gomer," Grinner said. "You called me up asking for shit and we came back to try to help you. Jesus, you are such a moron. You have no fucking clue." I handed him the last bag, and he tossed it in the back. "My beautiful, sweet, trusting wife, who actually believes that there is more to you than evil and ego—Christine insisted we come help you. She loves you, you stupid shit kicker, and you made her cry tonight. Fuck you, Ballard. I ought to kick your ass right now."

I leaned against the car and looked up at the glittering night. "And I'd let you," I said. "I do appreciate it, man, I hope you know that, but you know the Life don't cut anyone a break. I'm right. I may suck at how I said it, but it's time to move on."

Grinner leaned back too and crossed his arms. "There are people who are alone by choice," Grinner said, "and then there are the ones who are just naturals at it. After all these years, I still don't know which one you are, man."

He gestured for me to follow him, and we climbed the porch. He fished out a crumpled pack of smokes and offered me one. I grabbed it like a drowning man clutching at a life preserver. Grinner lit his, then mine.

"How the hell long did you have these?" I asked. Grinner, well, grinned.

"Since I got here. I just liked seeing you twist."

I uttered a few quaint vulgarities and thanked him for the cig.

"Okay, I got what you asked for," he said. "I wanted to tell you last night, but everyone, you included, seemed to be having a good time, and I knew you'd fuck that up sooner or later."

"Yeah, yeah," I said.

"Social engineering and programing have a lot in common," he said. "It's garbage in, garbage out. I think you finally asked the right question, Ballard, because I did find some very interesting linkages between James Berman, his lover, Trace, and the Life."

"Talk to me," I said. "What did you find?"

"Well," Grinner said, "you ever hear of an occult contract killer called Memitim?"

And then he told me what he had discovered.

"Okay," I said when he was finished. "If you're willing, here's what I would like you to do . . ."

I hugged Christine good-bye and thanked her. I apologized for being, well, me and shook Grinner's hand.

"Awww," Christine said. "I love you, Laytham. Even you can't be an asshole all the time."

"Take care of that baby and that idiot you married," I said. "And take extra good care of you, darlin'. The world would be a hell of a lot darker without you."

Pam stood with me as the Mazda struggled down the rutted gravel road in the darkness, its headlights bobbing crazily as the car bounced and then disappeared from sight. It was dark, and the moon was beginning its decent behind the shadows of the forest. After a few minutes, there were no more car sounds.

"Well," Pam said, "you got what you asked for. You're alone."

"How's Bruce?" I asked.

"Fine." She sighed. "Sleeping. Healing up until he finds another windmill to tilt at."

"It must be hard taking care of him," I said.

"Yes," she said. "But he'd die without me."

"Yeah," I said, "he would. Can you give me a ride to the truck stop?" I asked. "I'll find my way from there."

"Sure," Pam said. "I bet you will."

The door banged shut behind her. I looked up at the moon. Heavy clouds were chasing her, trying to devour her, caught between the black teeth of the forest and the narrowing sky.

TWENTY-ONE

It was the devil's hour by the time I walked into the Pilot Flying J truck stop on North Valley Pike in Harrisonburg. The Flying J was like most major truck stops across the country—an independent city, a freehold just off the interstate, wreathed in sodium light, rows, streets, cabs and trailers rumbling in the darkness. Showers and lockers, public laundries, bins of audio books and spinners of paperback westerns and action series. Walls of driftwood souvenirs and racing memorabilia. And best of all, people—beautiful, living, breathing, traveling, laughing, drunk, exhausted people. Sit in a truck stop long enough and you will see all of human drama and nature unfold before you. Sometimes I think Heaven may resemble a truck stop.

I bought a huge energy drink that I think may have included the distilled soul of the Aztec jaguar god as an ingredient, a large black coffee, and two packs of American Spirits. Oh, and a great big fucking ice-cold Cheerwine. I had a double cheeseburger and fries to accompany my various elixirs. I sat at a booth with my bags and ate, drank, smoked, and watched.

I was sitting next to the truckers' section. Occasionally I'd place my right arm on the table at the elbow, horizontal to my body. I'd place my right index finger on the left side of my face at the eyebrow and slowly run my hand across my face, as if I was rubbing my eyes.

I'd scan the restaurant for the appropriate response. About six thirty in the morning, in the raw-eyed dawn, I got an answer to my silent distress call. I stood and headed outside. It was cold, but after the heat of the Flying J, it felt good. People came and went, and numerous eighteen-wheelers and their loads roared to life in the early-morning light, pulling out of the lot and heading back on the highway.

A man in his thirties with blond hair, bright green eyes, and a scraggly beard swaggered out of the Flying J. He was a little over six feet tall and his build was pretty solid, but he was cultivating a solid beer gut over his worn jeans. His teeth were bad—yellow, brown, and a little crooked. He had on a faded black T-shirt with three wolves howling at a bright moon on the chest, over that was an open denim work shirt, and over that a black Air Force–style jacket with an American flag patch on the left arm. He wore a dark gray mesh trucker's baseball cap, which had one of the characters from *Squidbillies* on it. A golf-ball-sized lump of what I hoped was chaw rested in his right cheek. He looked me up and down, spit, and then walked over to me.

"Howdy," he said. "You lookin' for some help, chief?"

"Yeah," I said. "I need a ride to Covington, if you are headed that way."

"I can be," the trucker said. "You want to tell me why I should?"

"Ego quaero veneficus itinere meo custodiam vias fratrum. Mihi quaesiti iustum est, domine miles," I said.

The trucker replied without missing a beat. *"Ad iusta operandum, et viator quaereret bonum fraternitatis rotae praesidio ac tutela. Assumam te, mage,"* he said in heavily corn-pone-accented Latin. Then, "You ready to roll, chief?"

"Yeah, thank you," I said. "Much obliged."

"Company makes the road less lonely," he said. "The name's Jimmie Aussapile. Pleased to make yer acquaintance. Let's ride."

Jimmie's rig was a beauty, a Peterbilt 379, with all the bells and whistles. The cab was white and black with a red Jerusalem cross pattern on the hood and the doors, and he had added chrome pipes and a grille. The grille was also custom, carrying the mark of the Crusader's cross. We rolled out onto I-81 South and soon were headed toward Covington.

The cab was like a small house combined with the bridge of the USS *Enterprise*. Jimmie had an impressive surround-sound satellite radio and stereo that was currently playing "I'm So Lonesome I Could Cry" by Hank Williams Sr. There was also a police scanner, a massive CB radio, a hidden panel with a suite of radar detectors, a laptop on a swivel mount with full wireless Internet access, a couple of different cell phones, routers, and modems, several navigator systems, and satellite TV on a small flat screen and on a large one in the cabin/bunkroom/galley that was behind the main cab.

A Saint Christopher medallion, an amulet of Hermes, a small clay tablet depicting the Egyptian god Min, and dozens of other charms and talismans representing patrons, gods, and spirits dedicated to the protection of travelers and of roads hung from Jimmie's rearview mirror. This gear shift appeared to be a pistol-grip shotgun partially sheathed in the transmission well. The Crusader's cross was stamped on the pistol grip.

"So how many of you guys are left?" I asked.

"The Brotherhood? More than you might think," Jimmie said, turning down the stereo. "We keep a low profile. There are initiated members in over thirty countries now. The roads just keep gittin' more dangerous, and we're needed now more than ever."

In A.D. 1119, a group of nine crusaders became known as the Poor Fellow-Soldiers of Christ and of the Temple of Solomon—a militant monastic order given the commission of protecting pilgrims and caravans traveling along the roads to and from the Holy Land. This order would eventually grow in power, wealth, and fame to become the Knights Templar. In time, the Templars would be laid low, forced underground and into new roles as bankers, Masonic orders, and other agencies of power and influence. However, a small offshoot of the Templars endured and returned to the order's original commission, to defend the roads of civilization and to protect the pilgrims and goods that crossed them. Jessie Aussapile was of this line of Knights: truckers, state troopers, caravan cults, bikers—any of the folks that lived and worked among the asphalt arteries that crossed the land. They called themselves the Brotherhood of the Wheel.

"Historically, the health of a society is linked to the safety of its roads," I said. "Ask the Romans about that."

"Well, son, I can tell ya, it's gettin' scarier'n hell out here," Jimmie said. He shifted and spit into an empty Dr Pepper bottle. "You got possessed biker gangs, those weird black-eyed children-things, interstate serial killer competitions, and haunted rest stops.

"Then you got the evils that ain't so sexy—coyotes smuggling folks across the border, killing half of them in the crossing from neglect, or jist plain killin' all of them and taking their money and selling their organs. Dirty cops shakin' folks down, some of them creating their own little kingdoms between exits. Eighteen-wheeler pirates robbin' cargos and desolating whole little communities, and then there is the child smugglin' routes. I swear, if'n I had enough good folk, we'd burn that whole damn train down to the ground. Not to mention the sumbitch banks and mortgage companies always tryin' to find some way to take away a man's livelihood. You can get robbed with a gun or with fees and charges, late payment penalties and front-loaded interest; a gun seems more honest. It's getting tougher to make a living and help folks out at the same time, harder to keep rolling, to stay alive."

"Why do you do it?" I said.

"Shouldn't have to explain it to you, a wizard," he said. "You do the same things. You see all the ugly in the world, and you got eyes and hands and you got to act. Can't help it, like your foot tappin' to a tune—don't even realize you doin' it sometimes till you're ass-deep in it. Man got a means in this world to spit in the badness's eye, an' he don't, well, he's part of the badness, then, ain't he."

"I reckon so," I said. "Some days, now, I don't feel I got enough left in me to even spit, Jimmie."

Aussapile nodded, smiled. "I hear ya," he said. "Thing 'bout this world, though, is give it a little time and it give all the reason you need to get riled up again.

"My pa, when he was driving and I was on the road with him, would tell me stories, old tales. There's the one about King Arthur—he gets screwed over by everyone he loves, all he fought for goes to hell, and he gets run through by his kin, his own flesh and blood. He's sick and dyin' and wantin' to die, but he still believes, still tryin' to save the future. He has 'em toss Excalibur back in the water till it's needed again, and then he sinks into Avalon, to rest and heal. You fight the world long enough, and sometimes you need an Avalon. Not to quit, just to heal and remember why you keep fightin'."

"Wisdom," I said. "Technically, back home they'd call me a Wisdom, not a wizard. Wizards ride giant eagles, got them pimp hats, British accents, stuff like that."

"Where's back home?" he asked.

"Welch," I said. "West Virginia, McDowell County. Born and bred."

"I figured," he said. "Yew talk funny."

We both laughed, for what it was worth.

"So," Jimmie said, "what's waitin' in Covington?"

"Avalon," I said.

TWENTY-TWO

Jimmie arranged for me to meet up with one of his trucker buddies, who was local, and they would get me to Chicago when I was done here. It was late morning and I had time to kill and really only one place I knew I was welcome in this town.

Covington's a little city of about six thousand people, located where the Jackson River and Dunlap Creek bump into each other. It's a mill town—the main employer is a huge paper mill that's been there since 1890. It employs most of the city. You can see the mill pretty much from anywhere in Covington, huge plumes of white smoke rising into the brilliant blue sky. You can smell it too. Paper mills tend to give off a harsh chemical smell, like a massive fart. Some days that smell permeates the whole city and beyond. Folks who live here get tired of hearing about it. They're of a breed that tries to smell the roses and count their blessings. Covington was what I got for a home, and I have to admit, I had missed it.

When I ran away from Welch at thirteen, this is as far as I managed to make it. I stayed here till I was eighteen, more or less, and this became home. The only real home I ever had, after Granny.

Jimmie dropped me off on Durant Road, and I walked a few blocks through a quiet little suburb with rows of pretty little houses, most with porches. Today it felt more like early spring than winter, and that made me smile, like it was a present just for me, and maybe it was. There were lots of new pickups parked in front of houses with old paint. A chocolate-colored Rottweiler barked at me from behind a chain-link fence enclosing a yard.

I walked down Franklin Avenue—another quiet little street lined with huge oaks and tight rows of houses. The birds were singing. I could hear distant dogs barking, talking to the Rottweiler, and a cool wind crossed me and made the trees' bare limbs shudder. The third house on the left had a big tree next to the driveway and an open carport. I remembered splashing in the water hose in the backyard, games of tag, and lying on my back in the itchy grass in the hot, dark summer and watching stars.

There was a woman sitting on a swing on the narrow front porch, which was crowded with plant vases. A half dozen different wind chimes, arrayed around the edges of the porch and awning, tinkled in the wind. I noticed one of them had pieces made to resemble crescent moons. I walked up the sidewalk, my bags in my hand, and stopped at the walk up to the house.

"Here comes trouble," a warm, weary voice said to me. The woman's hair was blond and cut short. She wore a cream blouse with a red knit sweater wrap over it. She had kind blue eyes that had seen too much sadness. She stood as I approached, came down the stoop, and hugged me tight. I hugged her back.

"Hi, Karen," I said. "I missed you."

"Hi, yourself," she said. "Come on in, let's get you some coffee."

She led me inside. I dropped my stuff by the door and ignored the assault by the tiny poodle that yipped as I walked in.

"Still a fierce predator, I see," I said to the dog. He growled a little and hid around the corner of the couch.

Karen still made good coffee, and we sat down in the living room, her with her poodle on her lap, stroking it. The mantel above the TV was covered with gold-framed photographs. A much younger me was in some of the pictures. I was smiling in all of them.

"How is James doing?" I asked.

"Still in North Carolina," she said. "Doing well. He comes up to visit quite a bit, as much as work will allow."

"I'm glad you two still get along," I said. "I owe you and him a lot. You took me in off the street, he gave me work, and you both gave me a home."

"Thank Torri Lyn for that," she said. "She found you, brought you home, and she convinced her daddy to let some evil-looking little waif of a boy come live with us. She always could talk James into things—she was a daddy's girl."

Karen smiled, but the pain leaked through. I remembered, after the car crash, she was strong. She held up as well as she could for everyone, but in the private moments, the bolt-holes of privacy and quiet, she suffered the soul-flaying pain that comes with having to bury your child. I recalled what Bruce had said about outliving his boy. I sipped my coffee.

"How is her boy?" I asked. "How is Jareth?"

"He travels a lot with his work," Karen said. "He used to come most holidays after he went to college. But when he graduated, he got busy. He calls, and we Skype as much as we can. He's beautiful. He'd get onto me for saying that. He's handsome, and he's happy. Off having adventures like a young man should. Reminds me of you at that age."

There was an awkward silence for a moment as the old unasked question floated in the air.

"Where are Jenna and Mike?" I asked, trying to change the subject.

"They went out to the Humpback Bridge," she said.

Humpback was a covered bridge, one of the last ones in America. It had been built in 1857 near Covington. Torri and I had spent a lot of time at Humpback. It was also one of the guarded gates to the realm of the Court of the Sky, a fairy path. Very few knew that and fewer still could see it. Jenna, Torri's sister, had some Fae blood in her, and she often found herself drawn to the bridge, hoping to catch a glimpse of her sister.

"If they had known you were coming, they would have stayed," she said.

"But you knew I was coming," I said. Karen smiled and took a sip of her coffee.

"She told me in dreams," she said. "Last night. I miss having coffee with her in the mornings, like this, Laytham. After all these years, I still miss her sitting right there, on her spot on the couch. I miss her voice and her laugh."

Something tight was in my throat. "I do too," I said. "She visit?"

Karen sighed. "When she can, when she is allowed."

"I'm sorry about that, Karen," I said. "If I had any other choice, I would have taken it."

"I know," Karen said. "You did the best you could for her in a horrible circumstance. It's comforting to know she's still around, that I can still see her and talk to her, but I worry about her, if she's happy, if they are kind to her. I miss her all the time."

"I understand," I said. Karen put down her coffee and narrowed her wise-sad eyes at me.

"You didn't just come to see her," she said. "You're wrapping things up. You think you are dying soon, don't you Laytham?"

"Hell, no," I said, and laughed. "I am working a thing, and Torri Lyn can help. And . . . I miss her too."

Karen, gave me "the look," the one I had seen so many times, when I had done so many things wrong, when I thought I was so clever with some half-assed lie. "Whether you know it or not, you are courting dying," she said. "I can see it all over you. A man intends to die, he'll find a way to make that happen. Don't, Laytham. Please, just don't."

"Did she tell you where I could find her?" I asked.

"Of course she did," Karen said. "You two's old playground."

The moon was ascending, full, swollen, and bright when I jumped the wall at the Cedar Hill Cemetery. A weird sense of déjà vu took me. I remembered playing here as a kid with Torri. Later, we came here when we both began to explore our connections to the unseen worlds. Some summer nights, we'd lie on the hills, watch the night sky spin above us, and talk about dreams, fears, hopes, and love. I miss talking the nights away with her.

I walked through the rows of tombstones. I could feel with my Ajna chakra the faint stirrings of the Waiting near their graves. Ghosts were stirring at the presence of the living in the city of the dead. I didn't open myself to the presences, though. I had no intention of spending the evening listening to every haint in this place bitch to me. I walked toward the hill where Torri and I used to like to lie and watch the sky. I sat in the dark graveyard on the cold grass. I watched the stars in the clear sky. There didn't seem to be as many as I remembered when I sat here as a teenager. Didn't seem as bright, either.

I smoked most of a pack of cigarettes while I waited and watched the moon rise higher and higher. The moon was so bloated and bright I could see the craters and mountains on the surface, like ancient fortresses and ruined castles.

I thought about Torri Lyn; it seemed safe to let myself, here, alone in the necropolis. I had left town after a stupid, horrible fight. I was eighteen, and it was my fault. I was too proud and too egotistical and too selfish. Story of my life, and it cost me the love of my life. She had loved me better, with more purity and more sincerity than anyone else ever had. She gave without thought and she created joy freely everywhere she went. We seemed to complete each other, she and I, her light to my darkness. I came back in 2002, when Boj and Harel and I had called it quits. It was the best year of my life. We picked up like no time had ever passed. We were building a future together without even knowing we were doing it. Then the car wreck, that horrible phone call. And my future died.

Torri Lyn had the gift of power as well, but in a very different way. It was in her blood—more than a touch of the blood of the royal Fae. She had the powers of the Goddess—the Earth Mother. Her magic was in breath and herb, element and candlelight, stars and moon. She had introduced me to the Green spirits, the Fae, and the wee folk. She had been seeing them and talking to them since she was a baby. I taught her what Granny had taught me, but I selfishly held some secrets back. That is one of the many reasons I suck as a teacher, as a mentor. Torri taught me everything she could, freely, easily, with laughter and a voice like a song. She gave.

I felt my eyes getting grainy and hot. There was a heavy weight in my chest; it made my breath catch. I wasn't going to do this, goddamn it.

The moon was in front of me now, huge. A scarred pearl, silently burning with stolen light, the midnight sun, the silent, screaming heart of poets, lovers, and madmen.

There was a curtain of light in front of me, made of moonlight, getting brighter and more solid as I stood. It seemed to arc upward across the cold night sky, its origin point the crater fortresses of Tycho. A figure moved down the bridge, toward earth. I found myself brushing the grass off my pants and trying to adjust my clothes and straighten my hair. It was silly, but I did it all the same, just like I always did.

The Lady Selene, Guardian of Tranquillity, Mistress of House Tycho, Muse of the Moon, and the Adjudicator for the Court of the Uncountable Stairs, approached. She was silver light and living sculpture. Her gown was silver scales that flashed and sparkled with the passion of a lover's eyes. Her skin was luminescent diamond, ageless as desire, fragile as memory. Her hair was the color of polished copper; it snapped and fluttered in the astral wind like a hawk's wings. Her eyes were the color of sky on the best day of your life, burning, as the core of the flame does. Her regard, as kind as sleep, as terrible as dream, roared in my mind. I felt like a leaf clinging to a branch during a hurricane. I was a monkey standing before a goddess. There was so much beauty, so much light and presence pouring out of her, through her; she seemed too much for this fragile world to stand.

"Welcome home, Lady Selene," I said. "Your knave greets you."

Lady Selene stepped from the moon bridge onto the grass. As she did, the being in front of me changed, diminished, into something I could fully comprehend with my stunted senses.

She became a woman in her early thirties, auburn hair falling in gentle curls down past her shoulders. Her skin was fair, almost porcelain. Her eyes were blue, piercing, the kind of eyes that demanded your attention from across a room, that sent a charge through you when they were directed at you. Eyes that twinkled with humor and love and a hint of mischief. Her nose was prominent and tapered to a point; she wore a diamond stud by her left nostril. She had curves, the way women did before bulimia became a fashion statement. I remembered the way it felt to hold her. She was warm and soft and feminine. I could faintly smell her perfume—she smelled like lilacs and spring flower. She always reminded me a little bit of Tori Amos, but prettier.

Her shimmering gown had become well-worn blue jeans, sneakers, and a blue-gray T-shirt with a little walking time bomb character, named Bob-omb, from some Mario video game. She loved gaming. The shirt proclaimed I'M THE BOMB! She was also wearing a black winter coat and a red-and-blue-striped scarf that fell to her waist.

The moon bridge faded, a cloud had crossed the moon and broken it. It receded from the sky, fading quickly, and the part closest to her seemed to fold itself into the ethereal stone face of a rectangular moonstone pendant, which glowed silently for an instant at her throat. To me, she looked more beautiful now than she had in all her Fae regalia of office.

She looked around, smiled at everything she saw, smelled, and felt, giggled with a bit of delight at all of it. Then she looked at me. The smile got bigger, the eyes wider.

"Pickle!" she said. She had an odd accent: a hint of a southern lady's drawl in her voice, sometimes a slight nasally twang mixed with something a little more aristocratic, a subtle upward inflection that made her sound like a delighted or precocious little girl.

I sighed and tried to frown, but I was crying a little, so instead of giving her shit about her calling me that, I just scooped her up off the ground and hugged her as tight as I could.

"Hi, Torri Lyn," I said. "Hi, baby. I missed you."

She hugged me back equally hard, laughed, and kicked her dangling feet. I didn't want to let go. I remembered. I had held her cold hands and kissed her cold lips in the coffin. I remembered watching them slide her casket into the cremator, I remembered opening the door and seeing what was left of her after the fire embraced her. Her memorial marker was in sight of us now, up on the hill. Behind it the moon stood watching over us, like a chaperone.

"I missed you too, darlin'," she said. She pulled back and looked at me. "You look older, tired. Still pretty, just a little tired."

"You still look beautiful," I said, "exactly the same."

"Yeah. Pretty much, I guess. I felt you seeking me," she said. "You in trouble, sugar?"

"Trouble is my business," I said, and grabbed her hair, pulling her closer to my face. She groaned a little, and her eyes flared.

"You still running that tired old Raymond Chandler line," Torri said. "You found any girls dumb enough to swoon over that, shamus?"

"One or two," I said, as our lips began to brush. Torri pulled away and wiggled down onto the ground. She stepped back, obviously as frustrated as I was.

"I can't," she said. "One of their rules. No kissing. Tangles the souls up and all that. Kind of like a pact. I'm sorry."

"It's okay," I said. "I'm just glad to be able to hold you, talk to you. Really."

She arched a narrow eyebrow. "Sex is okay," she said and smiled. "Go figure."

We laughed.

"Come here," I said.

We held each other again. We lay down on our hill in our cemetery and made out like two teenagers, me and my living dead girl.

Time had moved the sky. We held hands and watched the moon and the stars and talked about everything. Time was different for her in the courts, different in each court she visited, different from earth. So I caught her up on things as best I could. She wanted to know about video games, and I tried to answer, but the gaps in my knowledge annoyed her.

"You are a celestial entity," I said. "You serve a court made of deities, elder spirits, and elemental forces, and you are mad at me because I don't know when the next Halo comes out?"

"That other stuff is my job," she said, and smacked my chest playfully. "*That* is really important. Besides, do you have any idea how tough it is to talk about Master Chief and Cortana relationship fan fic with the Etruscan god of plentiful grain production?"

Torri was quiet for a moment, then she sat up.

"How is Jareth? Mom? Dad? Jenna and Mike? Chelsea? They okay?"

"I talked to your mom today. She misses you. They all do. We all do."

Torri looked off in the direction of her marker. She nodded.

"I'm going to go see Mom in a spell," she said. "I managed to talk my way into some work down here for a while. There's a twelve-thousand-year-old man in Egypt, building a machine to devour gods. I have to deal with him."

"I feel sorry for the venerable bastard," I said, and ran my fingers through her hair. "I'm on the clock too. Got a black hat of my own to take care of. I guess we need to go, right?"

"Yeah," she said, and sighed. "I've missed you. I've missed everyone. It's lonely sometimes—you'd think it wouldn't be with all of time and space to play in—the colors, colors there aren't human words for, and the music. Can you imagine suns singing? Skies that rain emotion? And with all of it, all of that, I miss my little boy's laughter, the feel of holding a warm hand, the smell of Mom's coffee, you stroking my hair, singing and dancing with Jenna, tasting good sushi." Her voice quavered. Her eyes glistened as she blinked.

"I'm sorry," I said. "I'm so sorry, baby."

"You were seeking," she said, wiping her eyes, "the answer to a question. I felt the question calling."

"Yeah," I said, and wiped my eyes too. Scene change. "This man I am hunting, he calls himself Slorzack, and he apparently claims to be the avatar of the god Chernobog. At least one of Chernobog's servants thought so. He has protection from on high—a higher-order entity—someone you deal with, Torri. I need to know who is his patron, who has covered his tracks and why."

Torri frowned. "Chernobog is diminished, darlin'," she said. "He was a minor deity of evil, destruction, and darkness. Kind of low rent. The height of his power was in the twelfth century. He was mostly forgotten, and gods when they pass from the hearts of men diminish, fade. Memory is power, Laytham."

"So that god is just gone?" I said.

"Chernobog has become a shade," she said. "Powerless. His demesne lies in ruin, his throne shattered. Without worship or sacrifices, or even memory, he is . . ."

"Sacrifices," I said. "Sacrifices! Torri, is it possible for a mortal to take the demesne and power of a diminished god?"

"It's . . . I suppose," she said, shaking her head. She stuffed her hands into the pockets of her jacket. "A man would have to try to embody the very essence of the deity he was trying to supplant. Chernobog was a bloodthirsty monster, a god of darkness and terror. A man would have to embrace atrocity to his core to even attempt it, and he'd need power—sacrifices, and so many, so much blood."

"Slorzack has it on his hands," I said.

"Are you sure he is not merely a servant of Chernobog and is trying to fortify the god by—"

"I know him," I said. "I know him well enough to know he would never be anyone's servant, ever."

"Sounds like someone we both know," she said. "Well, I can tell you that Chernobog still slumbers in shadow and dust, and no member of the Court of the Uncountable Stairs, or any unaffiliated pantheons, have given this mortal aid or sanctuary. Trust me, I'd have heard word of it if they had."

"Well, the tricks he's pulled require that kind of juice," I said.

"That just leaves . . ." Torri let the thought drift off.

"Yeah," I said. "I was already headed in that direction, but I had to make sure."

"Are you going to . . . reach out to them?" she asked.

"Just ask a few polite questions," I said. "Not looking for no trouble."

She laughed. It was loud and it was boisterous and it was full of life. It was the universe telling you not to take it all so seriously. It was the most beautiful laugh I have ever heard. "Yeah, right," she said, snorting a little, "since when?"

I held her again, tight. "Thank you, Torri Lyn."

"I'm happy I could help you, Pickle," she said. "I best be getting on to see Mom. I'm glad you were here."

"Do you regret what I did?" I asked her.

"Yes," Torri said. "I regret what they took from you in exchange for me. I regret what that cost you."

"It was worth it," I said.

"Laytham, they took your joy," she said. "They cut it out of you like a surgeon. They amputated your emotions, sugar. No one is worth that."

"You were," I said. "'Sides, with you gone, I didn't need it anymore."

She hugged me fiercely. I felt her tears on my neck. "Oh, you stupid, stupid man," she said. "You know there are things I want to say, that I used to say, but I'm not allowed to say them here anymore."

"I know," I said. "The rules. It's okay, darlin', you said them all before. I remember them. Every day, I remember them. Your kisses too."

She pulled me close again. She was my world—her eyes, her scent, her hair, the warm softness of her skin, her smile, her lips. Her.

She held my head, her hands on either side. "Memory," Torri said, "is how I kiss you now."

I closed my eyes, swept my hands into her hair, and pulled her to me. Our lips were a breath apart.

"To hell with the rules," I said.

There were no lips, no Torri. I stood alone in the graveyard under the bright eye of the moon.

"Fine," I said. "I'll kiss you your way."

TWENTY·THREE

The ounce of heroin in my coat pocket would buy me the Rabbi's secrets—that is, if he didn't still hold a grudge over that whole Dybbuk thing.

I got out of the cab on Madison Street near the Wabash L line subway station and started the four-block walk to the Chicago Loop Synagogue. Harel had grudgingly agreed to meet me there this morning. It had taken the promise of the smack and my guarantee that I wasn't hanging around very long after that to coax him out.

It was very bright day, the sky was clear. I had thought it was cold in Virginia, but Chicago slapped me around and disabused me of that notion. It was still at least a month away from anything resembling spring, regardless of what the calendar said.

The trip from Covington had been uneventful. Jimmie had been good to his word, and his friend, a fellow trucker named Guthrie, had let me ride along while he drove a load of steel up to Illinois. Guthrie, a tall black man in his sixties, who seemed to have been born with a toothpick at the corner of his mouth, was also a damn good singer. He had played guitar and sung backup on a few tours with Buck Owens in '71, and we ended up knowing a few of the same old folks in the business. We sang a lot of old country songs, and by the time we rolled into Chicago, we were discussing names for the band.

I turned onto Clark Street, headed south. I loved this town. It was a wilderness of stone, glass, and light; there were dangerous predators on the street, in the halls of political power, in the markets. If you weren't on your A game, this city would eat you alive, feetfirst, so it could watch your expression. Don't get me wrong, New York will try to kill you if you don't respect her, but Chicago does it with a pipe wrench and the unabashed exuberance of a Teamster working over a scab.

The Loop Synagogue was next to a Wendy's. It was a beautiful building—the architecture was modern, sandwiched between older styles. There was a glass-enclosed lobby, and most of the façade was taken up by windows. A sculpture of twisted metal hands open in welcome. Behind the hands was a wall of words of love and faith carved in bas relief. The sculpture greeted me above the entrance. I liked it. It reminded me a little of magic itself—hands and words tied to divinity. It seemed a fitting greeting in a place where the ineffable spirit of God roamed.

I entered but didn't bother with the traditional donning of the kippah, or taking one of the siddurim, or prayer books, from the shelf next to the entrance to the Prayer Hall proper. Given what I was here about and who I was meeting, it seemed kind of hypocritical to do all that.

It was too hot inside the synagogue; someone had pumped up the heat to compensate for the cold outside. Harel was pacing near the huge stained-glass mural that took up most of the eastern wall of the synagogue, near the bimah, the platform where the service was conducted.

Harel Ettinger was about ten years younger than me, in his midthirties, but you'd be hard-pressed to realize it. Even as ragged as I looked, the years of shooting up had not been kind to him at all. He had dark circles under his hollow, haunted brown eyes, and his complexion bore the pale, waxy look of smack-chic. Harel was thin when Boj and I met him in '96 and skinny the last time I saw him six years ago; now he was cadaverous. His hair was black, sprinkled with white, cut short, and shaved tight on the sides; the top was a mop of dark curls. He sported a goatee and was wearing a dingy-looking trench coat, a gray collared shirt with a very fine purple pinstripe, black jeans, and leather shoes. It suddenly struck me by the way he was dressed how much he was the son of my and Boj's influence. We had helped shape Harel into the man he became. That realization made me sadder. Harel was known as "the Rabbi" on the streets of Chicago and in the Life, though he had been kicked out of rabbinical school in 2005, near the end of his studies.

"About damned time," Harel said. "You're late. You got the shit?"

"Nice," I said, looking around. "You want to shoot up in here too? You can cook it up right there on the bimah."

"Like you haven't done worse, Ballard."

He had me there. I gave him a casual handshake, which he returned with a scowl. I palmed and passed him the smack, which was in a small, taped plastic baggie. Instead of pocketing it, he cradled it like you might hold the last shard of your soul. Reluctantly, he slipped it in his pocket. An old Hasidic man paused from tutoring a young bespectacled boy to glare at Harel and me.

"You two will have plenty of quality time together soon enough," I said. "How you been, kid?"

"Are you fucking kidding me?" Harel said. "Like you fucking care, Ballard. What do you want?"

"Fair enough," I said. "And true. I gave up giving a shit about you when you tried to shake down Ellie Jackson's family after we got rid of that fucking Dybbuk."

I had told myself that if I wanted this to work, I needed to not bring up the last time Harel and I worked together. We had managed to cast out a powerful evil spirit of an old, dead Jewish mobster, which had possessed a little nine-year-old girl whose family lived in the infamous Cabrini-Green housing project here in Chicago.

I had wanted to play this cool, but every time I saw Harel, the little bastard pissed me off. It was one of the reasons the so-called Occult Rat Pack of me, Harel, and Boj had split up.

"You threatened to put the damn thing back in their little girl if they didn't pay you ten thousand dollars," I said.

"Pay *us*. They had it," Harel said, raising his voice. "Bunch of schwarze drug dealers, they could afford it. I've seen you shake people down plenty of times, Laytham, poorer than them. Remember that time with the nun when you—"

"Enough," I said. "You remember how this went down last time? You remember how it ended for you? Well, I've gotten stronger, and unless you really want to see how strong, I suggest you drop this shit right now before that fucking mouth of yours talks you right out of some work."

Harel shut up. The old man was obviously irritated. He was whispering to the little boy and trying as hard as he could to ignore us.

"You have a job for me," Harel said. "I can put aside whatever for coin of the realm, Ballard, even your bullshit."

"Regardless of what I think of you personally, Harel," I said, "you are the best damn kabbalist and summoner in the Life. I know that, and you damn sure know it. I've been on a caper for a few months now, and at every turn I am getting stonewalled and jacked by summoned entities."

Harel narrowed his eyes but said nothing.

"I need countermeasures and intel," I said. "Someone on your side of the street has been screwing with me. You know a summoner goes by the handle Memitim?"

"No," Harel said.

"I hoped you did," I said. "The name roughly translates to 'death angel' in Hebrew."

"Actually, it's *mĕmītǐm*," Harel said. "It means an angel that rains destruction on those the guardian angels no longer protect."

"Sure he couldn't be an old pupil of yours, or a fellow kabbalist?" I asked.

Harel shook his head. "No."

"Well, the guy is a contract killer," I said. "Specializes in hard targets, and targets in the Life. He's apparently done a little work for the Russians and the Sicilians."

"So what you want from me?" Harel said.

"I want you to help me find him, get all the info I can on him and his clients, and keep him off my back while I finish this job."

"And what's in it for me?" he said.

"This job I'm doing," I said, "it's for Boj. He's dying. He sent me after the man who killed his wife, who killed Mita."

Harel shrugged. "And I give a shit why?"

Back in the day, Boj was the cannon. When shit was too fucking powerful or too stubborn or evil to fall down when Harel and I threw words at it, Boj waded in with whatever weapon he could find and balls the size of Jupiter. He saved both of us more times than I could count and nearly died doing it as many times. Boj also took Harel under his wing—Harel was his stupid, naïve little brother. They had a lot of laughs together. Boj loved Harel as much as he was capable of loving anything after Slorzack carved out his heart by killing Mita.

This had been the test. I thought if there was anything that might bring Harel back to himself, it would be invoking Boj. I was wrong. The Harel I knew was dead and gone. I was talking to a hungry ghost.

The anger welled up in me. Anger at Harel for being too weak and too cowardly to keep the poison from eating his soul, anger at my part in all of it, and anger for the loss, the betrayal of someone who had been a treasure in this world and now was just debris.

I grabbed the little bastard by the lapels of his overcoat and forced him back until he crashed into the Ark. The old Hasid was up, bellowing at me in angry Hebrew. I spun and glared at him with crazy goyish eyes and jabbed a finger in his direction like a gun. The old man blanched and clutched his chest. The boy took the old man's hand and pulled him toward the front doors of the temple.

I turned my attentions back to Harel, still crushed against the cabinet that held the Torah scrolls.

"Now, that's more like the old Ballard I know." Harel sneered.

"You listen to me, you little piece of garbage," I snarled in his face. I could feel the flush of genuine anger on my skin. "I don't care how badass a kabbalist you are, were, 'cause I'm the mojo-murder-man, motherfucker. I can turn your skin inside out; I can burn your soul to ash before you were ever born. I can make it feel like you are jonesing for-fucking-ever, asshole. Do you get me, you little worm? I can and I will. You really want to test your powers against mine again? Do you?"

"No," Harel said, full of sullen fear.

"Good answer," I said, as I dragged him toward the lobby. "Now, I need that information in the next few days. Everything about this summoner hit man and what he was doing and who he was doing it with, plus anything about a Dusan Slorzack. You ever hear of him?

"No," Harel said. "Who . . . who is he?"

"The man who fucking murdered Mita," I said. "How about James Berman? You ever hear of him? I want whatever you can dig up on him too. They're all up to their fucking eyeballs in this shit."

"James who?" Harel said. He was sweating hard and cold now.

"Berman, Wall Street suit. Got murdered a few months ago. He was Illuminati—the Inner Cabal of the Five Boroughs."

Even in his present state, Harel snorted. "Fucking occult Kiwanis club. Posers."

"Flyweight, I know," I said, "but he was tied up in some much deeper shit, and I need to know what they were all up into and how it connects to this Memitim contract killer. I'm gonna pull it all out by the roots, and you are going to help me." I gave him the number he could reach me at. "Forty-eight hours," I said. "If I don't get it, then I swear to fucking God I will rain down on your ass. Now go cook up your shit, Harel; you're no fucking good to anyone straight anymore."

I let him go, and he slid away from me. His eyes were red coals of hatred.

"Yeah, okay. I'll get you something in forty-eight," Harel said. "No problem, pal. Just like the good old days, huh?"

He glared at me and staggered up the aisle toward the lobby doors and the bright outside.

"Whatever happened to you, Ballard?" he shouted as he pushed open the doors. "Lost your fucking sense of humor. It was your only redeeming quality. You used to be a riot at funerals."

The doors let in a gust of cold wind, like the breath of God, and then slammed shut in Harel's wake.

"Too many caskets these days, asshole. Too many. And now I have one more."

TWENTY·FOUR

I made my way to the hotel. I was staying at a dive off East Garfield in Washington Park. I bought another cloned cell phone off a guy on the street and used it to call Grinner's swept contact line.

"We're go as of thirteen hundred hours today," I said. "Let me know what comes back."

I waited. I drank. I smoked.

I kept remembering us the way we had been then and how the meat grinder had made us who we were now. Harel had been a bright-eyed young rabbinical student with a taste for the ugly side of the occult street, full of the fire and passion. He wanted so bad to have it all. He wanted to traffic in the forbidden but still help people. He was our light, but he yearned so for the darkness. Boj was the man, sharp as a razor, handsome, tactically brilliant, deadly, and so dead inside. He was beginning his slow courtship of oblivion through hypodermic communion. Not so lost in his pain yet that he had forgotten where the road was. His orbit had only started to decay. And me . . . I was a little stupider, a lot more arrogant. I was going to be the greatest wizard in the history of this world or any other—an occult rock star. I was willing to pay the price for knowledge, for power, and most of all for respect and awe—any price. I burned the taper of my soul at both ends and laughed while I did it. Okay, I guess I was a lot stupider.

When I called the hospice in New York, I was told Boj was going. He had slipped into and out of consciousness for the last several days.

"Can you give me any idea of how long he's got?" I asked the nurse. Her name was Rae, and she had talked to me a few times before when I had called.

"Three days, maybe a week. Anything you'd like me to pass along if he comes to again?" She paused and covered the receiver as she barked orders at a wandering patient to get back in his room.

"Yeah, you tell him the redneck said he's close and he needs to hang on, unless he doesn't have the guts to do that. Be sure you tell him just like that, okay, darlin'?"

Rae chuckled. "Yeah, I've gotten to know the tough little SOB. That should do the trick."

"I hope so," I said. "I'll be there by the end of the week. Thanks, Rae."

We hung up.

I was running out of time. If this plan didn't work, I was done, and so was Boj. It all came down to Harel. Part of me hoped he didn't let me down again, but another part of me secretly hoped he would.

I missed the Harel I met before his soul had been scorched away, leaving something blackened and coarse in its place.

In '96, a thing was killing young men in Chicago's worst neighborhoods. Without a shy, brilliant young rabbinical student named Harel Ettinger, Boj and I would never have found it, never stopped it. All Harel had wanted was the chance to keep helping us, to help more people, fight more monsters, and maybe take a little walk on the wild side of the Life.

That good man never came back. "Those who battle monsters" and all that . . .

I should have been preparing a defense for what I suspected would come next. I should not have been getting shit-faced drunk and listening to the gunfire down the street, while the idiot TV looped static, and the tiny blown-out speaker on the clock radio played "This Night" by Black Lab and I knew every word.

I took another drag on the bottle of tequila, lit another cigarette, and waited. It felt like a wake. Eventually, it didn't feel like anything anymore.

The bloodred numerals of the clock burned 3:15 A.M. into the stale, dark air of the hotel room when the cell phone rang. It had taken thirty hours, a carton of cigarettes, a bottle of tequila, and a bottle of Maker's Mark for the call to come.

I rolled over in the bed and answered the phone. "Yeah?"

There was a wet sound on the line, coughing, then Harel's rasping whisper.

"You bastard," Harel gurgled. "You set me up. I should have known better than to trust you, you son of a bitch. Always looking out for yourself."

"Where are you?" I said.

"Fuck you!" Harel screamed into the phone. There was a pause, more hacking, wet gurgling, and the sounds of great physical exertion by very damaged meat. The sound was sticky.

"I'm . . . ah . . . ah, old house in West Garfield Park. Oh, God, it hurts!" Harel said. "Turned on me, son of bitch turned on me. North . . . north of . . . Eisenhower Expressway."

"Where, Harel?" I asked.

More uncontrollable phlegmy coughing from the phone. I was up, the lamp was on, and I was fumbling for my boots.

"Four thousand block West Washington," he rasped. "Boarded-up house . . . look for the Mask of Melchom drawn on the door . . ."

"Okay, I'm on my way."

There was a barely intelligible barrage of profanity, and then the line went dead.

It took twenty minutes to reach him by cab. I threw a wad of crumpled bills at the cabbie and sprinted down the dark corridor of rotting houses and decaying concrete as he shouted after me to wait. My breath was pale smoke in the cold, wet night. My heart was thudding dully in my chest. I was still drunk, and I felt thick and stuffed with dirty rags. The cabbie shouted, called me a stupid peckerwood, and peeled off. Only a fool attracted attention in this neighborhood in the dead of the night.

Across town there were monuments of shimmering steel, venerable marble, and mirrored glass. Lakeview, Edgewater, Hyde Park, lit up like Heaven, guarded by blue-vested garbed knights ready to turn back the unwelcome with traffic stops and steel batons. In the land of many mansions, the homes of those who do, who have, in the Chicago you saw in the movies, on TV, decent folk were asleep in their beds, behind solid walls and protected by electronic sentinels. Their bank accounts were positive and their kitchens were full of food. Their bills were paid up, barely, so they had lights and heat and water and all the things those in God's country should have. They were anointed by the gods of credit and commerce: car payments, cell phone payments, mortgage, tuition bills, taxes. They were hardwired into the fabric of society. All it cost them was a small sliver of their souls, their freedom, paid in easy monthly installments.

But here, in places like West Garfield, it was the longest hour of the night. Here it was shadowed lots choked with weeds and crack vials, oil stains on asphalt, and distant gunfire, distant sirens. Here you worked as much, as many places, as you could; here you fought a constant war between a thin check and a thick stack of bills. A struggle between hunger and self-respect, bus routes, sick children with no magic card to grant them access to the kingdom to be healed. Here it was a war to convince your kids it was better to work yourself into an early coffin that they ended up buying for your ass on credit, as opposed to the fool's gold of cash in one hand, a gun in the other. Do the math of how little you actually make after you factor in the jail time and short life expectancy.

Either way, whichever zip code you called home, the result was the same—you ended up dead, you ended up in debt to people who made more in a month than you made in a decade. You ended up wondering if all the struggle, all the roadblocks, the wasted time and broken dreams, the stress, the tension, the crying, and the anger, if all that had been worth the trinkets, sealed to you like barnacles, the shit they couldn't bury you with anyway. What was your life worth? Your happiness? Your soul? What was the going rate on you?

I found the house. On the plywood sheet that covered what remained of the frame of the front door, among spray-painted gang tags, was the carefully drawn and painted mask of office for one of the infernal parliament, the demon lord, Melchom—Treasurer of Hell.

I could sense the powers churning inside, like the archive in D.C. A wound had been gouged into our world from elsewhere, and there were forces moving in that old boarded-up, dark house.

I pushed the door open. The hasp was already loose, and there was no padlock with it. Inside the house, old smells of shit, piss, mold, and the chemical stench of burnt meth competed with the overpowering coppery smell of fresh blood.

I didn't have a flashlight, so I left the front door open. I moved as quietly as I could, sidestepping a half-rotted cat carcass near a yellowed pile of abandoned mail and newspapers. I stepped into what had once been the parlor of this home.

Harel was a broken pile of jagged fractures stabbing up through sliced and bloody skin. Each blood-soaked cough made his entire tortured frame shudder in pain. I stepped toward him, but I abruptly stopped when I saw the crippled angel hovering beside him.

It was beautiful and terrible—a butterfly of divine light held together by a will older than human sin. It was vaguely man shaped. It had multiple faces, some of men, others of beasts, all wreathed, blurred, in light that I knew burned mortal eyes if they stared too closely. It had two sets of wings and cloven hooves made of angelic brass. The way it moved and flowed, liquid around time and space, seeping, vibrating, static, infinite motion, slipping through the cracks of the dimensions . . . the things it did to my brain as I tried to look at it. It was . . . a Chagall painting come to life.

I was no kabbalist, but it looked like it belonged to the Hayyoth order—from the seventh sphere of Heaven; thirty-six of them in the "camp of Shekinah." These were the beings that held aloft the pillars of Heaven, and it was hurt. Divine ichor, liquid fire, hissed as it spattered on the base matter of earth.

Only a master of the Merkabah, the ancient mystical system that predated kabbalah, could summon one of the Wheels of Heaven here. And Harel was a Merkabah master. It was impressive.

Across the room, partially embedded in the crumbling plaster, was a massive inhuman form, or what was left of it. Its gray, rubbery skin had partly been vaporized. Its face was toadlike and frozen in a grimace of pain and rage. Black blood spattered as it fell from the destroyed demon. The body was so mangled, I couldn't place the clan or the house of origin for the thing.

I approached slowly and bowed my head as the Hayyoth turned to regard me with a face that could lay waste to nations and turn men to salt. I heard Harel moan, and then a voice that I recognized as mine begin to chant. I was rusty in Dee's Enochian, and I felt the flesh in my throat begin to blacken and burn as I spoke.

"*Ol sonf vorsg, gohu',*" I croaked in the tongue of Heaven. "*Iad balt lansh calz.*"

The angel looked down at its charge and then turned away from the pain of material being. It faded into memory.

I spit sizzling blood out of my throat and knelt by Harel, pushing the sweat-slicked hair out of his eyes.

"You asshole," Harel hissed. "Set me up. You knew. You knew he would come after me. You knew and you used me."

"What was that thing?" I asked. I could see the light fading behind his eyes.

"It was a Vodyanoi, a Slavic demon. Very old, very powerful," Harel said. He hacked and coughed, and the jagged spears of his own bones jerked, impaling him again and again as he rasped and choked on his own blood.

"You knew he would come after me once you started talking to me about Slorzack and Berman, didn't you, old buddy? You haven't changed, Laytham. You're still king of the bastards, still always working your angle. You think you are so much better than me, don't you? You prick."

I tried to make him a little more comfortable. His coat was draped across a wooden sawhorse, near the plywood-boarded windows. I grabbed it and gingerly put it over his exploded body. His works, in a small zippered leather bag, fell out of the pocket. I took out the cook spoon and the remainder of the baggie of smack I had given him. I dumped all the heroin into the spoon. It was a strong dose. I put the spoon over one of the flaring spots of fire on the floor, caused by the angel's blood.

"Who did this to you, Harel?" I asked as the smack cooked. "Who?"

"Look in the fucking mirror, asshole," he rasped. "I can't believe I ever looked up to you. My life has been shit since I met you, Laytham. You going to keep that hit from me until I tell you what you want to know?"

I set the spoon carefully on the floor. I noticed the complex circles, hexagrams, and other summoning formulas meticulously drawn on the wooden floor along with overturned and still-guttering candles. It was a miracle the house hadn't caught fire yet, but I knew it would soon. A fitting tomb. I also noticed again that I cast no shadow in the jumping light. It was a jarring reminder of how right Harel was.

"I should, you little bastard," I said. "You were going to sic that Vodyanoi on me, weren't you? Send it off to kill me, because the Inugami in New York and Lady Neva in D.C. didn't get the job done. You use it on all those people who died while I was trying to make my way to Berman too? On Berman himself, when I got too close?"

Harel coughed and groaned. He made choking sounds, and I stopped what I was doing and lifted him gently, helping him turn his head to retch up some blood, then I held him up until the coughing fit stopped.

I finished putting together his needle and then carefully drew the cooked, liquefied heroin into the hypo. I leaned close to Harel. I could still see the young kid in him, up close, buried under pain and hard years, and I carefully injected him in his neck, the whole dose. He sighed and shuddered, but didn't cough or wince.

"Thank you," he said softly. I tossed the needle near the husk of the Vodyanoi. The candles and the angelic fire were starting to eat the edges of the room. "I guess you expect me to tell you now."

"Shut up," I said. "Don't matter. Rest, Rabbi."

"It used to make me so mad when you and Boj would call me that," he said. "Then the name stuck, and I was 'the Rabbi' to everyone in the Life, on the street. I got to like it." He hacked a little, but it was easier now. His eyes were softening too, as the pain eased. "Once I came in to help these people in Chinatown. They had this nasty Oni spirit plaguing them, and I came in the door all cool, and this old lady hugged me and said, 'Thank God, it's the Rabbi.'" He shifted a little and groaned. "Have no fear, the Rabbi is here," he said. I laughed and he tried to laugh. Some blood spit up and painted his lips. I wiped it away.

"It was the closest I ever came to feeling like a superhero," he said, "to feeling like you, Laytham. I really wanted to help people. I wanted to fight bad things in the dark and be a good guy." His eyes rolled back and I was afraid he was slipping into shock, but he came back after a second. "I got all fucked-up in it," he said. "But we stopped our share of monsters, didn't we, Laytham?"

"You sure did, Harel." My throat was tight, but at the core of me, I was calm. "Boj and me would have been dead a hundred times over if not for you. So would a lot of innocent people.

"Remember how we met? Remember how Gacy had figured out a way to come back through those fucked-up clown paintings? You found him, Harel, you stopped him from killing any more of those kids. You did that. You did good, Harel. Real good."

Harel coughed again, hard, but I could see the pain was moving farther away from him. "Not exactly the way I remember it, but . . . okay," he said, and smiled. His teeth were red.

"Is Boj okay?" he asked.

"He's dying, man," I said. "May already be dead at this point, I don't know. I told him he was a pussy if he didn't hang on."

Harel tried to laugh. A wet hiss came out. The room was getting brighter. The house was on fire. I didn't fucking care. I wasn't moving. I'd run out of future, and my past was turning to ash in front of me.

"That will keep the stubborn son of a bitch here," he said. "I'm sorry he's dying. I'm sorry about his girl. We talked about that a few times when we used to shoot up together. I wouldn't have started using smack if he hadn't been using. I know that's kind of a bullshit cop-out, but I think it's true. I thought a few times about trying to bring Mita back to him, but you know how that can go."

"Yeah," I said.

Harel managed to focus his eyes on me. "You did set me up, didn't you, Laytham."

"Yeah, I did," I said. "You remember Grinner? He tracked you through deposits from Berman to your dummy accounts. I should have been looking more closely at Berman, but I thought he was just the latest in a long line of dead ends, courtesy of you and your pets. Berman was Slorzack's right-hand man, and he hired you to clean up any loose ends he and Slorzack and their mystery patron left behind. You are the contract killer, you're Memitim, Harel, and you've been the one throwing roadblocks in front of me since the very beginning."

"Yes," he said, "I've been doing wet work for a few years. Not exactly superhero stuff, huh? Berman hired me when you started nosing around looking for leads on Slorzack. Memitim had a reputation for clean and quiet work."

"I knew you were involved, and I suspected you were Memitim," I said. "I figured if I showed up here and gave you the story, you'd contact your only living client in this mess and get instructions, or reassure him you could take me out. Grinner was keeping any eye on your phone and online activity. You were the bait to smoke out the silent partner, or Slorzack."

The fire was crawling up the walls and beginning to lap at the plywood that covered the windows. Smoke was starting to fill the room.

"Tricky bastard," Harel muttered. "Never trust you, Laytham. Never."

"Then Berman's and Slorzack's silent partner contacted you to close the circle and finish off Berman when I managed to stumble my way to him, right?"

It was getting hot, and the air was starting to claw at my throat. The smack was carrying Harel away.

"Berman hired me," Harel said, coughing a little. "Did . . . did I tell you that already?"

"It's okay, man," I said, looking around the room. I heard shouts outside the house. "Harel, can you tell me who hired you to kill Berman? Who paid you to send all the things at me since then? Who did this to you?"

"He turned my own summoning on me," Harel muttered. "That's some vigorish right there, man. Bastard has some power, to be sure. I summoned the demon up to try to kill you, the way it killed Berman, the others, and it jumped me. Good thing I had the angel ready. Always have a backup, that's what you and Boj taught me, Laytham . . . right? Always a backup."

The ceiling was a rolling cloud of fire now, and I heard the beams above me groan and creak.

"Yeah," I said. "Always a way out. Harel, who is it?"

"Harmon," Harel said. "Giles Harmon."

"Who is he?" I asked. "I think I know that name."

Harel was nodding out but he managed a grin. "You are such a clueless dumbass, Ballard. Harmon's third circle Illuminati, he's a big fucking hammer, serious juju. Untouchable. He's also the vice chairman of the Federal Reserve. He and Berman and Slorzack were all deep into something they wanted kept quiet. Thick as thieves . . . like you and me and Boj, Laytham. Thick as thieves."

"The Greenway?" I asked Harel as he was slipping farther and farther away. "Harel, was it the Greenway? What is that, Harel?"

"I'm glad you're here at the end of it," Harel said. "I wish Boj was here too. You guys are the only family I got left. Only ones that really loved me."

I was coughing. Everywhere was fire and smoke. I heard sirens off in the distance coming closer. I held him. His eyes closed.

"Thanks for not bullshitting me at the end about the setup," Harel said. "Tell Boj I said hello . . ."

And he died.

I held the meat that had borne him, the real him, as long as I could. When a flaming timber crashed down near me, I stood, covered Harel's face with his coat, and walked out the front door into the cold, dark morning.

I stood across the street and watched the old house burn until the sky lightened and the guilt settled into my bones alongside the cold.

Too many fucking caskets.

A crowd of locals gathered to watch the firemen battle to contain the blaze, but the house was lost. Finally, I walked away. I didn't look back. Never look back.

I heard a great flutter of wings; it was probably pigeons.

TWENTY·FIVE

I asked Grinner to undertake sorcery of a more mundane nature, to find out all he could about Giles Harmon using his craft—the true names found in Social Security numbers and the oracles of electron flows and databases. He read the digital entrails and, when he sent me his findings, I came to fear this Giles Harmon.

Harmon was untouchable. Everything I thought Berman might be when I had learned of his connection to the Illuminati, Harmon actually was. He was not someone I could just come straight at. He was one of the Unseen Masters, kings of this world, and I was a knave, at best. A knave with so much blood on his hands.

Sitting in a Starbucks, staring at Harmon's bland, tanned, perfect face on a computer screen, I knew what I needed to do to get past him and get to Dusan Slorzack. It didn't only seem necessary or appropriate, it seemed just.

I began the ritual the following night. I traced the blade of the athame along my left palm. The hotel room was a void dotted with islands of flickering tallow light, my nude body a highway of scars and tattoos. The newest tattoo had just been added that afternoon in preparation for tonight's rite.

The pain of the blade was sharp and bright as silver as it crawled coldly up my fate line. I let the midnight-black blood dribble over the edge of my hand and fall like fat, heavy drops of rain on the carcass of the goat that lay at the heart of the summoning circle.

It had taken a little doing by some friends in the Life here in Chicago and bribing some of the kitchen help at the hotel to sneak a live goat up to my hotel room, but where there is a will, there's a way. Besides, it didn't make noise for long.

A chain of complex formulas arrayed outward from the circle in numerous geometric patterns, each a part of the occult circuit, each a key and a door.

"Ave Guardianorum omnium Tenebrae," I began in Latin. *"Accipe sacrificium signum meum. Gratum et cautior in vestri coutuntur me."*

I lifted the dark green bottle to my lips. It held some of Harel's blood, my semen, mescaline, and cheap wine. I drained it as I clenched my bloody fist. I poured the dregs over the carcass to mingle with my blood.

"Ego nunc summone Dominus hostiam diabolorum, Magni deceptore Ipse, priusquam oculis meis. Oportet quod sit lumen tinea continetur clara sit, ut cogatur Officium Luciferi assumere, serve meus Consuasor."

It was hokey shit. I felt like I should be wearing a Metallica T-shirt and sporting a mullet. But my heart was black and sick with murder, and bloody fire burned behind my eyes. The ritual was a prop—they all were. The robes, the daggers, and the chalices—even the sacrifice— all theater. It was the will, the intent, and the karma that drove the bus, but the rituals and props put you in the proper mind space and kept you there. Those had value at times, especially when you were calling something to you from outside.

My vision wavered, like heat coming off an asphalt road. I spoke its name in Sumerian, in Aramaic, in Coptic, in Latin. The name became a curtain of language, of intent. The world became sound and flickering light. I felt a flush as the mescaline kicked in. Time became taffy, stretched, looped, and finally knotted. My tongue and my lips no longer served me; they were a machine to call across the waters between worlds, to sound a chime in the depths. I was like a flare in the dark night of eternity.

Then something moved in the deep. It glided toward the flare, toward our world.

The room grew brighter. The candlelight became the light of battery-powered lamps. I tasted more than smelled the choking grit of coal dust. The air in the hotel room grew stale and hot, like there wasn't enough of it.

It stood in front of me in the form of a man dressed in a faded Hank Williams Jr. concert T-shirt. His jeans were torn and bloody, and the helmet on his head had a deep crater to the left of the glaring headlamp. His face was shadows, but I knew what it looked like. It was my daddy's face.

"I figured you'd pick another face this time," I said after swallowing hard.

"I didn't pick it," It said in my father's thick, twangy West Virginia accent, "you did. You always do. So what do you want this time, O divine excrement?"

"Fuck you," I said, the anger welling up in me.

"Yes, that is it," It said. "*Fuck you.* That is *precisely* what I am here to do. Now, how do you intend to help me do that this time?"

"Three wishes," I said. "Same as before."

My father's face smiled in the shadows of the lamps. I never got to see Pa's face at his funeral. Carbon dioxide poisoning turns the victims purple, almost black. It swells them up like a balloon, too much sausage packed into too little skin. When the rescue party found him and the other miners, they knew the second they pierced the chamber's wall there would be no open caskets for these families.

"What makes you think you have anything left to barter with, Laytham?" It said. "I already have your shadow and the sliver of your soul that came with it. Word on the street is you let the Sugarplum Fairies slice up your insides and take some of your emotions. It's all supply and demand, and you are damaged goods in every possible way, Laytham Ballard."

"Three years," I said. "Three years of service, for three wishes."

"You? Service? The man who bows to no man, no demon, no god?

At least that was the pap you used to spew out all over the playground when you were a cocky little warlock. Service? Really? I'm keen to know why."

"I'm after a man," I said. "A man with the kind of power only a higher-order entity could give him, and the only one of those left on my dance card is you. I'm sure you gave him a similar deal to what I am asking for to hide his trail, to help him escape mortal justice.

"To find him, I must go through another man. I expect them both to be very well protected. I need the power to finish this."

"You need *my* power to finish this," It corrected me. "Say it."

"I need your power to finish this," I said.

"Who must you go through to find your prey?" It asked.

"Giles Harmon," I said.

The smile again. "Oh, Giles!" It said. "We play eighteen holes every other Wednesday with some mutual friends. Good follow-through." It leaned in as closely as the hexagram It had manifested in allowed and whispered in a conspiratorial tone, "Bit too fond of the mulligans, though."

"I need him to lead me to another man."

"Why not just have me take you to this other man? Or have him placed before you, wrapped in red-hot chains with a mouth full of bat guano? I am the Devil, you know?"

"I don't think you can reach him," I said flatly.

It frowned and tsked. "Ye of little faith. What is this gentleman's name?"

"Dusan Slorzack."

The Prince of Darkness's frown deepened.

"He," the Devil said, "is a very, very bad man. And I'm afraid you are right. I have power over this world, the one I helped to create. But Slorzack is not in this world and is therefore outside my authority, and my reach.

"He used the power I gave him to obscure all traces of himself on earth, even in the Akashic Record, to buy him time to discover a means to escape his pursuers, to escape everyone."

"He outsmarted you," I said, and it was my turn to grin. "Didn't he?"

The thing with my father's face looked at me, and I knew if It could reach across the chalk line of its prison of will and occult calculations, It would do far worse than kill me.

"You know what I find most irresistible about you, Laytham?" the Devil said. "You are a villain with a heart dipped in the blackest of blood and yet you still cling to the notion that you are a hero. You want to save the day, be the good man, make the noble choice. Do good. But you simply aren't very good at doing good, doing what's right. You try, you long to, but in the end you always do it the easy way, the dirty way, the way that hurts and uses people, and you always will. I can see all the way into the dirty, greasy core of you, like looking behind the fridge. Yuck. So let's not have any more talk about being outsmarted, shall we?

"Slorzack skipped out on me. He escaped me by means of some . . . unknown method and, therefore, I cannot draw him back to me through my power. He owes me a debt, and I'd be more than happy to collect. So you see, I am sympathetic to your plight and will be delighted to help you see justice done, yadda, yadda, yadda, and all that rot. Three wishes for the exclusive rights—"

"Four," I said, interrupting the Prince of Darkness. "Four wishes."

"And why should I give you four wishes, instead of the three?" It asked.

"Because I am going to get Slorzack for you," I said. "And the extra wish is my commission."

It stared at me for a very long time. Silent, expressionless. Then It smiled again.

"Four wishes for the exclusive rights to three years of service to me and the completion of my business with Mr. Slorzack. Done. Now, what do you want?"

So I told him. I made two wishes and held two in reserve, for a rainy day.

"And none of that 'I wish for more wishes' crap," It said. "I swear to God, that's the demonic equivalent of someone asking if it's hot enough for you in the middle of July. So lame."

"Amateurs," I said, shaking my head sadly. "No sense of decorum. Make all of us in the business look bad."

"Too true," the Devil with my father's voice said. "It's nice to work with a professional."

TWENTY-SIX

Giles Harmon's home in Bethesda was a fortress in this world and any other. A huge walled compound, armed guards, thermal cameras, motion-detecting sensors, magical wards, protections, and alarms that made what I ran into at Foxglove Farm seem like cheap magicians' tricks. There were alchemically transformed, genetically engineered hellhounds wandering the grounds of the estate, custom bred Inugami from the finest Yakuza families of Toyko, guardian demons, and chained human spirits. Houdini on meth with Aleister Crowley's cock in his back pocket couldn't have gotten in there without being noticed, nabbed, and nailed.

So imagine Harmon's surprise when he found me sitting behind his desk in his study two nights after Harel had died.

Harmon was as handsome a man as money could buy. He was not so much white as he was bronzed. He had sandy blond hair with a casual, longish cut, designed to make one think of Redford in his prime. The cut probably cost over a grand, easy. His eyes were blue, and his face had been sculpted, cut, tucked, and Botoxed. His body was the result of thousands of hours of personal trainers, Aspen ski vacations, and eating food not served in a paper bag off the value menu. He was shuffling along in a pair of pajama pants and a silk kimono.

He was perfect and beautiful and favored of the gods, and I hated him the moment I laid eyes on him.

"Hello," I said. "I wanted to talk to you about your personal relationship with God and drop off a few free copies of *Watchtower* magazine."

To Harmon's credit, the surprise didn't last long. He focused, exhaled, and gestured. The air between us burned. He was tossing around serious, high-order magic, the kind that would have put most practitioners in a coma to attempt. The curtains, the chair, the desktop all blackened and shriveled. It should have killed me. It didn't.

I smiled like a wolf. "That," I said, standing, "was impressive as hell."

He unloaded on me. I could feel the heat drain out of the room as he performed a dragon chakra kata, pulling the living fire out of the electrons in the room with the sweep of his arms and the breath in his lungs. The incantation was spit out as an angry curse. The room twisted like God was falling down drunk. Wood melted, glass burst into flame, and the air curdled. It should have killed me. It didn't.

"My turn," I said. I crossed the room and planted a solid right into Harmon's square jaw. He screamed, more in fear and surprise than pain, and flew backward, crashing into his massive aquarium. I followed and hauled him up to his feet, driving a few uppercuts into his six-pack abs on the way. I could feel his defensive magics flash and flare all around me. I shook them off like rain on my coat.

"Help me!" he screamed. There were no alarms raised, no shouts, and no sound of guards rushing to his aid, no summoned beasties manifesting to crush me into kibble.

One more quick jab to the face broke his nose with a hollow pop and a squirt of blood. He kind of slumped and stopped struggling. I swung him around and dropped him on his couch. He fished out a handkerchief and held it over his nose.

"Basdard," he muttered through broken cartilage and silk.

"Yeah," I said. "The definitive article, if you will."

"Whad do you wand?"

"Slorzack," I said. "I want him and you know how to find him."

"Who are you?" he whispered. "Who send you?"

"Cut the shit, Giles," I said. "You know exactly who I am. You sent a contract kabbalist to murder me twice. You killed Trace, you killed Berman, and you killed Harel Ettinger after he did all your dirty work. I'm the Devil's repo man. I want Slorzack, and I'm going to waste your WASP ass if you don't tell me where he is right now."

I started toward him menacingly. He raised his hand, the one not nursing his nose, to ward me off. "No, no!" he stammered. "I'll dell you whad you wand to know. Jusd gib me a second."

He gestured toward the bar. "Ged me a scodge, straighd."

I did, and poured one for myself as well. The sweat dripping down my back was cold and my legs felt like rubber. I had been scared that at the last minute the Devil was going to pull a fast one and let Harmon charm-broil me; he has a rep for that sort of thing.

Harmon leaned his head back and cradled the cold glass against the side of his broken nose. After he had drained his glass, had two refills, and cleaned himself up a bit more, he was easier to understand and a bit more willing to talk.

"How?" he asked. I was sitting on a leather barstool about five yards from him on the couch, finishing off my third drink as well.

"I wasn't kidding about the Devil part," I said. "Two investments—one to get me here undetected and one to defeat you, unscathed."

Harmon smiled. His teeth were stained red with his own blood. "Two wishes—you wasted two you-can-do-anything-in-the-fucking-universe-you-want wishes just to get me. I'm flattered. Now I know who you are, you're a fucking moron."

"Ah," I said, "my reputation precedes me."

"The reason there hasn't been a magical assassination performed like this in over a century," Harmon said, "is that no one is stupid enough to waste perfectly good wishes on it. You could have just wished me dead with no ill consequence for yourself and saved me the bills for a physician and a carpet cleaner."

"Dead is not an immediate option for you," I said. "I want to know where Slorzack is, and if you were pushing up the daises or been wished into oblivion some other way, I wouldn't get that little tidbit, now would I?"

"Why not just wish to know where he was, or have him brought before you?"

"Because . . . because the Devil couldn't find him either."

Harmon paused. I could tell he was damn pleased by that answer.

"Well, now," he muttered, "isn't that interesting? The tricky old bastard, it did work the way he theorized."

"Okay," I said, standing, "break time is over. Talk. Now."

"Actually, I am in an interesting position, here," Harmon said. "You need me alive and you need information from me. I think we are in a negotiation here, Mr. . . . ?"

I walked over quickly. I placed my hand over Harmon's hand that was holding the empty glass tumbler. I put my other hand and my knee on his chest and pushed down as I squeezed his hand. The tumbler exploded. Harmon screamed, and I squeezed harder, driving the jagged glass shards and splinters into his palm and fingers.

"Jesus!" he screamed. "What are you doing? Oh, God!"

"Let me explain this to you in a language you should be fluent in, Giles," I said, and squeezed his hand harder. He punched ineffectually at my leg and side with his free hand as the blood began to well up between his fingers. "The only negotiation happening here is if you tell me where Slorzack is with pain or without."

I squeezed the hand again. Harmon gasped and became pale. His eyes rolled back in his head. I eased up, and some of the color returned to him.

"Very well," he said through gritted teeth. "I'll tell you. Just stop this."

I released his bloody hand and climbed off his chest. I walked to the bar and fixed myself another drink and then fixed him a new one as well. I handed him the drink and a clean bar towel full of ice. He drained the drink while he mended his hand as best he could. He groaned and hissed as he pulled the jagged knives of glass out of his hand. He finished his ministrations pale and glassy-eyed. Harmon handed me the empty with his good hand. I refilled him and then sat back on my barstool, nursing my drink.

"What do you know," Harmon said, "about the founding of this country?"

"The Indians got fucked," I said.

Harmon laughed. "Succinct, but essentially accurate," he said. "Many of the Founding Fathers of this country were not only sociological and political pioneers, they were also serious scholars of the occult. Washington, Hancock, Franklin, and many others were Freemasons. Franklin dabbled in the infernal with the Hellfire Club, and Jefferson was a member of the Illuminati itself, as was Alexander Hamilton."

"The Masons are a means to an end for you Illuminati guys," I said. "You co-opted them back in the late 1700s, gobbled them up in a merger, like you've done with so many other secret societies. Illuminati is an umbrella corporation now, a franchise with a strong brand name. And like any huge corporation, you're everywhere and nowhere."

"That's right," Harmon said with an oily light in his eyes, "we are. The Illuminati, the Secret Masters of this world. The Freemasons, the Founding Fathers, the good old US of A, it was, and still is, a front for us, one of many. A tool to wield power over the huddled masses, yearning to be controlled, to be told who to vote for, who to hate, when to ignore, when to care and, most important, what to buy."

"So the faceless and the powerful run the world and the rest of us poor bastards have to sniff up a life eating your table scraps. This is not exactly a shocking revelation, Giles."

"Tell me, Mr. . . ."

"Are you trolling me?" I said. "'Cause you still have a good hand. You are honestly telling me you don't know who I am?"

"I do not," he said. "Berman handled the initial details of obscuring your investigation and, after your persistence required James be removed, I dealt through his man, Ettinger, or Memitim, if you prefer his nom de guerre. I understand you people enjoy your little street names.

"I saw no reason to be any more hands-on than that until your

clumsy attempt at the Bureau of Engraving and Printing activated certain mystical safeguards I had put in place. Again, I let Ettinger deal
with you, as he assured Berman and, later, me that he could dispose
of you easily. It's regrettable that I didn't close that loop with Ettinger
sooner, since he led you to my door."

"So did you even a give a fuck about the people you were having killed?" I asked, shaking my head. "Did you even know their
names?"

"So, tell me, Mr. . . ." Harmon said.

"Hillbilly will be fine," I said. Or Hoi Polloi, if you prefer," I said.
"Fancy fella like you might like Hoi Polloi."

"No, I think Hillbilly is more apt," he said. "Tell me, Mr. Hillbilly, have you ever killed another human being? I suspect the answer,
but I want to hear it from your own lips."

"Yes," I said, "I have. Many times."

Harmon nodded. "Tell me, what have you killed for in this life?"

The question made a greasy eel squirm in my guts. "The usual," I
said. "Survival, self-defense, anger, revenge."

"Never for love?" Harmon said, a smile on the edge of his lips. "The
most noble of the passions. That's a shame. Never for greed, for power?
Come now, Mr. Hillbilly, a man who traffics with the Devil surely
has some experience with these?"

"Yeah," I said. I knew this was not the conversation to be having. I
knew it was dangerous, and a man like Harmon was a master of emotional judo, but after Harel, after Boj—who was most likely dead by
now—and this all for nothing, after Torri and after driving away all
the people who hadn't known me well enough to know I wasn't good
to be around, I needed this from some anonymous asshole. I needed
confession, I needed to look into the black mirror at myself and speak
my truth.

"I've killed for things I wanted, coveted," I said. "Killed for knowledge I didn't have, couldn't learn on my own, and craved. Killed for
things I thought I deserved and someone else didn't. I've killed
people to prove I was more powerful than them, for bragging rights,

for my legend, my reputation, and my pride. Yes. I've killed for those things. Yes."

"Welcome to the human race," Harmon said. "You honestly think any of those troglodytes out there would give a second thought about killing me and my family, about killing you and yours?

"You think there is some inherent nobility in poverty? Extreme poverty does the exact same thing to a person that extreme wealth does. It burns away many of the pretenses about human nature we cling to in the dark, about good and evil that we thought were truth. You know the truth about humanity, the same truth I know, Mr. Hillbilly. Don't you?"

"We do what we have to, to survive and to claw our way to better," I said.

He nodded and smiled, raised his empty glass with his bleeding hand. I took it and refilled it and my own.

"Very eloquent," Harmon said. "So let us both dispose of the pretense that I am some master villain and you the dashing but world-weary hero. We are exactly the same thing, Mr. Hillbilly: predators in a world of sheep. You think some home invader or carjacker gives one drop of piss about who he's taking from, who he's murdering, any more than any other predator concerns itself with killing with fangs or claws or guns, taxes or foreclosures, interest rates or credit scores, laws and regulations, or downsizing? Some do the eating and some get eaten. How many did you kill or lie to or sacrifice to get to me, to get to Dusan Slorzack? So, ask me again, Mr. Hillbilly, about the names of those I had killed because they were a threat or an opportunity or an obstacle. Tell me how morally superior you are to me."

I handed him his glass, and he raised it in toast. "To the top of the food chain," he said. "Congratulations."

We clinked out glasses and drank.

"So," I said, "Slorzack. Where?"

He reached into his robe pocket, and I came at him fast.

"Stop!" he shrieked, and immediately hated me for making him do that. "I am merely pulling out my wallet. I have no desire to receive further pummeling. We have established that I cannot defeat you."

He pulled a thin leather wallet from his pocket and liberated a hundred-dollar bill. He held it up for me to see.

"When you killed," he said, "were there times you were hungry? Did someone you love need money, like this, and not have it?"

"Fuck you," I said, and yanked him off the couch by the lapels on his blood-crusted robe. He was still smiling. "Last time before I do some serious damage to you, Giles, where is Slorzack?"

He jammed the bill in my face. "Here, he's in here."

I struck him hard and let him fall to the floor. The Benjamin fluttered to the ground a bit slower than its owner had.

"What?" I said.

Harmon sat up. He laughed, the kind of laugh that begins when fear is cooking itself into madness.

"The Greenway," he said. "He's hiding inside the Greenway."

TWENTY-SEVEN

W hat the hell is a Greenway?" I said.

"*The* Greenway," Harmon corrected. "There is only one. It's . . . magnificent, a marvel for the ages. It's the philosopher's stone, the Holy Grail, a magic artifact in an age of dull skepticism and anorexic wit."

Harmon snorted in disgust as he climbed off the floor and then winced in pain from the exertion. He dropped back onto the couch and took another long pull on his drink.

"Mr. Hillbilly," he said, "do you have any concept of what drives the higher orders of magic?"

I shrugged. "I've heard lots of different answers to that question from a lot of different masters," I said. "None of them satisfied me. I say it's basic, unbendable will. You dominate the universe into doing what you want it to do. Mind over matter, in the simplest terms."

"Quite the simplest terms," Harmon said. "Magical theory from a street-brawling banjo player. Quaint. Your grasp of magic is as homespun as your accent."

"Okay," I said. "What's your take?"

"My *take*, as you so quaintly put it, is the true path to power in this world and others," Harmon said.

"The power of love," I said. "Huey Lewis and the News were right?"

Harmon ignored me.

"Faith," he said. "At its core, magic is about faith. The more you can engender, the more you can accomplish. With enough faith, the magus is no different than God. Magic requires unswerving belief, does it not, Mr. Hillbilly? You are able to do what you do because you don't just think you can, like the little engine, you *know* you can. Doubt cannot be in the lexicon of the wizard.

"The earliest miracle workers, the earliest of our kind, shared that characteristic with the most fervent priests and worshipers. They knew the gods were real, they knew they were watching, acting upon the universe in tangible ways, and that belief, that faith, gave the gods as much power as us. Faith can and did move mountains, did it not?

"The difference between the gods on high and us was, and still is, that our power comes from within us, while the gods have to go, hat in hand, trolling for believers. We believe in ourselves, or abilities, supremely. We have no other option. The best of us are egomaniacal, because we must be.

"There are a handful of us in this world—wizards, mystics, magi, call us what you will. We are woefully outnumbered by the huddled masses. They will never have the hardware to do what we do, but they possess the raw fuel of belief, and that was the genius of the Founders, the architects of America, and of the Greenway."

Harmon leaned forward with a groan and retrieved the hundred-dollar bill from the floor. He held it up for me.

"Faith," he said. "'Backed by the full faith and good credit of the United States government.' That's what they say, isn't it? Not gold or silver locked up in some vault, not anything real anymore, just blind belief that the giant will keep lumbering right along. The gods are shades, Mr. Hillbilly, starved long ago from nothing on their altars but dead flowers and ashes, but the green, ah, the green."

"Money," I said, "is some kind of magic?"

"The most powerful in the world," he said, climbing to his feet. "It creates matter out of nothing more than paper or base metals. It controls minds and behavior, can kill or save a life. It is the charm, the focus, of countless millions of human lives. It is considered as essential as air, water, or food, and it isn't real. Behold the greatest source of sympathetic ritual magic in the history of mankind—the currency system of the United States."

"How?" I said. "I saw the magical operating system on the printing dies and plates. That system was unlike any magic construction I had ever seen before. It was . . . poetry."

"It's uncertain with whom the idea originated," Harmon said. "What is known is that the rituals, the formulas, and the thought-form architecture were postulated, argued over, and eventually finalized and created by Jefferson, Franklin, and Hamilton."

"The system I saw changed and evolved," I said. "Long past the life spans of any of them, unless you're telling me they are still creeping around somewhere."

"No," Harmon said. "The architects are gone, but like their social and political experiments, they made the framework for the magical system tied to the currency of their new nation adaptable, flexible, and sturdy. It has been modified and amended and improved upon over the decades, over the centuries, by the seven occult scholars allowed to tinker with it officially—the seven engravers at the Bureau of Engraving and Printing. They are high priests of a sort, of a long-lost conspiracy that only a dozen individuals worldwide even know exists anymore. Seven engravers, seven—a powerful numerological, spiritual, and occult symbol, is it not? The Greenway was not originally created as an Illuminati venture, but as our influence grew in the nation, we eventually discovered the experiment and made it our own, for a time.

"The symbols you saw on the dies and plates serve the same purpose as those of any enchantment on an object or the formula surrounding a summoning or protection circle. It gives the power a foothold, an anchor to cling to and perform its function."

"And its function is what, exactly?" I asked.

"It takes the belief in and worship of a sympathetic object—in this case, U.S. currency—and transforms that faith into usable, workable magical power. Workable power that was then directed into a singular miraculous purpose, the creation and sustaining of the Greenway."

I stood and took Harmon's glass. I filled it and then mine. I had to open a fresh bottle of scotch to do that. Harmon drained half his drink quickly.

"That," I said, "is slick magic. So, in effect, you had a huge amount of the American population at first and then, pretty much the global population, participating in ritual magic for you guys twenty-four/seven. That's . . . wow."

Harmon was well past drunk now and feeling much less pain. He laughed again, that something-broken-inside laugh, and sloshed his glass around as he gestured.

"It took time. Faith can't be rushed, Mr. Hillbilly, it must be nurtured and given signs and portents. At first the currency, the notes, were an easier way to deal with large transactions, and it was backed by the blustering young nation's vast material wealth, but over time, as America's power grew, faith and belief in the money grew. Eventually it was coveted for its own sake across the world. Nothing more than an idea, bound to simple paper, enslaves the human race and controls all of us. It was genius."

"That it is," I said. "I have to admit."

"It wasn't just the money, either," Harmon went on. He was slurring a bit now. "A magical undertaking of this magnitude required additional underpinnings to ensure it would sustain itself. Occult architecture was employed. Pierre Charles L'Enfant and Andrew Ellicott were commissioned to help design Washington, D.C., with Jefferson's assistance, to produce an evolving, fluctuating mystic circuit of unimaginable size. Massachusetts, Rhode Island, Connecticut, and Vermont Avenues and part of K Street form a massive pentagram, a summoning symbol and the focus of the sympathetic ritual. The White Lodge, or White House, the obelisk, or Washington's monument. Lincoln's memorial is a Greek temple to the gods. All envisioned for the Greenway before they were ever physical buildings on this earth.

"They bound the Greenway to the other symbol of traditional power—the All-Seeing Eye, the pyramid. The thunderbird, or phoenix, became the eagle, clutching Apollo's spears in one foot and Athena's laurel in the other. Symbols have power, my hayseed friend. Making a symbol into a reality—that is the power of true magic. Control, harnessing the minds of the powerless to serve the powerful and keeping them ignorant that they are slaves, giving them a prize to strive for, a dream that might come true but never does. Person by person, child by child, generation by generation until they are willing cogs in an arcane process they will live and die never knowing about."

I had drunk too much. It was a bad idea. Giles Harmon, even in his present state, was one of the most dangerous men on earth. I had started drinking because I knew what was coming and I didn't think I could handle it sober. However, my booze-soaked brain was beginning to turn over some of the implications of what Harmon was saying, and the scope of it sobered me, somewhat.

"The whole damn city was a sympathetic model," I said. "The size of the focus would be . . . with that much power from all those people . . ."

Harmon leaned back on the couch and let his head loll. He laughed and held his empty glass in a toast to me. "The lights come on in Possum Holler! Bravo, Mr. Hillbilly. Bravo! Yes, they don't make them like that anymore, do they?"

"Trying to be like gods," I said. "The Greenway is a world—a magically manufactured world."

"They took the belief, the faith, the desire, and the love of greed, tied it to the currency, and created a world beyond this one," Harmon said. "A magician's paradise built in the dark corner of Jung's crowded closet. A world where all of that worship, all of that faith—from the peon shoveling shit for minimum wage to the priests of Wall Street, working in the holy temples—their belief holds the walls of the Greenway together. Made it real and kept it safe."

"So this place is some kind of Illuminati retreat, a place of power for working powerful, dangerous magic," I said. "A bolt-hole, a laboratory, a sanctuary."

"It once was," Harmon said. "The Greenway was designed to be very conducive to magic workings. It's built of belief, for Christ's sake. A wizard in the Greenway has access to far more power than he can summon on earth, and a master magus . . . they are gods in the Greenway."

"So why aren't you Illuminati assholes selling time-shares there?" I asked.

"The Greenway is a closed, isolated universe," Harmon said. "The workings you do in there can't affect anything anywhere else in all creation. It's also part of the reason why the Greenway can't be detected. And as far as time-shares, there have been numerous wizards who have inhabited the Greenway over the centuries and often fought wars to hold it or claim it."

"It's a pure research environment," I said. "You can do amazing magic there, I'd bet, but it has no impact on anything anywhere else. It's the ultimate in mystical masturbation."

"You," Harmon said, "are a tactless shit kicker. To think I was laid low by the likes of you. But I have a little surprise for you, Mr. Hillbilly. A very big surprise. I'm saving it for last."

He paused and rubbed his face. He was seriously drunk, and it was creeping toward dawn.

"Many of the inner circles found the Greenway too unstable," Harmon said, "too dangerous to risk their precious hides. After the stock market crash in 1929, the inner circle lost too many members when all of that faith suddenly blinked for a moment. Many of those who supposedly took their own lives, falling out of office windows, actually fell much farther—fell out of the Greenway when it faltered and were never heard from again. In that crash, most of the individuals in the world who knew of the Greenway's existence were wiped away, and it became lost lore, a magician's myth. Economic uncertainty, runs on the banks, currency and bond crises, market corrections, government bailouts—these are the weather of the Greenway. If that faith is diminished too much, the world flickers and goes away and anyone there falls between the cracks. The ultimate margin call, if you will. It became a forgotten relic, a vacant lot, known only to a few of the oldest members of the Inner Circle and the occasional free-range occultist."

"Like Slorzack," I said.

"Ah, Dusan. You remind me of him quite a bit, Mr. Hillbilly, ambitious, overreaching, arrogant. Dusan actually knew only vague rumors of such a place," Harmon said. "He had been playing at becoming a god, a true god, since the '80s. He had been working to supplant some moldy old Eastern European god of evil."

"Chernobog," I said. "He was really trying to become Chernobog."

"Yes," Harmon said. "Gods are like kings; If they grow too quiet, some hothead will come along and try to usurp them or rebrand them and make them sexy again. Happens all the time—ask the pagans about Christianity.

"Dusan made considerable progress, including becoming the earthly avatar of Chernobog, and had summoned and tamed some of the old boy's servants. I think Ettinger threw one of them at you in D.C."

"Neva," I said. "We met."

"However, Dusan racked up considerable karmic debts in the process," Harmon said. "Including a sizable bill with a very active and pissed-off Prince of Darkness. Your mutual business partner gave Dusan his start on the road to godhood, and the bill was coming due, with interest. Not to mention the more tangible disadvantages to being an international war criminal, hunted, hated, hounded everywhere."

"And you taught Slorzack about the Greenway?" I said. "Sent him in there?"

"I had been searching for the Greenway all my life," Harmon said. "I was born into Illuminati royalty. I heard a few hints and some old fairy tales. The Greenway is like Atlantis and Shangri La, a fable, a myth. It took me until the late '90s to discover the truth about it."

"How did you?" I asked.

Harmon smiled and shrugged. "You'd be surprised the things a two-hundred-twenty-year-old senile magus will tell you over a bottle of good scotch and an infant sacrifice."

"Where did Berman come into the picture?" I asked. "You didn't have to kill his lover, you know, Trace. He was no danger to you."

"Mr. Berman, a very minor associate of a fringe society," Harmon said, "happened to be something of an occult scholar himself. He was an ambitious little prick, I'll give him that. He had acquired some journals belonging to Alexander Hamilton and he leveraged those and their knowledge of the Greenway into an apprenticeship, a partnership with me. Supply and demand. He was capable but a little too eager to advance beyond his station. It's a very unattractive trait in the working classes, wouldn't you agree, Mr. Hillbilly? And I didn't kill Mr. Trace. You did, by involving him in this business. We'll add him to your tally of the dead on your quest to find me and Dusan."

I didn't take the bait. I was starting to get my courage up. Harmon was helping me.

"Dusan sought Berman out when he arrived in New York," Harmon said. "He knew Berman was the gate to me, and he knew he needed me to escape the forces closing in on him. I've often wondered if perhaps Slorzack and Berman met before he approached me with the journals, if Slorzack used him as a conduit, a filter. It doesn't matter in the end, does it? The point is Berman was used by everyone. He was the classic middleman.

"Among the three of us, we rediscovered the Greenway," he said. "We learned about the magical architecture that created it and its reinforcement in the dies and plates. The rituals and computations of the original architects proved too complex for us to fully comprehend, but we managed to puzzle out enough. We rededicated the gateway through the sacrifices of the nine/eleven working. The destruction of the twin towers—the twin pillars of global finance—a massive reordering of society and a breaking of the established order, the reworking of the Masonic Tracing Board, as a means to disrupt the stasis of the Greenway's matrix. The damaging of the Pentagon—another bound pentagram, a massive symbol of warding and protection, to allow us to bypass any wards, protections, or traps placed on the Greenway by former residents or visitors, to unlock the gate anew."

"You destabilized the global economy and started decades of wars, death, suffering, and hatred, just so you three could jailbreak the Greenway, like a cell phone," I said.

"In essence, yes," Harmon said. "And we did it."

Something had been clawing at me since I escaped from Rikers back in New York. A disconnect, but it suddenly made sense. I laughed and pointed at Harmon. "The Illuminati has no clue what the three of you have been up to," I said. "That's the real reason you were so keen to cover it all up, why you didn't use your Illuminati connections to take me and the others out, and that is the real reason you tolerated Berman. He threatened to expose you if you didn't teach him. The little hustler had you, the great man, over the fucking barrel, didn't he, Giles?

"The All-Seeing Eye would have your ass for staging something like nine/eleven without Inner Circle approval, and you didn't get it. They'd feed your guts to hungry demons while you were alive to enjoy it, if they knew. That and you didn't want to share the Greenway with them, did you? It was yours, your secret, and your power."

Harmon snarled, threw his glass at me, and missed by a mile. It exploded against the wall. "Smug little bastard!"

"Greed," I said. "Greed and fear of being caught. You're right, Giles—we are all the same, aren't we? Pretty simple to figure, aren't you?"

"Fuck you!" Harmon said, and fell partly off the couch.

"I want in," I said, setting my glass on the bar. "The Greenway. I want in."

Harmon laughed. "Of course you do, you're that kind of reckless idiot. A scavenger wanting a bite of the corpse now that the lions are finished."

I walked over, still smiling, and punched him in his broken nose. He screamed and cursed as he nursed it.

While he groaned and damned me, I took the time to move aside the curtains, open the sliding glass porch door to his study, step into the graying dawn, and suck in some cold air and try to get my head on straight.

This was way, way past me now. No one had been able to find Slor-zack; the fucking Devil couldn't find him because he was no longer on the earth. And I was about to go after him. *Go off the earth* . . . I wanted it. I wanted to go where only a handful of humans had ever been. I wanted those bragging rights, I wanted that rush. That was fucking stupid. This wasn't about a dumbass promise I made to a friend of mine who was probably dead by now and wouldn't mind anyway. To go any farther would be fucking crazy.

I looked at my reflection in the glass door, really looked. In my mind I did the gut check and I asked the questions: *You up to facing the fall-out of this? You ready, come what may? Can you hack it if it goes south? Well, rock star?*

I went back inside. Harmon was sitting on the couch again hold-ing his bloody nose with his bloody hand.

"Do you know who I am?" I asked.

"A dead man!" he sobbed as he gingerly patted his swollen, purple nose. I grabbed him by the perfect hair, and he whimpered like a puppy.

"I'm Laytham Ballard, the greatest fucking magus to ever walk this earth, motherfucker. I slay monsters and bed damsels. I traffic with demons and angels and everything in between. I walk wherever I fuck-ing well please in this world or any other. Now take me to the fucking Greenway."

It was the same juvenile ego-stroking shit I had been saying to my-self since I was a kid, since Granny was gone. For the first time in my sad traffic accident of a life, I really, really believed it, though. I could stride worlds and piss lightning. I could avenge a wrong, a genuine act of evil, for once in a lifetime of selfish intentions, weak will, and petty inhumanities. But the sad truth was, I knew why I was going, and it wasn't to avenge Boj.

I picked up a hunk of the broken glass, dragging Giles along the carpet as I collected it. "Now you say it," I hissed at him, and tugged harder on his mane. "Or I will open up your fucking throat right now and watch the comical expression on your face as you bleed out. Now, who . . . am . . . I?"

And he told me, repeated it verbatim as he soiled his pants.

"How do I get in?" I said.

"The way in is easy." Harmon wiped the tears from his eyes and whispered between sobs. "You, you just put yourself into a relaxed trance state. Very first-year meditation, apprentice kind of stuff. Then you focus on the doorway."

"And what is the doorway, Giles?" I said, my breath hot on his face. He pulled the crumpled hundred out of his robe pocket again.

"The doorway," he said. His eyes were glazed over like an animal's driven mad by fear. "No one sees it. Everyone covets it, wants it, but no one sees it. The new ordered world—'*Novus Ordo Seclorum.*'"

"You focus on the bill? Any bill?"

He nodded. "Coins too. The seal on the dollar is the template for the conduit for the power, but it works with all of them."

"The inactive gate is embedded in them when they're made," I said. "Brilliant. Doesn't even register as magic until it's active. How long has Slorzack been in there?"

"Almost eleven years," Harmon said.

"Eleven years? Doesn't he ever come back over? Is there food, water?"

"Once a year I find some eager young occultist to undertake a 'rescue mission' for me," Harmon said. "Dusan deals with them once they arrive. I purchase pallets full of MREs and bottled water, camping gear, books . . . other things . . . all with Slorzack's money. My lamb to the slaughter carries them across. Most machines don't work there. There's no electricity, either. Batteries seem to work okay."

"So you handle his money?" I said. He nodded with a grunt. I let go of his hair.

"Show me."

He booted up the computer. The monitor was built into the glass top of his desk, and in a few moments we had navigated the maze of dummy corporations and overseas banking institutions that laundered and hid Dusan Slorzack's treasure in Giles Harmon's name.

"Wow," I said, "I didn't realize committing crimes against humanity was so fucking profitable."

"Slorzack was one of Radovan Karadžić's inner circle. He was one of the men in charge of čelebići—it was a prison camp at—"

"I know what it was," I said. "How could he make all this money off of that?"

"You really are a bottom-feeder aren't you?" He cringed when I looked like I was going to strike him again. He went on. "Power. Power over lives, destinies. If you have power, then money comes easy."

"Well, right now I have the power, and the money is about to go. Here is what I want you to do."

He paled a bit when I told him, but he did it.

"I want all but two million to be transferred, as cleanly as possible, to the account of the Fund for Human Rights. I'm sure you can find it."

He did, and in twenty minutes it was done. I broke out the cocaine I found in Harmon's desk while he did it, and availed myself of it. "Now put the other two mil in this account," I said. His eyebrows went up.

"An alias of yours, Mr. Ballard?"

"Look," I said, "I've got expenses too; 'sides, how much you been skimming off old Dusan there, Giles?"

After the money was moved, I leaned over his shoulder and whispered in his ear. "Now, Giles, old boy, you are going to use all that awesome Illuminati muscle to spring a guy rotting in Rikers Island. His name is Darren Mack, and you are going to wipe his record and drop about a million of your own money into his brand-spanking-new account, with his brand-spanking-new identity. I want him breathing free air with a new life by sunup."

Harmon did it. I felt a small weight come off me.

"Trying to give yourself a moral foothold to cushion the jolt of what is to come?" Harmon said softly. "Honor among thieves and all that, Laytham?"

It was getting close to dawn. I had drunk all of Harmon's good booze and went through about four lines of rich-people-grade coke. My courage was as bolstered as it would ever be.

"Turn around," I said to Harmon. He faced the window behind his massive desk.

"So it's time," he said.

"Yes. When did you know?"

"I'm not an idiot. I knew it would end like this. Now I have my surprise for you. I promised, remember? I hope you prepared an investment like what you did for me for Dusan, because if you didn't, you will die. He's far more powerful than I, and he has passed so far beyond any shore of human thought or morality, he makes me look like Mother Teresa. I saw the look in your eyes, though, when you made me recite your ridiculous little credo. You haven't prepared for him because you are going in there to prove you're the better gunfighter, the greatest magus in the world. Pathetic. Slorzack doesn't trifle with guns anymore, he trucks in exterminating populations and seizing divinity. He will burn you, Laytham. I know. I know you; I've known your kind my whole life. You're a sad little white-trash shit kicker who finally got to get one over on someone who actually did something with his life."

I pulled the curtain. The sky in the east was the color of drunken sleep, bruised like the face of a staggering boxer. The sun's light was pushing its way through the night's last stand.

"I have children," he said, fear and tears finally creeping into his voice, choking him.

"Fuck you," I said. "You know the difference between you and me, Giles? I remember every single death. It marks me, burns me, eats me up some nights. Makes me sob and puke sometimes. Makes me hate me. I remember the faces, even if I don't know all the names, and that makes me one tiny drop less evil than you. I'll take that."

I killed him quickly, while I still had the amnesty of the night. It was quick, but not painless. He didn't deserve painless and neither would I when the time came. If you want to know how I killed him, the hell with you.

TWENTY-EIGHT

I sat on Harmon's couch in the early-morning light. His body cooled on the thick carpet. His trophy wife knocked on the door, tiptoed in, and gasped when she saw him on the floor. She ignored me. She had no choice; I wasn't there. Once she was sure he was dead, her expression changed to one of calm relief. She kicked his body and exited the room to call the police and her accountant, most likely not in that order.

I took a crumpled, old, ten-dollar bill from my wallet, smoothed it out, and took a deep breath. I regarded the U.S. Treasury building, massive stairs leading up to an entrance shadowed by eight Doric columns, on the back of the bill. I focused on the images—the tiny bronchial branches of the trees that framed the oval containing the image, the stippled green and white sky, with gentle banks of clouds.

My breathing slowed. I willed my cocaine-hammering heart to quiet itself.

The clouds moved. The branches whispered, and the flag atop the Treasury fluttered with a brisk snap.

A horrible suffocating feeling engulfed me. I couldn't breathe; my chest was tight. There was a dizzy, giddy terror. A sense memory—drowning as a child. I fought through the rising panic of suffocating, of being helpless. I retained my focus.

My body was there, but I felt thick and unconnected to it. The wind was in my face, but it was dry, with no sense of comfort or renewal. I felt sudden acceleration in my stomach, but my head said I was standing still. I wanted to shut my eyes, but when I did, I still saw the world in shades of green and white.

I tried to open my eyes, but I couldn't. I was falling with my feet on the ground. It felt heady, drunk, out of control. Another memory struck me. I was high on meth, clutching a paper bag of greasy fifties in one hand and a 9mm in the other. The alley was clear, and the alarm was a banshee at my back. I was the richest man in the world. I pulled the reins of my focus tight and held on, not allowing myself to charge off into euphoria. Then the acceleration stopped, abruptly.

I opened my eyes, effortlessly. I was no longer on earth.

The stairs were a few feet in front of me. I was standing before a statue, vaguely Greek in styling, dressed in robes and carrying a shield. The face was featureless—an empty mass of green shadows. I looked up at the stippled sky. There was no sun, no moon. The illumination was a sickly wash of vellum-colored light that seemed to stretch on into bland infinity. The clouds were gauze, the color of malachite, drifting into and out of white oblivion. It took only a few minutes to realize that the pattern of the clouds—their shape and how they moved across the sky—was fixed, like a looping gif.

I ascended the stairs. The scuff of my feet on them was the only sound in the universe. There were no birds, no murmur of human traffic, even the wind was silent and dry as a reptile's breath.

The handle of the door felt like frozen wood. I soon learned that everything here felt blunted and distant. The senses of touch and smell were almost nonexistent in this place.

Inside the Treasury were seemingly endless dark halls. The muted echo of thick marble walls and floors. The darkness reminded me of being in a cave, deep underground. I wished I had brought a flashlight with me. I used my lighter instead. The shadows it cast were olive.

After a few dozen levels of hollow, empty, tomblike rooms and stairs, I began to get confused. In fear of spending the rest of my life wandering lost, I hurried outside. It didn't help much to calm my nerves.

I started to walk down the street in front of the Treasury, past one of the large trees only partly seen on the back of the ten-dollar note. It was only then that I realized that the bill was still in my hand—a featureless piece of white cloth that was warm to the touch. It was my ticket home. I stuffed it into my pocket and kept walking.

About eight blocks later, I reached the edge of the world.

The sidewalk simply stopped, falling away into absolute white. It was as if the artist had grown tired of drawing the landscape, the buildings, everything. I stood at the edge of existence, feeling the gravity of oblivion tugging at the pit of my stomach and at my balls, like looking over the edge of a skyscraper, knowing with a horrible clarity that comes from the marriage of reason and instinct that if you take that next step, you will cease to exist. After a time, I turned around and started walking back toward the Treasury.

Wandering across the Mall, the massive field that divides the Capitol from the Lincoln Memorial, I discovered the ancient blackened remains of a wicker man made of human leg bones, a marrow man, I suppose. The grass around the half-collapsed thing was dead and "blackened," a dark shade of celadon. Hundreds of cold, discarded torches lay on the ground in a circle around the bone thing. There was a skeleton inside the rib "cage" of the marrow man. I could not determine if the mummified thing inside was the remains of a human or not. It appeared to have tattered wings under its arms.

The mirrored walls of the Vietnam Veterans Memorial leaked blood the color of spring leaves.

A fleet of black ships huddled in the docks just below the Kennedy Center—narrow, insectile vessels with barbed masts, lines that looked more like cords of knotted muscle than rope, and hulls of black, glistening chitin with a sheen of beryl.

I touched the oddly silent, gently, lapping waves of forest green that cradled the alien ships. My hand felt coldness and the pressure of surface tension, but when I removed my hand from the water, it was as dry as my mouth and throat.

I passed featureless cubes twelve stories high throughout the city. Some were completely covered in chalk symbols that were foreign to me, others were chiseled and carved in bas relief depicting gods and demons who I suspected had never been known upon earth. One cube simply had the word "mercy" written over and over and over in a child-like scrawl covering every inch of its massive surface.

A narrow, needlelike tower with terraces overlooking the half-finished skyline rose up out of Georgetown. It had no entrance, no ladders, no stairs.

A massive pyramid squatted near 19th Street. It was made of hundreds of thousands of tiny skulls mortared together.

Eventually, I found myself in front of the White House. I climbed the gate and dropped down onto the lawn. I seemed to fall slower than normal, but it was impossible to determine if that was my perception or the nature of gravity here.

I slipped in silently through the main doors. Scattered about the foyer were hills of decaying garbage. Mostly empty plastic water bottles, military MRE packages, and leaking, corroded batteries, but there were also mummified piles of human feces and shredded magazines and books scattered everywhere. I was thankful for the absence of my sense of smell in this place as I stepped over a copy of *Also sprach Zarathustra* that someone had wiped his ass on.

It was dark in here too. I found a Maglite flashlight on the floor in one of the rooms and I turned it on. A feeble circle of pea-colored light appeared, illuminating vast, intricate stretches of alchemical formulas scrawled on the walls with a Sharpie—green, of course. In one room, I found stacks of black-and-white photos of prison camp victims, mostly women and children. Some of them, the worst of them, were taped to the wall in the corner of the room next to a filthy towel. I tried to not think about the origins of the dried stains on the towel.

The door to the Oval Office opened smoothly. The room was well lit from the large windows that opened out into a courtyard that on earth was the Rose Garden. There was a dirty cot, a few tattered blankets, and towers of books and magazines. The walls were covered in magical formulas written in ink, shit, and blood. None of them seemed to be complete. On the floor was a Triangle of the Art, a symbol for summoning an entity, and a partially completed Sign of Ameth, a kabbalistic symbol that was supposed to contain all the names of God.

"They don't work here," a thickly accented voice croaked in English. It sounded like it had not been used in a very long time. I snapped my head in its direction and came face-to-face with Dusan Slorzack. "No demon of Hell, no angel of God, nothing," Slorzack mumbled. "We are alone here, my friend . . . alone. No one is watching."

TWENTY·NINE

Dusan Slorzack was cadaverous. He was nude, covered in bedsores, scabs, scars, and occult tattoos, many of which were twins of ones I had on my own body. His massive, unkempt gray beard hung almost to his knees and covered his loins. His eyes were the color of blood on fresh asphalt.

"*Bones effrego quod splinter,*" I shouted, as I gestured at Slorzack with my fist.

"*Boli okrenuti obrnuto,*" he spat back with a raised palm, turning my spell back on me.

"*Subsisto alica!*" I shouted, feeling the force of my own magic pressing down on me. It sent me flying back into a pile of books. I fell to the floor even as the spell's full power was dismissed by my counter-spell. I rolled to my knee and glared at the old bastard.

"You . . . you are not the grocery boy, are you?" Slorzack said.

"Nope," I said, standing and brushing myself off. "I'm the bill collector."

"Your accent," he said. "Cowboy. American. You have come to kill me, yes, cowboy?"

"Yep," I said. Slorzack waited for more, and then he smiled. His teeth were black and jagged with decay.

"I like that you do not say why you have come to kill me," he said. "You recognize that I most likely will not remember anyway. You came through much to find me here, to reach me, yes?"

"Yes," I said, and for a second, the weight of the trip settled on me. I shook it off. I couldn't afford a distraction.

"Good," he said. "That way it will be more satisfying to me when I kill you."

It was on.

He tried to cook my bones; I absorbed the heat and turned it into five hundred pounds of impaling invisible force moving at roughly eighty-five miles an hour straight into him. He dispersed it into a fragmentation rain, spraying both of us, cutting like a storm of nails and razor blades. The sacrifice play gave him the time he needed to follow up with a spear of devouring light. My partial lack of a soul actually gave me an upper hand in weathering it, which surprised the old bastard. I sent lightning into his spine, crisping his nervous system. He retorted by causing my lower intestines to rupture and boil. He knocked aside my defensive spell and gave me a concussion, which was supposed to shatter my skull. The push left him open, however, and I managed to counterstrike more out of reflex than any tactics. I made his blood boil like he was in vacuum. He countered and punched, and I countered it and punched.

A war of magic, a duel between wizards, isn't exactly like you see in the movies or read about in books. Sure, there are spells of harm and defense cast, but at some point, sometimes sooner, sometimes later, technique fails you, training fails you, and you are left with heart and spirit, blood and balls. As with boxers in the twelfth round, it all comes down to the will and the ego, and, trust me, wizards have plenty of both.

The fight dragged on longer here in the Greenway. The very air was dripping with power, and both Slorzack and I took it in in thirsty, ragged gulps to keep us on our feet, to keep us fighting.

We were both hurt, bones broken, organs ruptured, flesh burned and bruised. We had run out of cute tricks and flowery words—we were smashing into each other with raw, unrefined power now, sheer will and malice. And I wanted this more than him, I could feel it. I wanted to live; I wanted to beat the wizard who had beaten the Devil. I wanted to be standing when the music came up and the credits rolled. Just once, I wanted to be a winner, not a fucking loser, a joke.

I stepped into the blast furnace of heat and light, taking one painful step after another closer to the old man. I suddenly remembered a spell I had written in the old graveyard in Covington, when I was fifteen, with Torri, drinking stolen beer and smoking stolen cigarettes. Before the training, before the Latin, just power and passion and the joy of the universe unfolding to me, the joy of magic. It was based off an old Violent Femmes song—"Add It Up." Most of my earliest spells were lyric based, until I learned the fancy words—and, now, I uttered it through cracked, bloody lips.

A look of confusion suddenly crossed the old man's face. He struggled to understand the cadence, the theme, the thesis of the spell; he was being a wizard, and I was being a punk. I took a step toward him, then another.

Imagine being in a fistfight with someone and he suddenly decided he was going to kill you no matter what it cost him, no matter what you did. Slorzack couldn't understand what was going on, and by the time he did, it was too late. Another step, closer, so close . . .

I screamed. It was made up of rage, energy, will—all my anger, all I had in me, all my losses, my many failures, all my mistakes, every ounce of me that clawed to live and, just once, to win, roared out of me, a flame of a life, my flame, my life. Mine.

His barrage of destructive power fluttered and parted, and I was up against him, my hands on his throat. I saw the look of surprise on his face for just a second. I drove a fist into his face, and he staggered back, bumping against the desk in the office, towers of books tumbling to the floor, many catching fire from the energies rippling off me. I felt the skin of my knuckles rip with each blow. Slorzack's hands scrambled over the surface of the desk franticly as I hit him again and again and . . .

I felt a dozen red-hot sledgehammers smash into my guts, knocking the wind out of my lungs, burning their way through me, like someone was putting out cigarettes through my skin, through my body. Then I heard the thunder, filling up my ears again and again and again.

I opened my eyes. I was against one of the walls. Blood was gushing out of me and a snake made of hot, broken glass was crawling through my guts. I was dizzy and wanted to close my eyes and go back to sleep, but there was the horrible pain clawing its way through the numbness, chewing on my guts, my spine. Slorzack, bloodied and burned, eye swollen shut, held up a small revolver, still trailing emerald smoke.

"Guns," he said, "work just fine here."

He staggered over to the opposite wall and slid down. He checked the cylinder of the gun with a satisfied nod. A realization crossed my mind.

"Saved your bullet, I hope?" I said.

Slorzack smiled his blackened, rotting smile. "You certainly gave me quite a . . . how do you say . . . 'workout.' The best I have ever had. You are a master. Unfortunately, here I am a god."

"I won," I said, and paid for it by hacking uncontrollably for a few minutes. I almost blacked out from the pain. White spots danced in front of my eyes. "I was going to beat you."

Slorzack laughed. "You *are* American. Dying from multiple gunshot wounds and still calling it a victory. You got any cigarettes?"

I nodded and tossed the bloody pack and my lighter on the floor. He groaned in pain as he crawled over to them and snatched them up. He lit the cigarette like he was making love to a woman. His reaction to his first drag on it was the only human emotion I had seen in his eyes. He held the smoke nestled in his lungs for a long time and then let it drift out of his nostrils.

"This is the only thing I miss about earth," he said, holding up the cigarette. "Thank you."

"Your hands are trembling," I said. "You were scared you used all of them, weren't you? Used up all the bullets."

I went away for a little while, I wasn't sure how long. I was cold when I woke up, and nothing had changed.

"You can pray to me, if you like," Slorzack said, putting out the stub of the first cigarette on his arm, then taking another American Spirit out of the package and lighting it. "I'm the only god here, the only devil. I could save you now, heal you, if you beg me to and promise to worship me, cowboy."

I managed to work up enough strength to laugh. It was a mistake, and I suddenly realized exactly how Harel felt as he choked and drowned slowly in his own blood.

"That's okay, Dusan," I said. "As gods go, you aren't very sexy, even when you're the only one in the room. I'll pass. Besides, you're not really a god, you tried that with the whole Chernobog thing and you kind of sucked at it. So you ran away to your little pocket and decided to be . . . the god of ineffectualness? The god of hide-and-go-seek?"

Slorzack laughed as well and then hocked up some blood, spit it in my direction, and took another drag on the cigarette.

"You know those gut wounds are going to take a few days to kill you," he said. "I think I'm going to sit here and talk with you until you pass out or fall into a coma from the blood loss, and then I'm of a mind to fuck you. After that, I think I'll eat you. It's been awhile since I had any real meat."

"You're going to die," I said again. "I got to Harmon. He's dead. Before I killed him, I had him disassemble your supply lines. No more food shipments, no more water. Nothing. Just like you said, sport, we are alone here. And the way you checked that gun makes me think you wanted to make sure you still have a bullet for yourself, even though you don't have the balls to kill yourself. You can sit here and starve and die of dehydration and go even more batshit crazy than you already are. So eat up, asshole, 'cause I'm your Last fucking Supper."

He smoked the cigarette and watched me.

"I can leave anytime I wish to," he said. "Gather more supplies, return, and have lovely conversations and sexual intercourse with your boiled and polished skull."

"Yeah, except you and me both know you won't leave here," I said. "Satan is on the other side of that door, waiting to collect what you owe him. Remember him? Gave you your start in the god business? So please, by all means, head back to earth.

"Tell me why you came," he said. "Who did this to me and why?"

"No," I said. I was getting dizzy and my sight was narrowing. I was shivering, I was so cold. "You'll never know why. Enjoy that feeling, god."

He didn't say anything, and I think I passed out for a while. When I came to, the revolver was in my hand. My head was full of angry, stinging bees.

"Do it," he said, still against the wall. "I can't. I have seen too much, experienced things only God would understand—the power, the emotions, the blood, oh, the blood. I cannot end my existence. My lust to go on forever prevents it.

"So you, alone of all men in the world, have bearded me in my den. You, who have within you the power of a god but the failings of a man. It is only fitting that you end my life and go back into the world and tell the tale of Dusan Slorzack. I gift you with your life and with mine."

I realized how little distance separated us in every way possible. I felt very sick. I pulled myself to my feet, steadying myself against the wall. I almost threw up and passed out again, but I didn't. I refused to. I flipped open the cylinder of the revolver. There was one bullet left. I snapped the cylinder shut with a flick of my wrist and took aim.

"Remember this," Slorzack said. "Never forget the day you slayed a god."

I pulled the trigger, and his kneecap exploded.

He screamed and flopped around on the floor of the Oval Office.

"Bastard," he screamed. "Damn you to hell."

"You can keep the smokes," I said. I dropped the gun and staggered out into the dark hallway.

"Please" was the last word I ever heard Dusan Slorzack say. I shut the door.

THIRTY

When I opened my eyes, the ten-spot was whole and in my hand again, and I was sitting next to Boj's bed in the hospice. Back in New York, back on earth. I felt another blackout coming on, but I was so close to being done with it, I soldiered through it. The lower half of my body was drenched in blood, and I couldn't feel anything except cold all the way down into my bones.

Boj was in the bed. All the monitors, all the things attached to him to record the last struggles of his ravaged body with the disease, they were silent and dark. He looked peaceful. That's a lie; he looked dead.

He was dead.

I had not known what I was going to do up until this moment. Story of my life. Now I had one last battle before me. I fought it quickly, and in the end, I think I won it.

I leaned on the metal rails of the bed to stay upright. The nurses and the orderlies would be coming soon to put him in the bag and zip him up. They would burn him and put his remains in a cardboard box, the fate of people who couldn't afford a nice plot and a granite memorial. People with no family, no friends to stand for them, to secure their place in immortality, in the memory of man. Boj's fate was my fate. I was bound for a cardboard box too.

Leaning against a box of tissues on the stand next to his bed was an old photo of him and Mita. I picked it up and looked at the frozen slice of time. The emotional charge off the picture was like a warm light in the cold, dark forest I was entering.

I never got them a wedding present. Until now.

I knelt down next to his still-warm ear and I whispered to him. I told him a story of a much happier world than the one we lived in. This one had a happy ending.

One wish, two wish, red wish, blue wish.

I staggered back and kind of fell into the chair next to Boj. Darkness swam at the edges of my sight. I could see the forest. It was dark, and my breath was steaming before me. The ground was covered in snow and it was quiet, so quiet. I felt the pain drowning in an empty place that carried no name.

I entered the forest.

When Boj woke up, his body would be fine—the disease gone, the desire for the drugs gone. He would live a long and hopefully happy life, and he'd know I kept my promise. And his Mita would be beside him, waiting for him, holding his hand.

And I died.

THIRTY ONE

I opened my eyes. I was in a guest bedroom at Foxglove Farm. My chest was wrapped in surgical gauze and I had a drain in my side that burned like hell. I was alone, and my head was fuzzy from narcotics. The pain of my wounds was sore and deep but also distant. I rubbed my face, I was sporting a beard.

I managed slowly, over the course of about ten minutes of groaning and cussing, to get out of bed without tearing anything loose or bleeding all over the place. Next to the bed was an ice bucket filled with cold Cheerwine bottles and a green-glass vase full of black roses. Thirty-six of them, to be exact. There was a small envelope lying at the base of the flowers with my name on it. The calligraphy was exquisite. I steadied myself and tried to not fall back on the bed as I slid the card out of the envelope.

It was thick bond paper, very high quality, and the handwriting was intricate and beautiful in ruby red ink that seemed to glow on the page.

My dearest Laytham,

Congratulations on your success. You got your man! Thank you for attending to my interests in this as well. I am impressed with how you decided to use your final wishes. Very noble. I assure you I have kept my end of the bargain and your friend and his bride are enjoying their new life—your gift to them, even as your life ended.

Now, as you well know, returning souls from the dead is a very tricky and nasty business for mortal wizards like yourself, but my abilities are quite adequate to the task of breathing life back into your fragile little bodies of mud and making a few surgical nips and tucks to that silly space-time cage you people insist on living in.

While I stood over your corpse, your guttering soul in my palm, I considered how best to address this. After all, we had an arrangement for three years of your life for the power that allowed you to fulfill your obligation to your friend and to grant him a new beginning. While your soul defaulted to me, at any rate, I still felt somewhat cheated in our deal. I was considering how I might best torment you to get my investment out of you, when a friend of yours intervened.

We discussed the situation and she offered a solution that I found amicable to everyone. I think you will agree.

She has given me a favor, a silent friend within the Court of the Uncountable Stairs, whom I can rely on for a single favor. In turn, I have given you your life back, and I will exact three years of service out of you, from time to time, until your debt has been paid to me in full. You didn't think I'd let you pay it off in one big balloon payment, did you, my boy? Oh, no, in this agreement, the interest is front-loaded. I assure you I will extract every nanosecond of my investment from you. But I promise you the work will be diverting and worthy of a villain who longs to be the hero.

Enjoy your life, Laytham, or should I say *our* life? Though I am, by my very nature and function, hate, I cannot say I am unsympathetic to your desires. Once, long ago, I sought to be the hero of the story as well, but it became clear to me in time that I was most assuredly not. While I have nothing but contempt for you and your kind, there are others who look upon you as flowers in the garden, not the compost. Take time to enjoy the scent of the flowers, for winter eternally beckons.

As always, a pleasure doing business with you,

L

I looked up from the card, and the black roses were gone. I looked down and the card was gone too. Late-morning sun was falling through the windows, and it looked like spring had truly arrived. I hobbled toward the door; my wounds were stinging, and the drain was poking me too.

"Couldn't completely heal me, could you, you cheap SOB?" I muttered, and found myself laughing.

I opened the door and looked down into Pam and Bruce's living room. For a second I thought maybe I had died and this was Heaven, or maybe it would be pulled away from me in an instant, and I would realize the Devil had found his method of eternal torture.

In the living room were Bruce and Pam, of course; Grinner and a super preggers Christine; Ichi, looking exactly like he had the last time I had seen him; Didgeri; and a beaming Magdalena.

"Hi!" she said, looking up at me. "Look who's back."

Everyone stood, except for Grinner, who yelled about trying to watch the TV and waved to me absently.

"Hey, bro," he said, then went back to the tube. "See, I told you he'd be fine. Can't kill Elvis, baby."

Pam made her way up the stairs, black bag in hand. Magdalena raced up ahead of her and hugged me. I winced.

"Easy . . ." I said. "I'm kind of duct-taped together." Magdalena hugged me and kissed me gently on the cheek.

"You've been here for about two and a half weeks, since Torri brought you here, and Bruce called all of us to let us know," Magdalena said.

"Torri?" I said. "Where is she?"

"She said she couldn't stay," Bruce said. "Work."

"You were touch-and-go," Pam said. "But I'm pretty sure you are going to make it."

Everyone settled down, and things fell back into pleasant chaos as Pam ordered me back to bed and everyone back downstairs to give me some peace.

I leaned against the rail and watched and smiled.

"So pleased with yourself," Didgeri said. She hugged me gently, kissed me on the cheek, and walked away, shaking her head.

I was alive, living on credit. Hell, who isn't these days? I thought back to Boj and Harel and me. The Occult Rat Pack, the old band. I wish I had been able to give Harel a wish too. He deserved one. I guess everyone really does, but supply and demand says otherwise.

And now these people, trusting me when they damn well shouldn't, caring when they damn well shouldn't. I remembered what Harmon and I had talked about, about the true nature of life and the lesson it taught you.

"Who the hell has the remote?" I heard Grinner bellow.

"You shall get it back when your beautiful wife and I have concluded watching this *Bridezillas* program," Ichi said. "And not a moment sooner."

I watched a group of loners, freaks, oddballs, and outlaws enjoy the solace of not being lost in this cold, sharp world, at least not today. There was a treasure here more valuable than all of Harmon's gold, all of the Greenway's secrets, maybe even more valuable than being the most badass wizard alive. Maybe.

Anyone who has lived knows life is savage and unfair and cruel, painful in its irony. Everything we experience in this life is an exercise in loss and gain. We hang suspended between the two.

Perhaps for most of us it's not an equitable exchange between misery and joy, good and evil. In the end, we all know we rise and fall between debt and credit, windfall and loss. We hope God, or whatever it is that waits for us, is more forgiving than the tax man.

We hope for mercy, or at least a not-too-thorough audit of our accounts.

However, it's up to us to balance the books while we can, and as always, it's better to go out in the black than in the red.

I felt the debts of winter in my bones, but the flowers were waiting in the garden, and for today, at least, it was spring.

ACKNOWLEDGMENTS

This book was a long time coming. Writing it helped me to cope with an awful event in my family's life. I want to thank so many for their love, patience, and support during that journey.

Thank you to Leslie Barger, who was the first person to read this novel in its earliest form and gave me encouragement to finish the short story and make it into a novel. To Velvet Vernon, a brilliant editor, who saw the embryonic version of this book and saw potential there, and to Heidi Schmidt, who was a huge and passionate advocate that "The Greenway" should see print. I am in debt to all three of you for your kindness, talent, and belief in my words, even when I didn't believe in them.

I also want to thank my agent, Lucienne Diver, for immeasurable support in the writing of this novel and for believing in it, and me, enough to make its publication a reality. You are more than a wonderful agent—you are a wonderful person. Thank you.

As always, to my children, Jon, Emily, and Stephanie, who give my life its greatest happiness. You're my strength and my comfort. I love you.

To Katherine Milliner and Michelle Jirout, for joining our dysfunctional little family. Thank you for making it better and brighter. You are loved, and you always have a home here.

To my mother, Mable Belcher, and my sister, Vickie Ayers, who raised me through their own sorrows and losses, challenges, and struggles and always made me feel loved and supported. I count myself lucky to have had two such amazing people as my parents.

To my grandmother, Beulah Swanson—the real-life inspiration for Ballard's granny. She was always kind, wise, and strong in her faith and in her love for her family. We love you and miss you, Granny.

To Joyce Wallace, for her enduring and fierce love of my children and her love of life. You are a wonderful grandmother to my kids. Thank you.

To my awesome beta readers: Faye Newsham, Susan Lystlund, David Lystlund, and Kim LaBrecque, thank you for all the hard work and tough love.

Thank you to the unflappable Greg Cox, the incomparable Diana Pho, and the amazing Adynah Johnson of Tor Books, for all the support and assistance in every aspect of this novel.

To Steve Franco, Tim Delano, and Charles Kalanik: You saw me through so many good times and bad times, and I am honored to call you my friends and my brothers.

And finally, to Karen Bess Carter, James, Jenna, and Chelsea Carter, and Russ Bess for making me part of your family in its darkest hour. And to Jareth Saunders—you were your momma's life, her breath, and her greatest pride and joy, and you always will be. Torri Lyn is loving and kissing you all, and always will, in the gallery of memory.